Praise for the novels of Olga Bicos

"Bicos has definitely found her niche...
a sizzling summer read!"
—*Romantic Times* on *Perfect Timing*

"A terrific writer who knows how to keep the
reader turning the pages."
—Jayne Ann Krentz

"Wonderful characters and a riveting plot
make this a humdinger of a book. Stunning."
—*Publishers Weekly,* starred review, on
Wrapped in Wishes

"Intelligent and appealing...sprinkled with just
enough magic to be believable."
—*Library Journal* on *More Than Magic*

"The emotion is intense, the sensuality
powerful...creates both thrills and chills."
—*Long Beach Press-Telegram* on *Wrapped in Wishes*

"Romantic suspense fans can rejoice as
superb author Olga Bicos adds her voice to this
spellbinding genre. *Risky Games* reaches out and
ensnares readers from the first page!"
—*Romantic Times*

"Olga Bicos is a genius!"
—*Affaire de Coeur*

"Amusing and highly emotional... True romance."
—*Los Angeles Daily News* on *More Than Magic*

OLGA BICOS

DEADLY
Impulse

MIRA®

ISBN 0-7783-2211-4

DEADLY IMPULSE

Copyright © 2005 by Olga Gonzalez-Bicos.

All rights reserved. Except for use in any review, the reproduction or
utilization of this work in whole or in part in any form by any electronic,
mechanical or other means, now known or hereafter invented, including
xerography, photocopying and recording, or in any information storage or
retrieval system, is forbidden without the written permission of the publisher,
MIRA Books, 225 Duncan Mill Road, Don Mills, Ontario, Canada M3B 3K9.

All characters in this book have no existence outside the imagination of the
author and have no relation whatsoever to anyone bearing the same name
or names. They are not even distantly inspired by any individual known or
unknown to the author, and all incidents are pure invention.

MIRA and the Star Colophon are trademarks used under license and registered
in Australia, New Zealand, Philippines, United States Patent and Trademark
Office and in other countries.

www.MIRABooks.com

Printed in U.S.A.

For Lexi.

Prologue

Cheaters never prosper. Crazy how simple that sounds. Maybe too simple.

Simple isn't interesting. It's not...entertaining.

Here's entertaining: On a dark and stormy night while taking one of his award-winning photographs, Clayton Chase survived a lightning strike. It was as if the hand of God reached from the heavens and singled him out.

He woke up several hours later beside the body of his dead wife. He was covered in her blood. He claims to have absolutely no memory of what happened or how he got there. Now those are some shocking facts. Fascinating facts...and very entertaining.

Clayton Chase wants to entertain you, to make you believe he cheated death.

Unfortunately, his wife didn't. Jillian Chase was executed by someone she knew, someone she trusted. He stepped up close and shot her in the back without hesitation or second thought.

Ladies and gentlemen of the jury, Jillian Chase will never give birth to the child she carried, a baby the defendant claims he knew nothing about, a child who did not belong to the defendant. Another man's son.

So now he wants you to believe he's innocent, the real victim of the story. His attorney entertains you with smoke and mirrors. "Hold up," he says, "not so fast." This is no simple tale: a jilted husband murdering his rich wife.

Ladies and gentlemen, Jillian Chase was in love with another man. You've heard witnesses testify that Jillian was on the verge of filing for divorce, a divorce that would have left the defendant with very little under the prenuptial agreement he'd signed. Ballistics prove that the gun found in a Dumpster two blocks from the defendant's South Beach home killed Jillian. Fingerprints found on the gun belong to the defendant. The gun was registered to his father.

This isn't a movie. This isn't Steven Spielberg and his special-effects team making the incredible seem possible. This is murder, pure and simple.

Clayton Chase killed his wife.

Don't let him get away with it.

The State of Florida v. Chase; excerpt, state attorney's closing argument.

1

Piper Jordan sat up in bed, suddenly awake. The client files she'd fallen asleep reading tumbled to the floor as she slumped forward, knees to chest, catching her breath. Lightning flashed against the windowpane, briefly setting a match to the room as the patter of rain turned into a harsh, pitting hail.

As if it were a message from her dreams, Piper knew something was wrong.

"Simon," she whispered, shoving aside the covers.

Piper Jordan realized what silence might mean in her house during a storm.

She ran down the stairs, the floorboards biting cold. A camera flash of lightning flickered, making the portraits in the hall light up like the Haunted Mansion at Disneyland.

Don't panic. Don't let him see you freaked out.

Only hours ago, she'd tucked Winnie the Pooh covers under her son's chin and set the snooze function on the VCR to say good-night. She'd kissed her daughter and cleared the floor of Mandy's report due next week, stacking the note cards and books on her desk.

He'll be there. Simon's fine.

Down the hall, the door to her son's room stood ajar. The light from the hallway bled inside, Simon's version of a night light. Or, more likely, he wanted the connection to Piper sleeping down the artery of the hall. In either case, it seemed suddenly not enough...the room too far, her son too alone. She wanted more than anything to tuck him in bed beside her and fall asleep to the sound of his breathing.

Another flash of lightning painted Simon's room a near-white. The hall lights flickered—the house went dark. *A blackout.*

That's how she felt seeing Simon's empty bed, the covers puddled on the floor. *Blackout.*

"Mom!"

Piper turned to see her daughter. She almost collided with Mandy, then followed her frantic hand-waving down the stairs.

Around the corner, she saw the large oak door swinging open with the wind. Rain splattered on the tile inside.

She thought she would have heard something—the bolt on the front door, *snap, click*—his tiny bare feet on the floor. Anything.

By the time she reached the tiled entry, she knew her son had long since slipped over the threshold.

Standing in the rain, she screamed his name. The sky lit up, brilliant. At the end of the street, a palm tree blazed with fire from a direct strike as rain poured—a fire engine's siren wailed in the distance. Her heart pounding, she ran up and down the street, searching.

Please, please, let me find him!

In Piper's experience, it was when things seemed most urgent that the world had a trick of slowing down. The night Kevin had died, as she'd listened on her cell phone to Mandy crying, Piper had raced her Suburban through the storm to reach the house. She couldn't make the car drive fast enough. Couldn't click her heels and wish herself at her husband's side. She'd arrived too late, finding only the pulsing red of the ambulance light beating against the door.

Tonight felt the same. *Slow motion.* Piper turned in a circle, round and round, the fire engine flashing the same ugly red as she searched the manicured lawns and neatly trimmed yards of the cul-de-sac for her son…and found him.

He stood just down the street, his small body almost vanishing into the embrace of a man kneeling over him. Piper stepped forward, her heart suddenly too big for her chest. She couldn't see who it was—a neighbor, a stranger—only that Simon clung to him, his little arms tight around the man's neck.

Lightning like a flare overhead ignited the street. The man turned to look at her.

Some images don't make sense right away. They catch you by surprise so that you have to squint and wonder what's wrong or off or just plain impossible. You have to consider why the puzzle pieces don't fit. Like Clayton Chase holding her son in the middle of a rainstorm, some things just can't be….

"Simon!"

She rushed forward, the asphalt ripping into her feet, the rain dousing her soaked cotton-knit pajamas, none of which mattered to Piper. She could only think about Simon standing alone in the rain with Clayton Chase.

Clayton Chase. One of the names printed on the patient files Piper usually kept downstairs in her office—the very same folders that now lay scattered across the floor in her bedroom. Just that afternoon, Clay had been here at her home office for his session.

Reaching her son, she acted more out of instinct than

smarts. She scooped the eight-year-old up in her arms and took several steps back. Standing there in the cozy, middle-class suburb, frozen and silent, she thought: *Clayton Chase has come sneaking around my house in the middle of the night.*

But Clay appeared just as surprised as Piper by the situation. Battered by the driving rain, he looked like something out of an old-time horror movie, Dr. Jekyll facing the fruits of his nightly escapade. His eyes grew wider at the sight of her, his shoulder-length hair soaked and slick against the collar of his bomber jacket.

She considered the possibility that Mr. Chase had come to her door by coincidence. She almost smiled at him, inviting an explanation, which from experience she knew would be a long time in coming. His last two months of sessions with Piper had been more perfunctory than insightful, making her wonder at times why he bothered to come at all.

For his part, Simon stretched his hand toward Clay, not in the least intimidated by a man rumored to have gotten away with murder—a tabloid bad boy famous enough to earn her small practice a mention in the papers. Caught off guard by her son's smile, she watched his tiny fingers disappear into the other's grasp.

She heard Clay say gently, "I got you, big guy."

For the last two years, Simon had lived in morbid fear of lightning. Half a dozen times he'd woken from a deep sleep to race screaming into the mouth of the squall where Piper would find him staring at the sky, half defiant, half frozen in fear. But now, lightning arced and branded the blackness overhead and she couldn't feel so much as a shudder from her son.

The three of them stood in the rain, a tableau. The palm tree still ablaze, a fire truck throbbed its beat as firemen hustled to douse the flames before the fire spread to the adjoining homes. She didn't know what to say, adrenaline zinging through her veins, her amazement at odds with her confusion.

Clay shrugged off his coat. He angled his athlete's body so that he managed to shelter both her and Simon from the rain as he wrapped the bomber jacket around them.

To Simon in her arms, he whispered, "I think maybe you scared your mom, running out like that. Time to let her tuck you in and do all that good stuff moms like so much."

Her son took her face in both hands, turning her head so that she looked right at him. He didn't say a word, but in his eyes she could see what he wanted to tell her: *I'm not scared.*

Clay touched the boy's shoulder to get his attention and then raised his hand for a high five. Simon complied. "Just remember what I told you, okay?" Clay said.

He shouldered the bomber jacket like a superhero's cape, never acknowledging his strange appearance as he walked away. As if the whole exchange might have been commonplace. *Just stopped by to say, "Hey."*

In the middle of the night. In the middle of a storm.

Mandy stepped up behind her, taking Simon from Piper's arms. She had no idea how long her daughter had been standing there, watching.

"Who is that?" she asked.

In eight out of ten lightning strikes, the victim dies. Kevin, her husband, hadn't beaten the odds. But the aftereffects of lightning injury could be almost as devastating, enough that survivors like Clay didn't always count themselves lucky.

That's when Piper stepped in. Since Kevin's death, her children and her practice counseling lightning victims had been her reasons for getting out of bed in the morning.

Clayton Chase hadn't been the worst case she'd come across, but he'd been bad enough. He begrudgingly admitted to migraines and insomnia, though nothing more concrete. She suspected he suffered from more than the usual post-traumatic stress, given his wife's death and the murder trial. Twice a week, they met for an hour as part of a recovery program she'd designed. Sixty minutes he'd made clear were a complete waste of his time.

And here he is outside my door.

"Mom?" Mandy prompted. "Is everything okay?"

"Take your brother inside."

Piper stood in the rain in her pajamas, chaos unfolding around her, transfixed by the sight of Clay disappearing into the night.

She wasn't quite sure when she started after him, but at some point she figured she might as well try and catch up. She started running, a full-out sprint barefoot in the rain. She passed neighbors in their bathrobes peering out from the safety of their front steps, lured by the commotion of the fire engine. Coming up behind him, she grabbed his arm and, panting for breath, she screamed over the sirens and the storm, "What are you doing here?"

"You should go back," he said. "You're cold."

She wore only thin cotton pajamas. The top now plastered to her breasts was most likely transparent. She noticed he didn't offer his jacket this time, but she gave him credit for keeping his eyes on her face.

She crossed her arms over her chest. "I think I deserve an explanation."

She bit her tongue even as the words tumbled out. For goodness sake, she was his therapist…and everything she was saying and doing was completely wrong.

"Maybe we should go inside," she said, sounding too tentative. "I can call someone," she added with more confidence.

"You want to call someone?" He gave a lazy smile. "Like maybe the cops?"

"Is that what you think?"

"Come on, doc. I show up here in the middle of the night, and you find me with your kid. If that doesn't qualify as a 911, what does?"

He had a point. And still, she couldn't forget the sight of her son's tiny hand curled in his.

"Simon ran outside because he was scared," she said, telling him what she thought had happened. "You were standing here already. You saw him and came to help."

The few who still braved the storm kept a safe distance from the firemen at work, the flames no threat to the Spanish tile roofs of the cookie-cutter homes lining the cul-de-sac. She and Clay stood alone, their conversation unnoticed.

His smile disappeared. He tilted his head so that his collar-length hair hid most of his face. He gave a low whistle. "Very impressive, doc. ESP must come in handy talking to us nut jobs."

"If I remember correctly, we don't do a lot of that during our sessions. Talking, that is." She was almost shouting over the storm. "The mind reading, of course, I throw in to keep myself amused."

Clay had a way of looking at people, as if he were watching them through the lens of his camera. She imagined his hazel eyes would change color with his mood—not that she'd seen much emotion during their sessions. Add the vintage clothes and the careless hairstyle he favored, and he became the perfect image of a famous artist. That photographer's focus was almost too much. As if all the energy from the strike could still be there, lying in wait for the unsuspecting, ready to take his shot.

He didn't so much as blink as he asked, "So what's wrong with your kid?"

"Wrong?"

His question brought her up short. *Wrong* was a word she'd grown to hate. She'd heard it too often from teachers and her mother-in-law—from perfect strangers in the grocery store or the zoo.

She told him, "I'm your therapist, Clay. It wouldn't be appropriate for me to discuss the details of my life."

Again, that look. As if he were framing her for the camera.

"Why, doc," he said almost gently. "I believe you just did."

Lightning granted an eerie light to the horizon as he turned and walked away. He seemed almost to challenge the storm… or perhaps he believed that nature had long since done its worst. Piper squinted against the rain as the image of him strolling into the distance slowly grew smaller.

She'd never had a patient come to her house like this. She didn't fear the people she counseled; in fact, quite the opposite. Even a man accused of killing his wife—front-page news for the tabloids placing odds on whether or not he'd gotten away with murder—hadn't given her a moment's pause.

She considered herself a haven for people like Clayton Chase, a fringe member of an exclusive club of survivors. She'd made a promise to herself after Kevin had died that she would always believe the people who came to her for help, no matter how bizarre or absurd the case might sound to someone who hadn't been touched by their kind of tragedy. That's why she'd taken on Clayton's case despite everyone's fears. *He killed his wife….*

Inside the house, she could hear the blow-dryer in Mandy's room. She checked to see that Mandy had changed clothes and dressed her brother. With the electricity back, life appeared almost normal, but Piper still felt off balance.

She grabbed a terry-cloth robe from the bathroom upstairs. The light from the fire truck pulsed through the window and occasional thunder rattled the panes. In her mind, she could still see Clayton Chase standing in the street, staring down at her. Now she was the one being examined and judged.

Back in Mandy's room, she found Simon huddled in his sister's bed. Mandy was humming to him softly, brushing the chestnut wisp of hair from his forehead.

"Amazing, isn't it?" she told Piper.

Since Kevin's death, Simon had never slept through a storm.

"He looks so peaceful." Mandy leaned over to kiss her sleeping brother on his forehead.

Emotion constricted Piper's throat. That familiar vise around her chest when she looked at Simon happened too often these days, as if she could no longer swallow her frustration. Two years she'd lived a roller-coaster existence with her son since Kevin's death. What followed was a deathly fear of storms and an increasing inability to speak. Her son had retreated into himself. She'd tried to trick herself into believing in hope, that one day Simon would smile at her and rattle off all those words he'd been storing up inside himself for two years. The garbled speech he parceled out so stingily in embarrassment would be gone, his silent vigil ended. But she'd been fooled before in seeing progress…only to have her son shut down.

She didn't want to believe it could be this simple. That a stranger could walk into their lives one night and make all the nightmares go away. She didn't want to trust that kind of magic.

And still, she knew that this night something fundamental had changed for her son.

She touched Simon's hand. Even in sleep, his tiny fingers curled around hers.

Clay stood in the storm. He'd kept walking until he was sure she couldn't see him.

Great. Now, he'd always remember her like that. Staring at him as if he were some sort of ax murderer.

As if their sessions weren't difficult enough, he told himself. As if she weren't already staring at him with those big blue eyes of hers, wondering why he wasn't fixed yet. He could see the doc liked things a little more efficient.

He patted his pockets, hoping he'd find his car keys. He did—inside pocket of his jacket. That made him breathe a little easier. Especially when he saw the Jeep just ahead. *Everything's gonna be fine,* he told himself.

Only, he knew that too was a lie.

Opening the car door, he stopped long enough to glance in the car's side mirror.

There, just down the street, a silver sedan waited.

The guy didn't bother hiding anymore. Clay figured that was part of it. Letting him know he was being watched 24-7. A way of twisting the knife.

Ironic really. Because sometimes, just knowing the guy was there keeping tabs wasn't painful at all.

It was a relief.

2

Piper considered the possibility that she was dreaming, sleep-walking so that, like an episode of some soap opera, she would open the shower door and discover the last two years had been make-believe. Kevin would still be alive, a doctor with a thriving practice. She would be a stay-at-home mom, baking cookies, volunteering at school. *Wake up, Piper!*

Thunder rattled the windowpane, a familiar, painful sound. Her hands shaking from an overload of adrenaline, she opened the drawer of the bedside table where she kept a bottle of tranquilizers. She fumbled with the childproof cap.

The ancients believed lightning was a curse, marking those it touched for condemnation. Primitive cultures denied its victims burial rites, and even Neolithic drawings depicted lightning as an ill omen. Prophets and priests became effective weathermen, predicting the doom and gloom of battles and politics.

Piper had spent the last two years convincing herself those prophets were wrong. Her family hadn't been singled out by cosmic forces. They would get through the tragedy of Kevin's death and Simon's disability.

"I'm not cursed," she told herself.

Piper gave up on the bottle and shut the drawer, reaching

for her anger instead of the pills. She sat on her empty bed, glanced at the folders littering the floor beside it. She picked up the one with the name Clayton Chase typed on the label.

As shocking as the sight of him had been tonight, she suspected she knew exactly what had brought him to her door. Their session earlier today had been a doozy. She should never have asked him to bring his camera.

She closed her eyes and pictured him sitting on the sofa in her office, his legs pumping, the Nikon front and center on the coffee table between them. Past sessions had been marked by a cool indifference on his part. He was a man with better things to do than talk about his feelings. So she'd asked that he bring his camera, hoping to pry loose whatever it was he'd buried so deep inside he came diligently each week to her door to hide from it.

Piper practiced cognitive-behavioral psychotherapy. Her treatment goal was to assist clients in adapting to any disability or trauma suffered. The first twelve months after injury were crucial to the recovery process for the victims of lightning injury. Counseling at the outset to explain complications and reassure patients could head off problems down the line.

Unfortunately, Clay had had little or no counseling in the time leading up to the trial for his wife's murder, contributing to what she thought might be a panic disorder. He'd come to see Piper immediately after the court declared a mistrial, a man shadowed by the media and hounded by doubts. In the first few visits, she'd hit a wall with Clay, who swore he didn't need her help...even as he showed up without fail for each and every appointment. They'd met twice a week for the last two months without any sign of progress or change.

But that afternoon had been different. Suddenly, he'd fit the profile of a lightning-strike victim. Irritable, lacking focus, looking everywhere but at the camera on the table between them.

So she'd tried pushing a little.

She knew from reading court papers that hand tremors prevented him from holding his camera, putting an end to his career as a nature photographer. During their sessions together, he'd complained only of headaches and insomnia, avoiding the central issues of his wife's death, the trial and his failed career.

All he wanted was to sleep, he'd told her. His words: *to sleep like the dead.*

So she'd asked him to bring his camera, looking to jar loose those emotions cemented inside.

The session had started gently enough. She told him to pick up the Nikon, only that. Baby steps. When he hesitated, she reached for the camera herself.

Only to have him grab her hand.

"Don't," he told her.

She'd never been afraid of Clayton Chase. The newspaper clippings her sister sent her outlining the more sensational aspects of his trial for murder struck her as tabloid journalism at its worst, even though they were published in the local paper. Piper didn't fear the people who came to her for help.

Suddenly, that had changed.

"Why do you fight me, Clay?"

"I got blasted by a few thousand volts of electricity. In my book, that's not exactly a psychological problem, so pardon me if I haven't been accommodating."

"Then why come at all?"

"Look, doc. Give me a pill, strap me to some machine— yeah sure. I get the connection. But put a box of Kleenex on

*my lap and wait for me to cry? Now that's what I call a waste
of oxygen."*

"So it's my methods you object to?"

"And then some."

She'd been staring at his hand around her wrist, thinking,
be careful, when his fingers began to shake.

He let go immediately, as surprised as she by his reaction.

She'd reminded herself that lightning victims often suffered
severe personality changes, becoming fragile, irritable and
angry when experiencing even mild stress. *Don't push, Piper.*

But that afternoon was the first show of emotion she'd seen
from Clay, the kind of breakthrough she'd been hoping for.

So she picked up the camera and held it out to him.

With his collar-length hair and long sideburns, Clay really
did look like a "Renaissance man," as one newspaper had
dubbed him. He stood to face her, at the same time using his
hair like a shield, the bangs hiding his face. He shoved his
hands into the pockets of his pants.

"Don't."

"What are you afraid of, Clay?"

"You're the professional. You tell me."

"In two months of coming here, you haven't said a word
about anything that matters. How could I possibly know what
you're feeling right now?"

She remembered a change coming over him then, emotion
rising to the surface in stages like the photographs he'd once
developed. Slowly, he pushed his bangs back and cocked his
head to look at her. His mouth hardened into a smile. He had
an angular face, the kind that caught the shadows. Standing
there, he appeared incredibly intense. Cold and focused.

He stepped closer, his hands no longer hidden.

"So you think I'm afraid," he told her.

Within the rarefied group of individuals who survived a lightning strike, there existed vigorous independent risk-seekers—people whose career or recreation choice had put them in harm's way. Men like Clay tended to resist treatment efforts, intensifying the cycle of frustration and decline.

And still, she told him, "I think you're scared silly."

At that moment, he grabbed the camera from her and lifted the Nikon, taking her photograph, the motion smooth and effortless. For the first time, she caught a glimpse of the man he'd been before the strike. There wasn't anything indifferent about him. He was engaged and in control as he circled, coming closer, focusing between clicks.

"Tell me what scares you, Piper?" he asked, snapping his photographs.

She couldn't remember a time when someone had taken photographs of her. Not like this. One after the other as if she were a model on a photo shoot. Still, she couldn't imagine why it should make her feel so vulnerable. Exposed.

And then she knew.

Laughing with Kevin as they shoved wedding cake in each other's mouths. She and Mandy building a sandcastle on the beach. Simon's birth...Disney World with the kids and Kevin wearing that enormous Goofy hat with the flapping black ears.

The last time she'd been the object of a camera's lens, her husband had been very much alive.

She remembered holding up her hand, covering her face. She imagined how she must have appeared. A starlet avoiding the paparazzi.

"You didn't answer my question," he said, still snapping

his photographs, stepping closer until only the camera kept them apart.

He whispered, "I think I know what scares you, Piper. I scare you. I scare you to death."

That's when he dropped the camera to his side. They both stood staring at each other.

"Session over," he said.

That had been earlier today. Less than ten hours later, she'd found him standing in the middle of her cul-de-sac, comforting her son as he held him in his arms during a storm.

She wouldn't attribute cosmic powers to those touched by lightning. Just as she refused to believe them cursed, she didn't think them blessed with special abilities. Like healing her son.

With the storm still raging outside, she pulled out one of the articles her sister had given her from the Chase folder. The reporter alluded to the possibility that the lightning strike of the famed photographer could have been staged. Much had been made of the fact that Clay had no visible burns or injuries, relying on the popular "crispy critter" myth to cast doubt on his credibility. But Piper knew that, in reality, lightning could flash over the body, sometimes blowing off clothes and leaving no external signs.

The article suggested Clay had never been struck at all, explaining away the fact that the zipper to his jeans had been blown off and Clay knocked out of one of his shoes. The reporter tossed the question to the reader: Why only one and not both shoes?

The paper went on to describe a ground-current event. Lightning hits the earth, and rather than becoming "grounded," as was the popular belief, it spread along the surface, dirt making a fairly good conductor. When the current came in contact with a fence, or water, or in Clay's case, the human body, the electricity could surge to strike whatever was closest, sometimes jumping several feet to make its connection.

She flipped through the pages, ignoring the highlighted words her sister, a journalist, had marked for easy reading. Piper stopped at the passage quoting the state attorney's theory about the case, the words *convenient amnesia* underlined twice by her sister.

There were aspects of Clay's case that defied conventional wisdom. Although physical and cognitive complaints from lightning injury could be vague, after listening to victims and their stories these past two years, Piper had discovered a consistent pattern. The fact that Clay had taken a string of photographs in her office was just another indication to Piper that all was not as it seemed with Clayton Chase.

She stared at her notes. All along she'd been unsure whether his symptoms were due directly to lightning injury or were the result of some other trauma.

"Like killing his wife," she said out loud.

There was a real possibility that Clay's amnesia could be reactive. If he had killed his wife…he might not want to remember.

There used to be quite a few things that made Burton Ward smile.

This hotel, for example, the Breakers. The Palm Beach legend was a seaside Italianate palace, inviting guests with its fountains, courtyards and graceful loggias. The resort had been the brainchild of Henry Flagler of Standard Oil, an early developer who'd opened up the east coast of Florida in the late nineteenth century. With its string of luxury hotels, Flagler's Florida railroad had been called the Eighth Wonder of the World. In the past, Burton would come here to soak up the spirit of the man, hubris allowing him to make comparisons between their two fortunes.

Tonight's soiree was to benefit Florida wildlife, a pet project of Jackie's. The party was taking place in the Circle Dining Room, whose domed ceilings and Italian wall paintings made it one of the most spectacular restaurants in the country. But it was the view of the ocean framed by two-story arched windows that Burton found most impressive. A man could sit here staring out into nothing. He could remember all the things that used to make him smile.

"If I weren't the independent sort, I might feel ignored right now, Burton, my love."

He turned to face his wife, Jacquelyn. Friends had jokingly nicknamed her Jackie-O, only, it wasn't a joke to Burton. She had dark eyes and shining black hair. Tonight she wore her hair down to her shoulders in gentle waves, just the way he liked it best. Everything about his wife screamed class. Forty-one years together and the woman still looked amazing.

"I'm ignoring you?" He leaned down to give her a kiss. "Is that so?"

"Lucky for you that I am so independent. That's what I told that handsome young man who propositioned me just a minute ago. That you and I live completely independent lives."

"Young?" He searched the moneyed crowd that usually populated these types of scenes.

His wife nodded. "Very young, very handsome."

She pointed with her champagne glass at a man in his twenties whose posh clothes and hovering boyfriend made

clear hi...
well or s...

"Him, y..."

"As if I ne..."
granted him a...
gle. Half the pe...

"To try and ta...

"That may be so..."
the meantime, why...
of theirs?"

"For you, anything."

He looked into his wife... ...love and de-
votion a man could ever w... ...d watched Jackie
stroll through the crush of bo... ...eeting partygoers as she
passed. She walked with her back straight, her head held high.
Unlike Burton, his wife—who knew most of the people in the
room by name—smiled often. Never in a million years could
anyone guess those lovely shoulders bore the same weight of
tragedy that he'd allowed to bury him.

He'd met his wife during a similar stormy night at just such
an uppity affair. Wearing his first tuxedo, he'd been congrat-
ulating himself for having breached the coveted shores of
Palm Beach society. The rich food, the champagne—he'd
earned it all. Despite years of crawling through the dirt with
Miami's worst, at long last, he'd risen above the muck, a winner. That's when his greatest prize had walked into the room.

She'd been an art student at the University of Miami then;
he'd been celebrating his first million from the sale of a strip
mall, a paltry sum that didn't alter the label "fortune hunter"
her suspicious Fifth Avenue family stamped on him. A few
hundred million in real estate later, they'd come around.

window as if you can
plained, squinting into the

a crystal-ball effect. He imagined Henry
g out just such a window, thinking up some new
—a hotel or a railroad—anything into which he could
y his grief after the death of his daughter.

Jillian.

"Burton?"

"I'm all right," he told Jackie, squeezing her hand.

And then he was, catching sight of one of the hotel waiters making his way through the crowd toward him. He felt as if he'd been holding his breath, waiting all night.

The man came alongside Burton, informing him that he had a phone call.

His wife watched, a small frown creasing her brow. "Burton, you promised."

"I'll only be a minute."

He went to the nearest phone. Jackie had taken custody of his cell phone, but he'd given the number here at the hotel. Just in case.

He listened intently. His wife would think he was talking business. But this had nothing to do with Ward Enterprises. He could feel the blood pumping, these phone calls managing what Jackie's love for him no longer could.

By the time he hung up, Burton Ward finally had a smile on his face.

3

"*V-A-C-A-T-I-O-N.*" Crissa's voice spelled the word over the phone, enunciating as if she were talking to a woman whose first language might not be English. "It's this really cool thing that helps you get rid of those unsightly bags under your eyes."

"Ouch," Piper said to her sister, indeed checking out the luggage beneath her eyes in the downstairs bathroom mirror. Disgusted, she left the room and padded down the hall toward the kitchen. "Here, let me get some caffeine in my system before you deliver the hard stuff."

"Come on, little sis. A stretch of white sand, a hunky cabana boy rubbing oil into your sunburned shoulders."

"Saw the commercial. Not interested."

Her sister made a rude noise deep in her throat. "You don't watch enough television to see commercials." Then, after a beat, she asked, "How was Simon last night?"

Piper stared at the coffee she'd just poured. "He ran out again."

"Still?"

Because they had all been hoping he was getting better.

"My fault. I should have been better prepared."

"Dear God, were you actually sleeping for once?"

Piper ignored her sister's sarcasm. These last two years, sleep had been a luxury Piper couldn't afford. She should have been on storm watch, waiting for Simon to make his move. Instead, she'd fallen asleep reading client files in bed.

"Stop it," her sister said, apparently hearing Piper's silent guilt over the phone line. "You're way too hard on yourself."

"Life is way too hard." She watched Mandy walk in, skipping the waffle and orange juice waiting for her on the kitchen table. Under her sixteen-year-old daughter's eyes, Piper could see those familiar dark circles. *Like mother, like daughter.*

"I gotta go," she said, hanging up.

She grabbed the car keys from the countertop before her daughter could take them.

"Sit." She pointed to the kitchen table. "Eat."

"Can't. I have to go in early to pre-calculus. We have a test today and there's some stuff I don't understand."

Piper gave Mandy a hard stare before dropping the keys into her daughter's hand. She walked over to the table, grabbed a napkin and wrapped up one of the waffles.

"Thanks," Mandy said, taking the offering. She gave Piper a quick kiss and headed for the door.

Before Piper could give a last warning about what happened to the human brain if it didn't have sufficient food, the front door slammed shut.

Piper sat down, pushing grief away but knowing that like Sisyphus and his rock, it would soon return. Built into the nook in front of her, a series of staggered shelves held a photograph of Kevin, a rock from their first camping trip together and a cigar, which he had ceremoniously handed over when he'd quit smoking, the day they'd found out she was pregnant with Simon. The shelf had the appearance of a shrine.

She focused on the photograph, remembering the day she'd taken that particular shot. There had been a pie-eating contest at the school picnic and Kevin's face was covered in raspberries. He'd been threatening to come give her a huge kiss when she'd snapped the photo.

Piper stood and took the photograph off the shelf. She opened the kitchen drawer beneath and dropped the picture inside. She did the same for each memento. The rock, the cigar—one by one, they disappeared into the drawer.

She slammed the drawer shut. She stood back with her mouth covered, then laughed, falling back into the chair.

"Piper, you silly creature," she told herself.

A silly creature with a pile of bills to pay and two children to care for. Before Kevin had died, her main concern had been the emotional and physical well-being of her children. Mandy had been in training for show jumping with her horse. Simon had been reading since the age of three.

Now, Mandy cooked most nights, sneaking in riding lessons between school and working at the barn to pay for lessons. Simon did time in therapy: occupational, speech, biofeedback. Both kids helped around the house. Life insurance and the sale of their house in Coral Gables paid for their more modest home here in the shiny new suburb of Coral Cay. But only Piper's practice as a marriage and family therapist kept her from having to make that call to Kevin's parents, who were only too ready to step in and help…and take over.

Mandy isn't even yours, Piper….

Boy, if she'd ever wanted to pop someone on the nose, it had been her mother-in-law the day she'd said those words. Kevin not two days in the ground and Leah already at her. Mandy might not be Piper's biological daughter, but Piper had been the only mother Mandy had known since she'd turned five, thank you very much. And no National Charity League version of Attila the Hun was getting her claws into Piper's baby.

Piper sighed, trying to remember Kevin's parents weren't the enemy. The fact was, some days Leah and her bazillions seemed the lesser of the two evils, even with strings attached. Mandy needed braces. Simon's therapy bills were piling up, and Piper wondered if she weren't making a terrible mistake, working full-time, making them all struggle—keeping them trapped exactly here, the mice in the maze.

If only she didn't believe her mother-in-law was the devil.

"Holy cow, Piper," she told herself, standing.

At that moment, Simon raced in. He sat at the table, grabbing the morning comics before he began shoveling food into his mouth.

Piper stood watching, her coffee cup forgotten in her hand. Unlike his sister, who made it a practice to sleep until she only had time to splash some water on her face and pile books in a bag before running out the door, Simon often ate breakfast. But the night after a storm, this chipper appearance was completely out of character.

In the last two years, Simon had run out during a storm many times. She often thought he was testing his mettle, trying to conquer his fears by facing the squall. But afterward, he'd always spend the night curled beside Piper in bed, crying himself to sleep in her arms. He'd toss and turn as if he were still running from that nightmare storm that had killed his father and left Simon unable—or unwilling—to speak. It wasn't unusual for him to miss school the next day, sleeping in, exhausted in her bed.

She could feel her heart racing as she watched him looking so incredibly *normal*. She sat down beside him with her coffee and picked up one of his waffles, pretending to take a bite before he wrestled it back. He wolfed it down and smiled.

"So." She kept her voice up, acting as if nothing were different about her son this morning. "What's on the schedule for today?"

Simon reached up and gave her a big hug. He grabbed his backpack and headed for the door.

"Hey, aren't you forgetting something?"

He ran back and gave her a kiss before diving out the front door for the bus stop.

But not a word. Not one word.

"Baby steps," she told herself.

She thought about how ridiculous it was. A therapist who couldn't help her own child.

She walked over to the sink, staring at the pot of coffee as if she weren't holding a full cup in her hand.

Who was she fooling? These days, she couldn't help even herself.

Clayton Chase had come to believe that what others thought was destiny was actually just a matter of timing.

Last year, over a bottle of vodka, the whole destiny thing had come into focus. He figured it had been "a moment," like when Neil Armstrong had walked on the moon or when Jillian Ward had first kissed him on a damp Christmas night under the umbrella of a magnolia tree in his front yard. It had come on a day he'd tried to escape the hell of the airport, snagging a speeding ticket before sliding on home to find his wife waiting to tell him that she was leaving him.

Destiny, that's what Jillian had called it. *I'm sorry Clay. He's my destiny.*

But later, keeping company with that vodka bottle on the porch, Clay figured Jillian had it all wrong, confusing a practical matter of timing with the divine, as people often do. The way he saw it, Jillian's change of heart had nothing to do with destiny. The fact was she didn't love him anymore. Plain and simple, his time was up.

So when that finger of lightning struck, Clay hadn't made the same mistake of thinking about fate and the inevitable. Lightning wasn't his destiny, only his choice. He knew he'd just waited too long, wanting that last exposure, ignoring the storm alarm warning him to move along.

Only now, almost a year later, knowing everything he did about the screwed-up choices people made, he couldn't seem to get his footing back into the practical. He was standing in his darkroom and it was like he was watching a movie of himself stepping around the room, executing a carefully choreographed dance. He hadn't touched his camera equipment since he'd lost Jillian. He'd barely entered the darkroom in the last year. This man with the steady hands developing photographs couldn't be him. Not again. Not ever again.

The whole day felt so bizarre and out of sync that, if he didn't know better, he might be tempted to use words like *destiny* to describe what he was seeing. Standing in the darkroom, his eyes long adapted to the red light above, he kept staring into the shallow pan at Piper's submerged face, falling into that image, drowning in a surprising sense of the inevitable. On the wall to his right, proof sheets hung showing thirty-six little Pipers staring back at him in six neat little rows.

The familiar smell of chemicals made him think of Proust and his taste of madeleine cookie. Suddenly, he felt too much.

And now, he couldn't catch his breath, looking at the photograph he'd just developed. Piper's perfect likeness stared up at him, a surreal image that didn't seem possible.

Last night, before her son had come racing out into the storm, he'd been standing outside her door with his camera, plagued by that same sense of the surreal. *This can't be happening....* Just like the day Jillian had died, he couldn't make sense of what was going on. Couldn't fit the pieces together and say, *There.*

Using rubber-tipped tongs, he took the photograph of Piper out of the tray and clipped it on the drying line next to three others. In the eight-by-ten, Piper held her hand out in front of her face, captured forever in a pure diva moment. Her hand took up three-fourths of the photograph, showing glimpses of her heart-shaped face past the gaps in her fingers, those blue eyes and blond hair looking luminous in simple black and white.

When lightning strikes, the explosion that follows makes a man feel as if he'd just been turned inside out. He thought he'd never feel that again. He was dead inside. Just like Jillian.

Only now, staring at the photograph of Piper, knowing what it meant, he felt turned inside out again. Now nothing would ever be the same.

The phone rang, the sound sudden and shrill in the silence of his empty house. He didn't have an answering machine, nothing to stop the persistent ringing. After ten or so times, he headed for the kitchen, having finished developing the photographs of Piper. He figured whoever was calling wasn't giving up.

In the kitchen, he recognized the number on the phone's caller ID display.

Timing. It was all about timing.

He picked up. "Yes?"

"Clay."

It was Aidan, his attorney.

That feeling again. Like it was yesterday. Jillian there beside him on the ground covered in blood...

"Clay," he heard Aidan say. "I got the call from the state attorney's office. They're going to retry the case."

Shawna Benet stared into the full-length mirror, thinking people owed her. They owed her big.

Like Aidan. Shawna had given up everything for him, every little thing. And what did she have to show for it? Not much, that's for sure. Not enough.

He was supposed to take care of her, dammit. He was supposed to watch out for her, not the other way around.

And now he was throwing his career away to help Clay just because he felt sorry for him? Imagine, Aidan feeling sorry for the famed Clayton Chase? As if the renowned photographer and heir to Jillian's bazillions needed someone to feel sorry for him. Right.

"Ain't life grand," she told her image in the glass.

Shawna stood in front of the mirror wearing a red Donna Karan dress and strappy black heels, collagen lips in full pout. The contacts she wore turned her hazel eyes a sapphire blue. Her stylist kept her naturally blond hair a sophisticated black. She wore it straight and shiny, just the way Aidan liked. She applied rouge, working almost feverishly to look just right.

She worked hard to keep Aidan happy. Only lately, he'd been so preoccupied with Clayton and all his problems, he'd made her feel almost invisible. She frowned, staring at the mirror. She might be due for more Botox.

That was the problem. She always needed more. More

money, more love, more time. None of it was easy to come by, that's for sure, especially when she was forced to live by Aidan's rules. No one even knew they were together. It was their little secret, Aidan told her.

She thought she deserved more. From Aidan especially. The problem was, he wasn't thinking straight, putting them all at risk to help Clayton Chase.

Hadn't Aidan given up enough already, turning his back on the great Burton Ward? You didn't piss off someone like Burton and get away with it and that's exactly what Aidan had done, taking on the case of the man who had murdered Burton's daughter, helping Clay get away with murder. And there were others. Powerful people. People just like Burton who didn't forgive and forget.

She couldn't let Aidan throw it all away, could she? Sure, he'd made his name as a criminal attorney with the trial—not a bad thing in Miami, where men could throw away small fortunes to defend themselves. But he'd only succeeded because he was such a good lawyer. Who would have thought he could get Clay off with that stupid defense? *I was struck by lightning*....Yeah, right. And I was abducted by aliens.

But now, they were going to retry the case, because the first trial had ended with a hung jury. No way that lightning crap would work again. Last time around, Aidan had made the prosecutor look like a fool and the state attorney's office would be out for bear. Chances were, Aidan would go down in flames and everything she'd worked for would disappear with him.

And then she'd have nothing. Again.

Shawna snapped shut the Christian Dior compact she held in her hand, placing it on the vanity. Every time she thought she had something solid in her life, something she could depend on—a new beginning—it all went to shit. Just like her mother. That bitch had always sold herself cheap. *Don't rock the boat, Shawna.*

When her father had divorced her mother, the stupid cow hadn't even gotten a lawyer. Child support? Forget it. That bastard had just run off, leaving them with nothing, starting his own happy new life.

Well, now it was Shawna's turn at a new life. And she'd be smarter about it than her mother. She had to be.

Shawna stepped closer to the mirror, focusing there, forcing herself to see another woman altogether. A winner.

The woman Aidan wanted. The one he'd do anything to please.

Leaving the mirror, she dropped on the bed and picked up the phone. She dialed the number she knew by heart and asked for Aidan Parks.

She waited, getting the usual runaround. People did that a lot to Shawna. They thought she was some dumb bimbo they could use. But it wouldn't always be like that. No sir. She just had to watch Aidan's back and make sure he didn't blow it for them.

Finally, when they put her through, she had to listen to all his excuses about how busy he was and how important his life was until he finally agreed to have lunch. She needed to talk to him.

She stepped back to the mirror and smiled. Leaning forward, she planted a kiss on the glass, leaving behind a scarlet lip print. She knew what Aidan wanted. What they all wanted from Shawna.

Well, she was tired of being used.

Time to use them.

4

Beep. Beep. Beep.

The alarm chirped inside his head, the sound as loud and clear as if it were real and not just a memory. Clay figured if he told the doc about the sound, she'd be making up some weird theory about the side effects of a lightning strike. Maybe some sort of tinnitus crap. But Clay knew the sound was nothing, because he knew it wasn't real. Just his head messing with him.

Beep. Beep. Beep.

The sound was a warning. The same rhythmic beat used to tip him off to electrical charges building in the air, telling him to ignore the light show and pack up his gear, head for safety. But he'd never really paid much attention then. And he didn't now.

He was standing outside Piper's door, his heart racing. The time was near noon; there wasn't a cloud in the sky. And still, he could smell ozone burning.

Beep, beep, beep.

"Hearing you loud and clear," he said, reaching to ring the doorbell.

Clay had a nasty habit of falling into a storm, disappearing there against his better judgment. Waiting for Piper to an-

swer the door, he was falling into something just as dangerous, ignoring all the warnings.

Just like the old days.

When she opened the door, she didn't look surprised to see
him. She stepped outside, closing the door behind her, dressed
in her professional best. That was one thing about the doc.
Never a hair out of place, makeup limited to the bare essen-
tials. She might be blond and beautiful, but she wasn't here
to seduce. Quite the opposite…which was probably the most
seductive thing about her.

"I don't have an appointment," he told her.

A few emotions traveled across that face of hers before settling into an expression of concern. He could imagine. And
things were about to get a whole lot worse.

"There's going to be another trial," he said. "For Jillian's
murder," he added, as if he might need to clarify the point.

That's not where he'd intended to start. He'd been thinking he'd come over and explain about last night. Or call. He
should have called, of course. He was just a normal guy, not
some freak she should fear, thinking he might show up in the
middle of the night again, stalking her. But here he was, standing in front of her door, talking about trials for murder.

A freak. A regular sideshow freak.

"Clayton, I try to be available for my patients," she said,
maintaining that professional tone, not allowing even a little
tremor of fear to slip in and give her away. "I know this is a
difficult time for you. If you call beforehand, I can make time
in my schedule, especially if it's an emergency. If I'm not
available, I have people I trust who cover for me—"

"Yeah, I get all that. But will you see me now? Or should
I run back home and call first?"

More emotion on that pretty face. This time, it wasn't so clear what she was thinking. But she opened the door and stepped inside just the same.

"I happen to be available," she told him in that stoic-doctor voice he'd grown to hate.

He followed her into her office, a room in the back that appeared to be an addition of sorts. It was a typical home, filled with typical things. Ethan Allen furniture, photographs and knickknacks. Nothing like his home used to be.

Jillian came from money. Their house had been postmodern, everything white, glass or chrome. Sterile. He remembered how, after she'd been killed, that sense of emptiness suddenly felt like a perfect fit. *There's nothing left inside me.*

But here in Piper's house, everything was cozy normal. Here was every day. He could see she'd gone to great lengths to separate the living quarters from her office space, even turning the living room into a sort of waiting room. But he saw an action figure in one corner of the floor, as if the kid might have so many stocked away, the hoard would naturally spill over into other parts of the house.

It's what he'd noticed from the first, how much life there was in her home. She'd lost so much, but she hadn't given up. Not like him.

Because of the kids. They needed her. They needed their mother to be strong.

No one needed him. He could waste away and disappear and who would notice? Aidan, maybe. For reasons Clay still couldn't understand, Aidan was always there, pushing him to go on.

In her office, he sat on the couch. She probably thought he'd come here to make some sort of confession. Time to open up and bare his soul to the doctor. Only that wasn't the case. People like him had too many secrets to clear their consciences.

"So let's talk about last night," she said, starting in on him.

"I was waiting outside when he ran out," he told her, cutting off all the bullshit questions about his emotions. *And how does that make you feel?* The therapist's refrain.

"He was scared," he continued.

It had felt so normal to drop his camera back in the Jeep and step into the street. The kid ran straight for him, just a boy who needed reassurance.

So he'd stepped out from where he'd been skulking across the street, spying on the kid's house. He'd taken Piper's son into his arms and comforted him as if he had every right.

"You probably think I'm some sort of stalker," he said, stating the obvious.

Soon, he'd be worse than that. Pretty soon he'd be headline news again. Chase To Be Retried For Wife's Murder.

"I'm not a stalker," he told her.

She had this face. He could read her every thought in her expressions, which he'd always figured was part of the attraction. Maybe even why he came here twice a week, never saying a word that mattered but watching her, just watching.

Everything about her was perfect. Round blue eyes, shoulder-length blond hair framing her heart-shaped face. He'd read somewhere that there was supposed to be this perfect symmetry to the human face. The distance between the eyes, the length of the nose, the width of the mouth—it could all be made into some sort of mathematical equation. Given the right relationship in those numbers, the correct proportions, a person would be considered universally beautiful. It wouldn't matter the age or the culture.

He never thought he'd bring the camera. She'd asked, sure, but he hadn't thought he'd go through with it. Only, he'd known she was losing faith in her ability to help him. Two months and he'd given her zip to work with. He'd been a little afraid that she'd give up, tell him to go home and never come back, maybe even refer him to someone else. So he'd brought the camera, never expecting what had happened next.

He'd always been drawn to nature. The drama of a storm, the perfection of a flower. But sometimes, during their sessions, he would watch that face of hers, that perfect symmetry, and he would wonder about those photographs that he could no longer take, his fingers almost itching.

He should have known she'd be different. Yesterday had just given him the proof.

"I don't think you're a stalker," she said in that soothing tone he figured you had to go to school to learn. He'd liked last night better, the emotions she'd let ring in her voice—anger, shock. That had been the real her, not this careful professional.

"You were standing outside my house because of what happened during our session yesterday," she continued. "I asked you to bring your camera. I pushed you to take those photographs, and I apologize."

"That's right. You put me right over the edge, doc."

He said it with a smile. A friendly joke when she'd hit a bull's-eye.

"I'm curious. The photographs you took in my office. Did any of them turn out?"

"No," he said, not even hesitating to tell the lie.

"Really? Because I noticed your hands weren't shaking.

You looked so natural, taking the photographs. I just thought maybe something had changed."

"Nothing's changed."

He thought she might not believe him. He waited, holding his breath. And then he couldn't wait any longer.

"Look, I know I've been an asshole these past two months, coming here and wasting your time. But I really want you to help me," he said. "I guess I came here the other night trying to figure out how I could make that happen."

"And what did you decide?"

"I didn't. You might say I got distracted."

"Have I ever acted as if I might not want to help you, Clay?"

"Nah, doc. You've been a peach. But it might be a little different from now on."

"Because of the trial."

"Exactly."

He could see her mulling it over. It was one thing to take on a client who'd been tried for murder and had walked. There might be a little comfort in the idea that someone, even if it was only one lousy juror, had given him the benefit of the doubt. But here it was all over again, the idea that he'd killed Jillian, that he'd gotten away with murder. And now, at long last, justice would find him and she would discover that, all along, she'd been sharing time with a killer.

"Last night, you weren't frightened by the storm." She said it as though it was a fact. "Even after everything you've been through, it doesn't bother you to stand out under the sky with lightning blasting overhead."

"No."

"Well, Clay." She had blue eyes as clear as a cloudless sky. "Neither am I. I'm not frightened."

He almost smiled. "Good to know."

"So why don't we get past all the hemming and hawing and to the point? If you want me to help—" she spread out her arms, indicating the office "—I'm here. Please. *Let* me help you."

He could see they both knew this session was different. "You're right, doc. I wasn't afraid last night. But your son was."

He'd thought about it most of the night, the right tactic to keep those doors from shutting in his face. He knew the buttons to push. The kid. For her, it would be all about her son. If he played it right, if he was smart, the kid would be his ticket in.

"We're here to discuss you," she said, warning him.

"Trust me, I'm getting there, doc."

Of course, she wouldn't want to talk about her boy with him. Not right off the bat. If he were in her position, he'd react the same way. Just step right back into normal, normal being what she'd learned at school. *If the patient insists on taking over, becoming the therapist...* But he had a plan.

He leaned forward, pushing before either one of them could figure out that they were about to break the rules.

"You were talking about last night and the lightning. About not being afraid. Well, here's the thing. After the accident, when I was well enough to be out on my own, I used to go out during storms, the fiercer the better," he said, running roughshod over his doubts. "I thought for a while that I was daring the whole thing to happen again. Take me, dammit— but for good this time. But then I realized it was nothing like that. I just like it. The rain. The lightning."

"The drama."

"That's right."

A part of him wanted to tell her the truth. Just come clean. She was his therapist. Wasn't there some kind of confidentiality thing, a rule that she couldn't testify against him?

But it wasn't just about the trial coming up. There were things he didn't want her to know. He needed her to keep that chin of hers raised and her eyes staring right at him, believing she had nothing to fear.

"Yesterday, you wanted to know why I keep coming back. What am I getting out of coming here to see you?" He'd read somewhere that it was better to tell part of the truth in the lie. That it made it less likely he'd mess up later. "I thought maybe you had a point."

"And?"

"Well, I was standing outside your house thinking about it when your son came running out. And then there was just something more important to consider."

She took it in, giving him a lie-detector stare. For a minute, it even worked, making him think she could see deep inside to the rotted center of him.

But then he realized she couldn't. That was the magic of lightning. It cleansed you from real life. He was a clean slate, wiped clear by that blast.

"Your kid, he was really scared when he first came running out," he said, dangling the bait. "But then we talked."

Her body language said it all, tense, leaning toward him now. So did that pause before she asked, "What did you say to Simon?"

He realized he had her. For the first time since his wife had told him she was leaving him, he thought something might actually go his way.

"Sorry, doc. I can't talk to you about that."

"Clay, I think you're playing games," she said, suddenly sounding fierce.

But he didn't answer, not letting himself fall into that trap. He waited until she sighed. "He's my son," she added, letting that plea slip in despite all her attempts to keep things professional.

"And I can help him."

He was playing it by ear, not really sure what he was doing, the steps strange and awkward. He tried to remember the last time he'd tried to connect with someone. Tried to make them believe he might be worth the chance. He thought about the call from Aidan, and realized that, pretty soon, he wouldn't even be allowed near Piper's kid.

The doc finally took the bait. "For the last two years, Simon has had trouble speaking. At first, he made an effort, working through his garbled speech. Now, he hardly speaks at all. To be honest, I haven't heard him say a word in months. And his symptoms are getting worse. It's a phenomenon called electroporation. The electricity causes tiny breaks in the nerve cell membranes. Like a sieve, the cells can't hold nutrients, so they waste away. It's a slow-motion death at the neurological level. It takes years but the symptoms actually get worse, not better. Of course, I've taken Simon to all the experts in the field. We've tried several forms of therapy, with little or no progress. So you tell me, Mr. Chase. How can you help my son?"

He shook his head, keeping his smile. "That was a nice speech. The worried-mother soliloquy. But you see, doc, your kid doesn't have any of that," he told her, dead sure of what he was saying. "Simon is just plain scared."

For a minute, he thought maybe she'd tell him to leave. No

way it could be that simple. She probably had test results to back up all that nonsense she'd come to believe about the kid.

"You said something to him last night," she said, rather than telling him to get the hell out. "Something that made him *not* be afraid."

"That's right."

"And now you won't tell me."

"I promised Simon."

She gave him a look. "I don't think you came here for our normal session, Clay. I think you came here to bargain with me. You help my son. And, of course, you want something in return."

He leaned in closer from his position on the couch. The doc was in her wingback chair, a comfy throne from which she parceled out advice to her broken flock—misfits like him trying to survive what most people couldn't. He'd always liked how she looked sitting in that chair. That was part of the problem. Why he'd been such an asshole to her. Because he didn't want to like anyone.

"You keep seeing me," he told her, laying out his demands. "We keep our sessions. No matter what."

"Given what's already happened, I'm not sure I can promise that."

She would need convincing, of course. He'd figured that much out before coming here. But that kind of persuasion was something he'd never done. Jillian used to tell him that he was too relaxed about things. Go with the flow. Where was his ambition? Of course, when he'd found some, that had been the end of their marriage. So he'd learned never to care that much again.

But this time, he pushed. "It's not a big deal. Just don't believe everything you read in the papers."

She seemed to think about it. After a few moments, she gave a quick nod. "That much I can promise."

"I know my way out."

He whistled softly and headed for the door, able to breathe easily for the first time that day. Which didn't really make any sense, after his talk with Aidan that morning.

The trial was back on, and Aidan had said something about a new prosecutor with a bone to pick.

As the saying went: this party was just getting started.

Mandy was breaking one of her mom's sacred rules.

She felt bad about it. Piper would flip if she ever found out Mandy was driving someone in the Honda. She wasn't supposed to drive with anyone else in the car except Piper or Simon. And when she drove, she wasn't supposed to go anywhere but to school and back. Piper trusted her. Mandy was supposed to be smart, the responsible one....

"You okay?"

Mandy turned to Sean, sitting next to her in the Honda. "Yeah. Sure." Her hands tightened on the steering wheel.

He leaned back and smiled in that way of his. "You should just let me drive us in the Chevy."

She shook her head, just imagining what Piper would think of Sean's baby. *What, no air bags?* "Piper would just make a big deal about it."

She didn't want Piper to know she had a boyfriend, and the minute Piper met Sean, she would figure it out. That Mandy had actually kissed a guy. She needed to keep up the image of the perfect daughter getting perfect grades so she could go to the perfect college, with no distractions. She didn't want to let Piper down when everybody else had.

So every morning she drove over to Sean's house and picked him up. After school, they drove home together. Only soon school would be out for summer and it would be harder to keep her secret. Suddenly, it seemed silly to take these chances. She could feel her stomach turn and her hands go all clammy on the wheel.

"You hate this."

She made a face. "What do you know?"

"What's up with you today, anyway? Ever since this morning, you've been acting kinda funky."

"Hey. I'm the therapist's kid, not you."

"Yeah? Well, maybe it's rubbing off. Come on, something's wrong. Give."

The funny thing was, she didn't want to talk about it. She told Sean everything, but talking about last night would make it too real. Like maybe if she told someone she was afraid, that would mean there really was something to worry about.

"Pull over," he said.

"No way."

"Do it, Scout."

Mandy frowned. He called her Girl Scout because she always did the right thing. She fought the urge to listen and tried just to keep moving down the road, ignoring him.

"I'm going to be late getting home," she said, stopping the car just the same.

"Add it to your list of Things-I-Never-Did-Before. Hey." He turned her face to look at him. "You got me worried, okay?"

He had these beautiful eyes. Green, so that you just fell right into them. She'd met him at a party, one of the first she'd ever gone to. She remembered how he watched people, not like he was bored or afraid or uninvolved, but like he was *studying* them. And he wasn't afraid to use big words. He didn't do it to show off or anything. Those words were just part of who he was, like his big smile and his freckles, and his dark brown curls. He'd asked her for her screen name that night. That was ten months ago.

He'd been her first everything. First date, first kiss. First love. He was the only person she could trust with her secrets. So she figured she should tell him everything. Even this.

She took his hand in hers. "It's just that something weird happened last night."

"Yeah?"

She remembered Piper standing there soaking wet, staring after the guy as he walked away. And Simon. Even this morning, she'd watched him brush his teeth and it was like seeing this different kid. The last two years, she'd tried so hard to reach her brother, thinking that it was somehow her fault, what had happened. She should have been there to help, maybe she could have done something to stop the nightmare their lives had become. Instead, she'd been studying at Katie's house down the block, getting home too late to help.

Now some stranger had stepped into their lives and everything seemed to be changing in a way she couldn't understand—her brother most of all.

"One of Piper's clients showed up last night. I mean, in the middle of the night. Like almost midnight."

"Whoa."

"Exactly. And Simon ran out because he was afraid of the storm and we found him outside with the guy."

Sean whistled. "That's bad. I mean, he's got to be crazy, right? That's why he sees Piper?"

"You moron," she said, but he was already laughing and she knew he'd gotten the reaction he wanted.

"So what happened?" he asked.

She'd been thinking about it all morning. Last night with Simon, she'd been scared for Piper. She'd almost called the cops when she didn't come back right away. She'd never really thought about Piper's job before, that it might be dangerous. She only saw it as a burden on their lives. *If she'd only go to Grandma and Grandpa.*

But she knew that wasn't fair. Grandma was a real control freak. And she'd never really liked Piper, always making sure Mandy understood Piper wasn't her *real* mom— even though she was the only mother Mandy could remember. Mandy had only been four when Tami had died; she didn't have any memories of her mother. Grandma even tried to make her feel guilty that she loved Piper. Like maybe she was being disloyal to the memory of her real mom. Daddy used to tell her Grandma was just being ornery, that she'd been just as mean to Tami when she'd been alive and now Grandma talked about her like she was some freaking saint. Like maybe you had to die to earn Grandma's love.

And now this weird guy had shown up and Simon was acting all strange and Mandy didn't know what to think. Didn't know if she should be happy or scared.

"I don't know. It was just weird, okay?" She gave him a quick kiss. "I'm just being stupid. Piper knows what she's doing. I mean, she sees a bunch of these lightning people, and worse. It's nothing. Come on. I gotta drop you off and get home."

She let Sean drive, sitting back as he slipped the Honda back into traffic, telling herself everything she'd told Sean was true. If there was a problem, Piper could handle it. She would get rid of the guy, just like last night. She'd keep them safe.

Only, she remembered Piper's face out in the street, watching the guy walk away, then running after him. And Simon. The little guy cuddling next to her in bed during the storm like he didn't have a care in the world. And suddenly, her hands felt sweaty again and her stomach got all funky.

And she worried that nothing would ever be the same.

5

Burton Ward had always been able to see the other side of things. He'd come to believe that was what made him such a success in business: his ability to put himself in the other guy's shoes, to take a different point of view. He'd even read a few books on the subject, about different personality types and the things that motivated them.

If he knew what drove a man, he could make a connection, modify his personality to accommodate the other person and make him more receptive to Burton's position. He'd always been good at manipulating people. Especially women. It wasn't something he was proud of; it was just something he knew about himself. Women wanted to do things for Burton. The only thing that mattered to Burton was getting the job done. He liked to win.

But he'd failed with Aidan. He'd failed Aidan miserably, a man he'd once thought of as a son.

He hadn't been able to put himself in Aidan's place. Hadn't been able to understand how anyone could make the choices Aidan had made. Consequently, he hadn't made an impact on the situation with Clay. He hadn't been able to get Aidan onboard.

He didn't do this, Burton. Clay didn't kill Jillian. That's just not possible. He wouldn't hurt her. Never. You and I both know it.

He remembered Aidan telling him that…and remembered how much he'd wanted to punch his fist into Aidan's face as he'd said those words.

That son of a bitch, Clay, had murdered Burton's beautiful baby girl. He'd taken a gun and shot her dead. With Aidan's help, he'd gotten away with it, a damn jury letting the bastard walk because they couldn't reach a verdict.

Aidan, who had once been chief counsel for Ward Enterprises, had made that possible. And he'd do it again, if someone didn't stop him.

Rage, that was Burton's problem. A rage born on the day his daughter had been brutally murdered. That kind of emotion became a weight around a man's neck, keeping him down. It paralyzed him.

But he couldn't seem to get a hold on his emotions— couldn't find his way back to reasonable. His anger just swept over him so that he couldn't think straight, couldn't see beyond the red haze clouding his judgment to take on a different point of view.

Over and over, he'd imagined a different scenario with Aidan, that the scene with Aidan last year had played out differently. He wouldn't have screamed out of control that Aidan was dead to him. In his mind, Burton spoke calmly, telling Aidan how false his faith in Clay, how weak his arguments in support of his daughter's killer. He'd remind him gently that he'd once loved Jillian himself, had even asked her to marry him. He'd convince Aidan once and for all that they needed to work together to bring Jillian's killer to justice.

If he'd been able to do that, if he'd managed that moment,

maybe, just maybe, Clay would be waiting for some endless appeal on death row and Burton could finally rest.

But it hadn't happened that way. The day Aidan had taken on Clay's case, Burton had cut him off. Burton admired loyalty and Aidan had screwed him over.

Now Aidan was too powerful for Burton to threaten into submission, defending some of the richest men in Miami when the government managed to scrape together a RICO charge or two. Just one of Aidan's clients, Angel Barrera—the man who had given Burton his own start years ago—could float an entire law firm.

Looking back, Burton realized he'd made a mistake. He'd been shortsighted, letting his emotions guide his judgment. He hadn't been able, after all, to put himself in the other man's shoes. Hadn't been able to get into Aidan's head to convince him that Clay had murdered Jillian.

Now, almost a year later, he needed to be smarter. He needed to find a way to stop the past from repeating itself. And he was willing to eat major crow to do it.

He looked up to see Aidan walking into the restaurant. By all standards, the boy was a handsome man, tall and blond with a ready smile. But there was also nothing particularly outstanding about Aidan. He could blend into a crowd. Even in the courtroom, he was the opposite of the showman you'd see on those crime series on television. He quietly confided in the jury, relating what he thought was the truth…something that no doubt helped a juror or two lean toward the defense.

Burton wondered sometimes what life would have been like if Jillian had married Aidan instead of Clay. Aidan and Jillian had been high-school sweethearts, a relationship that hadn't survived Jillian going to college in New York and meeting Clay.

Perhaps that was half the reason Aidan had turned against Burton, siding with Clay and his claim of innocence. Some sort of twisted payback because, way back when, Burton hadn't been there for Aidan. He'd let his little girl follow her heart when Aidan had begged Burton to step in and ask his daughter to take a second look.

The truth was, there'd been a time when Burton, too, had chosen Clay, lulled by the man's charisma. He was a charming son of a bitch. If you wanted striking, that would be Clayton Chase, not Aidan. He would never blend into a crowd, not Clay. Those chiseled features, his presence—he'd be the first to catch your eye. They'd all been lulled by the man's talent, wanting to be part of something special—someone who could command magazine covers and major exhibits, even a documentary on the National Geographic channel about his work.

Back then, he'd told Aidan he couldn't get involved in his daughter's affairs, couldn't step in and tell her where her heart lay. But in reality, he'd chosen Clay over Aidan, seduced like everyone else by the man's genius. Artists did that sometimes—made you believe they were special and didn't have to bother with the rules like everyone else.

The hostess led Aidan to their table out on the terrace at the Brazilian Court, a charming sunny setting where one of Palm Beach's finest restaurants, Café Boulud, made its home. Burton smiled at his guest. Hypocrisy was another business talent he had nurtured over the years.

"Thank you for coming," Burton said, motioning for Aidan to sit down across from him beneath the umbrella in the interior courtyard. "How have you been, Aidan?" Burton asked.

Aidan shook his head. "Amazing that you can say that without choking on the words."

Burton kept his smile. "You know me too well."

"That I do, my friend. That I do. So let's cut to the chase. Why am I here?"

"I heard the state attorney is set for a retrial." He took a sip from the martini glass. "Don't take the case, Aidan."

"You give me too much credit, Burton. You always did."

"Bullshit. Without you, the bastard will hang, and I say let him. Jesus Christ, Aidan," he said, taking a different tack. "Do you really want to risk it? Look what you've built for yourself. Look what you have to lose if this case goes south."

Angel Barrera didn't associate with losers. And if Barrera cut him off, Aidan wouldn't find another job in this state, maybe not even in this country. Angel could do that. Not many people survived his kind of sabotage.

"You don't get it," Aidan said, shaking his head as if he felt sorry for Burton. "Clay didn't do this—"

Burton cut him off with a raised hand. A long silence followed. He tried to remind himself why he was here, tried to quell that voice inside his head screaming for him to grab Aidan by the throat and squeeze and squeeze and squeeze.

"I have a proposition," he said instead, setting aside the duck terrine he'd ordered in anticipation of Aidan's arrival. Aidan had always been impressed by all that foodie crap. Burt was more of a beer-and-pretzels guy, but he knew how to play the game.

He kept his voice level. "As you know, I am developing some Indian land. It's a lucrative project for the company."

The project went back several years, and Aidan had done most of the legwork to make it happen.

"But I'm getting old," he said, trying for self-deprecating. "I need someone by my side, and you, dear friend, need to get out from under Angel Barrera's thumb. I'm offering you a full partnership."

He was handing Aidan a gold mine, millions and millions of dollars just sitting there for the taking, as well as the chance to escape the tentacles of Barrera and his ilk—no easy task, as Burton knew all too well, having barely pulled himself free forty years ago. He let the offer hang between them.

Take it!

But Aidan shook his head. He stood, letting Burton know the meeting was over.

"I can't do it, Burt." Aidan looked shocked that he would have to disappoint his old mentor yet again. "I'm sorry. I really am."

Burton watched Aidan walk out. He could feel his blood pressure rising, a knot forming around his heart making it difficult to breathe.

No, he couldn't understand how Aidan justified what he was doing. Couldn't put himself in the other guy's shoes... couldn't imagine anyone who had ever loved Jillian siding with Clayton Chase after what he'd done.

Now he would have to stop Aidan, and he wouldn't be shy about his tactics. He'd learned a thing or two from Angel Barrera, after all.

He motioned the waiter over. He told himself it didn't matter; the meeting had been a courtesy. If he had to take Aidan down to destroy his daughter's killer, so be it. He couldn't afford those kinds of scruples anymore.

He just needed to get the job done. If Aidan didn't see what was coming, so much the better for Burton and his plans.

The last person Piper wanted to talk to was her mother-in-law. So, of course, Kevin's mother was standing at her door.

"I thought we could have lunch." Leah swept in with a bag from Cezanne's, the kind of expensive take-out place that had once been part of Piper's everyday life.

"Come in, Leah," she said to the empty doorway. "So nice of you to drop by." She shut the door. "To snoop."

By the time she walked into her kitchen, Leah had the food spread out on the counter and was pouring wine into two glasses.

"None for me, please."

Leah ignored her, handing Piper the glass and raising hers in a toast. Piper figured that whatever was coming, the wine might not be such a bad idea.

"So, to what do I owe the pleasure?" she asked.

Leah pushed aside the food that Piper knew her mother-in-law wasn't going to eat. Leah stood just under five feet and never weighed over a hundred pounds. She was the type of woman who loved to serve others food, as if she could appreciate the experience of eating vicariously.

"I read in the paper about this man, the one struck by lightning. The one who killed his wife."

"Allegedly killed his wife."

Leah waved away any doubts, drinking from the wineglass. "Mandy says he's one of your clients now. That he comes here to the house."

Piper tried to imagine Mandy talking to Leah about any such thing. She tried desperately not to feel betrayed by the notion, wondering why she should feel betrayed at all.

Leah pressed Piper's hand on the counter, giving it a compassionate squeeze. "Do you think that's wise, dear? Getting involved with someone like that?"

Piper felt something freeze inside her. Leah always knew how to push her buttons. "He's a patient."

"I know, I know. You believe you have a calling to help these people. Trust me, I understand. But I've read what they are saying in the papers. This man, this photographer, is different. Goodness knows, he could have faked the whole thing. I mean, he's some sort of expert on lightning, isn't he? And then there's all the money he would have lost if his wife divorced him. She was a real-estate heiress, you know. Imagine, the only child of Burton Ward. It could have all been part of some elaborate plan to do away with her. Anyway, that's what the papers say."

"That's not for me to judge."

"Is it the money?" Leah asked.

"It's my job," Piper said, used to these tactics.

"But does it have to be? By all accounts, he's dangerous, Piper. Are you sure you know what you're doing, seeing him here at the house? I've told Bob over and over you should have a real office. Let me put a stop to this right now." Leah put down her glass and reached for her Hermès handbag. "Let me write you a check."

"Leah, please. I don't want your money."

She flipped open her leather-clad checkbook. "Think of the children."

"I am thinking of the children and we happen to be doing just fine."

Leah gave an exaggerated sigh. "Have you asked yourself if this is what Kevin would want, Piper? This valiant struggle you're waging in his memory?" She reached for the Waterman's pen, a birthday present from her son before he'd died. "Because I am absolutely certain he wouldn't want Bob and me to stand back and let this happen to his family."

"I think I know what Kevin would want."

"The kids living like this? Their mother helping some murderer? I sincerely doubt it. I'm here to help, Piper." She began filling out the check.

"Leah—"

"How much, darling?"

"Stop it!"

Her voice echoed through the kitchen, with Leah's hand suspended over the check. The two women stood in a silent tableau.

Piper shook her head. "You're not much for subtle, are you, Leah?"

Her mother-in-law recapped her pen. She reached for the wine. After she tossed back the chardonnay, she said, "I find subtlety a waste of time."

She came around the table to give Piper a dismissive peck on the cheek. She whispered, "I thought you would, too."

Piper didn't bother showing Leah to the door. She felt as if she'd just gone a couple of rounds. *Is this what Kevin would want?*

She closed her eyes, feeling those words deeply. She was trying to do what was best for her children. She didn't want her daughter growing up thinking that wearing the right designer clothes and marrying well was all that mattered in this world. She didn't want Bob and Leah hovering over Simon, telling him he was broken.

Still, the doubts were there, a nice complement to Leah's accusations.

She packaged up the food, thinking dinner was now a done deal. The wine, she kept out.

* * *

Clay had been staring at her face all afternoon, memorizing the photograph. He'd captured her in a three-quarters profile. There was something incredibly seductive about that photograph, the expression he'd captured in her eyes.

The strange part? He'd been sitting across from her twice a week for the last two months and the one thing he'd avoided doing was looking at her eyes.

And her smile. His finger traced the lines around her mouth as he thought that he hadn't seen these grooves before, the kind women used expensive creams to try to smooth away. Lines that gave character to her face.

He remembered one assignment in Arizona three years ago. It was near sunset, and lightning flared in the clouds crowning the rock formation called the Three Nuns. Streamers, ribbons and spider lightning hopscotched from cloud to cloud—not dangerous, but getting there. With the backdrop of Sedona's fiery canyons, the photo shoot had been one of his best for *National Geographic*. All Clay had to do was find the guts to stick it out.

It wasn't general knowledge that by the time you heard thunder, you were already within range of a ground flash. When lightning came to ground, it struck with a temperature five times hotter than the sun. More than once, Clay had missed getting hit by a heartbeat. But close calls only encouraged him to pick up his camera and inch closer.

He stared at the photograph. A familiar sense of obsession warmed inside him.

He picked up the glossy. He'd thought he was a dead man, unable, after all, to desire anything, much less this.

Is that what he wanted? Another close call?

He dropped the photograph to the kitchen table and picked up the camera. He made his way to the front door. His conch house in Tavernier had an oceanfront view. Surrounded by tropical plants and huge banyan trees, it was a slice of paradise he'd inherited from his father. You couldn't beat the sunsets here in the Keys. But he had another destination in mind.

He put the Jeep into gear and raced down the road. He didn't want to think about what he was doing. He wanted to pretend that there would be no struggle. Everything would be effortless again, just like in her office.

He pulled off the road at mile marker 93.6. The Wild Bird Rehabilitation Center was an old haunt along the bay, where there were plenty of healthy, beautiful birds to capture with his lens. Here, you could see the real Florida Keys: solution holes, cap rock and the breathing roots of the mangrove rookeries that rose up from the shallow waters of the swamps.

He jumped out of the Jeep. He kept walking, Nikon in hand. He told himself not to allow even the smallest doubt.

There, just ahead. A flock of snowy egrets roosted on the tops of the mangroves. The sunset gilded the pool below. It was an incredible shot.

Focus, he said, raising the Nikon to his eye.

Immediately, his hands began to shake. It was almost a reflex. The palsy took over, making him drop the Nikon.

"Damn."

He picked up the camera, seeing with relief that it hadn't been damaged. He flexed his fingers until the tremors stopped.

He remembered his life before, how the camera had almost been an extension of him. The irony of that loss coinciding with his wife's death seemed somehow poetic. She'd made him famous. Why shouldn't his talent die with her?

He drove to three more places, getting the same results—the shaking hands, the splitting headaches—until he finally gave up and headed home.

The fact was, he hadn't been able to shoot a photograph since the night he'd woken up to find his wife dead in his arms. Until Piper. Now, suddenly, it had all come back, his sixth sense with the camera.

But only when he'd focused on her.

Back at the conch house, he picked up the photographs of Piper on the coffee table and headed to the darkroom. Inside, more photographs waited on the drying line. He picked up a file folder and wrestled them inside, shutting her away.

Before he closed the cabinet, he stopped. He slowed his breathing, counting: *one, two, three...*

He closed his eyes and imagined that face of hers in all its incarnations. Shocked by the camera flash, embarrassed by the focus of the lens, angry when he didn't stop harassing her with the camera.

His eyes still shut, he closed his hand over the file thick with her photographs, wondering what it might all mean.

After a while, he put the photographs away and shut the drawer. He told himself he'd had enough close calls for one night.

6

Graciela Calderon knew the case would be the end of her career. That's why that dickhead Armstrong had assigned her to Chase. He was cleaning house. And she didn't need her soon-to-be ex-husband telling her so.

"Jesus, Grace. It's a setup. Armstrong wants you gone." Chris had a habit of raising his voice when he was stating the obvious, so Grace was careful to hold the phone a good six inches from her ear.

"He doesn't want a Title VII case on his record so here he goes, letting you self-destruct."

"Unfortunately, I can't do anything about that, now can I, Chris?" she asked, making a note to herself on her legal pad. *Stop taking these calls!*

"Give it a pass, Grace," he advised.

"As if I could."

"Don't let that stubborn streak of yours do you in."

Like it had her mentor, Donnie Lincoln. Donnie had thought a front-page news case would make his career, maybe even grant him a talk show when he retired. Instead, Chase had turned into his O.J. Pretrial was a nightmare. The papers had a field day, making it clear Donald Lincoln had met his match in Aidan Parks. The lightning jokes alone killed Donnie. Come election time last November, Lincoln was out and Mitch Armstrong, his chief rival for the job, had stepped in to take his place.

Now, Armstrong was getting rid of the last of Lincoln's people and Grace, Lincoln's protégée, had a solid bull's-eye on her back. Hence she'd been assigned to retry Clayton Chase.

There was a knock on the door. "I gotta go, Chris."

"Put me on hold."

"This might take a while."

"I'll wait. I'm not near through with you, Gracie."

Not to mention afraid she wouldn't call him back. "I'm hanging up."

"Grace—"

She returned the phone to its cradle. She imagined him with his cell phone in his car, earpiece in place, and wondered who he'd be billing for his time. That was the problem with those stakeouts. So much time to kill. She really should file those divorce papers.

Another knock, this time louder. The eager witness was at her door.

"Come in," she said.

Grace did not consider eagerness a good quality in a witness. Eagerness made her suspicious of a person's motives. But here was the ever eager Shawna Benet, knock, knock, knocking on her door, wasting no time once the news of another trial had hit the papers.

"He killed her all right," she'd told Grace on the phone just that morning. "Jillian was leaving him and with the prenup and all, he wanted to make sure he got every penny."

Three hours later, enter the bombshell witness herself, Jillian Ward-Chase's assistant at the art gallery that featured

Clay's work. A striking brunette with a manicured appearance that screamed high maintenance, Shawna Benet was a woman who couldn't wait to make her plea in person.

"Sit down, Ms. Benet," Grace said, pointing to the chair in front of her desk.

Something about the Benet woman didn't sit well with Grace. Something all too familiar. A hunger of sorts, the kind that always came to no good in the courtroom.

But once she really got a look at her, Grace wondered if that sense of the familiar weren't something less ominous. She made a note to check and see if she'd met with Shawna Benet before. Or maybe it was just her polished appearance and stylish clothes, a look women seemed to cultivate here in the land of the nip and tuck. That glossy black hair, the perfect shoes and purse. Hey, Grace was a woman. She was allowed a little fashion envy.

Shawna sat down. After a few preliminaries, Grace started making notes. "You called this morning to tell me Jillian was having an affair?" she prompted.

"Of course. Clay treated her like shit." Shawna crossed her showgirl legs, settling in, center stage and enjoying every minute. "He was the star, you see. Always. That gets kind of old, as you can imagine. And he was gone all the time. On assignment." Here, Ms. Benet did her the favor of visual aids, using her fingers to put quotation marks around the words. "I mean, what did he expect?"

Grace always loved this part. I cheated because he ignored me. I cheated because he didn't understand me. I cheated because he worked long hours and I was lonely. Whatever happened to good old-fashioned loyalty and marriage vows?

But knowing the sorry state of her own affairs, Grace told

herself to listen up and stop projecting. "But you don't have any idea who this mystery man might be?" Grace asked. "The father of the baby?"

Shawna shook her head. "Jillian was discreet."

She was pregnant, Grace thought. The very definition of discreet.

The interview lasted another unproductive twenty minutes before Grace wrapped up. "I'm curious, Ms. Benet. Why didn't you come forward with this information the first time we tried Clayton Chase?"

Suddenly, Shawna's face fell into the picture of regret. In Grace's opinion, little Miss Shawna wasn't exactly Oscar material.

"I should have, I know. But I didn't want to cause trouble for Clay. I even thought that maybe he was innocent. I didn't realize what kind of a person he really was. Not then."

"And now you do?"

She nodded. "I've had a lot of time to think about it. And there's the gallery, of course. If he truly loved Jillian, he wouldn't have let that happen."

To be exact, Shawna Benet, the assistant to the victim, Jillian Ward-Chase, was out of a job. The gallery that featured Jillian's very famous husband's photographs had shut down. Since the death of his wife, Clayton Chase had chosen to close the gallery, despite Ms. Benet's pleas to allow her to keep it open, making her one disgruntled employee.

"Well, thank you for coming forward now." Grace stood, wondering if she was going to be able to use the assistant's testimony at all. Throughout the whole interview, she'd been going over in her head how to massage some of the facts Ms. Benet had so enthusiastically spilled. But Grace wouldn't put money on how well the woman would hold up under cross-examination.

"I really think I can help you, Ms. Calderon," Shawna said from the door, adding a smile for good measure. "Please, let me help."

Grace watched the woman walk out of her office. She'd gotten this office courtesy of Donnie Lincoln when she'd left her just-another-cog-in-the-wheel job at the state attorney's branch offices.

You and I are going places, Grace, Donnie had said.

But the only place Donnie had gone was right out the hallowed halls of the courthouse into private practice after he'd lost the election. And now, if the Chase case blew up in her face, Grace was thinking she might just follow him there.

On her desk, her cell phone chimed "La Cucaracha." Jesus, the man had timing. She flipped open the phone and punched Chris through.

"I know you think some people might have taken the hint by now," he said.

"What? And miss an opportunity to tell me all the mistakes I'm going to make with Chase?" She glanced through her notes from the interview with Shawna Benet, thinking, *Not good*.

"So just because you want a little space—let me emphasize here, *you*—I can't call and give you the heads-up on something like this? Come on, Grace."

"It's called a separation, Chris," she told him. "Look the word up in the dictionary if you're having trouble with the meaning."

The line went dead, Chris apparently having had enough of her scintillating wit.

Grace dropped her cell phone back on her desk. There'd been another word Chris needed to look up in the dictionary.

Faith. Three months into what she'd thought was a blissful marriage, he'd gotten cold feet. She was pretty sure he'd even used the words *ball and chain* during that last argument, when she'd kicked him out. Men.

She sat down, staring at the pile on her desk that contained the court record for *The State of Florida v. Chase*. The transcript alone was as thick as two phone books. A rainbow of colors sprouted where she'd tabbed about every other page.

She leafed to the first tab, the pit in her stomach starting to feel as though it might sprout an ulcer. At least she wouldn't have to worry about Chris yelling at her for working long hours anymore. These days, Grace's time was her own, the only man in her life one infamous photographer by the name of Clayton Chase.

"Stupid," Shawna said under her breath, punching the elevator button so hard she broke a nail.

"Stupid, stupid, stupid!"

She stuck the hurt finger in her mouth and stepped inside the elevator, careful this time when she pressed the button for the first floor. She wasn't sure what she should do now.

The meeting with the Calderon woman had been a mistake, a big one. She never should have called. She should have waited until the state attorney contacted her. She'd been Jillian's assistant, after all. An important witness.

Only she'd panicked. Because Aidan wouldn't listen to reason, telling her he was taking Clay's case no matter what she said or threatened. She'd thought if it looked bad enough—if Aidan believed the prosecution had something this time around—maybe he'd take a deal for Clay instead of going to trial.

And then they'd be safe.

So she'd called Graciela Calderon, thinking she could nail Clay. Shawna was one of the few people who knew what had really happened that night. If she played this right, she'd be free and clear.

"Dammit."

This was all Clay's fault. It was just like she'd told Graciela Calderon. He needed to be the center of attention. Always. He'd let Aidan coddle him and Aidan had wasted his life. *Just like Jillian.*

She played with the gold bangle on her wrist as she waited for the elevator to open. Jillian used to have one just like it. The Gucci purse, too, was identical to Jillian's...as were Shawna's new hair color and style. *Just like Jillian.*

But Clayton hadn't wanted any of it. Once, at the gallery, he'd made it perfectly clear, practically throwing her out the door when she'd made the mistake of coming on to him.

Shawna again sucked on her finger. She should have seen the violence in him then.

Maybe Aidan wouldn't find out. The prosecutor couldn't have looked less interested, Shawna thought, feeling a little better. She knew when she was being dismissed—she'd spent half her life with people doing just that.

But she needed to be more careful and not act so impulsively. *Think, Shawna!*

The best thing to do was work on Aidan, get him to understand that Clay wasn't worth the risk. The man had taken everything Aidan ever wanted and turned it to shit. He deserved what was coming to him with this new trial, that was for sure.

Aidan needed to start thinking about what was best for

them and forget about Clay. That was a problem...one she had to do something about.

Piper stared down at the congealed dinner that she'd taken the trouble to make despite the fact that she'd seen clients all day, driven Meowrice, their Abyssinian cat, to the vet for what turned out to be one expensive hair ball, and bought Cuban food for Mandy's project in Spanish class.

Now, she was staring at a spaghetti dinner that her daughter would not be eating and the third pink slip in almost as many days from her son's teacher because he'd forgotten to turn in his math homework yet again.

A typical day in the life of.

Megan and I have to study for a history test.

That had been Mandy's excuse for missing dinner, delivered via cell phone just minutes ago.

It wasn't the first time she'd received such a call. And Piper was beginning to smell a rat.

Back at the kitchen table, Simon waited.

"Go ahead, buddy. I'm not hungry and your sister's going to be late."

Piper watched Simon dig in. At least one of them had an appetite.

She picked up the phone. Mandy had given her Megan's cell-phone number, but that's not what Piper wanted.

Luckily, Megan's parents were listed.

As it turned out, Mandy was not studying at Megan's house. Megan was at a field hockey team dinner and wasn't expected back until later. And what was this about a history test?

Of course, Piper thought. Of course.

She stared down at the pink slip, another reminder that—

yes indeed, Piper!—she was failing as a parent. It would have been such a simple thing to go over Simon's homework with him, but she hadn't had the time. She'd only asked if he had everything he needed for school and rushed him to the bus.

And now, Mandy was lying to her.

"You want any dessert?" she asked her son. He didn't respond, she wouldn't have expected him to speak, but just sat staring at the pink slip. "I'm not angry," she said, pushing aside the pink slip. "I'm just…"

I'm just on hold. I can't think. I can't do this.

"I'm worried, that's all," she told him.

"Don't worry," he said. "She's with Sean."

She stared at her son. *Don't worry, she's with Sean.* Just like that. One complete sentence, flowing effortlessly from his mouth.

It wasn't that Simon couldn't talk. It was almost as if he'd chosen not to. Over the last two years, he seemed to mete out his words, each year seeming to become more stingy. Just as she'd told Clay, she hadn't heard Simon speak in months. She was losing hope just as quickly as he lost ground.

She couldn't remember the last time he'd uttered such a clear sentence.

And then, the proverbial lightbulb.

"Who is Sean?" she asked.

But Simon had retreated back into silence. He stood, picking up his plate and taking it to the sink. She watched her son raid the freezer for his favorite ice cream and excuse himself with a smile as he raced out of the kitchen.

"You better have your homework done and in your backpack ready to go, bucko," she told him, crumpling the pink slip in her hand.

To herself, she said, "Mandy has a boyfriend. Great. Just great."

She remembered when she'd first started dating Kevin. Mandy had been five years old, with a head of strawberry-blond curls and black button eyes. Little Orphan Annie come to life. Piper had vowed then that she would never hurt Mandy. No matter what happened between her and Kevin, Mandy was her treasure found.

She poured herself a glass of wine. She sat down on the couch in the living room, set the wine on the coffee table, and put her head in her hands.

Maybe Leah was right. This wasn't what Kevin would want for his family. Not by a long shot.

Two hours later, when her daughter came home from "studying" with "Megan," Piper was waiting for her in the living room.

Mandy didn't even bother to say hello. She just scurried for the stairs and a quick escape to her bedroom.

"How is Sean doing?" Piper asked.

Mandy stopped on the stairs, not saying a word.

"That's who I assume you were with, since Megan was at a field hockey dinner when I called her parents."

Her daughter looked like a woman weighing her options. "Look, he's just this guy I know. Okay? Don't make a big deal about it."

"That you're lying to me? Or that you don't trust me enough to tell me about your life?"

"At least he's not some murderer."

Piper's argument melted away, no longer relevant. A frozen minute later, she said, "Leah came by yesterday. She mentioned you talked to her about Clayton Chase."

"It's in the papers. It's not like I would miss it. That's the guy that we found outside with Simon, isn't it?"

"Mandy, if I thought he was any kind of threat—"

"How can he not be? Come on, Piper, he's not just your regular I-got-hit-by-lightning weirdo. That's bad enough. The guy killed his wife, and pretty soon he's going to go to jail for it. Unless they have you testify that he's nuts or something. Is that why he comes here to see you? Because you're some sort of lightning expert? Are you going to be his defense? Are you going to let him get away with killing his wife?"

She opened her mouth, about to give all the excuses she'd been giving herself, but not a sound came out.

"You know what, Piper? I think you're blowing it."

"Mandy—"

"What did he do to Simon?" Mandy demanded. "He's different now."

Piper stared into those beautiful brown eyes, seeing all her daughter's fears.

I wish I knew....

Instead, she said, "You tell Sean that he's invited to dinner next week. You pick the night." She stood, trying for regal as she passed her daughter on the steps. "Seven o'clock would be best. Tell him not to be late."

She made her way back to the kitchen where another dinner ended up cold, uneaten and in the waste can.

7

Burton remembered watching Jillian ride in her first horse show. She'd been eight years old and completely fearless, clearing fences almost as tall as she was on this enormous devil of a horse. He remembered paying a damn fortune for those lessons, fighting his wife every step of the way, asking Jackie in what universe was it okay to pay such an obscene amount of money to watch his kid put her life on the line.

But Jackie would just kiss him and tell him to shut up. Even when he'd told her he'd never forgive Jackie if anything happened to Jillian on that horse, his wife had only smiled and told him, "Don't worry, darling. I have big shoulders."

All those years worrying about the damn horses and the most dangerous thing his daughter ever did was get married.

He hadn't seen it coming, being completely ignorant about his daughter's life. She'd been alone in her despair, unable to confide in him. In the year since she'd died, he'd been working backward, trying to find the pieces she'd hidden from him.

He stared at the report from the private investigator he'd hired. There were photographs of Clayton, pages and pages of notes on his activities.

When Burton had gotten the call two days ago to meet with

the P.I., he'd thought there had been some sort of break-through in the case.

"What kind of crap is this?" Burton asked.

"I'm just being straight with you, Burton. I can't go out and prove the guy killed Jillian."

"Then what the hell am I paying you for? Dammit, you're supposed to be the best."

"And I'm good enough to know that I can't help you. I'm just wasting your money."

Burton flipped through the photographs, memories flooding him. The trial had been a nightmare. Four months of testimony and he hadn't missed a day, learning that Jillian had been pregnant with another man's child. During the Christmas holidays, he'd sat in that courtroom and listened to the coroner describe how Jillian, his baby, had died.

All along she'd been hiding a deep unhappiness in her marriage, the only reason she would betray her marriage vows. And he'd never known. God help him, he hadn't had a clue. Instead, she'd come to visit with a smile and hug, never so much as whispering of her pain.

She'd wanted kids. He knew that. He'd always wondered why she and Clay hadn't been trying. When he'd asked her about it, joking that he was ready to be a grandfather, she'd made some excuse about Clay's career just getting hot.

Now he knew the truth. That she didn't love Clay. That the marriage had soured. That she'd wanted out.

She'd loved someone else, enough that she'd chosen to have his child. Jillian wasn't stupid. She'd never make that sort of mistake. Not when it came to a baby.

Now, she would never be a mother. Burton wouldn't be

able to hold his grandson in his arms. Wouldn't be able to hold his baby, his Jilly Bean.

And the bastard was going to get away with it? No way. No fucking way.

"You want out because of the woman," Burton whispered. "The therapist he's seeing."

He'd hired the detective two months ago, right after the first trial had ended in a hung jury. He figured if the state attorney's office couldn't get the job done, he would. And now that he was close to finding something, the guy wanted to close up shop?

"Look, Mr. Ward, he's acting strange, okay? Who knows what your son-in-law is going to do next? Go to the police, that's my advice."

Burt slammed his hand against the coffee table. He fixed the P.I. with a hard stare. "With what, dammit? You haven't given me anything."

He was afraid for the therapist. The woman in the photographs that were part of the file the man had just handed over. The possibility that she could be Clay's next victim.

There were similarities. Both were beautiful women. Both had dedicated themselves to Chase in their own way.

And he'd been skulking around her home, watching her, snapping photographs when he was supposed to be a cripple who couldn't hold a camera.

He should feel sorry for the woman. She had children. A widow. A voice buried deep inside even told him the detective he'd hired was right. They were playing with fire, putting another life at risk. *Call the police....*

Burton thought about the possibility that history could repeat itself. That in trying to put his daughter's killer behind bars, he might cause another death. How that would feel, to know he could have done something to stop such a tragedy.

But then he remembered what Jackie had told him.

I have big shoulders.

"You find something, Mr. Cowan. Then I'll go to the police."

The detective stood, looking like he might argue. But then he surprised Burton. "Yeah. All right. It's not like they're going to put her on surveillance on my say-so. I'll try and get you something more. Something you can show the cops."

Burton watched the man leave his office. They were running out of time to make a difference. The state attorney was set to retry the case, to take one last bite of the apple. According to the law, no matter what the outcome, Clayton couldn't be tried a third time.

That meant they needed evidence, the kind that got results in a courtroom.

He looked down at the photographs and pulled out one taken with a telephoto lens. He could see the woman sitting in a room right across from Clay.

She looked nice. And that smile of hers? Well, the innocent expression said it all. Despite all her training, she'd been fooled by the bastard. Just like his daughter had been.

But this time wouldn't be the same. This time someone was on guard, watching.

No, he wasn't about to give up, not by a long shot. Clayton Chase wasn't about to get away with Jillian's murder.

He'd wait for the trial, see what he could make happen there. But if the law couldn't get him satisfaction, there were other ways to see justice was done.

* * *

Clay wouldn't look at her.

He stared at the ceiling. He memorized the pattern on the carpet. He played chess with the blown-glass animals on the coffee table.

They had agreed to meet at their regular time, acting as if they could just resume where they'd left off. *Thursday at two o'clock, right?* In past sessions, he'd draped himself in a pose of supreme indifference on the sofa, a virtual nonparticipant in his own therapy. Now before her sat a man who cared deeply. Or so it appeared.

He'd brought his camera even though she'd made no such request this time. He'd placed it on the table in front of him but hadn't touched it since. He avoided looking at the Nikon...just as he avoided looking her.

She kept hearing her daughter's voice in her head. *You're blowing it, Piper.*

"Why don't you just ask me?" he said.

His voice almost startled her. She hadn't wanted to push. Her game plan: let him do the talking.

And here he was, doing the talking.

"You want to know, right?" His legs began pumping. He held his hands clenched on his lap. "If I killed her? If I shot Jillian?"

"Did you?" It wouldn't help him if she played the coward.

He laughed, as if he hadn't expected her response. The sound didn't break the tension. Just the opposite.

"You brought your camera," she said, hoping to shift the energy in the room in a different direction.

He turned in a stiff motion to stare at the camera. Just yesterday, he'd seemed so confident, manipulating her into seeing him, dangling Simon as the carrot. Today, he reminded her of a puppet as he dropped his hands to his side, the motion seeming almost involuntary.

"Take my photograph," she told him.

She didn't know why she'd said it. She wasn't acting like a therapist, not with that tone. And still.

"Go ahead," she repeated. "Pick it up."

She knew that frozen state of his, recognized it for what it was: resistance, fear. But this fear didn't have a basis in reality. It was like a mirage, a spectral image haunting him that needed to be challenged.

It didn't take long for him to recoup. He reached for the camera and raised the Nikon to focus on her, watching her through the lens almost as if he'd been waiting for just this moment.

"This used to be who I was," he said, snapping her photograph. He cradled the camera in one hand. "This used to be effortless," he said, snapping another picture.

"It seems fairly effortless now."

He didn't stop, the camera clicking away as he stood up, trying different angles, always focused on her. The first time he'd taken her picture, there'd been an almost manic energy to everything he'd done. Not so this time.

"Quite effortless," she repeated.

"As in—is there really anything wrong with me?"

He had come around the coffee table, giving himself a clear view of her in the wingback chair. He seemed suddenly taller, stronger. Today he wore what looked like a black tuxedo jacket he might have worn to his high-school prom. But the T-shirt and jeans made the look somehow edgy and hip. She could understand now that charisma they talked about in the papers. That camera was almost a talisman. He stood before her a new man.

"Your hands," she said. "They're not shaking."

"No. They're not."

He had the most intense stare, as if he were still focusing the lens even as he held the camera in his hands. She could almost imagine him framing the photograph in his head, considering the light in the room, searching for a better angle.

As it turned out, that wasn't what he was thinking, at all.

"I read about this privilege thing," he said. "I mean, I can tell you things, things I might remember, and you can't go to the cops. Because you're my therapist, anything I tell you about the past is considered confidential."

She had a sick feeling in her stomach. The men and women who came to her for help had always been victims, innocents who felt condemned by nothing more than pure misfortune. *I was only talking on the phone inside my house; I was out playing golf and there wasn't a cloud in the sky....*

"I won't go to the police," she whispered.

"So I figured."

She waited, wondering if it would finally come, that knowledge she'd feared all along. *I killed her. Do you want to know how? Let me tell you all the details.* That need to confess and seek absolution.

"You think I did it, don't you?" he asked. "I can see it in your eyes that you think I killed her."

"That's not what you see," she told him, hoping that she was telling the truth.

He backed away, camera in hand. He walked to the door and stopped, still facing her. "What if I told you I did it, Piper? I killed my wife. That's who I am. A murderer." His voice grew louder. "What would you do?"

"What would you want me to do?" she asked.

He lifted the camera to stare through it, as if all the answers were there for him to see through his lens.

"Save the killer," he said softly, taking another photograph. "That's what you want to do, isn't it, Piper?"

He took several photographs in quick succession—*click, click, click*—cataloging her reaction.

"It doesn't matter what I want," she told him.

"Maybe it does to me."

In that moment, she felt a different tension in the room, one that had nothing to do with a therapist and a patient.

It wasn't unusual. People confided their deepest fears to her. She was their mother confessor. It was an easy thing to confuse the relationship, to see in it more than there was.

"Clay—"

"Yes," he said, dropping the camera and quickly turning back toward the door. "I understand."

Because he'd watched her reaction through his camera lens.

When he walked out into the hall, she heard a gasp, a sound ever so soft and very familiar.

She found Clay standing in front of Simon, her son staring at him with a stunned expression.

Until Simon turned and ran away.

Simon disappeared down the hall, his vanishing act punctuated by the sound of the door to his room slamming shut. When Clay looked back at her, the emotion on his face was suddenly too much. Now it was her turn to see inside.

He left without a word.

Her heart racing, she replayed in her head what he'd told her. *Save the killer.*

8

Nothing in Grace's life had ever been easy. The daughter of immigrants, she lived by one golden rule: Hard work.

"Graciela," her father had told her many times, "when we left Cuba, the government took everything. Nothing was ours, not our house, not our car. Not even your mother's wedding ring. Everything belonged to the state." He would point to his temple. "We could leave with only what was here, inside our heads."

So Grace studied. She went to law school, dismissed all the naysayers who told her everything she accomplished in her life had been handed to her on the silver platter of "diversity" because she was a woman and a minority. Never mind that she'd been ranked first in her class or graduated magna cum laude from a top school. She learned to cope with that, too—people underestimating her.

There was nothing Graciela Calderon loved better than a good fight.

"Grace, honey." The handsome black man across the table engulfed her hand in both of his. In his late fifties, Donnie Lincoln had always been a commanding presence, in or out of the courtroom. He'd hoped to leave the state attorney's office with a judicial appointment—which might still come his way—but the private sector had been good to Donnie, judging from that stunning Armani suit and the Design District eatery he'd chosen for lunch.

"I'll bring you on as a full partner. What do you say?"

"I'm not here for a job, Donnie. At least, not yet," she told him, because like Donnie, she might well find Chase on her career epitaph.

Grace had worked for Donnie back in the days when he'd been running the office as state attorney...until the Chase media circus had blown up in his face. Chase's attorney had called his bluff, opting for the defendant's right to a speedy trial, heading straight to court and catching Donnie Lincoln and his team with their pants down, ready for a whuppin' delivered courtesy of the defense.

At the time, Grace had been working on another case, a serial rapist she'd spent two years bringing to justice. To this day Donnie claimed she could have made all the difference on the murder case. Unfortunately, she was about to get her chance to find out.

"What I need, Donnie, is your help with Clayton Chase." Grace wasn't kidding herself. Donnie had enough eyes and ears back at the office to know that ticking time bomb had landed on her desk. She'd taken too many calls from him herself over the past months to think she needed to bring him up to speed.

"You, dear friend and ally," she said, "have the benefit of twenty-twenty hindsight. So fill me in, Yoda."

"Butter that toast, baby," he said with a smile. But his expression turned wistful. "What can I say? I thought we had him. The ballistics on the gun, his prints, motive...Jesus, did I have motive."

"But?"

"You know the old saying. A case is won or lost at voir dire."

The assistant state attorney who had prosecuted the case for Donnie had interviewed the jury afterward. It was the typical scenario. Some bleeding heart who'd bought the defense's argument about the burden of proof.

But that wasn't the whole story. The way Grace saw the case, no one in the office had taken the time to examine the evidence from any point of view other than a slam-dunk guilty verdict for the prosecution. They hadn't taken Aidan Parks seriously, seeing only some corporate suit trying his hand at criminal law. Now, the man was one of the most talked-about defense attorneys in the country, his name attached to a number of high-profile cases.

"Here's what I think," Donnie said. "I think you need to find yourself an awesome private investigator."

Grace sat up straight in her seat, suddenly alert. "No," she said. "No way."

"He's the best. You and I both know it."

She dropped her head back against the booth. "I was wrong. I really didn't want your opinion."

"Exactly," Donnie said, raising his beer with a smile.

She gave him a look. "I'm not sure even I want to win that badly."

"Grace, dear," Donnie said. "We all want to win that badly. Now get up, brush yourself off, and go take one for the team."

She left the bar, wondering how on earth she was going to eat that much humble pie and not choke…because the best private investigator in town happened to be her soon-to-be ex-husband. They'd met on a case five years ago, Donnie doing the honors of introducing them.

But that wasn't a call she was ready to make. Not just yet.

Back at the office, she spread her notes out over the desk, puzzle pieces she'd have to fit together to form a pretty picture for the jury.

There was the gun, of course. They'd found it in a Dumpster two blocks from the crime scene. Chase's prints were all over the murder weapon. The gun was registered to one McKenzie Chase, Clayton's deceased father. Defense counsel had made quite a show of the fact that there hadn't been any prints on the bullets themselves. Why load a gun wearing gloves and then cover the barrel with your own prints? It was beyond messy. It was stupid.

Grace had seen the "he couldn't be so stupid" argument work more than once, and Aidan Parks had argued the point more eloquently than most. She set aside the index cards corresponding to the gun.

Then there was Donnie's theory on motive, the old "she done me wrong." Only in Chase's case, they hadn't been able to prove that he knew anything about his wife's extramarital affair: no neighbor witness testifying about dishes crashing and heated voices, no waiter relaying information on a restaurant fracas. Nada.

She shuffled around the card she'd made for Shawna Benet. Tempting. So tempting. That eager witness now ready to point the finger. Shawna claimed to know all about the extramarital affair. *It was no secret.* Her words.

But Grace wouldn't take the bait as quickly as Donnie might have. She set the card aside, thinking she needed to push a little there. They'd never identified the father of the baby. If Shawna had known about the affair, she might know the father.

She came to the card with the name Burton Ward written on it, the victim's father.

She had a theory, of course. But unlike Donnie, she didn't need to prove Chase guilty. She'd go in with an open mind. The fact was, if Chase hadn't killed his wife, someone else had. She just needed to know who before they went to trial.

She put the card down, staring at the name. Burton Ward— a powerful man still hurting after the loss of his only child.... A man who would do anything to see Grace pull a guilty verdict out of her hat.

A man with a lot of enemies.

"As good a place as any to start," she said, picking up the phone.

Clay hadn't remembered anything about the night of Jillian's murder.... He hadn't even tried to remember. A dead man didn't have memories. He was empty of everything, living in a numb state sanctioned by Aidan, the only person who hadn't abandoned ship.

Don't worry, buddy. It's not a problem that you don't remember. It might even help. We'll get you out of this, you'll see.

Aidan had found doctors to tell him he couldn't remember, experts who testified at trial. Apparently memory loss was a common enough complaint after having your brain fried by a hundred thousand plus volts of electricity.

So he'd let himself fall into that frozen state of numbness. He'd held on to the sensation, cultivating that shield.

Only now, that wasn't going to be possible.

He looked down at his hands, opening and closing his fingers as if they might be attached to someone else. For the past year, he hadn't been able to take a photograph. But just hours ago, he'd developed his second roll of film this week. The photographs hung from the drying line, each and every frame perfect. More prints lay stacked on the dry bench.

He should feel different, he thought, somehow changed. Not the same old Clay with a camera in his hands.

Because with the return of his ability came the memories.

He'd been out in the Everglades, one of the places he loved best, a vast wetland wilderness that had become his changing canvas over the years until he'd memorized every marsh, swamp and encroaching residence. He hadn't been on assignment, something the prosecution had made a big deal about during the trial. How convenient that he should be off to such a remote location at the time of Jillian's murder.

They'd had a fight, he and Jillian. He'd been looking to lose himself in that storm.

He'd had the camera there beside him on the tripod. On the ground next to him he'd set out his gear, including various lenses and extra film. He'd chosen a wide-angle lens and screwed the cable release into the shutter button. There hadn't been a cloud in the sky, only the sound of far-off thunder and the smell of ozone to tell him he was close. But he had an instinct for these things, and he'd known he was in for a serious light show.

He remembered the sheet lightning illuminating a cloud from the inside. Streamers, ribbons and spider lightning crossing from cloud to cloud…arc lightning traveling horizontally. The perfect night for the perfect storm and he'd managed a front-row seat.

After that, the screen inside his head went blank. Nothing else—nothing more.

But it was enough. More than.

Flash forward to that horrible awakening: Jillian on the dining-room floor next to him, her hand in his.

He closed his eyes, blanking out the image.

"Jesus." He tried to catch his breath. He turned off the safety light in the darkroom and reached for the switch to turn on the overhead lights.

The stark white light gave him back a sense of balance, but didn't do anything for the sudden hammer blow of pain to his head. He staggered back and grabbed his temples. He tried not to tense up, knowing from experience that fighting the pain only made it worse.

It happened like that a lot. As if a part of him wouldn't remember, couldn't access the forbidden fruit of what had really happened that night. If he opened that door and walked through, he'd have more to deal with than a migraine and nightmares.

He sat down on the metal stool he kept in the room, facing his old Beseler enlarger, thinking about that wonderful numbness he'd lived in the last year and how much he hated that he wanted it back. He'd never been a weak man, but since that night he'd turned into a wreck, the kind of man who would sneak around, snapping photographs of the unsuspecting in a macabre experiment that might yet prove costly.

He'd gone to see Piper to push himself out of that nest of numbness. And now that it was gone, it seemed he was destined to live in constant fear. *What next?*

He took down one of the photographs: Piper, sitting on her throne of a chair, watching him. He'd been seeing her twice a week for two months. Yeah, she'd been frustrated by his lack of progress, him just sitting there, passing the time. But it wasn't like that for him. He came without fail to those sessions to take the measure of her. She was strong, a survivor. Someone solid, someone he could trust...

Did you kill her?

That's what they all wanted to know. The television reporters and the tabloids. What the cops and the prosecution—Burton and his private investigator—were all out to prove. That he was someone capable of killing Jillian. Some demented freak who could do that to the woman he loved.

He sat on the stool, letting the pain flow and ebb like a tide, sucking in a slow breath through the worst of it.

The night it happened, he'd been taken to the hospital, where Aidan had come to circle the wagons long before the cops got hold of him. Aidan had done most of the talking, and by the time Clay was in any condition to speak to the police, he knew the drill: follow Aidan's lead.

He didn't remember. He loved his wife. Yes, they'd had problems, like any other couple. No, he had no idea she was pregnant.

At least that much was true. He hadn't known about the baby.

He left the darkroom, grabbing a bottle of Advil off the kitchen counter and tossing back three extra strength with a beer before going out onto the back terrace of the small conch house that reminded him so much of his father. He missed his old man. Mac, as everyone had called him, would have been right here beside him. His mother had tried. So had his sister. But his dad, man. He wouldn't have given up.

He took another pull of the beer, staring out at nothing. Suspended over the mangrove swamps of the Upper Keys, this was where, as a kid, he'd listened to his father tell ghost stories. Listening to the crickets and frogs, he thought about all the things he did remember, like the fact that his wife had been in love with someone else. That she'd told him she was leaving him the night she'd died.

He would have admitted it readily if Aidan had put him on the stand. But Aidan hadn't, choosing to let the lack of evidence against Clay speak for itself.

I'm not telling you to lie. Clay remembered Aidan's speech vividly. *I'm just telling you to keep quiet. Remember, it's their job to prove you did this, not the other way around. And believe me when I tell you that if you go on that stand and talk about problems in your marriage, buddy, it is over.*

Clay stared out over the horizon. Positive charges on the ground are created by objects as simple as a blade of grass. Positive streamers connect with stepped leaders to create a lightning stroke. If upward streamers connect with a stepped leader with the photographer in their path, there's the danger.

Well, he was in the path of the lightning now. Because he'd seen her son's face. He'd felt it all the way down to his toes, the shame of that look.

What if I tell you I killed her?

Simon had overheard him, of course. He'd been standing there outside the door, no doubt waiting for his new superhero friend who'd taught him the secret of lightning.

He drank from the beer. "Where's numb when you need it?" he asked the warm night.

He heard a knock on the front door. The doorbell followed, insistent. He ignored both. More knocking, followed by the sound of footsteps coming around to the back terrace.

"Come on, Clay. I know you're there."

Aidan.

He thought about the photographs, his dirty little secret, Piper in her many incarnations captured on film. Maybe he'd known all along Piper would be different, and that's why he kept coming to see her. It made an odd sort of sense. If he just hung around someone so strong, couldn't some of that strength reach him?

When he'd read that article about her on the Web site for survivors—some guy basically saying she'd saved his life and all the stuff about her husband dying from a strike— yeah, he'd figured it out then. It was like lightning. He had an instinct about these things and Piper Jordan had something he needed.

And now he had his proof—photographs that he'd hidden in a secret file in his darkroom, afraid of what they might mean.

"Clay, dammit. We need to talk." Never a patient man, Aidan had come around the back. He walked up the two shallow steps that separated the porch from the beach.

Clay felt his shoulders tense, but forced himself to relax. What did he have to hide from Aidan?

"Aidan. What a surprise." He opened the back door and took Aidan straight through the house to the darkroom where photographs of Piper lay spread across the dry bench. He waited, letting Aidan judge the evidence for himself.

"Wow," Aidan said.

He let the word trail off, but Clay knew what he was thinking. Not a good time for a recovery.

"So I guess she's making you better, this therapist?"

He waited to see the suspicion in his attorney's eyes but didn't find any. But then, Aidan always did know how to pull off a good bluff.

He looked back at the photographs. He'd set them out in a series, like an old-time flip book where one image follows the next, as if he were in the act of bringing her to life.

"She pushed the camera into my hands," he said. "Man, did she make me good and pissed. Because I knew I couldn't take the shot and I wanted to, so very much. And then suddenly, I could."

"And now?"

"Only her. Nothing else."

Aidan stepped closer. "Can you remember anything about that night? Anything at all?"

When he didn't answer, Aidan grabbed his arm.

"Any little thing," Aidan whispered. "It could help."

Clay shoved him off. He left the darkroom, Aidan on his heels.

"Clay, they wouldn't be putting this trial back on if they didn't think they had something."

"Go home, Aidan."

"Jesus, Clay. I'm all you've got and you're pushing me out the door?"

"That's right. So get the hell out."

"Listen to me, you idiot. I loved her, too. And I swore on her grave that I would keep you safe. It's what she'd want, Clay. The only thing I can do for her now."

He turned. He grabbed Aidan by the shirt and pushed him against the wall.

Breathing hard, he said, "Jillian is dead. Don't do her any favors."

Aidan stared at him, those tepid blue eyes assessing. "Okay." He tugged Clay's hands off so that Clay released him. He straightened his shirt and gave a short nod.

"This is all that bullshit therapy talking, right? I mean, stuff is going on in your head and you need to work through it." Aidan took a step toward the door. "I understand. But don't shut me out, okay? Sooner or later, we're going to have to deal with this new trial."

When he heard the door close, Clay collapsed on the couch. The new trial.

He didn't want Aidan analyzing what was happening to him, already spinning the facts for proper presentation to a jury. He wanted to keep that numbness at bay when instinctively he knew Aidan would push him right back in, telling him how to think and feel, a director coaching his actor for his next movie role.

That was the funny thing about the truth. How it could change like lightning, shifting over time to strike again and again. Only this time around, Clayton Chase wasn't stepping out of the way.

9

Piper hated her sister's house.

At every opportunity when Crissa called, Piper would suggest a lunch alfresco or drinks at a trendy new restaurant in South Beach…whatever it took to pry her sister from her home turf.

Unfortunately, Crissa, who wrote a how-to column à la Heloise for the *Miami Herald,* worked out of her house in Coral Gables, a picturesque suburb where approval was needed for any new construction or remodel, keeping it free of Miami's high-rise developments and freeway overpasses. Like many writers, her sister tended to stick to her home like a hermit crab to its shell. The house, a lovely Mediterranean revival constructed of stucco and the famed coral rock that gave the area its name, was the local hub for the kids in the palm-lined neighborhood. It was no easy task to put off her sister's invitations to slip over for a little *café cubano.*

Crissa, who possessed a healthy overdrive of suspicion— another journalistic trait—didn't take long to catch on.

"What is it?" she'd asked. "Do I have a House of Usher thing going? Is it my lack of housekeeping skills?"

So Piper had confessed. "The house. It reminds me too much of Kevin."

Piper thought it was strange how a place could hold memories. And her sister's house would always remind her of the night her husband had died.

She'd been in the kitchen downing her second margarita with Crissa—a new recipe, her sister had informed her, one guaranteed to knock her on her ass. Just what the doctor ordered for the hit-and-run of philandering husbands. She'd been listening to Crissa plan Piper's eventual divorce from "that schmuck" Kevin. One that guaranteed to take him "to the cleaners" and make sure he paid for the "piece of tail" he'd indulged in at the expense of her baby sister's happiness.

That's when Mandy had called Piper's cell phone, giving her the 911 details of the lightning strike, extinguishing Piper's fuzzy margarita high.

To this day, Piper didn't drink margaritas. She'd sold her Coral Gables home, moving the family to nearby Coral Cay, a new suburb known for its scenic bluffs and wetlands, as well as its annual "Snark Hunt," when the locals dressed up and paraded the streets, the Snark being as famously elusive as Big Foot. And, whenever possible, she avoided Crissa's house.

But, but, but, she was a professional, after all. She could diagnose her avoidance behavior, knowing full well such things shouldn't be indulged. So on this lovely Saturday afternoon, she'd come for lunch, which led Crissa to plan the exile of Piper's new problematic client, one Clayton Chase.

"I just want to make sure you know what you're getting into," she said, stabbing a shrimp from the delicious salad she'd served to tempt Piper over for lunch. Crissa, who was always on a deadline, couldn't take the time to meet anywhere but her house, though she had more than enough time to spare to give Piper an earful.

"It's not like you're the only person in the world who can help this guy. Honey, I know you're good, but I say let the man be someone else's problem."

"Hmm," Piper said, quickly downing a shrimp. Crissa was on a roll. She wouldn't need much prompting.

"And how do you know this isn't all some scam? I didn't kill my wife because I was busy recovering from a lightning strike? Who believes that bunk?" She used the fork for emphasis, stabbing the air in front of her. "You explain to me how that can happen. How does this guy get home—on his own power, mind you—to find his dead wife and conveniently collapse there beside her? I read he even packed up his gear and loaded his Jeep for the drive over. What was he, a walking coma?"

Piper played with the shrimp on her plate. "The fact is, we know very little about the effects of lightning on the brain. A delayed response—"

"Bullshit." Again with the fork. "That's what he wants you to believe. But can he prove it?"

"The last time I checked, Crissa, it's not up to him to prove his innocence in this country."

Her sister put down the fork with a loud clank. "Ohmigod. This guy is getting to you."

"For goodness sake—"

"I've seen his picture. He's some hot-looking Viggo Mortensen type, right? All shaggy long hair and soulful eyes. A chin to die for. That's how he probably got away with it the first time. Turned on the charm and convinced some lonely heart on the jury to hold out on the guilty verdict."

"That would be a pretty nifty trick, Crissa. He didn't even testify at trial."

"I just don't get it. Why can't you see the regular Joes and Janes of the world? People who compulsively wash their hands or screw around on their wives? Why help the freak victims of lightning?"

"That is only a small part of my practice—"

"He did it, Piper. He killed his wife. Oh, maybe it was in some 'heat of the moment' thing, I'll grant you that he didn't plan it. That's why he came up with such a lame alibi."

"I can assure you, he's not a stupid man."

"Listen to you! 'I can assure you...' We're not in the office now, toots. You can drop that pretentious therapist crap."

Piper rolled her eyes. "Do you really think he would claim a lightning strike if he had any other choice? The very fact that he had such a preposterous alibi proves—"

"Nothing. You'll see. One day he's going to confess to you, and then it will be too late, because you'll be caught up in some weird professional ethics issue."

Now her sister was hitting a little too close to home, mirroring the very conversation she'd had with Clay. "Well, thank you for that vote of confidence."

"Christ on a crutch, this has nothing to do with your ability as a therapist."

"I disagree. It has everything to do with my objectivity."

"Objectivity? Let's talk about that, why don't we? You haven't seen a man naked in two years and some guy who just happens to look like God's gift to womankind survives the very accident that took Kevin from you. He shows up on your doorstep and begs, 'Fix me.' You don't think you might be a little vulnerable here?"

"Are you suggesting—"

"I'm suggesting I don't want this guy to be your fatal attraction."

Piper bit off her response. She wasn't going to convince Crissa...not when she'd made a very valid point. And that wasn't the half of it.

It seemed as if she were always defending Clayton Chase. To Crissa, to her mother-in-law, to Mandy...even to Simon.

After Clay had broken off their last session two days ago, she'd found Simon in his room, crying. She tried to schedule her patients when the kids weren't home. Simon stayed in after-school care on Tuesdays and Thursdays. But it wouldn't have been difficult for Simon to peek into her appointment book and figure out when Clay might show up next. Even though Simon rode the bus, his school was less than a mile away. He must have left early to try and see Clay.

She'd been completely caught off guard by her son's reaction until she'd realized that he'd been right outside her office door, overhearing what sounded like Clay confessing to murder.

Simon had launched himself into her arms and told her in one sputtering broken breath that Clay didn't mean what he'd said. He was only mad because people were saying that he'd killed his wife. She had to make Clay come back and tell her the truth, that he would never hurt anyone. And when she'd tried to explain to Simon that she couldn't force Clay to do anything—that wasn't how therapy worked—he started crying, begging her to promise that she would try.

All those words from her silent little boy, making it ever so clear that Clay had become a catalyst for Simon's recovery.

So she'd promised, thinking all along of the same reasons her sister had just served up alongside her delicious shrimp-

and-mango salad. That it was wrong. That it was unprofessional. That she was possibly falling for a client, a man who could give her back her son.

"He's trouble, Piper," Crissa added, reading her mind. "Nothing but."

The look Crissa gave her said it all: Piper was a woman with a mortgage, a teenage daughter with secrets and a son who was fighting demons she couldn't begin to understand.

"Why take this on?" Crissa continued, just in case Piper wasn't reading between the lines.

Piper put down her fork. "I once had a man tell me that he'd developed psychic abilities after surviving a lightning strike while speaking on the phone inside his home during a storm," Piper said. "Nobody, of course, believed him. I saw him for a year. I discovered he suffered from tinnitus, ringing in the ears, a common enough injury from lightning. His was a particularly severe case. The only way he could live with that sound was to convince himself it gave him some sort of superpower. Nobody believes these people. Nothing that happens to them makes sense. They feel hot one minute, cold the next. They have panic disorders and bizarre neurological problems that can't be documented. Eventually, they lose their job, their families break apart and they are left completely alone."

Her sister reached out and squeezed her hand. "I'm just saying, give this one a pass."

She thought about Simon, could still see that picture of him calm in Clayton's arms during the heat of the storm.

"I can't."

Crissa held her gaze. "Mother Teresa of the lightning set." She patted her hand. "I'll get us some ice cream."

End of subject.

* * *

Shawna used her key to let herself into her apartment, her arms brimming with shopping bags, including one from Alice's Day Off beachwear, where she'd bought a neon-pink bikini to die for. She'd gone shopping to keep those itchy nerves at bay. She'd left several messages for Aidan, none of which he'd returned. Not a good sign.

When she closed the door behind her and stepped into the living room of the trendy South Beach apartment Aidan paid for, she found him sitting on the green leather couch, his head in his hands. *Not good at all.*

He looked up. "Shawna, what have you done?"

She knew immediately that horrible woman at the state attorney's office had called him. *Stupid, Shawna. Stupid, stupid, stupid!*

"What were you thinking," he told her, "talking to an assistant state attorney?"

She put her bags on the dining-room table. She played with the bracelet on her wrist, the one just like Jillian always wore, and glided back toward him in that way he liked. She tucked her hair behind her right ear and gave a practiced glance. *Just like Jillian.*

"Stop it," he said, catching on to what she was doing.

He didn't want to play games, another bad sign.

She raised her chin. "I don't know what I'm being accused of, Counselor."

"Oh, come off it, Shawna. I know you went to see Grace Calderon."

Stupid!

She dropped down on the couch beside him, reaching for him. "I did it for you. For us."

He pushed her away and stood. "How in the hell does that work? My lover as chief witness for the prosecution?"

She stood to face him. "They're going to find him guilty, you know they are. You can't help him anymore."

"That's crap."

"He's going to ruin you!"

She could see he was upset, so upset he couldn't speak. She should have guessed that he'd find out. She should have known it would all blow up in her face. She'd hoped to claim she'd been summoned against her will, with no choice in the matter.

But suddenly, his expression changed. She watched his dawning disbelief. He shook his head.

He took two quick steps and grabbed her. He looked into her eyes, searching for the truth. "There's no way in hell you came up with this yourself." He gave her a hard shake. "Burton called you. He put you up to this!"

"What are you talking about?"

"You are such a bad liar. Of course, Burton. It's always Burton."

"I just thought it would help." Now she was crying, using tears where charm had failed. Because he was right. Burton had called last week, asking for her help. That's why she'd gone to see that stupid woman on Wednesday. "Burton said he had a job for you. But you'd turned him down because… because of this stupid loyalty you have to Clay. I thought if it looked bad enough—"

"I would tell Clay to take a plea?"

She twisted her arm free. "It's what you should do, Aidan. You're just too blind to see the truth. You think you can pull off a not guilty verdict? You're not God."

"But now you are? Making the decision for me and my client? Forcing my hand?"

"He's going to be the end of you, and then what happens? You tell me that, Aidan! There's no life after Clayton. Burton will make sure of it."

His eyes narrowed. "Is that what has you worried? You're concerned about me? How much did he pay you?"

"For goodness' sake!"

"How much!"

"Not a damn thing." For the first time, she felt true fear that she would lose Aidan, unsure what Aidan would do if he found out the truth. Burton might not have paid her, but he'd certainly let her know there was a carrot at the end of the stick. All she had to do was get Aidan to drop his representation of Clayton and all would be forgiven. Aidan would be Burton's number one again, taking over his empire when Burton retired. "What are you accusing me of, Counselor?"

She saw the shadow of doubt enter his expression. She pressed her advantage.

"Aidan, I've been there for you. Every step of the way I have held your hand. When Jillian died, who brought you back to life? Don't I get any credit for that, at least? All right. I made a mistake going to the state attorney. But I did it because I wanted this nightmare to end. Yes, for both of us. So we could go on with our lives."

She came closer. She placed her hand on his chest. She whispered up to him, "Burton is offering you the world."

"Burton isn't offering me shit. He just wants Clay dead and buried."

"And he's willing to pay whatever price you ask. Do you

really want to walk away from him again? And for what? For some loser like Clay? What do you owe him?"

He shook his head. "I'm not doing this for Clay."

"She's dead, Aidan. *Jillian* is dead." She took his hand and pressed it to her heart, letting him feel her pulse under his fingers. "Don't leave me for a dead woman."

She knew the exact moment he relented, could feel that tension in his arms slip away. He dropped down on the couch as if all strength had left him, his head once again in his hands.

"You can't talk to the state attorney, Shawna. Jesus."

She sat down beside him, her heart racing as she saw she would be forgiven. A close call.

"I won't. Never again." She kissed his face, over and over. "I made a mistake."

"A bad one."

"I'm sorry. I am." Deepening the kiss. "Forgive me."

"From now on, you come to me first with these wild ideas. You don't go half-cocked on some stupid whim of Burton's."

"Whatever you say."

"God, Shawna. You fucked up."

"I did." Now she was taking his shirt off, digging her nails into his back. "I really did."

He helped her along, lifting her skirt and pulling down her panties. "You have to fix this."

"I'll call tomorrow. Tell that Calderon woman I made it all up. I was jealous of Jillian. I've always been jealous. I wanted to hurt Clay. But I can't go through with it. I can't lie on the stand."

"Make sure she believes you."

"I will."

And Burton. She'd have to tell Burton.

She had to be smarter. Better. She'd tried to take a short-cut and shortcuts never worked. She'd have to find another way to get Aidan to see reason.

She lifted herself onto him in that way he liked, bringing back all those memories he longed for. That's what she could do for Aidan. The reason he needed her just as badly as she needed him.

"Whatever you want, baby," she whispered. "You just tell me what to do."

10

Pandora's box. A wedding gift to a curious woman. Once opened, all the ills of the world spilled forth like a party-gag can of snakes to plague mankind, never to be stuffed back inside.

The doorbell rang again. Piper rubbed her palms against her jeans.

"But at the bottom of the box," she told herself. "Hope."

Piper took a breath and opened the front door. It was Tuesday and Clay Chase was here. Time to face the music.

He had a habit of looking as if he'd slept in his clothes. At the same time, it was a "look," something she might find in a magazine ready-made for others to copy. Today was no different. A button-down shirt, the first two buttons undone, a T-shirt peeking from underneath. And trousers, the really fine kind that Kevin used to save for special occasions, only he'd paired them up with Converse high-tops.

"Thank you," Clay said straight away, the words sounding like an apology. "I wasn't sure you'd let me in."

Funny. Neither was I. "You didn't cancel. I expected you. Come on." She gestured for him to follow, her sister's warning playing a background tune in her head as they headed for her office.

Once he was settled on the couch across from her, she

thought about her training, how she'd convinced herself that their session last week was actually progress. A show of emotion from a man who had up until recently done nothing but hide from his feelings.

But there was another side to the story, the troublesome part…the part where she admitted that she wanted to see him again, that she no longer played the role of disinterested observer, functioning only as a sounding board, gently guiding his journey into self-discovery and healing.

The part where she admitted that she wanted something from him. Badly. That she was willing to take this chance to get it.

"A couple of ground rules," she told him. "No more games. This is real from now on. If I think for a minute you're putting me on, it's over. I can recommend any number of—"

"After the trial, my father-in-law hired a private investigator," he began, hitting the floor running. "He's been following me since the judge declared a mistrial two months ago. Always the same regular Joe wearing Ray-Bans in the same nondescript sedan. I don't think he even tries to hide anymore."

"How does that make you feel, having someone follow you?"

"I find it comforting."

She knew immediately why. "You're afraid of what you might do?"

"Yes."

"You don't trust yourself?"

"No."

"Do you trust me?"

He smiled. "I'm getting there."

"Well." She tried out her own smile. "That's a start."

She didn't want to be this keyed up, didn't want nerves to diminish their session into cute banter. She went over in her head all the reasons she helped people like Clay. She wasn't breaking the cardinal rule of her practice, using him as much as he planned to use her. But the fact was they'd made a deal, she and Clay. He'd practically dangled Simon before her.

"What's wrong?" he asked.

She shook it off. "Nothing. You didn't bring your camera today. Let's talk about that."

He thought a moment before answering. "It was getting in the way."

"I don't understand."

"Yeah, well. Neither do I," he said with a self-deprecating smile.

"Tell me what your camera means to you."

"Everything." He paused. "Nothing."

"Everything before your wife's death. And now it's meaningless. Is that how you feel about your life now? Without Jillian, life is meaningless?"

He stared straight ahead, almost as if he were afraid to look at her. "I love it when you get all professional on me. Has anyone ever told you that voice of yours is sexy as hell, doc?"

"We were talking about Jillian."

He gave her a quick glance, catching the warning in her voice. *Good.*

"She was going to leave me," he said. "I didn't know she was pregnant, not that. But I did know she was unhappy. And in love with another man."

"That must have been heartbreaking."

He cocked his head, hearing something in her voice. "Did your husband cheat on you?"

She imagined it was there on her face, the surprise that told him exactly what he wanted to know.

He nodded, acknowledging how easily he read her. "Well, now you know how it feels to be hit by lightning. You think you're happy. You think everything in your life is going along great—career in overdrive, money and security up the wazoo. The person you love will always be there for you. Love is sacred, after all."

"You felt betrayed."

"Didn't you?"

"We're not talking about me, Clay," she reminded him gently.

"I didn't know. I couldn't imagine. I thought Jillian and I were forever. She was my muse. The one who'd encouraged me from the beginning. We met in New York at a friend's loft in SoHo. I was just getting started, an assignment here and there. She invited herself over to see my work." He shook his head, remembering. "She told me I was going about it all wrong. That was Jillian. She'd step in and run the show every time. She had a plan, she wanted me to succeed. Apparently, I succeeded too well. The camera took over. She said she was lonely."

"You traveled a lot on assignment, I imagine."

"When she started to complain, I asked her to come with me…but she had the gallery. And she hated the road. She thought I was uncivilized, camping out in my Jeep. She said I'd never outgrown that boyish desire to commune with nature, mosquitoes and all. Jillian, she wanted a five-star hotel— a city girl, through and through. I think I suspected something. But I made excuses. I didn't really want to know. If I knew, I would have to do something. Give up an assignment, actually work on saving our marriage, that sort of thing." He looked around the room. "I knew she wasn't happy. I thought I had time to make it up to her. Change the situation."

"It happens a lot. Warring careers pulling a marriage apart."

"It was more than that." His gaze focused elsewhere. He seemed to withdraw inside himself, reliving the moment. "Jillian liked projects. I was one of her most successful. But once you succeed, you need to move on to the next project."

He glanced up, those arresting eyes of his giving away nothing. She held back from breaking the silence.

"Jillian," he said, "she moved on."

"That must have been very painful for you."

"Do you know what a mirage is?" he asked.

"Of course."

"My marriage was a mirage. Maybe they all are. The vision just dissipated faster for Jillian than it did for me."

"You loved her."

"Very much."

"Let's talk about how you felt when she told you there was someone else."

He smiled again. "Let's not and say we did."

"Sorry. Not allowed."

He pursed his lips. He was seated with his legs apart, his arms back over the couch, a relaxed pose for a man holding in a lot of tension.

He grinned, looking right at her. "I wanted to kill the son of a bitch who took her from me."

"You imagined her seduced away?"

"Yeah." He laughed, throwing his head back so that his hair fell away from his face, showing all those angles, his cheeks, that dimpled chin. "Right. Because, God knows, it had nothing to do with any lack in me. Some asshole just caught her in a weak moment. Took advantage of her unhappiness...or so the story goes in my head."

"Did you ever find out who she was seeing?"

"No. No way. Otherwise…"

He let the word trail off, catching himself, careful not to admit…admit what?

"Otherwise what?" she asked.

His smile turned into a smirk. "Otherwise, I would have beaten the crap out of him."

"That's not what you were going to say."

He nodded. "Very good, Piper."

"It's a gift."

She waited, knowing there was more.

"Otherwise, I would have testified at trial," he said, giving her a hard stare. "Because I think that's who did this. That's who killed my Jillian."

"You wanted to testify just the same."

His eyes narrowed. "A little too perceptive. I'm beginning to believe in this gift of yours."

"Everyone wants to have their say, Clay. It's human nature."

"Unfortunately, what I had to say would also incriminate me. So I stayed quiet. On the advice of counsel."

She told herself it was an old story. Lonely wife cheats on husband. Hardly a reason to kill.

"I would never have killed her," he said.

It was her turn to be surprised. "Apparently, my gift is catching."

"Or maybe we're just that solidly in tune with each other."

"Stop it," she said.

"What?"

"The flirting. It's inappropriate."

"Or very appropriate, depending on your point of view."

Careful, chimed a voice inside her head. But she told herself it was too late for caution. She'd broken all the important rules already with Clay. After talking to her sister, she'd thought long and hard about these next steps. Of course, there was everything he could do for Simon. But her decision to keep seeing him went beyond Simon. She wanted to help Clay. She still thought she could do that.

"Why do you keep coming back?" she asked. "What is it you want to accomplish with our sessions? For two months, you've hardly even spoken…but you always come back for your next appointment. Always schedule the next session. Why?"

He kept his gaze steady. "I'll tell you next time."

"I told you, Clay. No games."

"This isn't a game." He sighed, slipping his head back on the headrest of the couch. He glanced back. "I'm tired."

Apparently, that was all she was going to get.

"The trial," she said, "when will it start?"

"I don't know. Soon."

"What do you need from me?"

She wanted to know how to help. She couldn't imagine what it would be like for him, to go through all of that again. Even for someone without a panic disorder, the pressure of waiting, knowing what lay ahead, could prove too much.

"I want you to believe me," he said in a whisper. He was a man, after all. He hated to show weakness.

"Of course, I believe you."

He shook his head. "No. That's way too easy."

He wouldn't go for anything so lightly given.

"How about this, then—I believe *in* you, Clayton."

He smiled and stood. "Spoken with the proper professional tone. But it'll do."

He left the rest unsaid: *For now.*

When she saw him pull out a folded check from his pocket, she stopped him. "Please. No payment. These sessions…well, they aren't exactly professional, are they? I don't normally conduct myself—"

He pressed his fingers against her mouth. She could almost swear they moved just enough to feel the shape of her lips before slipping away.

"I get it," he said, putting the check away.

"Help Simon," she said. "That's all the payment I'll ever want."

He gave a quick nod. They walked silently to the door as if they'd both run out of words. But in her heart, she knew the truth. Theirs was a weighty silence. Whatever line they'd just crossed, there was no going back.

The little boy, Simon, was waiting for him in his car.

He hadn't bothered to lock the Jeep. He knew the kid was there the instant he shut the car door. The boy didn't bother to hide. He sat up, his face popping up in the rearview mirror like a jack-in-the-box.

Instead of putting the keys in the ignition, Clay waited. Truth be told, he was happy for the distraction. He'd gone to see Piper thinking he had the situation under control. He knew what he was doing…he'd be careful, watch his step. The next thing he knew he was stumbling all over himself, words he didn't know he'd blocked up pouring out in some sort of lame confession.

"What's up?" he asked, prompting the kid.

"Did you really kill her?" Simon asked.

Clay almost laughed. Kids were like that. No dicking around, just straight to the point.

But he knew this wasn't the time for the truth. The truth was complicated. Simon, an eight-year-old boy, wanted simple.

"No," he said. "I didn't kill anybody."

"Did you really get hit by lightning?"

Their eyes met in the mirror. "Oh, yeah."

The kid had big blue eyes, just like his mother. Only on that angelic face—the chestnut bangs just brushing over his brows, the mouth full and soft—those eyes took on an eerie glint, looking almost too large for his face.

"Tell me what it feels like," Simon demanded.

A test.

He remembered Simon's confession during the storm. He tried to imagine what it had been like for this child to experience what Clay had: a lightning strike. "When I came to, I was paralyzed. Couldn't even move my pinky," he said, recalling those first few seconds before the horror of his wife's death had struck. "And I had this funky taste in my mouth. Like I'd been chewing on a piece of silver."

That was exactly what Simon was waiting for, a detail only someone in their exclusive club might know. The kid nodded once, then scrambled over the seat into the front.

He sat there for about five minutes, just staring straight ahead. Clay noticed he didn't even reach his shoulder, just this tiny mite of a kid. Smaller than a typical eight-year-old, his head looked almost too big for his body. That's what he'd thought that night out in the rain, holding him. *He's so small.*

They clocked in another five minutes of silence. Simon wore Dickies shorts and a black T-shirt with a skull and cross-bones that announced Abandon All Hope. His shoes looked too big for his feet, but Clay figured that was the style.

Another five minutes passed.

"Your mom says you don't say much," he said, unable after all to wait the kid out.

"Nope."

He was still staring ahead. A couple of boys sporting surfer-trash hair and board shorts sped by on their bikes. A woman in a crazy muumuu gown with enormous blue flowers walked a poodle the size of Clay's fist across the street.

"You don't seem to have any trouble talking to me," Clay said.

"You're different."

"Okay."

Any minute now, Piper would come running out that door, he thought. She'd have that same frantic look on her face she'd had the night of the storm.

Simon saw him watching the door. "Mom had Mandy pick me up after school. She thinks I'm at the neighbor's with Mandy," he said. "She makes sure we're not around when she's seeing people."

Another mind reader in the family? Must be genetic. "Where's Mandy now?"

Simon made a face. "Making out with her boyfriend."

"Really?"

"Nah. They're doing homework at Katie's house. But no one notices when I take off."

"You must be good at it."

A secretive smile. "Yup."

There was a lisp, and some garbling of consonants, but he could understand the kid just fine.

"So. Anything else you want to ask me?"

"I don't want you coming here to see my mom anymore."

The kid was looking straight ahead again, the cozy intimacy of the last few minutes decidedly chilled. Clay could imagine what he was thinking.

"I won't hurt your mother, Simon."

But Simon gave him a look. He didn't seem the trusting type. Clay thought about what Piper had asked of him. *Help Simon.*

"Tell you what," Clay said. "You want to learn how to use a camera?"

Again, the kid didn't say a word, those wide blue eyes just taking it all in, assessing.

"I thought you couldn't take pictures anymore. That's why you come to see my mom."

"Yeah, but that doesn't mean I can't teach you. It will be like therapy," Clay said. "For both of us."

He seemed to think about it, giving the idea the proper rumination, then nodded. "Okay."

Clay held out his hand. Simon's disappeared into his as they shook on it.

"You better get back," Clay warned. "Before Mandy gets wise."

He watched as Simon scrambled out. The kid used proper spy tactics to sneak around a house two doors down. Before he disappeared into the backyard, he turned around and waved, giving the all clear.

Clay smiled, jamming the key into the ignition and putting the car in gear.

He thought how much his conversation with Simon had paralleled his session with Piper earlier, when she'd asked if he trusted her.

It was a start.

11

The first time Grace had looked at crime-scene photos of a dead body had been in law school. Advanced Criminal Procedure class.

She'd come to class, hoofing it inside with all the other third-year legal eagles who couldn't wait for the day they passed the bar and prosecuted or defended their first case. She'd been early—Grace was always early—so she'd gotten a clear view from her seat in the front row.

The eight-by-ten glossies had been posted on the board, the body of a woman half-hidden in some brush on a roadside, discarded there like trash. There'd been no warning, just her professor setting out books and lecture notes on the podium. At first, Grace hadn't realized what she was looking at. The body was twisted in odd angles, not looking quite human.

When the lightbulb came on, her stomach pitched as if they'd strapped her chair to a roller coaster and she'd just hit that long dive down. She thought she was going to be sick right then and there.

She'd been staring down at her legal pad, pen in hand, taking deep breaths, thinking… *This is what I want to do for a living—and I can't even look at those photographs! I can't!*

Just as Grace began planning her career as an estates-and-trusts lawyer, she heard her professor tell the class, "Don't worry. You get used to it." He took a moment to produce a smile. "Just be happy I took pity on you and didn't bring the color photographs."

By the end of class, Grace was right there with all the other hotshots, examining each and every glossy, looking at the body from all angles. The woman was naked from the waist down. Together, they gathered around to discuss the evidence with her professor, a prominent defense attorney in the community. They talked about what looked like remains of duct tape on the wrists and ankles, taking note of the cigarette burns on the woman's arms and legs. They'd discussed mens rea, the idea that here was obvious evidence to support a charge of first-degree murder.

Now, whenever she looked at crime-scene photos, her first thought was always of her professor. That he'd been wrong. She'd never get used to these photographs.

With a sigh, Grace opened the folder on her desk and dealt out the color glossies of Jillian Ward-Chase. She'd bled out on what looked like a very expensive area rug in her dining room. The dining table and chairs were something ultra chic and very modern. Japanese prints hung on the wall. A single orchid posed in minimalist splendor at the table's center.

Other than the fact that half her torso was covered in blood, Jillian Chase looked peaceful. One hand lay, palm up, resting beside her head as if she'd just tucked some bothersome strand of hair behind her ear.

They'd found the gun in a Dumpster two blocks from the South Beach pied-à-terre where Jillian had lived with her famous, now infamous, photographer husband, Clayton Chase. His prints had been all over the gun, a Colt .38 revolver registered to his father, a man who'd passed away a few years back of a heart attack.

Unfortunately for Lincoln's theory of the case, Clayton had made the call to 911 himself from the kitchen phone. He'd also been covered in his wife's blood.

The defense had made quite a show of these facts, basically telling the jury that there was no way Clay could have dumped the gun, then run back home to make that call and wait for the police to show. If he had, where was the handy prosecution witness to testify about the man covered in blood running down the street? Why hadn't the jury heard the prosecution's expert discuss the bloodied footprints leading out to the sidewalk? And while they were at it, why hadn't they explained Clayton's dipshit idea to come back to the house after he'd dumped the gun?

These were what Donnie Lincoln referred to as MLFs, Messy Little Facts…the kind of stuff that a good defense attorney used to blow smoke in front of the jury's communal vision. In the real world, the pieces didn't always come together to make a pretty picture, Donnie would say, hence the MLF factor.

Donnie, of course, had his own theory. Clayton Chase had never touched his wife's body before he'd left to dump the gun. He could have returned to the scene of the crime for any number of reasons. Maybe he'd run back to see if she really was dead, thinking he was sorry for what he'd done. Maybe fear and guilt had overwhelmed him—maybe he'd even thought about turning himself in before self-preservation had taken root and he'd begun to case the rooms for evidence of his guilt. Or maybe he'd come back for just that, to double-check, make sure there wasn't anything tying him to the crime.

With an MLF, Donnie always said you needed a good story, one better than the story trotted out by the defense. Unfortunately for Don Lincoln, someone on the jury had liked the defense version better.

Grace hated MLFs, hated even more that Donnie had made up the name. That's what bothered her about the whole legal system. How many defense attorneys had she heard blather about the importance of rigorously defending their current scumbag client, even if they knew for a fact the guy had blown away a mother and her two kids for a six-pack of beer, because, hell, isn't that what makes this country great? And prosecutors like Donnie, thinking they were the good guys so it was okay to gloss over little inconsistencies, revving up the massive government resources at their disposal to secure that guilty verdict under the theory that where there's smoke, there's fire.

Well, Grace wasn't so sure. She'd seen one too many cases where institutionalized thinking and prosecutorial cutting of corners didn't amount to much justice. She needed the pieces to come together. She supposed that, just like the jury, she wanted that pretty picture.

She stared down at the photographs, again getting that weird sense of the familiar. She'd never worked on the Chase murder. If she'd seen these photographs at all, it had been only in passing.

After a few minutes, she stacked up the glossies and slid them back into their envelope, thinking she didn't have the stomach for it, not today. She turned her attention to her day planner, where she'd written the name Burton Ward.

She'd returned his call last week, reaching the man himself after a cursory screening by his secretary. He'd sounded happy enough to speak with her…a normal reaction from a family member. Too often, the ones left behind after a murder felt ignored. You were never doing enough. It wasn't possible.

What they didn't understand was that the worst always came at the end. Even if there was a conviction, the family never felt whole. Vengeance became a useless exercise. Once the trial was over, there would be no more meetings with the prosecutor, no more days at court dodging the media. There was in fact nothing but the horrible emptiness of that final verdict, which could never fulfill its role of comfort. Comfort could be found only in striving for the goal of justice. Once that was reached, there came the realization that their loved one was gone forever, and now there was nothing to do but mourn their loss.

Burton Ward hadn't gotten there yet.

After the first trial had ended in a hung jury, Burton had called the office almost every day. A man like Burton had a lot of friends. Like the new state attorney. Burton had been a big contributor to his election fund. Word had it that Burton hadn't been too happy with the prosecution pretty early on. He'd made damn sure Donnie Lincoln didn't keep his job after he'd let the Chase case get out of hand.

So it hadn't surprised her when Burton had called her direct line. He probably knew she'd been assigned to the case long before she'd even gotten a whiff of the possibility of another trial, much less that she'd be lead counsel.

Luckily for her, Mr. Ward had a hole in his busy schedule today. The great man himself would make an appearance here later this afternoon. Grace planned to be ready. Because there was something else Grace had learned from her Criminal Procedure professor. When you got nothing, try adding a little pressure, and see what comes crawling out.

In the meantime, she had a call to make. She braced herself. *What a pain.* But not everything Donnie said was slick professional bullshit.

She dialed from memory. He picked up on the second ring, no doubt recognizing her number on the LCD display of that damn cell phone he should have surgically implanted into his ear.

Note to self. Never marry your P.I. And then try to divorce him.

"Chris," she said, forcing a cheerful tone. "Got a minute? Listen, I have a favor to ask."

An hour later, Grace found herself navigating through the difficult waters of yet another tricky conversation, this one in person. Burton Ward had at long last made his appearance.

It didn't surprise Grace that Burton Ward was not a patient man. Those who live by the Lord-Of-All-I-Survey creed often lack people skills, especially when dealing with underlings like Grace. Burton was no exception.

"You are wasting time," he told her, his face set in the expression of a man ready to lose that tight rein on his emotions. "This is all old ground, Ms. Calderon."

"But that's the thing, Mr. Ward. We need a fresh look."

"What you need is to strap Clayton Chase to a gurney ready to receive his due—a lethal injection for the murder of my daughter."

She took a minute, hoping to stop the slippery slide of their conversation. If she wasn't careful, it wouldn't take long for the whole thing to blow up in her face and Burton Ward to storm out of her office asking Armstrong for her head on a platter.

"No one wants a guilty verdict more than I do. But I need

your cooperation. Burton," she said, making that eye contact, going for sincere. "We need to keep one step ahead of the defense. And trust me when I say that Aidan Parks will float all these trial balloons, hammering the jury about who we might have overlooked in our rush to judgment."

Those words brought an angry twitch to Burton's eye, which was exactly why she'd said it. The defense had made liberal use of the phrase during trial, a favorite tune in the courtroom: Rush to judgment, cha, cha, cha.

"Burton, the fact is, I need to know how to shoot down *all* their theories. It doesn't really matter what you and I believe to be true. It's the jury that counts."

He nodded, now on the same page. And it had only taken half an hour.

So the theory she was working on with the good Mr. Ward was the possibility that someone—someone he knew, someone with a grudge—might want to cause his daughter harm.

"Currently, you own the exclusive right to develop Seminole lands, is that correct?"

She could see that patrician jaw tighten. Even at sixty-five, Burton Ward was incredibly handsome. Pewter-gray hair, vivid blue eyes, still fit and looking good in Prada. She remembered seeing photographs of that profile during trial and thinking he could probably slice through papaya with that jut in his chin.

During the trial, Burton Ward had never shed a tear…he'd never broken down. Even during the coroner's testimony, he'd kept that inscrutable expression.

"Your current plan for development includes a casino, correct? In fact, several casinos, I believe?"

She got a short nod for her trouble. It didn't bother Grace. They were making progress.

"I understand that Angel Barrera—"

"Stop right there," he said, holding up his hand as if she needed the visual. "I have never had any dealings with Mr. Barrera."

Grace nodded, showing that she was listening. "But did Angel Barrera want to have dealings with you, Mr. Ward? Did he approach you in any way about the very lucrative business of gambling? And what was Mr. Barrera's reaction when you, a very civil-minded professional with ties to the community, turned him down?"

If she'd hit home with this little fantasy scenario, Burton Ward didn't give anything away. Angel Barrera was Miami's version of John Gotti. His specialty was money laundering, Miami being a hop, skip and a jump to the black hole of financial institutions in the British Virgin Islands. He had several legitimate businesses the feds had been watching since God created man. He always came up clean. Always.

Interestingly enough, Angel Barrera was one of the few angles the defense had not followed during the first trial. Heck, they'd practically implicated the milkman in their attempts to make sure the jury knew the police had overlooked the "real killer" in their "rush to judgment." But Aidan Parks had never mentioned Barrera—which she thought intriguing, given that his mob-like connections made him the obvious choice as a scapegoat. Now, Barrera had become a valuable client for Parks.

She'd found a few other intriguing things about the Jillian Ward-Chase murder, now that she'd started taking a hard look. Things that went far beyond Donnie's MLF theory.

"Angel had nothing to do with my daughter's murder," Burton stressed.

"And I'm sure that my saying so after defense counsel

brings up the theory of a mob hit will shoot down any concerns the jury might have."

"Aidan would never point the finger at Angel."

And there was the reason she'd brought up the subject in the first place. A hunch.

Aidan, the son of a childhood friend of Jacquelyn Ward, had been working for Ward Enterprises practically since he stopped wearing diapers. He went to work for Ward straight out of law school, obtaining the lofty position of chief counsel for Ward Enterprises with the minimum of fuss.

And now this certainty on the part of Ward himself that the man who had stabbed him in the back by doing the unconscionable—defending his daughter's murderer—would not bring the most obvious suspect to the jury? Not to mention that Aidan Parks might have his own reasons for keeping Barrera out of the limelight.

She thought back to her conversation earlier with Chris, who had brought her up to speed on yet another interesting coincidence. *You know how Burton got his start in real estate in Miami, don't you, Gracie? Angel Barrera.*

She shuffled some papers on her desk, getting herself ready for the plunge into what would certainly be turbulent waters. She might not trust Chris when it came to her heart, but in the detective's world of intrigue, the man never took a misstep.

"Mr. Ward," she began. "It's come to my attention that you know Angel Barrera."

He waved away the connection. "A social acquaintance, nothing more. I see him during the usual round of charity functions, that sort of thing."

It didn't surprise her that Burton Ward, leader in the community, would not fess up to a past with Angel Barrera, major thug…unless that connection could shed light on the death of his daughter. And Burton didn't look like the kind of man who was watching his back right now, his sole concern being justice for his daughter.

She shuffled to the page where she'd written a few notes from her conversation with Chris. She knew she was on a fishing expedition, and still…

"Over forty years ago, you purchased your first strip mall. You had a silent partner in the enterprise, correct?"

"There is no way you can connect me to Angel."

He said it with a smile, but she heard the warning.

"I am trying to find out who murdered your daughter," she said softly.

Burton stood, the action saying it all. End of interview.

He leaned in, whispering, "I understand you're doing your job, Ms. Calderon. And I do appreciate the effort. But my daughter's death was a crime of passion, not some mob hit. When you start focusing on bringing the real killer to justice, you'll have my complete cooperation. Until then, don't waste my time."

She watched him head for the door. Before he could leave, she called out, "You seem to think a mob hit excludes a crime of passion. I happen to know that's seldom the case."

Burton Ward turned. The look on his face.

Bingo.

"I'm just asking you to think about the possibility," she told him. "Call me if you remember anything—anything at all."

"Of course," he said.

The door shut quietly behind him. Grace fell forward, elbows on her desk, her head in her hands. "And away we go."

Burton Ward…Angel Barrera.

And Chris, the man with all the theories.

"Cripes."

Divorce papers were being drawn up and now she owed Chris dinner?

Where was justice when you needed it?

Burton pulled off his tie. He couldn't seem to catch his breath. His lungs felt like collapsed balloons in his chest.

In the summer, the air here in Miami could be hot and thick and difficult to breathe, like breathing soup. But he knew that wasn't the problem. Not now.

Angel Barrera.

She was just making the obvious connection, one he was surprised he hadn't made himself.

He started walking toward his car, held out the control to unlock the door so he could hop in. Once he had the air-conditioning on full blast, he felt better.

A long time ago, Angel Barrera loaned Burton a hell of a lot of money. A long time ago, Burton had done Angel a great wrong. Not that Angel knew anything about it. There was no way he'd ever know the truth about Burton's indiscretions. And even if he did, nobody, especially a hothead like Angel, waited almost forty years to settle a score.

Burton merged into traffic thinking that the Calderon woman was only fishing. Angel Barrera was a son of a bitch, but he hadn't killed Jillian.

He felt it in his bones, Clayton's guilt. A father couldn't be wrong about that sort of thing. Jillian was part of his DNA. In his dreams, she urged him on in his cause to find justice for her murder.

Gunning the Cadillac's engine, he remembered that frantic drive to the hospital. He hadn't believed Clay could kill Jillian back then. He'd thought there had been some horrible mistake. He'd been thinking only about poor Clay, the pain he must have been feeling after coming across Jillian's lifeless body. The same pain Burton had been feeling.

When he'd arrived at the hospital, he'd been like a lion defending his cub, telling the police to back off, summoning Aidan to Clay's hospital bed to make sure he said nothing to incriminate himself.

He knew Clay. He and Jillian had been married for five years. He was kind and gentle. An artist. Certainly he wasn't a monster capable of such a cowardly act.

He'd even put up the bail for his son-in-law. In the beginning, he'd been his staunchest supporter, right alongside Aidan.

His wife had always told him he was too quick to judge. A year ago, he'd learned the hard way she was dead right.

Later, when the evidence had come forward—Jillian's affair and her pregnancy—when he'd watched his son-in-law's slow decline into a lifeless man filled with guilt, he'd realized his mistake.

Ms. Calderon could explore all her theories, but Burton knew the truth. And throwing the bogeyman of Barrera into the mix didn't change a damn thing.

Clayton Chase had killed his Jillian. And Burton Ward would make certain he died for it.

12

Piper remembered the day Mandy had turned thirteen. It wasn't a particularly pleasant memory.

She'd been driving Mandy home from the barn where they'd kept her horse, Emma. They'd been arguing, Mandy incredibly bitter because she wasn't getting a new horse. All the other girls at the barn—most of whose parents wouldn't blink at purchasing a small island in the Caribbean, much less a new jumper—had already moved on to bigger and better things. Emma, a beautiful chestnut warm-blood, apparently didn't make the grade, unable to jump over three feet. Something about the tendons in her front legs.

Piper remembered losing her temper, telling Mandy that she'd always known the horse world was a mistake. This was the sport of kings, after all, and while they were quite well off on Kevin's income as a doctor, they were not by any means capable of spending a hundred thousand on a horse, the price tag for a decent jumper.

To which Mandy had responded: like you care? You're not even my real mother.

They hadn't spoken for the rest of the drive.

Later that night, there'd been the weepy reconciliation… initiated by Piper, of course, the adult in the relationship. But

Piper recalled that during the drive—when Mandy had pulled out the heavy artillery of her parentage—Piper had had the eerie sense that she'd been arguing not with her child, but with her husband. Throughout the obstacle course of ill-timed traffic lights, she'd begun to wonder: Who had taken her beautiful Mandy Candy and replaced her with this recalcitrant foreigner?

She'd realized then that she was dealing with a completely separate being. Mandy was no longer a child to whom she could dictate terms. Mandy had fallen into the world of teen angst. *No one understands me, nothing I do is ever good enough.*

Her newfound need for independence had alarmed both Piper and Kevin because it had arrived with the barrier of silence. Mandy had closed off the PUs, the parental units, choosing to deal with the issue of adolescence all on her own.

Over tonight's meal of steak and potatoes, Piper recalled that turning point because this evening felt exactly the same. Mandy sat across from her at the dining-room table, a foreigner staring daggers at her, making Piper wonder once again: *Who took my daughter?*

And then there was Sean. The boyfriend.

"Would you care for more broccoli, Sean?" Piper asked.

A beatific smile spread across his face. Sean had dark brown curls and vibrant green eyes. For lack of a better term, he was *hot*.

Basically, he was the embodiment of every mother's nightmare.

"Thank you, Mrs. Jordan," he said, taking the plate.

Piper didn't want to like Sean. But, of course, Mandy had made that impossible, too, having chosen wisely in this, her first foray into the tricky waters of romance.

During dinner, Piper had discovered that Sean liked magical realism, Isabel Allende being his favorite modern writer. He'd also discovered this cool article about the origins of the universe in *Popular Science*. Something about "string theory." Of course, he didn't understand it, but he planned to ask his physics teacher all about it. Not to mention, he'd made it a habit since middle school to read *Newsweek* and *Time* cover to cover. He thought it was cool to be informed.

He had impeccable manners. He wrote poetry and surfed. He'd taught himself the guitar. And, most importantly, he looked adoringly at Mandy.

Her daughter had discovered that most rare of the species, the teen Renaissance man.

Piper knew she shouldn't be surprised that Sean was just about perfect. After all, like her father, Mandy was a perfectionist. She'd never dated, hadn't even attended a formal dance at school. She'd never had a crush. Instead, Mandy had bided her time until somebody truly extraordinary crossed her path.

So, of course, it was impossible not to like Sean.

Still, Piper was selfish. A part of her wished him gone, no matter how happy he might make Mandy at this most difficult of times in a young girl's life…because now Piper would have to deal with a complete new set of rules.

Mandy was all grown up. And here was Sean to prove it.

It was almost comical, the tension in the room. For his part, Sean hadn't known how to react. He was trying to make a good impression. At the same time, he was obviously concerned by Mandy sitting beside him doing some lovely impressionist work with her food. Her tense silence during dinner made it clear to all that Mandy was not happy about this forced encounter. That she in fact thought the entire episode "weird" beyond belief.

Piper could almost hear Mandy's complaints. *Nobody else's parents needed to have the boy-of-the-moment come over for dinner. Leave it to Piper to make a big deal about everything. After this, how could she avoid becoming a social pariah?*

When the doorbell sounded, it was almost a relief. Piper excused herself, thinking that she'd been insane to ask Sean over to dinner. Such an official encounter only made her daughter more nervous about what were surely difficult emotions.

And still, Piper didn't feel she had a choice. She couldn't break yet another of Kevin's golden rules. He'd always said that before the children could date, "the suspicious character under consideration" must have dinner with the family.

If Kevin were alive, they might have discussed other options. She could have convinced him to pursue the more acceptable interrogation on the sofa, the living-room lamp spotlighting the boy's face. They could have had a good laugh about it.

But she didn't have that choice. And she lacked the strength to ignore those rituals Kevin had planned so carefully for his children.

When the doorbell rang again, she frowned. Whoever was at the door, they'd come at a damn inconvenient time. She didn't exactly appreciate a lack of patience.

She reached the door just as her uninvited guest switched to knocking, the last hope for those suspicious of doorbells. When she opened the door, her intended sharp words died on her lips, making her realize that life had become entirely too complicated.

Clay was standing before her. He pushed his bangs out of his face with impatience, his hazel eyes wide and bright.

"I remembered something," he said.

Her children were inside—a first dinner with the first boy-friend. She should tell him it was late. He'd had his session yesterday. The right thing to do would be to send him on his way.

Leave. I'm busy now. Come back tomorrow.

But here he stood with that look of revelation. And she found herself again too weak, unable to say the words.

"Wait for me in my office," she said, motioning him in, shutting the door behind him.

She stepped back into the dining room. All three children sat staring at her.

"It's him, isn't it?" Mandy asked, accusation in every word. "It's that weirdo."

"I'll be just a minute," she said. As if that were explanation enough.

She could feel her heart pounding in her chest. A therapist should never feel this way about a patient, those all-important personal barriers and rules of professional conduct couldn't be suspended, even once. And still, *I remembered something.* She couldn't let that go. As she walked down the hall to her office, she tried to believe that somehow she could make this work, for both their sakes.

Get a grip, Piper. Keep control.

The moment she stepped into her office, she forgot all about control. But it wasn't a bad feeling. She realized she'd experienced this rush some time ago, before marriage and children. She'd been studying for her master's degree, facing the challenge of not having the answers but feeling confident of a breakthrough. Those were the old days, when she still had the luxury of focusing on her career.

She sat down. He didn't wait for her to settle in.

"When you take a photograph," he said, "you have to follow a certain procedure. During a storm, I have an alarm. Because I tend to fall into the moment, do you understand?"

His eyes looked hot, on fire. This was what she'd trained for, to bring a patient to this moment.

She nodded. *Game on.*

"I lose myself in the storm," he said, "so I have an alarm. When the storm gets too close, the alarm goes off."

She waited, keeping silent but sensing that edge drawing toward her…that point where she could peer over the ledge to see what her patient had been hiding all along. On television, she reflected, they always showed the therapist as the detached observer, sometimes so bored, they're actually multitasking with a grocery list or a crossword puzzle. On the couch, the patient rattles on, unaware that no one is listening.

That had never been the case for Piper. If anything, the opposite was true. She cared too much, could fall into the moment as easily as Clay fell into his storms.

"I remembered the alarm," he told her. "From that night out in the Everglades."

Suddenly, she understood, peering over that ledge to see what he himself had just discovered.

The alarm. A first memory. Something they could pry loose to reveal the events leading to his wife's murder.

"Piper?"

She turned to the door. Mandy stood at the office entrance, her hand on the knob so that she stood pitched forward on her toes, half in, half out. Just minutes ago, Piper had worried about Mandy. Now, it was Mandy's turn to question Piper, to worry about the choices she'd make and the consequences that could follow.

"I'll be just a minute more, Mandy."

She watched her daughter give a terse nod. But the look on her face was heartbreaking, reminding Piper that they'd all been forced to grow up too fast.

Mandy disappeared, slamming the door shut behind her.

"I shouldn't have come," he said, hearing another alarm in that slamming door.

He seemed embarrassed. Out of place. Almost as if he were just waking up to realize that coming here at dinnertime without even a call to give warning might be considered inappropriate. The day before, they'd made their silent pact, marching into unexplored and dangerous territory. Now, he seemed unsure.

"No," she told him, trying to reassure him. "It's all right. I want…"

But she stopped herself, knowing suddenly what she wanted. That excitement again. How long had it been since she'd felt that rush of discovery?

He nodded. "I'll go."

She stood with him and awkwardly almost stepped into his arms. He seemed to walk into the embrace, forcing her to scoot back, out of reach.

"Come back tomorrow," she whispered, looking away.

She didn't know how long she waited in her office after he left, her hand on the door. She took a deep breath.

"Enough," she said, and headed for the dining room, knowing it was long past time to face the music.

"What's wrong?"

Mandy didn't even look at Sean, afraid he'd see what she was thinking. What Piper was doing was wrong. Weird and dangerous and completely out of character. And it scared Mandy more than she wanted to admit.

"Mandy?" Sean repeated, staring at her.

She glanced over at her brother. Simon had folded his napkin into a triangle football, in his own world.

Mandy was remembering a story she'd read in the paper. How this defense attorney had fallen in love with her client in jail. So she'd come up with a plan to bust him out of prison. In the end, she was the one who got caught, ruining her life forever.

She remembered thinking how stupid that was, falling for some loser like that. But then she'd met Sean, and she could understand a little. How sometimes, those things weren't always in your control.

"Mandy?"

She looked over at Sean. She tried to smile because he was so worried, but she knew it had come out all wrong.

Instead, she pushed back her chair, deciding to give it another go. She couldn't just sit here and do nothing, waiting for some ax murderer to seduce Piper.

"I'll be back."

She raced down the hall. She didn't know what she planned, but suddenly she was running straight into Piper's arms.

"Mandy?"

Mandy grabbed her and hugged her. She was taller than Piper, so she could whisper in her ear, "Why did you do that? We were having dinner. You should have told him to leave and you didn't."

The accusation hung between them. She didn't know when it happened, when she'd started becoming the one in charge, the one everyone depended on. But that's exactly how Mandy felt. And now, her mother was screwing up. And Mandy was scared.

"He left, Mandy," Piper said in this strange calm voice.

"But he'll be back." She could hear her voice getting louder, higher pitched. "Mom, don't you get what's happening?"

She felt Piper tense in her arms. Mandy hugged her tighter, refusing to let go. She didn't call her *Mom* often. That had just slipped out, as if she'd needed the extra footing—needed to remind both of them what was at stake.

"I've done everything I'm supposed to do," Mandy whispered. "I work around the house and at the barn. I get good grades—I watch Simon."

Because Mandy was the only one he even talked to a little. And even then, it was hardly at all. Not like before.

Hadn't she been there for everyone? Hadn't she done everything? What had she forgotten? What more did Piper need?

Piper held her face in her hands. "Hey, this is not your problem. He's a client. A patient, only that. And if it bothers you that he comes here, I can see him somewhere else."

Piper had that I-am-the-mother look, the expression that had been missing when Mandy had seen her in the office with the lightning guy. And her voice sounded strong, telling Mandy that whatever happened, she'd keep them safe.

But she hadn't said what Mandy wanted to hear. She hadn't said she wouldn't see the guy—just that she'd take him somewhere else for their sessions together.

She shook her head. "It's not that…"

"What then?"

But how did she explain the look in Piper's eyes when that weirdo was around? Mandy knew now what it felt like to love someone and how it made you do things you shouldn't. She felt stupid even bringing it up. As if Piper could be that silly, like that woman who broke her client out of jail.

Looking at Piper now, Mandy started to second-guess herself. Piper was levelheaded. She'd gone to school and learned about how people could get broken inside like Humpty Dumpty. There were rules on how to put them back together.

Just the same, she whispered, "I'm scared, Piper."

Piper kissed her on both cheeks and on the top of her head. "Don't worry so much. You're not the mother here. I am. And I'll take care of us. I promise."

Hugging her again, Mandy frowned. Piper had said exactly those words when they'd been at the hospital, waiting to hear about Simon. Dad had already died. Piper had done the exact same thing, too, this little ritual of hers. She'd wrapped Mandy in her arms and kissed her three times, telling her everything would be all right. That she would take care of them.

Mandy felt her heart thumping so loudly she thought for sure Piper could hear.

But Piper couldn't make everything all better as she claimed. She wasn't Superwoman, after all.

She pulled away to smile at Mandy, brushing her bangs out of her eyes. "You know what scares me, Mandy Candy?" she said. "That handsome boy eating steak at my table."

She looked into her mother's face, and for a minute, it seemed like it was going to be okay. That the only thing they had to worry about was the normal stuff, like Mandy starting to date.

"Sean's okay."

"The seal of approval." She turned Mandy down the hall. They both headed back toward the dining room, their arms around each other.

But Mandy knew their life hadn't been normal for a long time. Simon had all this stuff wrong with him. The kids at school teased him…and he didn't even know enough to care. He was like one of those autistic kids. Stuck in his head.

And now some weird guy shows up and he looks at Piper like she's hung the moon. And Piper wants to pretend they're all okay. No problem.

Mandy knew that, too, was a lie. And she couldn't pretend that she wasn't scared that it could all get a lot worse.

13

Clay was lost.

He'd taken a couple of right turns, then some lefts. By now, he had no idea where he was. Everything looked pretty much the same, what he called Nouveau Mediterranean. Slap some stucco on the walls and cap it with red clay tiles and voilà, a suburban maze. And he was the rat, with no idea where he was heading.

Not that it mattered. Getting somewhere wasn't the point of the drive. Quite the opposite.

He'd been out of his mind to go over to her house. But that pretty much summed up his mental state these days. Out of his freaking head, always making the wrong choice, accepting the collateral damage that might come along with his bad judgment.

Aidan pointed it out all the time. After the trial, he'd advised Clay to sell everything and just take off. Clay couldn't do it. Maybe because that's what Burton expected. Then he could point the finger. *There, you see? I was right about the bastard. He wanted her money.*

Money. As far as Clay was concerned, he had too much already. He didn't want a single dime of his wife's. Most days, he just wanted to disappear. Or maybe open his eyes and see

Jillian there in front of him, telling him the nightmare he'd been living the last year was over.

So he didn't take the meds the doctors gave him—didn't make plans to go abroad either, as his lawyer advised, searching for a new life.

"What are you waiting for?" Aidan had asked. "Get the hell out of here."

Get away. Far, far away.

Don't stay frozen in the past.

Words to live by, according to Aidan. *Clay, you have to move on. It's what Jillian would want, Clay.*

But what did Aidan know? Jillian, like her father, might very well want him dead and buried. He didn't share Aidan's optimism about his future. Not by a long shot.

How could Clay move on when he couldn't remember a damn thing about what had happened the night Jillian died? How could he pretend everything was okay, when he couldn't sleep at night and his head felt like someone had buried a hatchet in it? Post-traumatic bullshit, whatever.

At least a couple of times a week, he had the nightmare. He'd wake up and stare down at his arms, reaching for his wife's dead body, grabbing only air.

That's why he'd gone to see Piper. He needed to get inside his head. He didn't care about pain—headaches and insomnia didn't matter to him. He wanted answers. And he couldn't even get that right.

After their session yesterday, he'd been at his house, staring at Piper's photograph, one of many he now had hidden away in his filing cabinet. He wondered sometimes why he did that, hid everything, as if he half expected the cops to show up with a search warrant and find all that incriminating evidence.

Yesterday, after Simon had left him, scurrying back to the neighbors, Clay hadn't driven straight home. Just like now, he'd circled around. Only, after an hour, he'd ended up parking a couple of blocks from her house, hoofing it to just across the street, careful that no one see him. He'd taken photographs of her, pictures shot with a telephoto lens.

He'd told himself he was conducting an experiment, pushing the parameters. But it was just like when they'd been in her office. As long as he was focused on Piper, there wasn't a damn thing wrong with him.

I'm obsessed with my shrink.

Because he could photograph her and only her. When Piper was in his camera's field of vision, he became the old Clay, the guy who held a camera in his hands as if it were an extension of himself. For those few minutes, he could disappear into his lens. There were no headaches or nightmares to worry about. No trial. He was in the moment—and if that wasn't magic, damned if he knew what was.

When he'd gotten home, he'd gone back into the darkroom, thinking of that ever-growing file of photographs, knowing there was something dark and twisted about what he was doing. At the same time, a part of him wondered if that wasn't what he'd needed all along. To get in touch with that darkness inside himself, see if it couldn't lead him to murder.

He'd done the same today. He didn't know how long he'd been sitting there staring at the eight-by-ten of Piper's face. Long enough that the sun had set. But he'd started feeling like he was in one of their sessions.

He'd imagined her right there in front of him. He'd be looking into her eyes rather than the photograph. He'd be wondering what he saw there that could make him feel new again. Make him want to pick up his camera and take another shot. Why it was that only Piper could steady his hands.

Then, bam! That jolt of memory had rocked him back. He'd been there again, in the humid thickness of the Everglades with his camera. The day Jillian had died.

The magic of the storm had returned with full gale force. He'd been squeezing off the automatic shutter button at the end of the cable release as the sky had exploded with lightning. That's when he'd heard the alarm.

Beep, beep, beep.

That sound. He'd heard that same rhythm when he'd stood outside her house last week. At the time, he'd thought it was a warning of some sort, his head telling him to back away before he sucked Piper into his nightmare. But now he knew it must have been the same memory slowly rising to the surface.

Beep, beep, beep.

"Hearing you loud and clear." He'd said it out loud, just as he always did when he heard the alarm.

He couldn't sit still after that. He'd grabbed his keys and headed out, almost as if he were afraid to think about what he was doing because then he'd have to stop and acknowledge how crazy he was acting. Logic would sink in and stop him from starting the Jeep and backing down the drive. If he'd considered what he was about to do, he would have stopped. He would never drive over like a maniac to knock on her door. He hadn't lost that much control.

Or had he?

He'd gone into automatic after that, ringing the doorbell. And when that hadn't worked, he'd banged on the door, the echo of the sound pounding in his chest.

He hadn't even felt bad about what he was doing. Not by then. Quite the opposite. He'd felt exhilarated, thinking only about some stupid wish fulfillment.

He'd wanted to see her. Talk to her. Tell her everything.

I remembered...

A gold star for the crazy guy.

Only, once inside—once he'd started talking, letting it all spill out—something else had happened.

Another memory...one not so good.

The kid had interrupted at just the right moment, sticking her head in the door as if something karmic had timed the interruption. She'd distracted Piper, stopped her from seeing the expression on his face.

He'd been telling her about hearing the alarm when, out of the blue, a second image had flashed in his head.

His hand holding a gun.

His hand. And a gun.

He stared up into the rearview mirror, caught sight of the gray sedan. The guy wasn't even being careful anymore. Clay squinted, imagining the man's expression as he drove. Bored, no doubt. Wondering what the hell Clay was doing driving in circles at this late hour.

He'd been driving for at least twenty minutes. Not a lot of traffic here in the sleepy streets of Coral Cay. Not so easy to tail him without being seen. Not that his shadow gave a shit. The guy had gone into automatic long ago, probably just happy to cash Burton's checks and play babysitter.

When he'd gone to see Piper, Clay had been running on this fantastic energy. Elated. He'd had this stupid idea that he could remember now...that he could trust himself again. Maybe, just maybe, the nightmare was over.

Only, that hadn't been the case. The fact was, the nightmare was just beginning.

He stared up into the rearview mirror and pulled over alongside the curb. He waited as the car approached, ready to pass.

At the last possible instant, Clay pulled out fast, swooping in front of the guy's Acura. He slammed on his brakes so that the car, not expecting the move, rear-ended his Jeep.

Clay hopped out of his car and ran over. He motioned for the guy inside the sedan to roll his window down.

Clay leaned in, all smiles. "License and insurance," he said.

"What?"

He motioned toward the rear of the Jeep. "You just rear-ended me, buddy. So I need your insurance information. And by the way, don't worry. I'm fine."

The guy looked like he was going to argue. Clay thought he'd save him the trouble.

"Tell Burton we need to talk. And trust me, he's gonna want to hear what I have to say."

He left Burton's expensive detective wondering how he was going to tell his very demanding boss that the target was on to him. His problem, Clay figured.

He slipped behind the steering wheel, revved the Jeep's engine. He didn't give a crap about the bumper on the Jeep, but the Acura looked like it had taken a good hit. He wondered if the guy would bill Burton's account.

Within the hour, Clay was back out over water, riding the rail of the highway down the Keys.

The beauty of a photograph was its ability to freeze a moment in time, captured forever. That's what he'd told Jillian when she'd asked him why he loved photography so much. Was it the artistry? Composition? Communing with nature?

For Clay, it had always been about the ability to freeze time. To capture something majestic, a power that he could never quite forget.

On the drive back to his house, he remembered that power. How it had hit him right between the eyes, knocking the breath out of him. The picture stuck in his head: His hand holding a gun.

His hand.

His gun.

Just like that, a moment in time, frozen forever.

Piper stared up at the ceiling, the television off for once. Beside her, Simon slept, his breath warm on her arm as she stroked his soft chestnut hair.

Simon was the spitting image of Kevin at his age. Her mother-in-law showed her pictures all the time, proclaiming Simon a Jordan through and through. Her way of stamping her grandson one hundred percent hers: *You see? None of this belongs to you.*

Mandy, she looked more like her mother.

When Mandy had been four years old, her mother had died. Her death had been quick and unexpected. An aneurysm. Piper had met Kevin a year later. Mandy had had strawberry curls and black button eyes, a walking, breathing Orphan Annie. To this day, Piper couldn't say whom she'd fallen in love with first. Kevin or Mandy.

Simon sighed in his sleep, snuggling closer. It was one of those hot, muggy nights, so that even with air-conditioning, Piper could feel the weight of the air against the windowpane.

A part of her knew Mandy was right. Piper was playing with fire. If Clay had killed his wife, Piper was taking a huge chance, the kind she couldn't afford. Not with everything her family had been through already. Not with Simon the way he was.

She stared down at her son and sighed.

"What did he tell you that night, baby?" she asked softly, so as not to wake him.

What had Clay said to Simon that had erased that look of fear, so that, even now, her boy slept soundly, despite the approaching storm?

Clayton Chase, man of mystery. Survivor.

Her sister had given her the heads-up. She'd told Piper she needed to be careful, not to fool herself into falling for the allure of a man who'd survived what Kevin could not.

At the time, Piper had scoffed at the idea. She'd told herself Crissa didn't understand Clay's true draw…that he'd somehow reached Simon. Whatever had happened that night during the storm when Clay had held Simon in his arms, he'd made the kind of difference nothing else had managed—not the hours of biofeedback, not the months of speech therapy. Nothing had made a dent in her son's wall of silence, until Clay.

But tonight, Mandy had come to give the same warning. The fear on her daughter's face should have been enough to make any mother reevaluate.

First Crissa…now Mandy. The people who knew her best.

Well, maybe they were right. It was time to stop. She couldn't take these risks after all—couldn't fool herself into believing this was all for Simon.

The truth was, Clay brought back that sense of discovery, what had taken her into psychology in the first place. She couldn't let that wonderful feeling seduce her into making a mistake. Because what she felt for Clay wouldn't stop at the professional high of accomplishment, or the hopes of a mother for her recovering child. He'd brought back other emotions. Those butterflies in her stomach fluttering up to her heart, how long had it been since a man had made her feel that?

Stroking Simon's hair in his sleep, she told herself this wasn't her youth. She wasn't free to use up her life in any way she chose. Simon and Mandy depended on her. And lately, they were all starting to show cracks.

She would let him know at their next session. She couldn't help Clay, not anymore. She'd refer him to someone else. Someone better. Stronger.

It's what he needed. What they both needed.

She turned on her side, Simon fast asleep beside her, as the heaviness in the air turned to rain. Somewhere in the distance, she heard the roll of thunder.

14

Burton had always considered himself a careful man. In his life, he'd taken only calculated risks—in business, even more so. He didn't like to gamble. His dealings with Angel Barrera had been one of those calculated risks.

When he'd first come to town with nothing but a hundred dollars in his wallet and a dream in his head, he'd been bloated with his vision, swelled with the possibilities. Buy a little piece of something in Miami's ever-growing real-estate market, develop the same with hard work and the sweat of his brow, then leverage it to buy the next property, then the next.

He'd even taken a class back home in Martin, Tennessee. Not like the classes they taught at the university. His father, a factory worker, had no money to give any of his five children a formal education. Burton, whose real name was Bert Wardensky, had been working at the same Goodyear factory where his father had toiled his whole life.

He'd worked nights and he'd always had trouble falling asleep when he got home. So he'd watched television, often drifting off in his father's Barcalounger in the den.

The day his life changed, he'd been flipping through the channels after a tough day, Budweiser in hand—the king of beers—when he remembered this Gus Matsen brochure some guy had been handing out at work.

At first, reading about the men and women whose lives had changed using the "Matsen Method," he'd thought: *Bullshit.* But seeing those happy faces in the brochure and reading their incredible stories got to him. And after his fourth Bud he started thinking: Why not me? Why the hell not me?

So at nineteen he packed up his duffel bag and headed for the sunny shores of opportunity...only to end up working nights at another factory.

The fact was, the Matsen Method was, as he feared, bull-shit. In the end, he had to make up his own rules. Which meant getting in with Angel Barrera.

At the time, he knew all about Barrera and his family, ru-mored money-laundering kings. Barrera liked him, saw a lit-tle of himself in Burton's hunger to succeed. And there was his wife, Lydia. She liked Burton, too...he'd always been good with the ladies. He was charming, a hard worker. At first, he was nothing more than one of Angel's thugs. But that soon changed.

From the beginning, he told himself working for Barrera was the means to an end. He drew up a plan, played on Angel's desire for legit business ventures, promising the moon and the stars if Angel just took a chance on a young kid with dreams.

They never discussed where the money came from, just that Angel was happy to invest. Angel took him under wing. At the time, Burton didn't give a shit how Angel made his money.

Burton made them both a small fortune. And then he asked Angel to cut him loose.

That wasn't so easy. Angel knew a good thing when he saw it. He and Lydia had never had kids and he kept talking about how much he loved Burton like a son, even though Angel was only some ten years older. This was just the beginning for them.

So Burton took his first real risk, breaking a cardinal rule of business, big time. Worse yet, he acted out of desperation, not even putting that much thought into the consequences if he failed. By then, he'd met Jackie. He knew there was no way a woman like her could be a part of his life with Angel in the picture.

The plan had been spur of the moment, not his style at all. He'd been almost shocked when it had paid off. But he'd always had that special way with women and Lydia had come to his rescue. A year later, at his wife's pleading, Angel had let Burton go.

But now the Calderon woman had him thinking, bringing back the specter of what could have been a big mistake.

"There you are, my love." His wife, Jackie, looped her arm through his. "I thought I'd never escape that dreadful Steward woman. Shame on you for leaving me to her."

As usual, Jackie looked like a million bucks dressed in a simple black dress. She'd been doing something different with her hair, some kind of subtle highlights, and Burton liked how it looked. She wore it up in a French twist, showing off the patrician features of her ancestors. But it was how she held herself that had made him want to marry her. A woman with that much spine.

"Burton, dear." She took a sip of her champagne. "Why are we here?"

"Beluga and Cristal," he said, motioning to her long-stemmed glass. "Don't I only bring you to the best places?"

"Nice try," she said. "Since we have a refrigerator full of things you like much better."

She was talking about his Budweiser and those little ween-ies that came in the jar. Burton could put on a good show, but at home, he was that same guy sitting in his dad's Barca-lounger.

"Just some business, darling," he said. "Nothing to worry about."

His wife lifted her hand to his face, getting his attention. She didn't say a word, but the look she gave him…

Burton didn't conduct business anymore; he'd lost his taste for it. He'd been dead ever since they'd lost their only child, and nothing—not counseling or alcohol, or even Jackie's great love—could bring him back to the world of the living. All of which his wife knew only too well.

"So let me repeat the question you are so diligently avoid-ing," she said. "Why are we here?"

She knew how much he hated just this sort of gathering, these vapid people and their need to be seen and heard. There had to be a goal, a reason that had nothing to do with the busi-ness excuse he'd given. But it was one that he wasn't about to share with Jackie, not by a long shot.

"Darling," he said, "why don't you get me some of that fine Cristal while I mingle?"

"Burton?" Her tone let him know he wasn't fooling the woman he'd lived with almost forty years.

But he walked away just the same, knowing that Jackie wouldn't follow. Her style was more gentle nudging, not the hammer blow of butting in. It's one of the things he loved most about her. That she'd always given him the space he'd needed.

Of course, there was a purpose for putting up with this shitty champagne and uppity caviar. And there he was, hold-ing court by the window.

Angel Barrera.

Burton strolled over, knowing that while Jackie wouldn't stop him, he'd have plenty to answer for once they got home. But Grace Calderon had put the germ of an idea in his head. Last night, it had sprouted and grown into this tangle that wouldn't let him sleep or eat. So he'd come here to follow through, seeing if she could possibly be right. That he'd overlooked something as obvious as Angel Barrera.

He stood on the periphery, waiting to catch Angel's glance. In his mid-seventies, Barrera looked ten years younger—the product of living right, he would probably say. He was short and stocky, ill suited for the fine clothes he favored. His hair was the same shade of silver it had been when Burton had first met him over forty years ago, though there was a lot less of it now. Burton watched, trying to discern if this man indeed was responsible for his daughter's death.

Eight years ago, when Burton had first acquired the right to develop the Seminole land, Angel had approached him. Remember what a team they'd been? Burton was a rich man, now, after all.

He'd left the obvious unsaid. Angel didn't have a taste for the obvious. He was a man who cherished the subtle. He'd let Burton fill in the silence: Rich, because of Angel.

He'd caught Burton off guard. Angel and his wife Lydia—the lovely woman who had lived in Angel's shadow for years—were part of Burton's history, a deal he'd made with the devil that he thought he'd put in the past.

But there he'd been again, asking about the Seminole lands.

Burton had known gambling would be a perfect front for money laundering.

Angel hadn't tried to bully him. Maybe he'd known that

by then, Burton had resources at his disposal, a powerful man in his own right. Or maybe it had been Lydia coming to Burton's rescue again. She'd been recently diagnosed with cancer. Angel had had his hands full. He loved his wife and she was most certainly going to die.

But Burton hadn't been certain. He couldn't have taken the chance that Angel was a different man, focused on his wife and her health rather than his endless quest for power and money.

So he'd hired a bodyguard. He'd kept a close watch. Burton knew how to take care of his own.

But now the Calderon woman had him thinking. A man like Angel could be patient. Burton, believing he and his family safe, had let his guard down.

Angel caught sight of Burton watching him. His face broke into a grin. Immediately, he excused himself, moving past his entourage, hangers-on who didn't care that the man was linked to organized crime. He had power and money, a seductive combination, one that Burton himself had tasted.

Angel stepped over, held out his hand. As both men shook like old friends, Burton thought: *Once I did you a great wrong. Did you find out? Was Jillian your revenge?*

"Got a minute?" Burton asked, nodding to a more private corner.

Angel gave a wry smile. "For you, my friend, always."

Both men stepped outside. Angel pulled out one of those cases that held two cigars, the kind that could fit inside the pocket of the fine suit he was wearing. Angel had his suits made by a guy in Hong Kong. Same thing with his shirts. Burton remembered they were monogrammed, Angel being the kind of man who liked to advertise himself.

Burton, he wore whatever his wife told him to wear. He

couldn't even match his socks without her. He was color-blind. Now he was wondering if that blindness went beyond the menial to something sacred.

Angel offered him a cigar. Burton shook his head. He waited for Angel to light up. He wanted his complete attention.

When their eyes met, Angel gave him an expectant look.

"What can I do for you, my friend?"

Burton moved in, getting a close look. He wanted to be sure. He needed to know the truth.

He said, "Did you kill my daughter, Angel? Did you hurt my little girl, you piece of shit?"

He watched Angel, looking for a change in his expression. There was none.

"What in hell kind of question is that?" he asked in a mild tone.

Burton kept his gaze steady. He didn't even blink, afraid he would miss something. But he saw nothing.

He should have known. After all these years doing the kind of trash Angel was into, killing Jillian would be like drinking a glass of water. Nothing to it.

"I heard they're retrying the case. Is that what this is about?"

Angel took a lazy puff from the Dominican cigar. Angel smoked only Dominican cigars, telling Burton once that the Cubans were all hype now, that Fidel had ruined even that. In the old days, those Cubans were smooth. Rolled on the thighs of lush Cuban girls, Burton remembered Angel saying just that.

"I talked to the state attorney," Burton said. "They seem interested in our past relationship."

Grace Calderon had spoken to him about Angel to let him know she'd discovered that link in his past. But as he'd said to her, he also knew she couldn't prove the connection. But that's not why she'd brought it up.

Angel stared at the tip of his cigar almost as if he expected to find it wasn't lit. He didn't look at Burton, just spoke in the same mild tone, "Lydia has three months to live. Maybe not even that long."

He glanced up, looking Burton dead in the eye. Something hung in the air between them.

Angel stepped closer and whispered, "I wish I could take credit for your little girl. But I can't. You fed your own to the sharks. You let your Jillian set up house with a killer. And then, to top it off, you let him get away with it. Shame on you, Burton." He stepped back and gave a shake of his head. "Shame on you."

Burton watched Angel return to the party. He waited outside, his gut burning. Almost forty years ago, he'd cut his ties to Angel Barrera. He'd been watching his back ever since. But now he wondered if he'd been up to the task.

That look Angel had given him. He knew that look.

And now he couldn't be sure. Because either way, whether it was Angel behind Jillian's murder or Clay, Angel was right about one thing. It was Burton's fault she was dead.

He hadn't been careful enough, hadn't kept a good enough watch. His daughter had been murdered, most likely by the man she'd loved...or by the sins of her father.

And he'd let it happen.

Whatever the case, Angel couldn't have spoken truer words. Shame on him. Shame on him.

"So what's up with that guy?" Sean asked. "I mean, showing up at dinner like that. It was weird, right?"

Mandy turned toward him. They were parked outside Sean's house; she'd driven him home after dinner, with Piper's blessing. Mandy liked Sean, a lot. In fact, she loved Sean. She'd even told him so. At first, because it was what he wanted to hear. But later, she realized she meant it. That she wasn't afraid of that emotion anymore.

For a long time, she had been. She hadn't wanted to love anyone. She couldn't afford to get close. If you love someone and you lose them, it's the most terrible feeling in the world, something she knew only too well.

No, she hadn't wanted to love Sean. But she did.

You're not the mother here.

That's what Piper had told her. And she wanted to let go, not to worry about the people she loved. But over and over, that hadn't worked out so well.

"He's just some stupid patient. He had a crisis or something, so he showed up to talk to Piper."

"Does that happen a lot? People just dropping by like that?"

"No."

"So was it okay? I mean, he left pretty fast."

"No. Not really."

She couldn't talk about it, her throat felt all thick and tight. She thought maybe nothing would ever be okay again.

"Hey," he said. "Tell me what's going on."

She knew how hard it was for Sean that she kept things inside. He wasn't like that. He had this wonderful view of life where you get the happy ending. He could still afford an open heart. He never hid anything. It's what she loved best about him. That he didn't carry any burdens.

She didn't want to put any on his shoulders, either. Not the kind she'd been carrying. So she tried not to say anything.

But sometimes she could see it was worse not to talk about it. Because he worried that she was keeping things from him. About them. And if she didn't tell him the truth, he would start thinking just that.

"Sometimes," she said, leaning back into his arms. "It just feels like it's hard to breathe, you know?"

She knew that's what Piper meant when she told Mandy she was taking on too much. But what else was she supposed to do? Her father had wanted her to go to some Ivy League school, just like him. And she felt like she owed it to him, no matter how hard that was—the grades, the SAT scores, the AP tests—all those chances to screw up. And Simon needed her, too. Because she was that last little bit of Dad. Just like she was for Piper.

But she thought it was more than that weighing on her heart right now.

"So many things have changed since my dad died." She sighed. "I guess I don't want anything more to change."

"And this guy is going to change stuff?"

She kept thinking about that look on Piper's face. "Yeah. Maybe. And not in a good way."

No matter what, Mandy didn't want to lose anybody else.

15

"I got the 411 on the attorney heading up the prosecution," Aidan told Clay. "Graciela Calderon. Smart, with a take-no-prisoners mentality. Last year, she put away that dirtbag rapist Holden."

Sitting on the couch, Clay listened to Aidan talk on. He thought it was cute how Aidan—attorney to dirtbags—could use the term with such panache.

They were sitting in the living room of Aidan's apartment. As chief counsel for Ward Enterprises, Aidan had never been hurting for money, but he'd certainly moved on in the world as a top criminal attorney. The place was new. Danish glass tile accented the minimalist furniture, plasma-screen televisions adorned the walls of both the living room and master bedroom. Jillian would have loved it. And then there was the million-dollar view, beautiful if you liked your slice of beach lined with high-rise apartments and hotels.

"She's going to be tough, especially after the beating they took the first time around. The prosecution isn't going to want a repeat performance, believe me. Still, it's all circumstantial. Frankly, I'm surprised they're even bothering. Some political infighting, no doubt. But I don't like surprises, so we'll try to stay two steps ahead. It's never too early to talk strategy."

Aidan liked circumstantial evidence. Direct evidence—an eyewitness or even admissions Clay might have made tying him to the crime—were more difficult to defuse in court. He also loved to talk strategy. Aidan, in fact, loved to talk. He was a performer, at his best in front of an audience.

Sometimes, Clay thought it funny how different the two men were—almost to the point of reaching the ridiculous. Clay worked alone. Out in the field, he could go days without talking to a soul. Aidan needed to bounce ideas around, processing information by talking.

They looked nothing alike, either. Clay, the taller of the two, had light brown hair and hazel eyes, his features hardened by the elements. Aidan with his slighter build appeared a good ten years younger than his thirty-five. He used his blond tousled hair and pale blue eyes to good effect with a jury. You wanted to believe Aidan with his boyish looks. He was the good guy…while Clay's long hair and perennial five o'clock shadow had him halfway to villain.

And still, the same woman had loved them both. Two such different men. Aidan, a friend of the family, had been Jillian's childhood sweetheart, part and parcel of a privileged background that included private schools and supper clubs. While Clay had been exploring the mangrove swamps with his grandfather's Brownie Hawkeye, Aidan and Jillian had been learning how to dance at Cotillion. They'd even shared their love of horses. Jillian, an experienced equestrian, often had gone to watch Aidan at polo matches.

"Our strategy will be the same as before," Aidan continued. "Shoddy police work—a rush to judgment. Yes, it was your gun, but they can't explain why there was no residue on your hands."

The prosecution had claimed he'd worn gloves, but hadn't been able to explain his prints on the gun…other than to say Clay had made a mistake in the heat of the moment, handling the gun after he'd gotten rid of the gloves. Aidan had effectively pointed out at trial the prosecution couldn't have it both ways. Clay had either planned his wife's murder, wearing gloves—gloves the prosecution had never produced—or he hadn't fired the gun.

Clay remembered the moment perfectly, Aidan the performer giving his closing remarks to the jurors. *I don't know about you, folks, but I'm not buying the prosecution's "now you see them now you don't" theory on those gloves.*

"Discovery will let us know if they have anything new. And the witness list. We'll keep you off the stand—"

"No."

Aidan took a moment. This was old ground for the two men. "Clay, I understand how you feel. But you're not getting on the stand."

"It's going to have to be my call, Aidan."

"Is this that bullshit therapy talking? Clay, you leave these decisions to your attorney. That's why you have me, to stop you from making a big mistake, and that's exactly what it would be, my friend. A huge opening for the prosecution."

My friend. Aidan had called him that a lot this past year, which always made Clay wonder. Before the trial, Aidan had never used the term. There had always been that tension between them. *She chose you instead of me…* Aidan didn't like to lose.

Clay could understand the man's need to keep Jillian's memory alive. What he couldn't comprehend was the strange link Aidan had made between keeping Clay out of jail and fulfilling some obligation he had to Jillian. Certainly, Burton Ward made no such connection, quite the opposite. For his daughter's sake, Burton had vowed to see Clay in hell.

"Clay?"

When Clay didn't answer, Aidan pressed a hand to Clay's shoulder, his annoyed expression turning to one of sympathy.

He told Clay, "Listen to me. This is going to end. You're going to get through this. You're going to be okay. Life will go back to normal."

Because Aidan the Great would be there at his side, ready to defend him. And then Clay could return to his hellhole of guilt and confusion. To a life where his wife was dead and the doubts that lingered would haunt him with a lifetime of what-ifs?

What if he hadn't gone out that night? What if they hadn't argued and he'd stayed home?

What if his wife had still loved him?

Or maybe he had it all wrong, always making it about Jillian's decision to leave him. It could have been the other way around. Maybe he was the problem—maybe, as Jillian had claimed, he just hadn't loved her enough.

A marriage didn't fall apart overnight. There'd been cracks. Okay, he'd always thought those fissures came with the terrain. Nothing was perfect, right? They'd talked about seeing a counselor, but there was his travel schedule…and then they'd stopped talking.

No, he wasn't going to be okay. Okay would mean he could sleep at night. Okay would mean that he wouldn't be plagued by memory loss and nightmare doubts. That he could hold a camera with someone in the viewfinder other than Piper.

Okay would be Jillian alive. Hating him, sure. Leaving him for some other man, fine. But alive.

"Look, I know you're having a rough time," Aidan said, filling in the silence…because, for Aidan, silence was an opportunity to step in and guide those who would listen. "I wish to God you didn't have to go through another trial. But I need you to focus here, okay? For just a little longer, I need you to give me one hundred percent."

"I'm testifying."

Aidan gave him a hard look. "All right. Let's say you do testify. What do you have to say? I don't remember? Pretty please, believe me? Do you think that's going to cut it with the jury?"

"Do you ever wonder how things would have turned out if she'd stayed with you?" Clay asked.

The question leveled both men, almost as if neither could quite believe Clay had spoken out loud.

"That was a long time ago," Aidan said.

But once he'd started down the course, Clay didn't want to put on the brakes. "If she'd stayed with you, she'd still be alive, wouldn't she?"

This time, Aidan remained silent. Clay knew the drill. As his attorney, there would be this double-edged sword. Aidan couldn't perpetuate a fraud on the court if Clay confessed or handed over evidence. At the same time, he was obligated to provide a rigorous defense. A good attorney walked that fine line by making it clear to his or her client that he didn't need to know anything the prosecution couldn't prove. Let the prosecution bear the burden of proof…that's the way the system worked best.

But this was different. Aidan had loved Jillian. He'd asked her to marry him in sixth grade and had repeated the offer after law school. Watching him now, Clay could see Aidan the attorney losing the battle to Aidan the man.

"What are you saying?" Aidan asked, the question there in his eyes. *Did you kill her?*

Had Aidan suspected him all along? Clay wondered. Had he always had those doubts?

And the answer: *How could he not?*

Aidan shook his head, breaking the spell holding both men. "Apparently, this isn't the time to talk strategy. Go home, Clay. Get some rest."

Clay stood, more than ready to get out, wondering if that shouldn't have been his goal all along. To stop talking "strategy," and just get the hell out.

At the door, Aidan told him, "You're wrong. I never believed you killed her. I wouldn't defend you if I had the slightest doubt."

Clay didn't turn around, his hand on the door. He said, "Have you ever noticed how often you say that?"

Aidan might be the best, but tonight, he wasn't fooling anyone.

Shawna came out of the bedroom where she'd been waiting for Clay to leave. She glanced over at Aidan and walked to the bar. She poured him a drink of the very fine Springbank scotch he loved.

"You should have told him he killed her," she said, handing him the glass. "You just sat there, letting him see the truth in your eyes. Why are you still trying to protect him?" She sat down on the couch. "Just tell him he did it. It's what he deserves, after all."

He hadn't been expecting her. She had her own key, just like Aidan had a key to her apartment. He'd told her he was meeting Clay, hinting that she should go. But Clay and their strategy session had only made her want to stay, so she'd stalled, insisting on making him dinner.

Every day, she went on gourmet.com and found new recipes to entice him. Jillian, the one true love of his life, had been a gifted cook. Shawna had made him a lovely chowder soufflé, which they'd just about finished when Clay had rung the doorbell.

Aidan had asked her to leave. Instead, she'd told him she'd wait in the bedroom, not make a sound.

"He's in hell already," he said now. "Why should I turn up the heat?"

Shawna bit her lip to keep from answering him. She patted the couch beside her and waited as Aidan sat down. She dug her fingers into his shoulders—trying to massage away his tension or get out her frustration, she wasn't sure which.

"Did you make the call to Calderon?" he asked.

She sunk her fingers deeper into his tight muscles. "I started thinking it might look suspicious. I just met with her last week. It might be better if I wait. I might even help Clay, just like you want. If I change my position at the last minute."

He shook his head. "She'll nail down your testimony long before she'd ever rely on you in the courtroom."

She made a face. "What's the big deal, anyway? I'm not the only one who knew she was cheating on Clay."

"Make the call, Shawna."

"I said I would, didn't I?"

Honestly, she'd be happy to get off the woman's radar, but she didn't like his attitude. No one was supposed to know about her relationship with Aidan, and Aidan seemed to like it that way. It hurt that he wanted to keep her his little secret.

Sometimes she thought she embarrassed him. She wasn't as smart as Jillian—she wasn't as pretty.

I'm not dead, either.

Shawna allowed herself a small smile.

Burton, of course, knew about her relationship with Aidan. No one kept much from Burton—which was the point. To stay on the winning side. She wished Aidan could understand that, wished he'd give up on his misplaced loyalty to Clay. What about Shawna, the woman he supposedly loved? Didn't her opinion count?

"The way he talks to you," she said, her frustration coming through loud and clear despite her best efforts. "He doesn't even appreciate all that you've done for him."

"Sometimes it's important to do what's right, Shawna, no matter how hard it seems."

Oh, great, Shawna thought, massaging his shoulders. That's all they needed…Aidan at his sanctimonious best.

She hated all that moral crap of his. He was just like her mom. The worse her father had treated her mother, the harder she'd tried to please him. And Clay treated Aidan like shit.

Still, it didn't help Shawna's cause to push so hard. He wasn't listening to her, in any case. Quite the opposite. Lately, he'd been acting as if he were suspicious of her, accusing her of playing Burton's stooge. But Shawna was nobody's fool. She was looking out for number one.

Of course, Burton had approached her. He'd probably known even then that they were sleeping together. But this wasn't about manipulating Aidan into pleasing Burton. She had to look out for Aidan. Here he had this beautiful opportunity and he was going to turn his back on what Burton had offered? With Jillian gone, who else could Burton leave his company to? Not to Jillian's murdering husband, that was for sure. It only made sense that Aidan step in and take over Ward Enterprises. Which meant making sure Clay got his due.

She changed her grip, pressing her thumbs into the spot at the base of Aidan's neck where he kept most of his tension, thinking about what Aidan had said—that sometimes, you had to do what was right—seeing it from a different angle. If you really loved someone, like she loved Aidan, you had to protect them. Sometimes, even from themselves.

If Jillian had listened to her, wouldn't she still be alive?

Stupid, stupid, Jillian. She had had everything a woman could ever want in life, and she hadn't lifted a finger for any of it, either. Everything had just been handed to her on a silver platter. Her career running her gallery, a cute husband who, if she'd played her cards right, probably wouldn't have been gone half the time on assignment. But Jillian wouldn't pander to anyone's needs. *Stupid!*

Shawna felt her anger rising. Aidan thought Jillian was this great love he'd lost. Her death only confirmed it, basically granting the woman sainthood. Well, Shawna saw things a little differently. Aidan had fallen for the boss's daughter. What could be more obvious?

And she'd never loved him. Not like Shawna. For God's sake, she'd left him to marry Clay, and still Aidan carried this torch for her?

She whispered, "Why can't I be enough for you?"

He turned, startled. "What are you talking about?"

She told herself to hold back, not to break the illusion they had so carefully crafted. It wasn't so much that she'd become Jillian for Aidan. She could never do that. But as the woman's assistant for five years, watching Jillian strut around like she owned the world, Shawna could do a fair imitation. Neither of them wanted reality…only she felt the tears coming.

She reached for him, kissing him. With Aidan, it was always the same. He'd only give this tiny piece of himself, holding back. Honestly, the man was breaking her heart.

She told herself she had to be smarter. She was running out of time. Burton had set his sights on his daughter's killer, Clay. One way or another, he'd bring him down, and he wouldn't worry about any collateral damage.

She curled into Aidan's body on the couch, wrapping his arms around her, suddenly cold in the air-conditioned room. She wondered at her own power. She was taking a big gamble, talking to Burton behind Aidan's back. Had she miscalculated? After all she'd done for Aidan, would her love be enough?

She stroked his arm, thinking that she needed something more, something more tangible. A way to make certain Aidan did what she wanted.

But then she remembered what she'd overheard from the bedroom, Aidan talking to Clay. What Shawna Benet needed was a strategy.

The idea came to her suddenly, spectacularly, the risk making her heart pound.

"Do you love me, Aidan?" she whispered.

"Of course."

She smiled. Now, he just had to prove it.

16

He was driving too fast, his hands at two and ten o'clock gripping the steering wheel. The long slick road ribboned ahead, tempting him. He pressed his foot on the accelerator.

He remembered how carefully Piper had brought up the subject of suicide during one of their first sessions, tiptoeing in so as not to misconstrue or give offense. Suicidal thoughts were common after lightning strikes, depression being a result of both the trauma and the neurological damage—something about electricity seeking out the path of least resistance, targeting the heart, brain and spinal cord. She'd talked about how important it was to seek counseling following injury. She even used words like *courageous* and *recovery,* calling their sessions an important first step.

He remembered thinking that it was all such bullshit. He'd thought about interrupting her nice talk to ask what kind of mental problem came along with waking up and finding your dead wife in your arms, the cops pointing the finger at you.

He pushed the accelerator a little harder. The needle trembled past the 80 miles-per-hour mark.

He admitted readily to being an adrenaline junkie, but he'd never thought about suicide. Never. And he wasn't about to put that label on what he was doing tonight. There was just this idea in his head about ripping down the access road off Highway 41 down to the Glades, maybe turning the wheel hard to the right. Executing a perfect doughnut across the abandoned road.

Just slam on the brakes and spin the wheel.

The impulse to do just that poured over him, making him all loose inside. He pictured the move perfectly in his head, anticipated the forces tugging at him and what he'd do to keep control. He imagined a sensation like pulled taffy.

He could feel the wheel tremble under his hands as the dark marshland sped past.

Do it! Do it now!

That impulse inside him grew, pushing him, heating him up...but at the last minute, he eased his foot off the accelerator. He pulled the Jeep over to the side of the road.

He sat in the car, the air-conditioning set on high. He found himself catching his breath, as though he'd been running right alongside the Jeep. After a minute, condensation beaded the outside of the window. He pressed his palm to the glass, still breathing hard. It was hot outside, a thick soup of a night.

Do you ever wonder how things would have turned out if she'd stayed with you?

What a stupid question to throw in poor Aidan's face. Not for one minute did he believe Jillian had ever loved Aidan. He'd been just another one of her projects, one that had run its course, just like Clay.

When she'd told Clay she was thinking of leaving him, he couldn't help but make the comparison. He remembered what she'd told Clay when she'd left Aidan.

Jillian had known Aidan since grade school. He'd been her

first kiss. They'd had this thing where they always spent Valentine's Day together, no matter who they were seeing at the time. At first, Clay had argued against the tradition—they were married for God's sake—but eventually he'd seen the ritual for what it was: a sacred ceremony between friends.

She'd called Aidan her "go-to" guy. If she needed a date for the prom—if she turned into a spinster with twelve cats.

But that spark, that zing in the gut when you even thought about the person…that had never been part of the picture.

That's how she'd explained it to Clay. He hadn't broken them apart; they technically hadn't been engaged. Aidan had wanted the relationship so badly, she'd just fallen in line. And her father had loved him. He'd been practically part of the family already. She'd been sorry she would hurt Aidan. She'd made a mistake getting engaged.

You can't guide your heart, she'd told Clay.

It was a pretty little speech. She'd said the same thing to Clay the night she'd told him there was another man. *I can't guide my heart, Clay.*

Clay turned the car back onto the road, thinking, *No truer words…*

He ended up in front of Piper's house. This wasn't the first time he'd sat here, a voyeur in her life. He'd have to explain himself soon. He wasn't stalking her. He just couldn't seem to keep his focus unless she was in the viewfinder.

Let's explore that, shall we, doc?

Right.

He'd have to explain quite a few things to Piper. Like the possibility that he might have killed his wife.

He turned off the engine and stared down at the keys swinging from the ignition. It wouldn't take long for the heat to seep in from the outside.

He *was* sorry for Aidan. How it must hurt Aidan to have that knowledge of Clay's guilt come to him slowly. Clay could understand how, at first, Aidan had wanted to help. Jillian was gone, after all. Clay was all he'd have left of her. A connection. Burton had felt the same in the beginning. They'd all wanted to come to his rescue.

Once committed to defending Clay, Aidan probably couldn't let himself doubt his innocence. He called him "friend," and defended him vigorously. How could he admit to himself that he could be wrong, that instead of fulfilling Jillian's wish, he'd helped her killer? No, he'd need to believe in his cause. He'd need to save Clay because he hadn't been able to save Jillian. Piper could probably explain all the mental shenanigans the guy had gone through.

But tonight was different. Tonight he'd looked Aidan in the eye and he'd seen nothing but doubts.

Sitting in the Jeep, he thought about the old days, when fires were a common event in the pinelands and prairies of the Everglades, summer lightning often the cause. The fires would burn until they hit a natural barrier like water or mangrove, burning in irregular patterns, leaving a mosaic of burned and unburned vegetation.

Well, lightning had burned through him in just the same way. There were places inside him that didn't feel different. He could call his sister in California and speak to his nephew and niece about birthdays and school. He could close his eyes and pretend that he was still a good man. That he would never have hurt Jillian, not in a million years.

But then there were the charred and broken bits of him,

places so dark, he couldn't see the truth. Snapshot images would bombard him: his hand holding a gun, Jillian dead in his arms, her blood everywhere.

Aidan didn't want him to testify. The prosecution would have a field day, he'd told him. But Clay thought Aidan's reluctance came from someplace deeper than fears over the state attorney's case.

He was beginning to think that, just like Clay, Aidan feared the truth.

Piper was dreaming of Kevin. She was begging him not to leave. She didn't want to sleep in their cold bed alone. He should come back to bed.

She'd had the dream before, many times. A silly dream that had nothing to do with the deep problems in their marriage. Kevin had been a doctor, often on call. She'd learned to sleep alone. In real life, she'd never complained.

Tonight, she woke up to find the bed empty, just like all the other times. Only now, the sheets had been thrown aside.

Beside her, a shallow indent in the mattress showed where Simon had fallen asleep.

She reached over and touched the sheets. Stone cold.

She was out of bed and heading down the stairs, calling his name. There wasn't a storm tonight, no reason for him to disappear. He was probably in his room, or snuggled in bed with Mandy.

Only there was Mandy standing in the hallway. She'd heard Piper call Simon's name. She'd gone into automatic, checking on Simon herself.

"He's not in his room," she said.

Both women ran for the front door. It stood ajar, just like

all the other times...which didn't make any sense. There was no storm tonight, not even the hint of one in the air.

Piper threw the door open and stared out into the dark, disoriented. Somehow it made it all worse, this change in pattern.

"He's right there," Mandy said, her eyes adjusting to the dark first. "Sitting on the curb."

Piper heard the relief in Mandy's voice and tried to take comfort in it. But when Mandy tried to step around her, Piper stopped her.

She waited for her heart rate to approach normal before she whispered, "Go back to bed."

She stood at the door, watching her son unnoticed. Simon did not look the least bit agitated. He sat on the curb, his small arms cradling his knees to his chest. Clearly, he was waiting for something.

Or more precisely, someone.

Piper stepped outside and walked down the path toward him. She sat down next to her son and put her arm around him.

"What are you doing here, pumpkin?"

"I'm waiting for him. He'll come back. He promised. He was going to show me."

All those word from her silent little boy.

Lightning injury often resembled brain damage. Disturbances in language and verbal memory were not uncommon. Neither were somatoform disorders, physical symptoms that have no corresponding medical condition. But a conversion disorder—emotional distress expressed through physical symptoms—usually resolved itself in a matter of weeks. Two years later, Simon hadn't been getting better. Quite the opposite.

Until the night she'd found him in Clay's arms.

Ever since the storm, Simon had begun to communicate, stringing together words. The notion that his speech problems were purely psychological was no longer a hope or a fear, just a fact. The likelihood that he suffered from a hysterical condition brought on by trauma didn't make his recovery any easier.

But it did give her a key.

"What was he going to show you?" she asked, still holding him.

But the moment was gone. Simon was staring ahead, once again falling into his silent vigil.

She had years of experience with this sort of thing, training to guide her. And still, at that moment, she was just a mother worried about her child.

"You want to see him again, don't you?"

The minute she said those words, she wanted to call them back. She'd spoken too soon—she hadn't thought through all the ramifications. But it was like trying to put the genie back into the bottle.

Simon looked at her with such longing.

She stood and picked him up, cradling him against her. In another year, he'd be too big to carry. His feet already brushed her calves as she walked back into the house.

She thought of all her resolutions. How she'd promised herself she would find Clay another therapist—that she would finally put an end to their dangerous bargain. But her resolve was meaningless in the face of the battle she and Simon waged.

"Whatever it takes, baby," she said, nuzzling him, smelling the baby shampoo in his hair. "Whatever it takes."

He watched Piper carry Simon back into the house. He was parked down the street behind a string of cars. She hadn't even noticed the Jeep, of course, being focused completely on Simon.

In his career, he'd specialized in nature photography. He remembered one of his toughest shoots, a night shoot in Puerto Rico for *Condé Nast Travel* magazine. That night in the water, he'd tried to capture the beauty of one of the area's famous Biobays, photographing the phosphorescent plankton in the lagoon. The water had lit up with even the slightest movement, the manta rays on the ocean floor, the flying fish skipping over the surface like skimming stones.

Every time anything had agitated the water, it had turned the color of a glow stick. Dipping his hands, he'd watched the water slip over his skin like diamonds dripping from his fingers. He'd gone through roll after roll of film and had nothing to show but frustration for his efforts. He couldn't even come close to getting that beauty on film.

He felt the same tonight. No camera could capture that image of Simon in Piper's arms haloed by the streetlight.

His heart hammered inside his chest. He was back on that access road, fighting the impulse to jam the Jeep's steering wheel in a hard right and slam on the brakes.

Jesus, he couldn't catch his breath.

There was absolutely no doubt in his mind that Simon had been waiting for him on that curb.

He ticked off the mistakes he'd made with Simon. He'd been premature, telling him he'd teach Simon how to shoot a camera.

Simon was just a couple of years older than his nephew, John. At that age, he knew how kids could anticipate, growing excited by the prospect of something special. How many times had he seen John's face light up with that kind of energy at Christmas, when Clay walked through the door carrying presents? Well, he'd offered Simon a huge present: freedom from his doubts.

Simon wouldn't understand how easily it could go wrong. Clay had no business stepping into a young boy's life, acting as if he had all the answers. He was trying to put back together the fractured pieces of his own life and had little enough to offer. Once the trial started, he'd have even less. He'd be the man in the headlines. A murderer.

He turned on the ignition and pulled into the street. He looked into the rearview mirror, the action almost a reflex.

There, down the street, a silver Acura with a bad bumper slipped into the street, a quiet reminder of what he really had to offer Simon and his mother.

17

Piper knew there were things over which she had no control. It wasn't something she'd read in a feel-good book or learned about in school. That lesson had been hammered into her by Kevin's death. It was something she woke to each morning…what put her to sleep at night. A knowledge that she believed helped her counsel others who had experienced a similar loss. *Let go…accept.*

After last night, her son's condition no longer fell into that category.

A door inside Simon had been cracked open, a light allowed to slip inside. Clayton Chase had managed to do what Piper and a slew of doctors and professionals had been unable to accomplish. And now Piper was left with only one choice: What was she going to do about it?

She sat at her kitchen table, the morning sun creeping in through the blinds. Her sister, Crissa, poured each a fresh cup of chamomile tea, her newest discovery, from a shop in town that specialized in holistic brews.

Like pieces on a checkerboard, color copies printed off the Internet covered the glass table in Piper's kitchen alongside a magnificent coffee-table book. She'd bought the book when she'd first started seeing Clay, hoping to get a sense of who he was through his work. The other photos she'd downloaded off the Internet last night after she'd tucked her son in bed. Each and every photograph on display appeared the product of a magician.

"No, no, no," Crissa said suddenly, trying to cover the photographs with her hands. "Take that look off your face."

"What?"

"The mesmerized thing—the oh-my-god, what-a-man look."

"You're being ridiculous."

"No, I am not. I saw that look when you met Ricky Metzger, the singer from that trashy garage band, in ninth grade. I knew what it meant then, and I know what it means now."

Piper looked her big sister in the eye. "You couldn't possibly."

Because Crissa had not lost her husband, and it wasn't her child who'd disappeared into a world of silence for two years, then suddenly reached a hand out from that abyss. Yes, Crissa had held a front-row seat to Piper's tragedy, had embraced her pain and shared its burden the last two years. But in the end, she'd been only a spectator to the battles Piper fought on a daily basis.

Not that it mattered as far as Piper's sister was concerned. Crissa was never one to go quietly, her style far from the squeeze of a hand and silent support. Crissa, Miss Fix-It— the actual name of her column in the paper—always had an answer, whether you wanted to hear it or not. If she could take out a bloodstain from a silk blouse, by golly, she knew how to run your life.

"You know what the problem is here?" Crissa swept her hand over the photographs on the table. "You want to figure out your life from a photograph? How about this one?"

From her purse on the floor at her feet, she produced some folded sheets of paper. With little drama, she smoothed out the pages to show a newspaper article. Front and center, a color photograph of Piper was featured on the top page.

Piper picked up the printed sheet in disbelief. She remembered the photograph from her days working at a local clinic before she'd married Kevin. It was one of those head shots they kept on file for publicity purposes. The headline read Murder Suspect's Therapist Lost Husband to Lightning.

"I debated whether to show it to you," Crissa said. "But I can see I need to bring out the heavy artillery."

The article was about her husband's death and her valiant attempt to keep Clay, a lightning survivor, from facing the death penalty. Of course, there were tawdry allusions to a relationship that went far beyond what was professional.

The article was recent, an Internet version of the local paper, which had basically serialized the trial like a soap opera. *Stay tuned!* It was the sort of sordid story that had never been a part of her life before Clay Chase. She tried not to read it word for word, her eyes skimming quickly, just the same absorbing the not-so-subtle subtext. The author put into print all her sister's fears, how the charismatic photographer could put any woman under his spell, particularly the vulnerable widow who counseled him.

"Where did you get this?"

"Deidre sent it to me in an e-mail."

Deidre was a co-worker of Crissa at the *Herald* and a busybody to boot, the kind of woman who would write for the *Herald* but might secretly scour the tabloids at the grocery store for a juicy story.

"I know you feel violated," Crissa said, hitting a bull's-eye once again. "I did, too, when I read it. I worried about how it might affect you and the kids, this kind of publicity. I mean, it's one thing to help people, but do you really want to be swept up in this kind of drama?"

"I can't worry about newspaper stories," she said, handing the pages back to her sister.

Crissa sighed, then threw her hand in the air. "I'm dying here, Piper. I see this train steaming down the track, ready to mow you down, and I can't seem to put on the brakes or push you out of the way."

Piper made a dismissive gesture, putting a stop to Crissa's attempts to mother her.

"Okay. I never said he wasn't a good photographer," Crissa admitted, taking a different tack. "And maybe he can help you with Simon. But you need to be careful here. Everything that article says isn't pure drivel. You are in danger of losing perspective, and don't give me this I-am-a-professional blarney of yours. The last thing you and Simon need is for you to get some weird knight-in-shining-armor complex over this guy."

"That's not going to happen."

"Really? Maybe I'm only the lowly stay-at-home mom with a silly column for housewives—certainly, I don't have the experience or education of an important psychologist like you—"

"For goodness sake, Crissa—"

"But I am your big sister. I don't want to see you hurt, Piper. Not again."

Piper sighed. She gave herself a minute, not really knowing how to blurt out anything but the truth.

She looked at her sister. "I'm not sure you can stop me."

Crissa pressed her lips into a straight line, shaking her

head. She allowed a minute or two of silence before she picked up one of the photographs from the table. It showed lightning reflecting off the surface of a lake. Threads of light cut across the magenta-and-purple background of the night sky, the streaks appearing blurred and indistinct on the placid waters. On the horizon, dark hills marked the change from sky to water.

When she glanced up again, Piper recognized her sister's change in expression. *Time for plan B.*

Crissa made a face. "Okay, he's a genius. There, I said it." She dropped the photograph back on the table. "But the question, darling, is not whether the man has talent. The question, dear sister, is whether or not you can trust him with your son."

Piper threw her hands up. "It just seems that I have an obligation to try."

"Okay. Good point. Here's another one for you to ponder." Crissa pointed to the photographs littering the table. "So you want to get to know the man behind the art?" Crissa shook her head. "Nice try. But these photographs are not going to give you any answers. Trust me, life is never that easy."

When Piper said nothing, her sister let out an exaggerated sigh. "All right. I can see that I'm going to have to helm this little investigation."

Crissa put aside the teacups and reached across the table to take both of Piper's hands into hers. "Honey, focus here. Have you not spent a considerable amount of time with the man delving into the inner workings of his psyche?"

Her sister didn't really need an answer. The fact was, Piper had been seeing Clay for more than two months now, and yes, many of their conversations could be termed *intimate,* particularly these last two weeks.

"If I am not mistaken," Crissa continued, "that would include discussing the subject of the wife?"

"That's right."

"And?" Crissa pressed. "I'm not asking you to break any confidentiality, for goodness sake. This isn't about ethics. Close your eyes, clear your head, and ask yourself. Did Clayton Chase kill his wife?"

A valid question, she thought, knowing that every once in a while, her big sister scored a hole-in-one.

Piper closed her eyes. She pictured Clay sitting on the sofa across from her. He'd push back hair that barely touched his collar, giving her a clear view of the rugged face, the sharp planes and angles. He had a strong jaw, with a dimple that couldn't be ignored. And his eyes, hazel to green depending on his emotions, could indeed mesmerize. She thought about the articles she'd read, the possibility that he could manipulate women with those fine looks of his.

But then he would open his mouth and say all the wrong things. He'd never been particularly cooperative. He'd never tried to convince her of his innocence. Each and every step of the way, it was Piper who had to do the work, getting him to trust her, pushing him beyond his survivor's guilt to try and understand that, no matter what, he deserved this chance to recover.

She recognized all the dangers her sister had pointed out. That he was handsome, a romantic figure of mystery. But he was also a man in pain, someone who needed her help, desperately. So she dug deeper.

She remembered Clay speaking about his wife's infidelity. He'd compared it to a death. It was a romantic notion, the idea that love lost could be likened to a life inside you, so that when that light was snuffed out, a part of you was lost forever.

She'd wondered about the comparison ever since that night. And she'd pondered the idea that, like Clay, she'd experienced both marital infidelity and death.

Certainly with both came regret, as well as a sense of betrayal. It had taken everything she'd had not to leave Kevin when she'd discovered his infidelity. Her anger had been searing—something so hot, she thought she couldn't bear to live so close to it. Instead, she'd walked away and searched for calm.

She hadn't had the luxury of indulging in anger. Not with Simon and Mandy to consider. She'd had to bear the heat of Kevin's betrayal, had to keep a tight rein in her fury and frustration.

There'd been times she'd thought herself a crazy woman, needing to raise her head to the sky and scream about the injustice of it all. Or grab a plate off the dinner table and throw it in Kevin's face.

Instead, she'd swallowed all her anger, letting it warm her inside until it became a friend.

The night Kevin had been killed, she'd gone to her sister's. She'd known he'd been planning to see his lover. Leaving him at home with Simon had been her way of controlling the situation, making it impossible for him to leave.

Making it possible for him to die.

That pain, Kevin's death, was so much worse than any betrayal she'd felt.

She opened her eyes and reached for the book featuring some of Clay's finest lightning photos. The image she turned to filled two pages, a centerfold. She found herself wondering what the actual photo would look like without the unfortunate crease in the middle. She realized she wanted to see the real thing and not a reproduction.

She pressed her hand to the photograph. Before she'd searched out these photographs, she hadn't understood what he'd lost. But now she did.

His wife, his marriage, and this...this ability to find magic and capture it forever.

"Are we channeling here, or what?" Crissa prompted. "Did he kill her?"

"I don't think he knows," she said, revealing what she'd suspected all along.

"And how could he not know?"

"I can't say for certain—"

"Stop with the caveats, just spell it out for the nonprofessional." Her sister took the book out of her hands. She squeezed Piper's hand between both of hers, looking her dead in the eyes. "Talk to me."

Piper nodded. "There is no way I can know if his amnesia is the product of the lightning...or if, as I suspect with Simon, he's blocking something because it's simply too painful for him to remember."

Crissa stared at her for a minute. "Holy smokes. You think he did it."

"No," she said, very certain about that much. "But I think he's worried that he may have killed her. I think he's scared he's a murderer."

"And this is who you want to mentor Simon?"

She shook her head and gave a deep sigh. "Oh, Crissa. I want my son back, desperately. After everything Simon has been through the last two years—losing his father, being unable to speak. Every day just becoming more...silent. If Clay can help Simon, do I really have a choice?"

She'd once read an account in school about unorthodox

treatment measures. That sometimes you had to shock the patient into recovery.

Mandy wanted her to be careful, but Simon wanted nothing to do with caution. Because just as Clay had brought life to these images, he'd shown her son something in the lightning storm that first night. And Simon wanted more.

She looked at her sister. "Is this who I want to mentor Simon? If Clay can help him?" She nodded her head. "You betcha."

Grace put down the phone. She looked across her desk to where Chris, her still-husband and now-private-investigator, sat waiting.

"That was Shawna Benet," she told him. "She wanted to let me know that after careful reflection, she has now decided she's made a terrible mistake suggesting that Clayton Chase might have had a motive to kill his wife. In her words, she's done him a terrible injustice."

Chris smiled. Unfortunately, it was his cute smile, the one where that magic dimple appeared at the right side of his mouth. That same smile had lured her to his apartment when they'd been working on a homicide case together four years ago, when she should have said no. The very same smile had made her fall in love.

"I'm starting to like the assistant," he said.

"As a suspect? No way."

"Lookit," he said, going with it. "She ran the gallery for the last five years, right? Suddenly, she starts to feel entitled. Happens all the time. People cross that line to believe they deserve a little more than they're getting. Maybe she starts to take a little of the credit for the gallery's success, but she's behind the scenes. Not fair, right? She comes to let Jillian know she wants more…maybe she even knows about the lady's secret life with her mystery lover and threatens to tell the hubby? Or the papers? Big important family like that? Does Jillian Ward-Chase really want that kind of publicity for her gallery and artist husband?"

"Nice," she acknowledged. She'd only called him for help a few days before. He'd already done some substantial background work. "But it doesn't fit with an execution-style killing."

Chris rocked back in the chair across from her desk. "I'm not convinced that's what happened here."

"Explain?"

"I'm not sure I can—not yet. Call it a hunch." Chris and his hunches. "Just go along with me a minute. What the husband claims is true. By some weird miracle of lightning, he gets struck but can't remember getting back to the house. He's in some sort of weird shock, doesn't remember what happened, just that he wakes up to find his wife dead. Lucky break for Miss Benet. He gets tried for murder, being the obvious choice—only, hold the phone, the prosecution can't make good on the charges. Hung jury. Miss Benet gets a little desperate the second time around."

"So she comes to me and points the finger. Trying to make sure that we seal the deal with Chase?"

Chris nodded. "Forget about who's behind Door Number Two."

She was impressed. There wouldn't be powder burns on the husband's hands because he'd never fired his gun. "It explains a few of those MLFs of Don's."

"MLFs?"

"Never mind," she said, pondering the puzzle pieces of the

case. She didn't like it, the loose ends. Aidan Parks could have a field day with the jury.

Chris's hand covered hers, forcing her to look up at him. "Feels good, doesn't it?"

She looked up at her husband's face. This was just the sort of back and forth that had made them such a good team, both in and out of the office. "Don't."

"Hey, you called me," he said, already sounding defensive.

"That's right," she said, pushing his hand away. "And I do appreciate the work you're doing."

But he didn't leave off. Instead, he gave a deep sigh and shook his head. He didn't look at her as he whispered, "Gracie, I miss you."

She slumped down, hating this part. The temptation. "I wasn't the one who left." Because it was Chris who had broken her heart, getting cold feet after their quickie Vegas wedding, wondering if they couldn't just go back to the status quo of living together. She'd known all along the chance they'd been taking. Chris's mom had already moved on to husband number four. For all Chris's professed love, with that kind of background, it would be tough to believe in happy endings.

"Yeah?" He gave her a hard look. "But you're the one who won't let me come back."

"Don't. Don't you dare make it sound like I was the one who gave up on us."

"I'm willing to take all the blame here, Gracie."

"I knew this was a bad idea."

"Or a really fantastic one."

The double-edged sword that was her relationship with her husband.

She shook her head. If she were analyzing, which she sure as heck didn't want to do, she might even think that she'd done this on purpose, letting Donnie convince her that she needed Chris's help.

She stood and walked to the door. She opened it, standing there waiting.

"Go home, Chris." She was a prosecutor. She knew about intense emotions and where they could lead. "I'll call you later."

Life. It was complicated.

18

Clay missed his next appointment with Piper.

He figured it was for the best. He was taking a break, not sure of his next step. He needed time to figure out what was going on inside his head, that image of his hand holding his dad's gun bizarre and disturbing.

He hadn't gone near his camera since he'd taken those photos of Piper outside her house four days ago. And he'd stashed all the photographs in the file cabinet in his darkroom, another place he'd given a wide berth.

The last three nights, he'd dreamed of Jillian.

She stood in the dining room of their place in South Beach, the same room where she'd died. But in his dream, she was very much alive, waiting for him with a smile. He could see she was trying to say something, but there was no sound to the film spinning in his head, just his wife mouthing a single word.

Each time, he woke up clutching his head, a pain like a sledgehammer having a go at his skull.

He had a medicine cabinet full of stuff—none of which he ever bothered to take. For him, it wasn't about numbing the pain. Ever since the trial had ended in a hung jury, he needed those memories back—needed to know the truth.

That's why he'd pushed so hard with Piper. He couldn't ac-

An Important Message from the Editors

Dear Reader,

Because you've chosen to read one of our fine novels, we'd like to say "thank you!" And, as a **special** way to thank you, we're offering you a choice of <u>two more</u> of the books you love so well **plus** an exciting Mystery Gift to send you — absolutely <u>FREE</u>!

Please enjoy them with our compliments...

Pam Powers

Lift here

Peel off seal and place inside...

The Reader Service — Here's How It Works:

Accepting your 2 free books and gift places you under no obligation to buy anything. You may keep the books and gift and return the shipping statement marked "cancel." If you do not cancel, about a month later we'll send you 3 additional books and bill you just $4.99 each in the U.S., or $5.49 each in Canada, plus 25¢ shipping & handling per book and applicable taxes if any.* That's the complete price and — compared to cover prices starting from $5.99 each in the U.S. and $6.99 each in Canada — it's quite a bargain! You may cancel at any time, but if you choose to continue, every month we'll send you 3 more books, which you may either purchase at the discount price or return to us and cancel your subscription.

*Terms and prices subject to change without notice. Sales tax applicable in N.Y. Canadian residents will be charged applicable provincial taxes and GST.

cept the prosecution's interpretation of the facts, couldn't imagine a scenario where he might want Jillian dead. He'd never felt that kind of rage and he couldn't imagine a situation that could tap into some Neanderthal inside and give him life. But here in the Keys, he was plagued by doubts.

For days, he'd been holed up here in the house he'd inherited from his father. Tavernier was a quiet community just south of Key Largo. It was a favorite destination for eco-tourists searching for the solitude and beauty of lagoons and mangrove swamps. His father, who'd worked for the parks and recreation department, had loved it, the turquoise sea and waving palms. His mother, an artist whose ceramic creations still decorated almost every horizontal surface of the small conch house, loved the community and came to visit occasionally. Before his father had died three years ago, they'd both found peace here.

That's what Clay had been searching for the last few days. Peace. Not that he'd found any.

So instead, he'd been trying to figure out a strategy for his meeting with Burton. He'd told the P.I. to give Burton the heads-up, that the two of them needed to talk, but he hadn't heard squat. The P.I. was still there, of course, his little shadow.

Clay wasn't sure if Jillian's father would see him. If he knew Burton, the only thing he'd want was to put a bullet through Clay's heart. Not that Clay could blame him, not if Burton really believed he'd killed Jillian.

When the front doorbell rang, he imagined Aidan making another go at him. No one else ever sought him out here in the Keys. Since their last meeting at Aidan's place, Clay had refused to return his calls. It would be just like Aidan to hunt Clay down.

He was wrong. It wasn't Aidan who'd come calling.

Piper's daughter, Mandy, stood on his doorstep. And she wasn't alone.

Next to her towered a boy taller than Clay's own six foot one, wearing baggy clothes and a backward cap over his dark curls. Before Clay knew what to make of the two, Simon nudged the lanky teenager aside to come stand next to his sister. He slipped his hand into hers.

"My brother," Mandy said. "He asked me to bring him here. He wanted to see you."

There was all kinds of accusation on her face, not to mention attitude plus. She was the complete opposite of Piper. With her fiery curls and dark eyes, she looked ready to tear into him if he gave her half the chance. And she was just getting started.

But Simon wasn't the patient sort. He dropped Mandy's hand and ran around his sister to disappear inside.

"Simon!"

The girl took off after her brother. The kid in the cap ran after her. For a man who had spent a good part of his life alone, the sudden invasion felt surreal, slowing his response time.

"Simon!" Mandy screamed from inside the house.

Clay shut the door, his heart thumping in his chest as if he were facing the mother of all storms. During the eighteenth century, wreckers had used this part of the Keys as a base, searching the reefs at night for booty from ships they'd caused to run aground. He felt a bit like the hapless victims washed ashore by the power of the sea. He smiled, realizing it wasn't a bad feeling.

He found all three standing around a framed poster in the living room, a gift from Jillian before they were married. That poster had been used to announce his first high-profile exhibit, featuring a photograph that had put him on the map as a fine-art photographer and won him a fistful of awards—all Jillian's doing. He just took the shots; Jillian made the photos famous. That's how it had always worked.

She had given the image some cutesy name like "Fire from the Sky." She'd named all his work. It had been this big joke between them, Jillian coming up with the most commercial (her description) and treacly (his take) titles she could.

The photograph showed lightning against an orange sky, a fire blazing in the forest below. Jillian described it as chiar-oscuro, straight out of the Dutch School. She'd dubbed him the Rembrandt of the photo world in all his promo material. That had been her great talent, the Big Sell. All three kids stared at the poster in perfect silence.

He'd seen similar reactions to his work—they meant nothing to him. Once he printed the photograph, he was done. Those pictures had no connection to him. He'd hand them over to Jillian and start concentrating on the next shoot.

He tried for the first time to see what they saw, but to him a photograph had always been about technique, the artist's eye and his work in the darkroom. It was too hard to look at the finished product and not begin to analyze every little flaw.

He turned his gaze to Simon instead. The boy stood next to Mandy's mystery friend. Simon looked incredibly small by comparison. A little guy with a big secret.

He tried to imagine someone Simon's age taking on the same burden Clay carried. The headaches, the sleeplessness, the fear that it could all get worse…because that was the na-ture of the beast that had touched their lives.

But Simon was just a boy. It was way too early for the little guy to give up and hide. Even as he told himself that he wasn't the person to help, Clay wanted to step in and take it on.

"That's what I want you to teach me," Simon said with perfect timing, as if somehow he'd been inside Clay's head catching the whisper of that desire.

Clay waited for Mandy's reaction, but she gave nothing away with her tense frown and dark eyes. He knew she rode horses, just like Jillian. He'd seen photographs of her atop some huge horse taking a fence. He knew from experience horsewomen were tough.

"Okay," she whispered after a minute.

Clay realized he'd been holding his breath.

"Come on," he said, holding his hand out to Simon.

He took Simon back to his darkroom, showing him the equipment there. He talked about the Nikon FG20 35 mm SLR—automatic and manual shutter-speed setting with manual focus, resilient against the elements—and the 50 mm lens he preferred for lightning shots. He showed Simon one of the wooden tripods and the lengthy cable release he used, the irony being, of course, that despite these precautions he'd been struck.

He used a low F-ratio to take advantage of ambient light. He explained about shutter speed and how Simon could control the length of the exposure. For black and white, he liked Ilford's Pan F 50 film for its fine grain and contrast values.

Simon never said a word, never asked a question. He listened with an almost eerie focus, handling all the equipment, taking it all in. Whenever Clay finished one explanation, Simon looked up at him with an expression that seemed to ask, "What's next?"

He hadn't been around kids much. After his father had

died, his mother had gone to live with her sister in Manhattan. His cousins all lived there as well. His sister and her husband had transplanted themselves to California. Of course, they'd all rushed in to help him recover from Jillian's tragic death and his own injuries. But the trial had taken its toll on those loyalties.

Or had it? Thinking back, he wondered if he hadn't pushed them away. Carla, his older sister, and his mother most of all. Like Simon, had he sought to hide in silence, cutting off the people who cared about him most?

All interesting questions, questions he pondered as he and Simon worked in the darkroom. Mandy and the kid who was most likely her boyfriend—poor Piper, they were coming at her from all directions—kept to themselves in the front room. Watching Simon fiddle with the Nikon, he realized he felt something approaching happiness. Like he could close his eyes and imagine this was his normal life. Just a fun Saturday afternoon. He smiled, remembering he'd told Simon this could be therapy for them both.

Yeah, maybe. Simon had seen his father killed. Clay would like nothing better than to help him find new images to fill his head using the camera's lens.

"What do you say?" he asked Simon. "Do you want to take a few shots?"

Simon nodded. Camera in hand, Clay led the way outside.

The classic conch house of the Keys had multicultural roots, blending architectural styles designed for the New England seacoast with tropical adaptations made for the Caribbean. Clay's house rested on piers to prevent rot and help keep it cool. There were louvered windows to block out the tropical heat of the afternoon and allow circulation of the sea breezes. An encircling veranda gave shade. Each room was a sturdy box built to resist hurricanes. At the center of just such a cube waited gale force winds in the guise of Mandy, seated on the couch.

The boy next to her watched Clay with obvious suspicion. Mandy had her arms locked across her chest. From the body English, Clay figured she'd been second-guessing her decision to bring Simon here. Clay handed Simon the camera, watched him walk past his sister and head for the great outdoors with the Nikon. Mandy stood, setting a course to intercept, the boyfriend right behind her.

Clay opened the door for Simon, telling him to go ahead and knock himself out with the roll of film in the front yard. He nodded at the boyfriend. "Mind if I talk to Mandy alone?"

The kid, whose name turned out to be Sean, seemed to think about it a minute, as if maybe he had a choice in the matter. *Ah, youth,* Clay thought.

Sean looked over at Mandy. Eye contact between the two let Clay know who was in charge.

"It's okay," she said.

Sean headed back inside to keep his spot warm on the couch. Clay and Mandy walked out, then stood staring at each other on the veranda, neither saying a word. Clay smiled to himself. He liked a woman who wasn't easily intimidated.

"I was just wondering why you brought Simon over?" he asked, leaning against the rail.

She shrugged. "He's talking again," she said, keeping it simple.

She turned to watch Simon out in the yard with the camera. Apparently, the kid liked flowers.

Clay knew Mandy was Piper's stepdaughter; they weren't

related through blood. Just the same, chewing on her bottom lip just then, she looked so much like Piper, it hurt.

Strange how living with someone, picking up voice intonations and gestures, could make people do that. That's how it was with his sister and his mother. They looked nothing alike, Carla taking after the Chase side of the family like Clay. But the way Carla arched one brow at you, that soft lilt in her voice...yeah, that was Mom. It was just like that old argument, nature versus nurture. He'd bet on nurture every time.

"Does Piper know you're here?" he asked.

She shook her head. "I told her I was taking Simon to lunch and a movie. Trust me, if she thought you could help Simon, she would have brought him here herself."

"And you wouldn't want that?" he guessed. "Piper coming here?"

"What do you think?" she asked.

Before he could answer, she turned to look at him, her eyes assessing him. "Look. I don't know what's going on, but Simon likes you. Don't blow it."

Having had her say, she turned back to her brother, calling out, "Come on, Simon. Time to go home."

Simon came charging back, mission accomplished. He handed Clay the Nikon, but Clay didn't take it.

"Keep it. Finish the roll," he told Simon.

Mandy looked like she might argue with him, but Simon raced inside with the camera, the deal sealed.

"I'm not sure when we'll come back," she said, heading inside to gather up the posse.

Or if, Clay added, watching silently from the veranda as the kids made their retreat.

* * *

On the drive home, Simon wouldn't stop talking.

He rattled on about f-stops and shutter speeds, lenses and tripods, the sound of his voice strangely high-pitched. She figured he was excited. In her head, she always remembered his voice lower, scratchier. More like Dad's.

Before the accident, Simon had talked all the time. He'd driven her crazy, never even taking a breath as he'd march out every boring detail about some stupid video game or movie. Gawd, he could be so annoying.

She used to call Simon "on-and-on," complaining to her parents that she should get paid double for babysitting because he talked enough for a dozen kids.

She glanced over at Sean as he drove. He was cracking up, loving the nonstop photo babble. He glanced over at her and mouthed: *Wow!* She reached over and gave his hand a squeeze.

Wow. That just about covered it.

After the accident, she hadn't really worried about Simon not talking. She figured he'd be okay. He was alive, right? And Piper said he'd get better with therapy. She'd almost seen his silence as a blessing back then. She'd been in such pain, wanting to go deep inside herself and not have to deal with the outside stuff, people asking her all the time how she was doing…trying to make her feel better when that wasn't possible.

The first year, she and Simon had both slept in the big bed with Piper during storms. What had Piper called it? Some kind of storm phobia. There was a word for it. But Mandy remembered waking up one morning a couple of months after the accident and looking down at her brother sleeping next to

Piper. She'd been half-asleep when she'd thought: *He's not going to get better.*

It was like this lightbulb had gone on inside her head. Simon had a problem. Her baby brother wasn't "normal" anymore. He might spend his whole life in that silent world in his head, slipping away like those kids who had autism.

Remembering the boy he'd been and the kid he'd become, it was just sad.

And here he was talking nonstop again. And she liked the sound of it, the words pouring out his mouth so that she didn't have to listen to each and every word, didn't have to respond or make sense of it. It was like music. She just sat back and enjoyed.

I did the right thing taking him, she thought with a smile.

She knew the days Clayton Chase was supposed to come over. Ever since she found out he might be this murderer, she'd started monitoring stuff like that more. She knew when he'd skipped his appointment Thursday. And she'd seen Piper's reaction. Piper was in what Mandy called her "holding pattern" mode.

That's when she'd gotten this idea. Why let the whole thing spin out of control? Why not step in and take action? Sure, Piper wanted Mandy to believe she had everything covered, but did she really? Simon was Mandy's brother. If this Chase guy could help him, why let Chase call the shots, telling them when and where that would happen?

It wasn't hard to find his address on the Internet, the guy was pretty famous. And with Sean along, she thought they'd be okay.

She glanced up in the rearview mirror. Simon was still talking, explaining the different parts of the camera. Yeah, things had worked out…for now, anyway.

A few hours later, Sean turned into their street and Simon

suddenly stopped. It was like he'd used up his batteries or something. Mandy turned to see what was wrong.

He was holding really still, like maybe he was waiting for something bad to happen.

"It's okay, Simon," she told him, figuring it out. "I won't tell Mom."

He smiled and turned his attention back to the camera. When the car stopped, he jumped out, heading for the backyard.

She knew the garage door was his "secret entrance." He wouldn't want Piper to see the camera. She bit her lip, watching Simon as he disappeared behind the gate, suddenly not so sure about what she'd done.

She felt Sean's hand on hers and turned.

"Hey," Sean told her. "I have to show you something."

He pulled a paper out from under his shirt. He'd tucked it there so that no one could see it. Only it wasn't a paper at all. It was a photograph.

He'd folded it up into this square. Her heart started thumping in her chest as she watched him unfold it. She couldn't believe he'd take one of those beautiful photographs. Sure, the pictures were amazing—she could understand the temptation— but she'd never thought Sean would do anything like steal.

Only, she saw right away that Sean hadn't stolen for thrills. He'd had a completely different reason for taking the photo.

Because it wasn't a picture of a storm or lightning. It was a photograph of Piper.

Her face was blurred in places. Clay had shot the photograph in the middle of some motion. But it was beautiful, just the same, like the blurring only served to give the photo life.

"Where did you find this?" she asked.

She couldn't touch it. She just stared at the photograph of Piper there in his hand. The folds bisected her face, making it look like a target, the crosshairs over her mouth.

"I went into the darkroom while you guys were outside talking. He had a file cabinet in there. Look, I don't know why I did it. I guess I just don't trust the guy. So I started opening some drawers, you know? Looking around, checking it out. And I found this file full of photographs of Piper."

Sean looked really serious. Mandy didn't like that expression. She braced herself.

"There were a bunch of them. A lot, Mandy. Like tons. It was weird. I thought the guy couldn't take photos anymore. That's why he goes to your mom, right? To get fixed?"

Her heart started beating really fast. She couldn't catch her breath. She took the photograph from his hand and folded it carefully again, following the creases.

"I know you said you wouldn't tell, but it's too weird, okay? He's like…stalking her. You have to show your mom."

Sean had told her from the beginning they should talk to Piper. She was the adult—the therapist. If Clay really could help Simon, Piper would know.

But Mandy had thought she could handle it. No, she'd *wanted* to handle it.

Stupid, stupid. Trying to fix everything.

She got out of the car and shut the door. She stood there, feeling like Simon, because she didn't have the words anymore.

Sean came up beside her. "You want me to come inside with you?"

She shook her head and squeezed his hand as she left, the photograph clutched in her other hand. She knew Sean would be out here waiting for her when it was done.

19

Piper remembered the first time she'd seen one of Clay's photographs. The book had been a coffee-table book entitled *Strokes of Genius*. A single bolt of embossed silver split the black-and-white cover in half as lightning struck an African tree in the savanna, a baobab tree, she thought they were called. The photograph had been taken at dawn or dusk. A lazy orange ball of a sun floated on the horizon.

On the kitchen counter, Piper smoothed out yet another one of Clay's photographs. This one, too, held incredible power. He'd captured "a moment" in her expression. Now Piper's face told the story instead of nature.

"Sean said there were a lot of them." Mandy shifted her weight nervously to her other foot. "Tons, he said."

Piper knew the exact moment he'd taken the photograph. She could tell by the clothes she was wearing. That first day, when she'd asked him to bring the camera to their session— the photos she'd egged him into attempting.

When she'd asked, he'd made it perfectly clear none of those photographs had turned out. He'd led her to believe he couldn't take photographs.

And here was this perfect photograph. Of her.

"What are you going to do?" Mandy asked.

Piper closed her eyes, blocking out her image. She'd been told he was a liar. Her sister had warned her the lightning injury could be a hoax. She hadn't believed Crissa, of course. Piper was the court of last resort for people like Clay, victims whose stories were never believed.

She stared down at her shadowed face in the photograph. How magical he'd made her look through the trick of photography. She wondered how many more illusions he'd created for her.

When she'd first seen his photographs on the Web sites dedicated to his work, she'd felt such supreme loss. His talent was something special. She remembered thinking how dearly that ability of his would be missed.

"Mom?"

She turned to look at Mandy. She could see the worry on her daughter's face…. Mandy didn't call her *Mom* very often. She reached up to stroke her cheek to reassure her.

What are you going to do?

She knew her job: to raise her children to the best of her ability. When she'd married Kevin, raising his child—adopting Mandy as her own—had been both a privilege and a responsibility. With Kevin's death, the welfare of their children had become her duty alone.

She folded the photograph in half. She wouldn't belittle her daughter by trying to hide her reaction.

She told Mandy, "Don't worry, sweetheart. I'll handle it."

July 14th. The French called it Bastille Day. The day an angry mob stormed the famous prison in Paris during the French Revolution. Burton remembered his first trip there with Jackie years ago. The French had erected some sort of monument at the site and he remembered thinking he was going to see the real thing, a medieval fortress right out of *The Count of Monte Cristo*. Instead, there was this puny spire with a plaque commemorating the day.

July 14th. The date crept up on Burton. *A year away, six months, two months...* The anniversary of Jillian's murder.

Sometimes Burton worried her memory would fade. He'd test himself, closing his eyes to conjure up her brilliant smile. He would picture that special way she'd roll her eyes heavenward and tease him. *Oh, brother, Daddy,* she'd say. At thirty-one, she was still his princess. Anything she wanted, if he could manage it, it was hers. He'd always wondered how he'd ever deserved such a gift as his daughter.

Jackie had wanted more children, but it wasn't in the cards. Not that it mattered—not to him. Because life had given him this one perfect jewel.

He closed his eyes. No, her image hadn't faded. She was right there.

"Mr. Ward? About Lydia Barrera?"

Burton held up his hand. "Give me a minute."

And now, this piece of shit detective he'd hired wanted to change that image of his little girl in his head? Turn her memory into a shadow at the periphery of his vision, something he needed to duck away from, a ghost haunting him?

"Lydia Barrera is dying," Burton said.

The man nodded. "Cancer, I know. Been sick a couple of years, I understand. Angel Barrera makes the rounds for all the charity events looking for a cure. But I'm sure you know that. You support the same organizations, right?"

Burton looked away. *Jesus.*

Cowan walked up, saying softly, "You know, toward the

end, they take a lot of drugs. For the pain. Sometimes, these poor people, they're so out of it, they don't even know what they're saying."

Burton closed his eyes. He hadn't seen Lydia since she'd been diagnosed. He'd severed those ties a lifetime ago. He hadn't exactly threatened her, but he'd made it clear that it was in their mutual interest to stay away from each other. She was a good Catholic woman, after all. She would keep their secret.

When he'd left Tennessee, he'd changed his name and never looked back. Sure, he sent his family money, but that was the extent of his contact. Here in Palm Beach, he'd become a new man. He'd hoped to shed his past with Angel just as easily. And now this?

He looked back at Cowan. When he'd first hired the man, he'd been told he was the best, his intuition and methods, flawless. He could see now what he'd liked from the beginning: the man's intelligent eyes and probing stare.

Burton stood and walked over to his desk. "I believe you were right, Mr. Cowan. You can't help me anymore." Burton pulled out his checkbook. "We're finished here."

First the Calderon woman and now the detective he'd hired, pointing the finger at his dirty little secrets.

He tore out the check and held it out. Burton wondered how many times he'd done that, used money to buy absolution. But he knew there wasn't enough money in the world if his sins had taken his baby's life.

Cowan took one look at the number on the check and broke into a smile. There were a lot of zeros, enough to buy anyone's silence.

"Wow," he said, taking the check from Burton. "That's... well, that's just darned generous."

Unbelievably, he handed the check back to Burton.

With deadly earnestness, Cowan said, "But this one's on the house."

At the door, he told Burton, "There's something I forgot to mention. Your son-in-law, he wants a meeting. If I were you, I'd set it up. ASAP, you know?"

Burton felt his legs go out from under him as he dropped into his chair. He still held the damn check.

He and Lydia had something else in common besides the past. Losing his little girl was like a cancer growing inside him, her loss taking everything, so that sometimes he couldn't catch his breath. Some mornings, he couldn't even get out of bed.

The only defense he'd had was his search for justice. That energy and focus, the same drive that had brought him millions, had kept the cancer of her loss at bay.

Burton looked down at the check. All that money and it meant nothing to him. Absolutely nothing. He'd give it away to have one day with his Jilly Bean.

Only that wasn't going to happen. Much more likely was the possibility that he'd cost his little girl her life.

Shawna lay beside Aidan in bed, feeling his chest rise and fall. On the bedside table lay the gold bangle bracelet she always wore. She reached across and picked it up, holding it up to the light.

Jillian had worn one just like it. Shawna closed her eyes, remembering the day at the gallery when Jillian had found her bracelet in Shawna's purse.

What the hell is this?

She remembered Jillian saying just those words, shaking the bracelet in Shawna's face. When Shawna had demanded to know why Jillian had been searching through her purse, things had gotten ugly.

Jillian was no fool. She'd known what Shawna was up to, mimicking her style in clothes, even her voice. *For God's sake,* she'd screamed at Shawna, *stop acting as if you own the gallery!* How many times had she caught Shawna telling patrons to contact her and not Jillian if they were interested in a particular piece? And did Shawna really think Jillian hadn't noticed how she flirted with Clay?

Well, here's a news flash, honey. He's not interested. He's barely interested in me. Clay has only one love, his camera.

Shawna remembered how she'd started crying, pleading with Jillian not to fire her. The gallery was all she had. She didn't want to end up like her mother, a woman in her sixties stocking shelves at Wal-Mart. Jillian should be flattered. Shawna wanted nothing more than to better herself. So what if Jillian was her inspiration? And she couldn't be more wrong about Clay, that much Shawna would deny with her last breath. She was smart enough to know some things couldn't be forgiven.

What made it all worse was the fact that Jillian had taken a chance on her because she'd felt *sorry* for Shawna. Jillian had been one of those do-gooders, hiring Shawna from the women's shelter. So what if Jillian had trained her to help with the office stuff, eventually letting Shawna run the gallery as her assistant? Did that mean Shawna owed her? Hell, hadn't Jillian benefited just as much from the relationship?

But she remembered how Jillian had watched her with that bracelet, assessing the situation. No way she'd let the thing go. So Shawna had tried a different tack.

I know about you and that guy....

Shawna turned on the bed, slipping the bracelet on her wrist. She'd made Aidan buy her the very same bracelet once they'd started sleeping together.

She sighed. Shawna knew the value of information. But she also knew its danger.

Now that she had everything she'd ever wanted, she couldn't go back to the yearning and the wanting, always wondering how to get what she deserved…what life and her shitty family had denied her.

She'd come here to become someone important. And she had. Once that bitch, Jillian, was gone and dead, Shawna finally got a taste of the life she'd earned. Like this bracelet.

But she couldn't lose it. No way. She couldn't go back. Because that would be twice as bad.

And here they were so close to losing everything. There was still the possibility that Aidan would again do his job too well, that he would get that bastard Clay off and they'd still be looking for Jillian's killer.

She couldn't allow it.

Aidan didn't understand. He was too emotional about everything. He couldn't seem to shrug off the grief that was weighing him down. His focus was strictly on Clay, how to protect the bastard.

As if Jillian would ever care what happened to Clay. Aidan had never really known Jillian, not like Shawna had. He'd always idealized Saint Jillian. They all had, Burton and Clay included.

But Shawna knew her. She understood. Jillian had always been about Jillian. Shawna had made one stupid mistake, taking that bracelet, and Jillian had been ready to throw her to the wolves. After everything Shawna had done, making the gallery the best in South Beach, giving Jillian the time she needed outside the gallery to lead her double life with her lover.

Jillian had been using them all, making them all miserable. She'd deserved to die.

Shawna had to talk to Aidan. Make him understand exactly that. He shouldn't throw everything away. Not for some ghost.

But it scared her a little, her plans. How to use the information that she'd held secret the last year to her best advantage.

She slipped her hand under her cheek. She could feel the cold of the bracelet against her skin. She'd always wanted to be just like Jillian—have everything that was hers. And now she could…if she had the courage.

Tomorrow. She'd tell him, tomorrow.

She cuddled closer to Aidan, timing her breath with his. How deeply he slept. A man with a clear conscience.

She smiled. She'd gotten this far. In the end, she'd get just what she wanted. She wouldn't let anyone take away what she had.

Not even Aidan.

20

When Grace had first thought about becoming a criminal attorney, she'd wanted to become a public defender. She was going to be Perry Mason to the downtrodden. Her father, a very wise man, had supported her choice one hundred percent. In fact, he'd been so gung ho that, after her first year in law school, he'd made it possible for Grace to shadow one of the local public defenders for a day.

That day had begun with a child-molestation case. Grace had taken one look at the client and had known the guy had done it. He had soft hands, greasy hair and unnaturally white skin. His milk-blue eyes had shifted away any time he caught you looking. Big-time creepy. But there was the P.D.—she couldn't remember the guy's name—with his arm around his client's shoulders, conferring in intimate whispers.

The twelve-year-old victim had been easily brought down on cross-examination. As the public defender had told Grace later, he'd been pretty sure the girl had had some kind of mental disability. In his words, tearing her testimony apart had been a piece of cake. He'd felt kind of bad about it, but there you have it. Justice at work.

Next came a three-martini lunch at the local watering hole where private investigators and defense attorneys had gathered to regale each other with war stories about their rapist, child-molester and homicidal clients. After that, Grace had given the afternoon session a pass.

So her father had gotten his wish. Grace worked for the prosecution. But she'd always kept a healthy suspicion about "the machine" of the state attorney's office and how much power "the man" wielded. She knew how easy it was to get sucked into your role and shift into automatic, prosecute to the fullest extent of the law, even when it didn't make sense. She'd always been careful not to overreach. And now, Grace was having a crisis of conscience.

She didn't quite consider what she was doing unethical. After all, the woman's name had been published in the paper. And, in all honesty, Grace was still in the investigative stages. Her inquiry could just as easily lead to dropping the second trial.

But the truth was, she'd been getting a lot of heat from the state attorney to move on Chase. She was running out of time. Grace knew she was easing down that slippery slope, justifying her actions. Still, in for a penny…

Now she stood on the doorstep before Piper Jordan, MFT. Grace was a woman who prided herself on her ability to make things happen out of nothing. Getting information from the defendant's therapist was unlikely. But if she could manage it, it would be solid gold.

Piper Jordan was a good three inches shorter than Grace, slim with a gentle face. The combination struck Grace as fragile. Or maybe it was just the blond hair and blue eyes. Grace had olive skin and dark hair and eyes. She had a tendency to consider all blondes delicate. But she figured, given what the lady had been through, she was tough enough.

"I'm not asking you to reveal any sort of confidence, Ms. Jordan. But you are considered an expert in the field of lightning injury. All I ask is that you look at the evidence for yourself."

This wasn't the first time she'd shaken that tree branch to see what fell to the ground.

Chase's medical records had been a hotly contested issue in the first trial, his attorney claiming privilege…which was a load of crap, since the defendant himself had made his physical condition an issue.

Unfortunately, courtroom roulette had put the case in Judge Tracy's hands, the most liberal judge on the bench. He'd ruled that the possibility of prejudice outweighed any evidentiary value.

Which didn't mean she couldn't use the evidence to pry something loose here.

"I'm sure you're familiar with all the tests administered by our expert, a qualified neuropsychologist. Look at his evaluation. My understanding is that nothing about Clayton Chase even mildly fits lightning injury."

"Miss Calderon, you're talking about highly subjective tests, amenable to a plethora of interpretations."

Plethora. Good one. "Which is why I brought along the complete file, as well as our expert's report." You had to love anyone who could throw around words like plethora. Intellect as a weapon. *Oh, yeah, I'm intimidated.* "Look at the data yourself, Ms. Jordan. You make the call."

It wasn't so much that Grace believed Piper here would suddenly fess up to knowing the man's guilt. *Oh, my God, Ms. Calderon, thank God you came! He told me all the horrible details….* But the therapist privilege was a tricky thing, nothing like the attorney-client privilege. If Jordan knew something, and she was the decent sort, you never knew what she'd leak. Sometimes, people just needed someone to step forward and ask.

And Piper Jordan actually looked as if she might say something, glancing up at Grace, assessing. Only, at the last minute, she backed off. Instead, she stared at the file with her arms crossed tight over her chest, her lips pressed flat.

Included in the pile of medical papers were the results of a battery of tests taken by Chase—against the advice of counsel—to show a characteristic pattern of deficits in memory, organizational ability and other how-the-brain-works type functions. Luckily for Chase, Aidan Parks had been able to exclude their expert.

Maybe it was Piper's body language—or Grace's own bad timing in the area of romance—but Grace suddenly remembered the article in the paper, the one that made Chase out to be some sort of Svengali who mesmerized women like Piper Jordan. The article hadn't been subtle about it either, intimating that his therapist, a woman who had lost her husband to a lightning strike, was easy prey.

Grace had seen the guy in the courtroom and she hadn't gotten any of the vibes mentioned in the story. Sure he was cute, but so what? If anything, he'd had this strange sadness about him. To Grace, he'd looked just like a guy in shock. Nothing Svengali-like about him.

Guys like Clay Chase were the ones Grace worried about, the defendants who didn't even try to help their cause. They'd just sit there looking like a train wreck, making her wonder if maybe, just maybe, they *were* innocent…or superb actors. You could never tell.

At the same time, she wondered what kind of effect a guy like Chase might have on the young widow. He'd somehow escaped what her husband couldn't. Piper Jordan had dedicated her life to helping people like him. Grace suddenly wondered what the guy had done for Piper. Certainly, the woman hadn't looked pleased to see her.

"Ms. Jordan?" she prompted. "Could you just take a look?"

"I can't help you."

Grace nodded. She tried on a cheerful smile. *Worth a try.*

"Why don't I leave this with you," she said, handing Piper her card along with the file. "If you think you have something to say, just give me a call."

Even as Grace turned to walk away, she saw Piper crumple the business card in her hand. The gesture struck Grace as very personal and extremely telling.

Grace thought of her own recent misfortunes in the area of romance.

"I feel your pain," Grace said to herself, heading for her car.

Piper waited in her office. Today, she knew Clay would not miss his session.

She thought back to the conversation she'd had with the state attorney, Grace Calderon, and the woman's suggestion that the injuries Clay had suffered were all a ruse. Piper, as a trained professional, needed only to look over the report from their expert to see the error in her ways. Only, someone had beat Ms. Calderon and her expert to the punch.

Piper had shoved the photograph Clay had taken of her in the kitchen drawer. She didn't plan to wave the evidence in front of Clay today—exhibit A! She'd leave that sort of thing to the authorities. Now Piper waited, hoping she could muster a measured response when Clay arrived and quell the temper she'd felt rising inside her.

He'd lied. He'd used her son. And he might very well have killed his wife.

The lies, of course, would be her focus from now on. She knew of therapists who had been in her situation, lulled into believing what a patient was convinced was true, losing that all-important objectivity. But even that would be giving Clay the benefit of the doubt.

She looked at the small television monitor in her office. The security camera showed the front entrance to her house. There was a bench for patients, ferns spilling from pots and a small fountain. On the screen, she could see Clay pacing back and forth. He was wearing jeans with a shiny black satin smoking jacket that looked vintage Hollywood. He hadn't rung the doorbell.

She'd just had the security system installed, after Mandy had handed her the photograph. The television was there to let her know when her next patient had arrived—at least that's what she'd told herself when she'd ordered it.

She watched him, trying to discern what she could from his body language. Occasionally, he bit his thumbnail. She'd seen Simon do the same thing a million times. He continued to pace, now in a tight nervous circle. She could see the tension in his shoulders.

She tried to understand how far the subterfuge went. What *did* Clay remember about the night his wife had died? How much of what he'd told her had been lies? And his magic with Simon, had that all been part of the ruse? Had he planned all along, as Mandy had implied, to use Piper as some sort of witness in his defense?

But the idea only left her exhausted. In the end, she stood to open the front door, unable after all to wait him out.

He seemed surprised to see her. He hadn't, after all, rung the bell. Or maybe that perfectly blank expression showed only guilt. Once again, he'd been caught in the act.

"Come in," she told him with a professional smile, contributing her own sort of subterfuge.

When they stepped into her office, Clay dropped a file on the coffee table. A pile of eight-by-ten photographs slipped past the edge of the red folder. There must have been twenty or more photographs.

Which explained the pacing outside.

"You've seen one of the photographs, of course. I keep them in a special sequence, so I knew right away which one was missing. The boy, Sean, I'm sure, couldn't resist. Mandy would show it to you. You'll have questions."

She stared at the photographs. After a long silence, she reached out and pulled the top picture from the folder. It showed Piper in three-quarters profile, a sort of *Girl with a Pearl Earring* pose.

Questions? About a million of them—none of which would do either of them any good.

"No questions," she said, dropping the photograph. "I think the next step is fairly clear. It's time you seek help from someone else, Clay."

She looked away, having practiced this little speech several times. She took out her props, a pad of paper with several names on it. She made a show of tearing off the top sheet, folding it in half as she told him, "I have here the names and phone numbers of two very good therapists. They're both familiar with lightning injury. I'm certain either one would be willing to take your case."

She held out the list to him. He seemed frozen in place, unable to respond.

"Don't do this," he said.

His eyes never left that piece of paper. She could hear the edge in his voice, a man on the verge. And she wasn't near done.

She dropped the paper on the table within easy reach. "I should also tell you that yesterday the prosecutor came to see me."

"When it rains…" he said.

"Apparently, you took some tests at the behest of the state attorney. We call them neurocognitive or neuropsychological. Anatomic tests, like a CT scan or an MRI, are useless. The mental changes after lightning injury are functional, not anatomic. Tests measuring how the brain is working are much more helpful in these situations, although expensive. I'm sure you remember taking them, six hours of pen-and-paper tests."

"Yes," he said, looking up.

"They're usually not necessary but can sometimes be useful in litigation. Lightning survivors show a characteristic pattern."

"Let me guess," he said. "I flunked."

"I can't help you anymore, Clay. Maybe I never could."

"Because I wasn't honest?"

She sighed, feeling extremely tired. She glanced up. He had the most beautiful eyes. It almost hurt to look at him. There was such energy coming from him, a spark, as if he almost dared people to think the worst, reveling in their bad opinion.

"Honesty would have helped," she said. "But that isn't the whole story and you and I both know it."

He nodded. They were on the same page now. Theirs was never the normal therapist/client relationship.

"Ever play poker, doc?"

It had been so long since he'd called her that. She'd never corrected him. He understood she didn't have a medical degree.

"Do you know what a bluff is?" he asked.

She thought very carefully about her answer. "Was Simon a bluff?"

"I was scared, Piper."

"I understand."

"But here's the thing. I don't think you do. Even with your great telepathic-therapist powers, you don't know the real story. I made sure you didn't. My mistake."

He came around to sit on the couch in front of her and opened the file. He started dealing out the photographs like cards, covering the table, reminding her painfully of her own checkerboard of photographs on the kitchen table with her sister just last week.

She remembered being in awe of his talent then. Her reaction to these pictures was quite different.

The photographs showed her in various poses and in different locations. There was even a picture of her gardening. Piper frowned. She could feel a prickling at the back of her neck, the eerie realization coming to her.

"When did you take these?"

"A week ago. I didn't plan it. I left after my session and just kept driving around. I ended up back here. The camera was in the Jeep. You were outside, gardening." He shook his head, as if realizing how weak his excuses sounded.

She closed her eyes, leaning back in her chair. *Dear Lord...* She opened her eyes, but the photographs were still there, on the coffee table.

"You don't know what it's like," he said, providing the narrative to the disturbing images, "being able to hold the camera again. I started taking photographs with one of those old Brownie cameras. It was my grandfather's. I was about Simon's age. I almost can't remember a time when I wasn't holding a camera."

She picked up one photograph. She was standing in her front yard wearing a floppy straw hat with enormous plastic daisies on the band. She remembered the kids giving her that silly hat for Christmas, laughing at her every time she put it on.

"That first day when you told me to bring my camera, do you remember how I lost it? Those angry photographs I took? I didn't even realize it at first, but you did. My hands weren't shaking. I was on automatic again, everything coming together as I snapped those shots of you."

"Why did you do this?" she asked, not looking at him, staring instead at the photograph.

"Because I *could,* Piper."

She stared up at him, confused. He gestured to the photograph.

"They're perfect. Everything just came into focus. It was like magic. For a year, I couldn't even hold a camera, then suddenly, I could. But only when you're in the picture. Only with you."

She shook her head. He still wouldn't face the truth. Everything he'd just told her was the epitome of obsession.

"Why didn't you just tell me about the photographs?"

"I was supposed to trust that?" he said, pointing to the pile of photographs. "One moment of screaming at you in your office and I was cured?"

"But later, after you developed these?" She lifted two other photos.

"It was like some stupid miracle. And I didn't trust it. So

I tried to take more photographs. I went to all the places I knew so well, where I'd taken thousands of shots. Only, I couldn't. The same thing happened. My hands started shaking uncontrollably. That's how I ended up here, in front of your house, trying to figure it out."

He sat down again, rummaging through the photographs on the table. He singled out one or two and slipped them forward.

"Don't you get it? After what happened in your office, I had to test myself. I only photographed you the one time," he said, as if to reassure her. *I only broke the rules once.* As if she could believe anything he said.

"I know it's weird. But this is *me,* Piper. This is what I do—who I am. I have all the equipment for the perfect shot." And when she didn't say anything, stunned, he continued, "I wanted to see if it was possible. Dammit, I wanted my life back."

He could take photographs, but only when she was in the picture? She shook her head. She stood, backing away from the table and the photographs.

"You should have told me" was all she could manage to say, knowing that theirs had become a mutual obsession. *I can only take a photograph when you're in the picture—Simon, he's talking again.*

He stood, coming around the table to stand before her. He grabbed her arms. "There's a lot of things I should have told you. I'm ready now."

But she kept shaking her head. "You say you want your life back." She pointed to the photographs. "But at what price? Am I supposed to be the sacrifice? Is my son?"

He leaned forward, intent. She could see the plea coming even before he opened his mouth. He dropped his hands, taking a step back. "I screwed up. I know that. But imagine what it's been like this last year. Everything I do is questioned. Everyone I know is suspicious. When it wasn't the paparazzi, I had a private investigator on me, cataloging my every move, writing a report, taking photographs with a telephoto lens." He pointed at the photographs. "For once, I wanted to be in control. I wanted to understand what was happening to me. I needed to understand this," he said, gesturing to the photographs again.

She remembered her sister's warning, worried that Piper would become obsessed with Clayton, a man who had somehow managed to survive what had killed Kevin. But Piper hadn't given enough thought to what effect she might have on Clayton.

"You think I don't understand?" She shook her head. "More than you know. And that only makes my mistakes greater."

"Please. Don't shut me out, Piper. Not now. Not like this."

She focused somewhere behind him.

"You think I'm faking?" he demanded, frustrated now.

"Those tests," she said, raising her voice, for the first time on the edge of losing control. "I've administered those very tests, Clay. Don't you understand? I don't trust you to tell me the truth anymore. And without that…I can't help you, Clay. I just can't."

He stepped back in defeat. At the same time, there was an intensity in his eyes.

"Don't do this," he repeated.

"What choice do I have?"

They faced each other in a standoff, neither moving nor saying a word.

Piper broke the silence. "I think you should leave."

He stared at the photographs. He picked up one.

He said, "You were my own little miracle, you know that?" He shook his head, dropping the photo. "And I blew it."

When he walked toward the door, the only thing she felt was this strange relief, seeing that he wouldn't fight her.

Only he didn't walk out. He stopped, not turning around at first, just waiting at the door. "When I lost Jillian," he said, "I thought I'd lost everything."

He turned around, taking a long hard look at her. She could see that photographer's gaze, imagined his mental picture. *Saying goodbye to Piper...*

When he shut the door behind himself, she knew what he'd left unsaid.

21

Grace hadn't known that Florida was the lightning capital of America, central Florida in particular earning the name "lightning alley." But included in the Chase trial record was a map showing flash density per square kilometer and Grace was now armed with the knowledge that only tropical Africa had more red zones on that map than the place she was standing right now.

Funny, the things you learn prosecuting a man for murder.

Grace—basically a "bag of electrolytes," according to the expert testimony she'd read in the transcript—watched Chris pace off steps on the ground, completely oblivious to the gathering clouds and the roll of thunder. It had been drizzling off and on.

Chris had brought her out to Everglades National Park straight from work and Grace was still wearing her suit. Silk, of course. But after weeks of researching lightning injury for the Chase case, she wasn't about to use the umbrella stashed in the car.

The suit would be ruined. Just another casualty to add to the long list, she told herself. She squinted at the horizon. Difficult not to see the coming storm as a symbol for everything that had gone wrong in her marriage.

"Chris? Did you know your chances of getting struck by lightning are a lot greater than one in a million?"

He wrote something in his pocket-size notebook. "What?"

"You know how they're always saying you have this one in a million chance of getting struck by lightning?" Sure enough, those looked like thunderheads heading toward them. "Well, it turns out, the odds are something like one in three thousand."

"No kidding?"

She also remembered reading somewhere that lightning could appear out of the clear blue. "And the faster the storm travels, the more violent."

"Hmm?"

"I think this is a fast storm, Chris. Experts say that by the time you hear thunder you're already in danger of getting struck by lightning."

"Okay."

"Chris, I hear thunder."

"Gracie?"

"Yes?"

"Shut up."

She frowned. "So what exactly are we doing here?"

Here turned out to be the exact location where Clayton Chase had claimed to be taking one of his famous photographs when he'd been struck. Of course, they'd never found any film to prove it, something else Chase had never been able to explain.

This wasn't her first trip to the Everglades. When her cousin and her kids had come to visit from Iowa, Grace had taken them on one of those tours where they load you on an airboat and zoom around the humid vegetation and some guy who's missing a few fingers wrestles an alligator. She remembered the guidebook calling the Everglades a "river of grass," the mangrove swamps and coastal prairies creating an ecosystem home to hundreds of species.

They were standing in the dry uplands, where pines and palmettos coexisted with orchids and Spanish moss. This was the warm and wet season and the mosquitoes were fierce. But you couldn't question Chris, not when he was in the zone.

She'd worked with him before, on several cases to be precise. And while she didn't always agree with his method, she had to admit, he rarely struck out. Which was probably why she was still here despite the ruined suit and the greater than one in a million chance of becoming a crispy critter.

He looked around, then smiled. "This was the spot where it happened."

A sudden realization came to Grace. *Of course, of course!* She shook her head, knowing all along that she should have figured it out. But Chris knew how she felt about this sort of "evidence," that she'd never agree to anything less that the strictest of standards of protocol. Which is probably why he hadn't mentioned what he was up to when he'd brought her out here.

She turned and headed for her car.

"Grace!"

"No way."

"Come on, Grace. You know I get results."

She waved him off. "Not happening."

She kept walking. Sure, anybody else at the state attorney's office might have gone along with this little stunt, given Chris's success rate. But dammit, she was married to the bum. He should have told her. He knew how she felt about his "Ouija board" approach to discovery.

As she walked, she tried not to let her less-than-sensible heels—shoes being a weakness of hers—slip into the moist earth. And maybe she could still salvage the suit. It was only water, right?

She heard Chris running up behind her. He grabbed the keys out of her hand before she could push the unlock button.

"You know what your problem is, Gracie?"

Oh, boy. Here we go. She crossed her arms. "No, Chris. Why don't you tell me? Again."

"You give up too easily."

"We're going there, are we?"

"It's an observation."

"I gave up? I'm not the one who—give me those keys, dammit."

Chris pulled the keys out of her reach. "Okay. I got spooked. We ran off to Vegas and the next thing I know, it's the ball-and-chain."

She made another dive for the keys, but he held her off. He grabbed her shoulders. She looked up at those beautiful brown eyes and felt that horrible melting in her stomach. Stupid man. This was just the reason they'd ended up in Vegas in the first place.

She said softly, "Don't ever call our marriage the ball-and-chain. It may have been Vegas, but it was sacred to me."

Chris looked like she'd slapped him. That, of course, was her specialty, verbal evisceration. Chris always claimed he'd never had a chance, as if she hadn't handed him her heart on a plate.

He dropped his hands, aimed the keys at her old Volvo and pressed the unlock button. With a little chirp, the door locks opened. He handed the keys back to Grace.

"There you go, Gracie," he said. "Because God knows, I never get the job done."

She closed her eyes, reminding herself that calling him for help hadn't been about the past. It had been about Chase and doing exactly what Chris said: *getting the job done.*

She told herself to focus on the case, forget about navigating the hot coals of her failed marriage. The papers were being drawn up, for the love of all. She just needed Chris to sign, and sign he would, eventually. After he figured out that he wasn't going to wear her down. Once bitten, right?

She took a breath, opened her eyes. *Focus, Grace.* "Chris, as you know, I am not fond of the Ouija-board school of prosecution. I need admissible evidence."

"Which I can get you. In my own special Ouija-board way."

She covered her face with her hands and shook her head. *What the hell, Gracie. You've got nothing else…*

"All right," she said, dropping her hands, giving in. "Ouija away."

He smiled, looking his tanned and buff best. He'd just gotten one of those cute feathery haircuts that she liked so much. And the sun had given his normally brown hair these highlights. She remembered Chris telling her that he'd been scouted as a model in high school. *Oh, yeah.*

"You won't be sorry."

"You want odds on that?" she mumbled to herself as Chris walked back to his Expedition, what he called his weekend-warrior car. To Grace, it had always been just the gas guzzler.

Chris's Ouija-board detective work involved putting himself in the place of the victim or perp. He would do extensive research on the persons and events surrounding the case. To Grace, it smacked a little too much of those psychics who helped cops sometimes, a last resort for the lost cause. Chris claimed that he put himself so tightly in the other person's shoes, he could almost channel their thoughts and emotions. In his mind, he'd replay the events surrounding the crime. Almost always he'd discover some hidden sequence or motive the cops had missed.

Grace preferred good old-fashioned detective work. She'd been under the impression that's what she'd signed on for when she'd called Chris to help her with Chase. Again, he knew how she felt about the hocus-pocus stuff.

But the fact remained: Chris *was* good at this. At the same time, she was cold and wet and tired of watching the genius at work. And she didn't want to second-guess herself about their marriage, which would be inevitable if she kept spending time with him.

She watched Chris at work and felt that twinge of regret. God, she missed him. But how many times did you hand over your heart and let someone stomp on it? Okay, he hadn't cheated on her, sure. But he'd walked out. He'd told her their marriage was a mistake, the proverbial stab through the heart. He'd lost faith once. What would stop him from doing it again if she gave him half the chance?

"Could we at least speed it up?" she asked, thinking that, no doubt, she would live to regret this.

"Give me fifteen minutes. Twenty tops."

She glanced at her watch. "Ten."

The man did have a brilliant smile...especially when he got his way.

Out of his car came a tripod and a camera, Chris apparently ready to become one with Clay Chase. Grace felt the whole thing had the look of a lightning rod. A red flag in the face of Mother Nature. Jesus, was that thing made out of aluminum?

"God, I hope he makes this quick," she muttered under her breath.

She took off her jacket and tossed it on the passenger seat. It was warm enough that she didn't need the jacket. Watermarks on the skirt wouldn't be as noticeable.

Chris had been working on the case for the better part of a week, learning about Clayton Chase, his method, and photography in general. Still, she was impressed as he revved up for a reenactment of the evening.

Chris called it "method" P.I. work, but watching him always reminded her a little too much of her mother and her superstitions. Her mother always threw salt over both shoulders when it spilled, just in case. She never raised a glass of water for a toast. The first year of her life, Grace had never gone anywhere without her mother first pinning her *azabache* on Grace's clothes—a small pendant made of jet that warded off the evil eye. Cubans were very superstitious, and her mother, despite her advanced education, was no exception.

Thirty minutes later, Chris gave her a look. "Something's off."

He said it with a smile. Because that's what he wanted, why they'd come here in the rain to risk a lightning strike. To put himself in the perp's place, playact the events leading to the crime.

And now the conclusion. Something was off about the story given by Chase.

"He wasn't here alone," Chris added.

How the hell can he know that? Not that she'd give him the satisfaction of asking.

Then again...

"How the hell can you know that, Chris?"

"Because. It was an amazing night," he turned, his eyes shining with the excitement of discovery. "The storm was coming over the horizon from the west—the moon was just starting to disappear behind the clouds."

He flipped through the notes in his little book. The man did do his research. "Lookit, Grace. When the murder happened, Chase would have been in the middle of this fantastic storm. The light and timing would have been perfect for his kind of work. He would have gotten some amazing photographs— award-winning stuff." He shook his head, emphatic. "He never would have left if he could stay. Someone forced him to leave this light show."

Grace frowned, not liking it. "Or maybe he had better plans. Like killing his wife?"

"No. Her death was a crime of passion, see? It wasn't planned. He didn't leave here to have dinner with the wifey or hash out some old argument. I'm telling you, Grace. That night was perfect." He gestured ahead where, indeed, lightning flickered across the horizon, almost on cue. "There is no way someone like Clayton Chase would walk away from this."

"Yeah?" But Grace wasn't convinced. "Says who?"

Again, he flipped through the notebook. "In the world of lightning photography, Chase leads the pack—that's from *The New York Times Book Review*," he said, reading from his notes. "Lord of Lightning—the real deal—from *Popular Photography*. That's just part of the guy's press." He shook his head. "No way, Gracie. He didn't leave. Not for some crime-of-passion murder." He gestured over the horizon. "Right here is our guy's passion."

She nodded, hating how much she respected his talent. If only the idiot hadn't broken her heart.

She sighed. Oh, well. At least he was still useful here.

"Okay," she said, heading for the shelter of the car. "Now, let's go figure out how we prove it."

Clay found Simon standing next to the Jeep. He had the idea the kid wasn't supposed to be around. Getting wind of what was happening, Simon had hidden out here, waiting for the verdict.

"You're leaving," Simon said.

Bingo.

Clay knelt down, taking Simon's hand in his. He wasn't sure when the kid had dug a hole in his heart and settled in, but this wasn't going to be easy for either of them.

"Remember everything I told you, okay? Someone else can help you now."

He thought it was supremely ironic that he was giving Simon the same lame excuses Piper had tossed at him in her office. *I can't help you anymore…maybe I never could. My mistake.* Now it would be up to someone else to take Simon down that next step in his recovery.

Of course, the boy would have a similar response. Just like Clay, he wouldn't appreciate a change in tactics. He'd just had the rug pulled out from under him. Simon had barely started to trust Clay—it had been painful enough to take these first steps. No way he could just stop and move on to another confidant.

But like Clay, Simon wouldn't have a choice.

"Goodbye, big guy," he said, giving him a pat on the shoulder. "Make good use of that camera, okay?"

He didn't have the heart to look back as he got into the Jeep, knowing what he'd see on the boy's face. His own misery mirrored back at him.

Pulling away from the curb, Clay stared at the storm clouds gathering on the horizon. There had been a time in his life that he'd liked nothing better, a sense of excitement starting to brew with the darkened sky. He'd developed this weird sixth sense of where lightning might strike. He remembered telling Simon about it back at the house when he'd been showing him the Nikon. But now, all that excitement seemed distant, something from the past that was no longer a part of his life.

You may never have been struck by lightning.... You were able to mimic the effects.

His life on display...his life as an act.

He turned onto the highway leaving Coral Cay. The storm was coming in from the southeast. Soon enough, the rain lit up the black tarmac, the Jeep's lights reflecting off the slick surface. Twenty minutes later, he hit Highway 1. It was a straight shot home from here.

He was a man with an emptiness he didn't want to fill. He missed the drama of numbness. And now he'd just wait for the inevitable, knowing that, despite all of Aidan's efforts, someday justice would find him.

He'd gone to come clean with Piper. He'd wanted to tell her everything. That he knew he'd failed Jillian. Was even afraid he was somehow responsible for her death. Jillian had always told him he needed to want something bad enough to push, not just sit back and let life happen. Well, here he was, pushing. Dammit, he didn't want out of Piper's life.

Inside his conch house, he tossed the keys on the kitchen counter. He dropped into the recliner and stared at the phone.

He wanted to call her even now. Wanted to tell her it was all some stupid mistake. *I screwed up, but you can forgive that, right?* He hadn't really given them a chance because he'd been holding back from the beginning. He should call her. He should fight for another chance.

Coward, the phone seemed to whisper back.

He let his head drop, remembering the good old days when he could lose himself in his Nikon. It was this wonderful abyss that required all his concentration, so that he could disappear there into the calculations of ambient light and shutter speed, sometimes forgetting to eat or sleep. Never worrying about the people around him.

At her most acrimonious, Jillian had called him The Magician. She'd said that once he picked up his camera, he made everyone around him disappear.

Amazing how the one thing you loved about a person could be the very thing you came to hate.

Jillian was this amazing bundle of energy. Nothing could contain her. She was front-page stuff. The center of attention. Always. When he lost focus on that, he lost her.

He'd confronted her with the evidence, a hotel slip and a receipt from a romantic restaurant when she was supposedly at work. Jesus, he'd known she wasn't happy, but this?

He'd thought she'd deny it. That she could come up with some story he'd try not to believe. Hell, he'd been halfway to making up the excuses for her, so blown away was he by the idea that his marriage was over.

Please lie to me.

That's where it had gone wrong with Piper. He'd wanted the lies. She hadn't.

She wasn't a woman who ran from the truth, not like him. She'd want only to dig deep into those dark places he avoided, knowing all along that it was only a matter of time before the past would catch up, making all the hiding irrelevant.

She wouldn't want a flawed man who couldn't help her find those places inside herself. She wouldn't want him.

Suddenly, he picked up the phone. He pulled the connection out of the wall and threw the whole thing across the room. The phone crashed into the wall. Pieces of it ricocheted across the floor.

He stared at the mess, wondering what the hell was wrong with him.

Right then, the phone began to ring.

He was trying to catch his breath, thinking that the phone couldn't possibly be ringing. But then he realized the sound was coming from the bedroom, from the phone on the nightstand.

He raced into the room and picked up, his heart pounding when he saw the caller-ID number.

"Simon, is he there?" It was Piper on the phone.

Immediately, he knew what had happened.

"He took off," he said into the handset. It wasn't a question.

"He's supposed to be at school. I sent Mandy to pick him up. But he knows your appointment time." He could hear the tears in her voice. "I was hoping—I don't know, I thought maybe he'd sneak into your car or something. Do you have any idea where he might be?"

Because they'd had this secret life, he and Simon.

"No. No, of course not. What can I do to help—"

But she'd already hung up.

He stared at the handset, imagined her already running down the sidewalk in the rain. She'd be racing up and down that street, searching for Simon. Clay would be the last person she'd ask for help.

In his head, he imagined himself going back out there to her house, the drama of giving her a shake and telling her that she couldn't just turn him away, that he wouldn't allow it. He cared about Simon, no matter what she thought. He almost picked up the phone for another round, until another idea came to him.

Goodbye, big guy…. Make good use of that camera.

A sudden flash of lightning illuminated the room. The crash of thunder quickly followed, shaking the house. The lights flickered.

"Jesus."

He picked up the phone, suddenly knowing exactly where Simon had gone.

22

Piper hit the wipers and cleared the fogged-up windshield with her hand, forgetting which control on the dashboard would do the job for her. Her head felt on overload, the little things beyond her. She needed to keep moving, to do *something*.

Simon was gone. And she didn't know where to find him.

There was this small part of her that still spoke of caution. The slick streets posed a danger. Her hands trembled on the steering wheel with her panic. She couldn't afford to make a mistake. Not when her children needed her most. She needed a cool head.

Focus, Piper. Focus!

Only the truth was her little boy was gone, and if she couldn't find him right now, this very second, she thought her heart might just stop in her chest.

This wasn't like the other times. She hadn't stepped outside to find him crying in the rain or sitting on the curb waiting for Clay to show.

He was missing. He'd run away.

Mandy had found the note, scribbled words that spoke of longing and sadness Piper had had no idea dwelled inside her son. She hadn't been paying attention; she'd let her own issues with Clay interfere. She'd played the parent, believing she knew what was best for her son.

She'd known all along his relationship with Clay was complicated. For reasons neither would divulge, Clay had delivered Simon from what Piper now knew was a self-imposed silence. She hadn't thought about Simon's immediate reaction when she'd dismissed Clay summarily from his life. She'd considered only what was right for her son in the long run—to be out from under the influence of Clay, a man she considered unstable. She thought she would have time to explain the better course to Simon. He was only eight years old. She hadn't thought to bring Simon into the decision-making process, not until she had better control of the events.

And now he was gone.

She remembered the day she'd lost Kevin. At the hospital, she'd held her vigil at Simon's bedside while the doctors worked on Kevin in the E.R. She'd kept praying for one of those movie miracles. Somehow there would be a machine or a pill that could wake Kevin's heart and bring him back to his family.

She'd been sitting in the dark alongside Simon's hospital bed when the doctor had come in to give her the news. Simon had been in a deep sleep helped along by medication, completely unaware.

She'd known immediately Kevin was gone. The telltale signs had all been there. The doctor's slow walk toward her, his expression—he'd been bracing himself to tell her the news.

She remembered she hadn't been able to cry, because she'd made this strange pact with God. He'd let her keep Simon. Kevin had been the sacrifice.

And now, Simon was gone. And she couldn't breathe. There was nothing left she could sacrifice.

Her cell phone on the passenger seat began to ring. She reached for it with one hand while driving with the other. The whole time, she searched for Simon on the sidewalks and in the shadows. By the time she managed to wrestle the phone free of her purse, it had stopped ringing.

"Dammit." She tried to remember which button to push to find out who'd made the missed call, but that kind of recall seemed beyond her.

She should call the police. Let them know Simon was missing. She should call her sister, get her involved in the search. Crissa could be levelheaded in a crisis.

But she did none of those things. Instead, she threw the phone on the passenger seat, knowing that if it was Mandy calling, she'd try again. She doubled back toward the house. She tried a different route. She hoped against hope that she'd see her little boy walking along in the rain. Or maybe she'd find him waiting for her back at the house.

She meant to hit the brakes, but her foot smashed against the accelerator instead. She took the turn too fast. Suddenly, she was fighting the wheel as the car skidded. She found the brake, the car spinning out of control on the wet road.

She just managed to hit the curb, bringing the car to a stop.

The rain poured over the windshield as she caught her breath. She pounded her fits on the steering wheel, screaming her fear and frustration.

It hadn't been like this with Kevin. She'd been with her son at the time, worrying about him, knowing in her heart that Kevin had been beyond her help. So she'd focused on Simon still breathing there in the hospital bed, never allowing true fear. But now she felt overwhelmed by the possibilities.

Simon wouldn't know of all the dangers parents feared. Drunk or careless drivers. Child abductions. He was out in this storm alone, helpless and scared.

She'd thought he'd been getting better. She'd thought he'd be fine. Clay had opened the door and she'd had knowledge enough to help her son walk through. They would find their footing together. There would be life after Kevin's death.

Beside her, the cell phone chirped to life once again.

She realized she was crying. She was, in fact, on the edge of hysteria. Nothing she was doing made sense, and it wouldn't help her find Simon.

She'd thought he'd be with Clay. She'd been so sure. Somehow, he'd waited in Clay's car, or managed to flag him down. If he was with Clay, he'd be safe.

The world didn't make sense anymore. She was a good person, someone who worked hard to help others and take care of her children. What had she done to deserve punishment? Why would God single her out again?

The cell phone continued to ring beside her.

She picked it up, brushing the tears from her eyes. Her heart was going a mile a minute when she heard Mandy's voice.

"Simon?" Piper asked.

"I think I know where we can find him," she heard her daughter say.

Listening carefully, Piper caught her breath and started the car. She told Mandy to stay where she was, in case her brother called or came home.

As long as she was moving—as long as she had someplace to go, something to do—she'd be okay.

He remembered how much Simon liked flowers. It made sense to him that now, in a time of crisis, Simon would seek out nature. So Clay tried to imagine where the little guy might make that connection with the Nikon in the storm. Someplace close.

He found Simon on the bluffs behind Piper's house. Clay remembered there was a beautiful view of the wetlands. After Piper's phone call asking for Simon, he recalled a conversation with Simon in his darkroom, how the boy had talked about just that, already planning his shoot with the Nikon. It's where Clay would have gone.

The first thing he saw was the blue tarp. Not far away, Simon lay half-hidden among the shrubbery. He'd rolled up into a ball, his hands tucked under his armpits, the rain pouring down his slicker as he used his body to shelter the Nikon from the rain.

Clay dropped down beside him. Immediately, Simon threw himself into his arms.

"I thought if I could do it," he spoke in that same halting speech Clay had grown used to, the crying making it worse as Simon tried to catch his breath. "I thought if I could take the picture, she'd let you stay."

"I'm not going anywhere, buddy," he said, holding him tighter.

He was making promises he couldn't keep. He'd made a mistake; he could see that now. He'd stepped in to help and only created the situation. And now he had to make it right.

"Let's go home, Simon."

But the boy shook his head, pushing him away. "You can help me. If I take the photograph, she'll know I'm not afraid anymore and she'll let you stay."

"No, Simon," he said firmly. "A photograph isn't going to change anything. Not tonight."

"But it has to!" Simon screamed, pushing him away when he reached for him. "All those pictures I saw at your house. They changed things. That's what I want to do. But I got scared."

He brushed away his tears, the gesture almost angry. "But you're here now. And I'm not scared anymore."

He glanced at the tarp Simon had set up for shelter over some bushes. He'd planned well, using heavy rocks to keep the tarp from blowing away. There was another pile to serve as a sort of tripod, Simon knowing from their talk in the darkroom that he'd need long exposures. Coming here, facing the storm, Simon was trying to change something inside himself that had nothing to do with the photographs he so dearly wanted.

From the moment Simon had whispered his awful secret that night in the rain, Clay had tried his best to help him. He'd kept his promise to Simon, telling no one—not even his mother—what he'd confessed. He hadn't wanted Simon to lose faith in him. He felt the same way now. Maybe he didn't have Piper's training, but he had experience. He knew what Simon was going through, why he'd come here to face his fears.

He knelt down beside Simon. He nodded, giving Simon the answer he wanted, thinking that he'd helped him before, he could help him again.

"Taking a photograph," he said slowly, "is like capturing a moment. Your timing has to be great. You have to be fearless," he said, speaking from the heart. "And on rare occasions, if you're patient—if you're really good—God shows you all his secrets."

He thought about the choices they faced, he and Simon. How pivotal this moment. How critical his timing.

He called Mandy again, letting her know Simon was safe and where Piper could find them. He knew that phone call put him on the clock. They wouldn't have much time.

Back at the Jeep, he took out the wooden tripod and a

shutter-release cable, equipment that always traveled with him, even after a year of gathering dust. Some things were just part of who he was. Clay understood that dreams could be the most difficult thing in the world to give up.

He took Simon's hand. "Come on."

Together, the two men walked out to face the storm.

Running up the bluffs, Piper found them taking photographs of lightning.

Relief and fear rushed in her bloodstream. She walked slowly, then ran again, the rain driving against her as she reached them.

They hadn't seen her yet—they couldn't hear her cries. The wind just swallowed up the sound of her voice calling to Simon. But as she drew closer, she slowed her step, seeing something magical.

With only a camera before him and Clay at his side, Simon was facing the storm.

She felt frozen with indecision, not knowing what was best for her boy. The therapist inside her said this was what he needed, to challenge his fears…. The mother in her wanted to drag him to safety, knowing she'd sacrificed too much already to take this risk.

She settled for stepping slowly alongside her boy, but it was Clay and not Simon who saw her first. Meeting her gaze, Clay's expression dissolved from joy to guilt. But on Simon's face, she saw only the joy.

The camera was on a wooden tripod several feet away aimed at the black sky ahead. Simon was standing incredibly still, his finger on a button topping a long cable attached to the camera like an umbilical cord.

"Now," Clay whispered.

She watched her son push down on the button to keep the shutter open as Clay slowly counted to five.

Clay checked his watch. He said, "Okay."

Simon released the shutter, still focused ahead. She heard Clay talk to Simon softly, explaining about the rhythm of the storm, timing the photographs for the best exposures. The two repeated the same steps through the course of the film, until Clay finally put an end to it.

"Okay," he told Simon. "That's enough. You got it, Simon. You've captured the storm."

Simon stepped back. He smiled up at his mother.

"I did it," he whispered. "I changed everything."

She took him into her arms, holding him as he hugged her. She whispered, "Yes, Simon, you did. You most certainly did."

It took them only a moment to pack up. The boy at her side was no longer in a hurry or scared. He talked nonstop about the images he felt sure he'd captured, telling his mother about the cloud-to-ground lightning that strobed, requiring a longer exposure than the faster lightning strikes that took only a fraction of a second. He told her he couldn't wait for the next day when he and Clay would develop the photographs in his darkroom.

Clay grabbed her hand when they reached her car. "I called Mandy."

She nodded. "I know. She reached me on my cell. Clay, I don't know what to say."

"Don't say anything," he told her, adding softly, "not yet."

Once Simon was back in the car, he grabbed his mother's hand.

"It's all right, isn't it?" Simon asked. "That I came here? That Clay helped me?"

"Now you want my permission?" she said, tousling his hair and giving him a smile she didn't feel.

Because she didn't know what to say. She wanted to tread carefully. She didn't want to make more mistakes, damage this fragile courage beaming from her son.

"Everything's going to be fine," she answered as she looked up at Clay, giving them all the pabulum.

23

Burton sat in the dark watching the storm through a wall of glass. The second-floor room had a pristine view of the Atlantic. He remembered Jackie telling him she chose this room for his home office because the view was supposed to remind him of everything he was giving up if he should stay holed up here too long.

The architect she'd hired had given him some bullshit about bringing nature indoors. There wasn't a room in the house that didn't have a view of water. Even the laundry room had a glass window in the door to take advantage of the ocean and sun. The laundry room, for Christ's sake.

Now lightning ripped across the night sky, reminding him not of nature but of something much less gratifying.

Another finger of lightning lit up the sky. These were just the sort of images Clay had brought to life, making a fortune off those damn photographs.

He remembered how Jillian had nurtured each and every piece, giving them names like children. Burton himself had purchased several works for his corporate offices and his homes, all of which he'd donated to charity after the trial.

He stared down at the glass of whiskey. After a minute, he

sighed and placed it back on the glass-top coffee table, untouched. Tonight, he needed a clear head.

He couldn't imagine where it had all gone wrong. When had he convinced himself that his guilt had nothing to do with the tragedies life had dished up and served him cold?

And now, he was mulling over his options, knowing full well that he had a debt to his wife…a debt he'd put in jeopardy if he continued on this course.

He stood and walked over to a Wyland painting of marine life. His wife and daughter had always told him his taste in art ran to the pedantic. *So shoot me,* he thought.

He flipped a switch on the desk. The painting slid aside to reveal a small safe. He spun the combination and reached for the handle, but stopped.

He had never been a good Catholic. Although he had taken all the sacraments, he hadn't gone to church, letting his wife hold the spiritual course for them both. But after Jillian's death, he'd stopped caring about any lack of spirituality on his part.

Now he was making a final step down that road. *So shoot me.*

He reached for the gun, a 9 mm Beretta. He loaded it slowly. It had been years since he'd practiced on the firing range. But the weapon felt warm and very much at home in his hand.

Jackie wouldn't approve. A silly thought, but there you had it. The last person he didn't want to disappoint. And he would. If he checked out now, if he gave in to that temptation to eat a bullet and put an end to his pain, what about Jackie?

He sat down, staring at the gun, holding it tight. He was thinking about the women in his life, Jackie, Jilly Bean, Lydia. Thinking of how he had disappointed them all. He didn't know how long he just sat there, but he looked down at his hands holding the Beretta and saw that they were shaking.

He stood and placed the gun back inside the safe. He spun the dial.

Not tonight.

Instead, he picked up the phone. He punched the number from memory, wondering if the guy would even take his call. Burton had acted like a real prick trying to pay him off. Funny thing, when he'd turned down that check, Burton had been almost disappointed.

He'd wanted him to be just another asshole out for a buck. Actually, he'd wanted the guy to be dead wrong.

When he picked up, Burton smiled.

"About Lydia Barrera," he said. "There might be something. If you're still amenable, we should talk."

Piper waited until breakfast for any revelations. She had two reasons for waiting. First, she hadn't wanted to confront Simon during the storm. No matter how strong her little guy had appeared last night after his feat on the bluffs, she didn't want to make that kind of push. They were going to be that little engine that could, she and Simon, making slow and steady progress.

So she kissed Mandy goodbye and watched her head off to school. As Mandy hopped into Sean's car, Piper frowned at the dilapidated Chevy she thought most certainly did not have air bags, much less good brakes. She thought it might be time to insist on the Civic for their communal use. She turned just in time to see Simon rub the sleep from his eyes.

"You didn't wake me for school?" he asked.

He still had a slight lisp. The syllables didn't flow as well as they should, stumbling at times from a lazy mouth that needed practice. But standing in his Spider-Man pajamas, he'd spoken as if language had never been a challenge.

Simon was back.

"Hey," she said.

"Hey," he answered, still sounding pretty sleepy. "What about school?"

"What about it?" she said. "Pancakes?"

His eyes lit up. No school *and* pancakes for breakfast? Simon had just hit the jackpot.

"I'll make the batter!" He raced to the kitchen pantry.

She still couldn't listen to him talk without her heart rising to her throat. She kept waiting for the miracle to fall apart. Good things didn't happen here at Club Jordan. Oh, fate might tease her a bit, dangling the possibilities just out of reach. But the real premium stuff always slipped through her fingers.

But here it was, primo, grade-A, good stuff. She was standing beside Simon at the kitchen counter. Pancake-batter circles bubbled on the electric griddle. In order to reach the griddle, Simon stood on a chair in his pajamas. Piper held her arm around his waist to steady him and watched as he sprinkled M&M's into the pancake. She waited just a minute before she flipped each perfect circle. Simon liked his pancakes fully loaded.

"A glass of milk with those, okay?" she said as they headed for the kitchen table, each carrying a plate piled high.

She waited until he was halfway through the heap before she put down her fork.

"Okay, buddy," she said. "How about we get down to business here and talk about yesterday?"

Some of the animation left his face. He'd probably figured out there was some price to pay for this day of luxury. He scrunched his lips and started making circles with his fork in a pool of syrup on his plate.

"What?" he asked, falling back on monosyllables.

She smiled. Even that small pearl was progress compared to the last two years.

"Last night," she said. "Those photographs. I could tell you really liked taking pictures with Clay."

He nodded, still playing with his food. She let the silence carry. That's one thing she'd learned as a therapist. When to show them and when to hold them.

"I'm sorry," he said, breaking the silence.

"You don't have to apologize, sweetie. I think I understand."

He stopped toying with the pancakes. He looked up, biting his lip. "I don't want Clay to leave."

She nodded. "Yeah, I get that. But I need to know something, okay?"

"Okay."

"That first night when you met Clay. He was out there during the storm with you. He said something to you. Something that made you not so scared anymore."

Again, that silent nod. She could see he was frightened. There was something there, something he didn't want her to know.

"Well," she continued, "during one of our sessions, I asked Clay to tell me what you guys talked about. I wanted to know because I wanted to help, too, you know? Because I love you." She took a breath, pushing back the emotion that was right there, ready to choke her. It wouldn't help the situation. She needed to keep an even keel. "I love you so much, big guy. It's hard to say it enough sometimes."

He nodded. Simon knew about love. Mandy, she played it close to the chest, throwing in that hug or kiss every once in a while. But Simon was still young and full of that kind of demonstrative love that a mom just lived for.

"But you see, Simon, Clay didn't think he should be the one to tell me. I think you must have asked him to keep it a secret."

She could see the tears well up in her little boy's eyes. "I don't want to tell you, Mommy."

"Okay." She hugged him again. She kissed the top of his head. "I guess it's something you think is bad. That maybe I'll be angry."

He didn't say anything, looking down at the pancakes.

She picked up his hand. She shook her head. It was tearing her heart in two, seeing Simon like this.

"Honey. I think you and Mandy forget sometimes just how much I love you."

But he was shaking his head.

"Okay. You don't have to tell me," she said, trying to reassure him. "I just know it's hard to keep things inside sometimes. It's like that monster under the bed. It's always better to look and see that nothing is there."

And how many times had they done just that, making a game of it? See, baby? Nothing under the bed. She wanted to help Simon take a peek at his fears and make them disappear.

So she pushed a little. "I think maybe that's why you were so quiet for so long," she said. "Because you were afraid of what you might say."

He looked at Piper, silent tears sliding down his cheeks. "Yeah. Maybe."

Piper stood. Simon jumped to his feet with her and she swept him up in her embrace.

"No, honey." She kissed his cheeks. "Don't you be scared. I'm here. I'm always here. And I love you. No matter what. I know that's hard to believe sometimes. But it's the truth,

Simon. You think about how much you love me. And you'll know there's nothing that could change how I feel about you."

He was crying now, gulping for breath. "Mommy, I want to tell you."

"Okay. I'm listening."

"It's my fault Daddy died."

"No. Never. What happened to Daddy is no one's fault."

"Yes it is. Because I ran outside. Daddy told me it wasn't safe, and I didn't listen. I wanted to see what it felt like to just stand in the rain. And that's why we were outside when the lightning started. Because of me. Because Daddy was trying to get me back inside the house."

He was crying hard against her shoulder, his whole body shaking.

"Oh, Simon." She closed her eyes, hurting so much for him. "You couldn't be more wrong. Daddy's accident wasn't your fault. Why didn't you just tell me?"

But she knew, of course. The very same reason she hadn't talked to anyone about why she hadn't been home that night. Guilt, one of those sticky stages of the grieving process.

"Simon." She hugged him harder, kissing him over and over. "I know it's hard to believe—that there's no rhyme or reason to such a terrible loss. You try to make sense of it. But that's not how these things work."

She didn't know how long they stood like that in the kitchen, the smell of syrup and chocolate lingering in the air as they hugged each other. But eventually, Piper pulled away.

"You know something, Simon? I have a confession, too. For a long time, I blamed myself for what happened to Daddy." She could see his eyes get bigger. "That's right. Because we had this big fight, and I made him stay home instead of going to work like he was supposed to. I kept thinking if he'd gone to work, he wouldn't have died. So I thought it was my fault."

She pushed his bangs out of his face and sat down. She pulled him up on her lap. He put his arms around her neck, his body curling into hers.

"It's hard not to feel bad after someone you love disappears. Especially the way Daddy died. Because it doesn't make sense. It's not like one of those math problems in school where everything gets to add up. So we try to make up reasons why it happened. We try to connect the dots and start wondering what we could have done different or better. But the truth is, we couldn't change what happened. Do you understand? We just don't have that kind of power."

He nodded. "That's what Clay told me. He said lightning strikes only from above, and by the hand of God," Simon recited the very grown-up words from memory. "And when I asked how he knew, to see if maybe he was lying or just trying to make me feel better, he said he'd been hit by lightning. But he lived. And that God had let him live because he was supposed to find me and tell me it wasn't my fault about Daddy. So I would stop feeling bad. God didn't want me to feel bad anymore."

Piper felt those softly slurred words fill the room. Her heart suddenly felt too big in her chest. *God had let him live because he was supposed to find me and tell me it wasn't my fault....*

She held her son's face up to hers. "That's right. The hand of God." Her voice cracked a bit. "It was just Daddy's time, okay? I know it made us really sad, and that we miss him a lot. But it's not something we have a choice about, okay?"

"Clay told me I had to believe him. Because he wanted to do a good job for God. On account of him getting to live when Daddy didn't."

She wrapped her arms around Simon. Simon hugged her, crying softly now, the tears a release. Just like hers.

"I couldn't have said it better, sweetie," she told Simon. "I couldn't have said it better."

Shawna didn't like that sad look in Aidan's eyes. Aidan, when he wasn't happy, could get a bit of a hound-dog look, especially around the eyes. Not attractive.

She leaned across the restaurant table and stroked his cheek. She didn't want to hurt him. But it was time for her to step in and take over.

"Don't be mad," she whispered.

He took a quick sip of wine. It was almost as if he couldn't look at her. On the other side of the restaurant, a married couple sat silently across from each other, not saying a word. She wondered if that was how it would become between her and Aidan.

"Aidan?"

He put down his wineglass. "You're twisting my arm to drop a client—a man who is most likely going to end up strapped to a gurney with an IV drip for a lethal injection without my help. And I'm supposed to be happy about it?"

"Don't say it that way."

"You don't like my spin?" He took another angry drink.

'That's right," she said, getting courage. "Because that's all it is. Spin. I mean, look at it from my point of view. Aidan, we have our whole lives ahead of us. Do you really want Clayton Chase to be what destroys us?"

"You don't understand."

She reached across the table and squeezed his hand. She'd practiced this speech. She knew all the words, the sympathetic expressions needed to hit sincere. "Honey? I don't understand? Please. Aidan, I have been here from the beginning and I have seen how that man has used you."

He turned away, not listening. He didn't want to hear anything bad about Clayton Chase. He wanted to pretend the man was some freaking saint just like the little wifey he'd put a bullet in. Saint Jillian and Saint Clayton. Let's all light a candle and say an Ave Maria.

"I don't know why you're acting like this," she said.

"Look." Aidan was good and pissed. He even shook a finger at her. Aidan never shook his finger. "This is my career. You can't dictate who I represent."

She leaned over the table, a little riled herself. "Listen to me, Aidan. I don't give a shit if your entire clientele is drug lords and mobsters. You can represent Angel Barrera, his cousins and his uncles, for all I care."

Aidan looked shocked. *I just bet.* She was silly little Shawna. What did she know about Angel Barrera? A lot, that's what. That's how she'd finally gotten the courage to talk to Aidan. Because she'd realized she held all the cards. Even over Angel Barrera.

"I'm not going to interfere," she said, settling back in her chair.

She loved this place. The glass-enclosed restaurant located poolside at the Clinton was already a celebrity hot spot. She'd heard Gloria and Emilio Estefan, Miami's power couple, had hosted a party here. And Cher loved their takeout. Shawna looked down at the plate of stylishly presented Chinese food, tried to compare it to the greasy takeout she'd once considered a treat. Well, her life had changed—but only because she'd taken a chance. She smiled at the waiter keeping her wineglass filled. This is what she'd been waiting for her whole life. Hovering waiters and fine wines.

"You're not going to interfere? What do you call what you're doing now?" he asked mildly after the waiter had stepped away.

"Okay. I won't interfere...too much." She smiled, taking the sting out of her blatant manipulation. "I love you, Aidan. For me—for us—you can do this."

He nodded, gesturing for the check. She sighed, looking down at the food and her plate that apparently would go un-eaten, because Aidan had already finished his meal. She, of course, would have to follow and soothe his nerves. Well, maybe she was expecting too much. It's not like he'd be happy about what she'd told him.

"So you'll call him?"

"Yes," Aidan said, dropping his credit card on the table. "I'll call."

"And you'll tell him."

"I said I would, didn't I?"

She could almost see him grinding his teeth.

Well, it's not like it mattered. Aidan would get over it. Someday, when they had their house and their babies, he'd come to see that she'd been right all along. Clayton Chase would have ruined Aidan. That man would have been the death of them both.

Time to cut him loose.

24

Even before he'd shown Piper the photographs, Clay knew he'd made a mistake keeping them secret. He wasn't under any delusions about how he'd be judged either. He'd stolen those images from her. He hadn't needed her look of disbelief and shame to nail it home, but he'd sure as hell deserved it.

He'd gone behind her back to capture hidden moments. That hadn't been his intent, of course, but intent didn't matter here. Piper wouldn't care about his take on it. In his mind, he'd been like one of those scientists conducting double-blind studies, his goal only to replicate results, confirm the limits of his newfound ability. He'd been stretching muscles he'd thought atrophied beyond all hope, looking for a second chance. Or so the bullshit went in his head.

The truth was a whole lot uglier. Because he'd used her. Even worse, he'd hidden from her a grisly possibility in his past: that abrupt memory that had flashed in his head. His hand holding his father's gun.

The truth was he'd killed Jillian—he most certainly had.

He couldn't pretend now there wouldn't be a price for such wrongdoing. He couldn't go on with the fantasy that he could return to a normal life. He'd spent the last year in numbing darkness. And now he needed the courage to step into the light, unearth whatever he'd buried inside himself. If he wanted Piper's help, he'd have to come clean on every score.

And once he found out the truth, he'd make good on it. He'd call the police.

When the doorbell rang, he stood to answer the door. He'd called Piper that morning, asking her to come out to his house. He'd half expected her to turn him down. *It's gotten too complicated, Clay.* But, of course, this was Piper, the woman who had agreed to take his controversial case in the first place. She'd come despite her good sense. She'd made good time.

"Thanks for coming," he said.

She followed him into the living room and sat down on the couch. He tried to remember what it had been like when Mandy and her beau had been sitting there, he and Simon working in the darkroom. The whole day had felt like a fantasy. Roll the orchestra music, cue the lights…here comes cold reality.

"How is Simon?" he asked.

She took a moment, but granted a tired smile. "Champing at the bit to come here and develop his film."

He released the breath he'd been holding. "He's better, then."

She gave a short nod as she wrapped her arms around herself. He wondered if it helped, holding in all her fears like some cocoon.

"Clay," she said, "I spoke to Simon this morning about everything. He told me what you said to him that first night. How you made him believe he wasn't responsible for his father's death."

He nodded. He was sitting on the love seat across the coffee table from her, trying for relaxed. He was anything but, of course. But here was Piper, launching in fearlessly.

"Thank you," she said.

"Irrelevant," he answered.

"You think so?" She smiled, shaking her head. "I disagree."

He shrugged. "He's your son."

She gave him another tired smile. "Meaning?"

"You're his mother. You want good things for him. It doesn't matter how it happens."

"Wow." She shook her head. "I'm still confused about the 'I shouldn't be thankful' part."

He sighed. "Come on, Piper. You were right yesterday. About everything. I lied to you. I used you. Christ almighty, I may have killed my wife. But heck. Simon's all good, so forgive and forget?" He shook his head. "I don't think so, Piper."

"Such cynical words from a man who talked about the hand of God?" She leaned forward, dropping her arms to her sides. The gesture struck him as almost symbolic. Piper, setting herself free, ready to take flight.

"You know the part that made it pure magic?" she asked. "When you said he had to believe you because God saved you so you could find Simon and help him."

He could tell she was having a hard time. There were tears choking up her voice. She rubbed her eyes in an impatient swipe of her hand. "That was a nice touch, of course. You understand that I tried everything to help him start talking again. I even told him his father was watching him, that Kevin didn't want him to be so sad. But I couldn't help Simon, you know? Because I wasn't the one struck. But here you walk in, the very thing he needed. A fellow survivor with a secret."

He smiled, liking that last bit. "It's poetic, don't you think? I go to you for help and suddenly I can take photographs. To hold my camera again. It was huge. Then I skulk back to your house with my camera like some idiot, telling myself I'll just stand here and see what happens. I had my camera in my hand when Simon ran out of the house. Suddenly, the camera didn't matter. I dropped it in the car and ran out to see what was going on."

He remembered standing outside the door. It was almost midnight. The storm was hitting full force and he was thinking about crawling back to his car, getting on home. And then he saw Simon.

The kid just blasted out of the house, like a shot. Almost at the same instant, lightning hit the palm tree just down the block. He'd gone into automatic, thinking he had to make sure that little boy was going to be okay. It still shook him, thinking about it.

"Suddenly words come pouring out of my mouth I never could have come up with in a million years. All those dominoes just lining up?" He looked up at Piper, meeting her gaze. "Tell me that's not meant to be."

"So now we're talking about the hand of God again?"

He grinned, liking the irony. "Who knew a cold-blooded killer could find religion?"

"That's not what I meant."

He frowned. "Don't sound so frustrated."

"What else?" She threw her hands in the air. "This whole thing, you and me—you and Simon. It has me going crazy. I know about obsession, Clay. I know all the steps. It's part of my training. Psychology 101."

"You think I'm obsessed with you?"

"Don't do that," she said, sounding angry for the first time. "Don't pretend this isn't happening."

He took a minute, catching his breath. "So I'm obsessed? Because I can take your photograph?"

"And vice versa. You think that doesn't make me feel special? Dear lord, man, you're like the Triple Crown of psychology. Famous photographer loses his touch. But no—hold the phone. The magic is back...but only when *I'm* in your viewfinder. And it doesn't stop there, folks. Oh, no. After two years of watching my son slip away."

She stopped, closing her eyes. He could tell she didn't want to lose it. She glanced up. Her hair, like silk, covered half her face. She took a moment to loop it behind her ear, giving him a clear view.

"After watching my son slowly slip away," she said, her voice firm now, "I saw you throw him a net."

It was hard for him to hear what she was saying. He didn't want to be some stupid hero, not with his past. But he understood how powerful that had to be for her. "Okay."

But Piper wasn't finished. "Do you know how unprofessional I sound? I don't talk to you like a therapist."

"And here I thought that was a good thing."

She shook her head. "We're just *pretending*. I'm not helping you, Clay. Not like this. After Kevin died, I told myself I wouldn't believe all those myths about lightning. I was the hardened scientist. Certainly, there's a lot we don't understand about lightning and its effects, but there is nothing supernatural at work here. Nothing magic. Then you step into our lives." She looked away. "Talk about magic."

He could see she was battling her emotions. "Piper?"

She held up her hand, taking a minute. When she finally looked up, one single tear slipped down her face. "I'm supposed to trust these emotions?"

He said quietly, "Maybe there are things we need to do even if we don't trust them."

"You think I should just continue seeing you? Even if I don't trust you? Because something good might come of it?"

He took a breath, wondering if he should just plunge right in with her, after all. "You know what I think? Sure you're pissed that I lied…but maybe there's something else there, too. Something not so obvious. Like the fact that I helped Simon when you couldn't."

That stopped her. He'd been right about her all along. She was a woman who wouldn't want to turn away from the truth.

"What do you want from me, Clay?" she asked.

She looked so tense sitting there, almost as if she expected the worst. *I want it all, Piper. The kid, your love, and I won't stop until it's mine….*

"I want you to help me," he said, feeling a shaking fear rise up inside him. The fear that he did love Piper—and that he was a man who had too many demons lying in wait to love anyone. "I want you to help me remember what happened that night. Even if it's bad. Even if it's the worst."

In the end, that's why he'd called Piper. It's the same reason he'd gone to see her in the first place. Too late to back out now.

"I need to know if I murdered my wife."

Shawna stood in the doorway, fuming. She checked her watch. He'd told her ten o'clock. It was almost eleven o'clock at night and he still wasn't here, dammit. And now she was waiting outside some dumb-ass mom-and-pop joint on main street Tavernier, some stupid hellhole of Americana. Jesus.

Just standing here gave her the creeps. Maybe because the place reminded her a little too much of her childhood. She'd grown up in just such a dismal place. You could almost close your eyes and pretend the world stopped half a century ago. Nothing to do but get drunk and go cow-tipping for fun…and have sex. The guys in town had loved Shawna. The girls had called her a whore.

She looked down at her Marc Jacobs pumps. The shoes had cost $340. She wondered how many of those cow-town girls even knew about Marc Jacobs. She allowed herself a small smile.

She'd been surprised when Clay had called. Shocked even, after not recognizing his voice, thinking it was someone else entirely. She wondered how he'd gotten her cell number. But she figured Aidan had told Clay he wouldn't represent him anymore. Clay was just plain out of luck.

She could see it now. Once Aidan let him know all bets were off, Clay would try to negotiate. Aidan would let him know it wasn't his call. He'd have to speak to Shawna, the girl in charge.

Shawna smiled, liking the scenario. Her whole life, Shawna had been at the whim of others: her mother, her asshole dad and that idiot she'd almost married. Tommy had put her in the E.R. so many times she'd finally had to leave with only the clothes on her back and hop a Greyhound bus out of town, ditching him after he'd passed out from one of his drinking binges. That's how she'd ended up at the women's shelter where Jillian had found her. She'd been hiding from Tommy.

At first, she'd been so grateful to Jillian. But then she'd started thinking about the differences in their lives. Here was Jillian, filthy rich—anything she wanted handed to her by Daddy. What had Shawna's father ever given her?

It had seemed so unfair. That's when she'd gotten the idea to start dressing like Jillian, mimicking everything about her.

Why not? Jillian had been teaching Shawna what she'd known about society and art. Pretty soon, a lot of doors could have opened up for Shawna.

What she'd needed was a transformation, to become another woman altogether. A woman no one from her past would ever recognize. Never again would she be that blond bimbo everybody had used. Now, she was the one pulling the strings. And it felt good.

She glanced at her watch again. If this was some stupid attempt to get her to cave, Clay was blowing it, big time. Not that she'd ever cave.

She smiled, thinking about Aidan and the future. It was all on track now. Aidan would have called Burton and told him he'd dropped Clay as a client, just as she'd instructed. Burton would in turn keep his end of the bargain, bringing Aidan back onboard to run his company. Eventually, it would all be Aidan's, because who else would Burton give his money to? His only child was dead and buried.

Shawna didn't believe in right or wrong. She only believed in making sure she got what she wanted. She'd learned a long time ago what happened to women who didn't fight back.

"Where the hell are you?"

She said it out loud, like whistling in the dark.

She looked up at the inky-black sky. There'd been a big storm yesterday but now there wasn't a cloud in the sky. It was unnaturally quiet out here. Shawna liked the noise of the city, its bright lights and manic energy. Here, it was spooky quiet. She'd practically broken her ankle on the uneven pavement.

She wondered about a man who wanted to live out here. What had Jillian seen in the bastard to choose him over Aidan?

That stupid cow, Jillian. She'd always gotten everything she'd wanted. But in the end, it hadn't mattered. In the end, Shawna had won.

She heard footsteps behind her. Finally! With a smug smile, she turned.

"It's about time—"

She stopped abruptly when she saw the gun.

"No, don't!"

She heard that pop they talk about in the movies, the kind that happens when the gun has a silencer attached.

Funny. She heard the sound, but she never felt a thing.

Piper leaned back against the front door, taking a minute. Even at this hour, the humid heat had the power to suck up any ounce of energy a person could manage. Add to that feeling of lethargy her surreal meeting with Clay, shake well and pour, and you had yourself one exhausting cocktail of a night. And it wasn't nearly done.

Waiting for her in the living room was Mandy and the new fixture in their lives, Sean. Piper gave a tired smile as Sean stood and told Mandy he loved her. He waved goodbye, exiting stage left. The door shut quietly behind him.

I love you. Sixteen and already so sure.

"Don't," Mandy said.

"What?"

"The lecture." Mandy crossed her index fingers in front of her face as if warding off the evil eye. "It's right there on the tip of your tongue."

"That transparent, am I?"

Mandy shrugged. "It's a mom thing."

Piper came to sit down next to Mandy. She put her arm

around her daughter, delighting in the warmth of Mandy's slack body against hers. A rare moment, this.

"So," she said after a while. "To what do I owe the honor? Obviously, you're not waiting for my scintillating motherly advice about boyfriends and such ilk."

Mandy turned and looked at Piper. "Sean's nice."

"Sean's a peach," she said, playing with Mandy's strawberry curls. "He seems to have a brain, which is a good thing," she said, not wanting to give too much away.

But Mandy wasn't going to be diverted. Her brown eyes focused on Piper, she pursed her mouth into a frown.

"Okay," Piper said. "Go ahead. Ask me."

Mandy seemed to take it in stride that Piper knew what was bothering her. She simply asked, "What happened tonight with the lightning guy?"

Piper sighed. "His name is Clay."

"Whatever."

She kept playing with Mandy's curls. She remembered how much Mandy had hated her naturally curly hair. She'd even begged Piper to let her try that Japanese straightening technique. Apparently, it permanently straightened the hair shaft. The hair had to grow out to wave again. Judging from the head of hair that had just walked out the door, curls were no longer a problem.

She looked into her daughter's worried gaze, wondering how much to tell her. She settled on the truth. "He took those photographs because he discovered that when he focuses his camera on me, suddenly, his hands don't shake, his head doesn't hurt. It's like the old days. He can take pictures again. But only of me."

"Wow," Mandy said, mulling it over. And then, right out

of the blue, she said, "He can't remember what happened the night his wife died, can he?" she said. "Like maybe he's worried that he really killed her."

Piper, shocked, didn't know how to respond. But Mandy didn't need the confirmation.

"He must be really scared," she said.

"And then some, honey," Piper answered.

Mandy seemed to think about that, the idea of really not knowing what had happened, how awful that must be. "Can you help him?"

"I hope so, sweetie."

"You don't sound so sure."

She turned on the couch to look at Mandy. She knew how difficult the last years had been for her, the older sister and fellow survivor, trying to fulfill all her father's ambitions.

"I'm as sure as I can be," she told Mandy.

"Do you like him?"

Piper allowed a tense silence. "Yes. I do like him."

"Like Daddy?"

She smiled because Mandy was leaving so much unsaid. She shook her head. "No."

How to explain her relationship with Mandy's father? Kevin had been everything that was right for so long. A handsome doctor with a beautiful little girl. A widower. The "should" in her life when Clay Chase could only be the "don't."

"Mandy," she said softly. "I know you're afraid. So much is changing so quickly. It's difficult sometimes to keep up."

Difficult for a sixteen-year-old not to be frightened. Mandy had lost both parents. Why wouldn't she believe that once such tragedy touched her life, she was somehow on track for more? As if misfortune were catching like a cold, and they were more susceptible now. After Kevin's death, they'd been walking on eggshells, waiting for the other shoe to drop. Only next time around, they might not have the emotional resources to make it through.

Piper knew those fears, battled them daily. The idea that she was worn down, weakened by Kevin's loss, too fragile to survive another blow from fate. *Go away. Destroy someone else's life.*

"What are you afraid of?" she asked Mandy.

"That it's somehow all a trick," she said, staring down at her clasped hands in her lap. "That we'll wake up tomorrow and Simon will be just like he was before. Or we'll find out that Clay is really this big crook and he killed his wife." Her eyes locked on Piper. "That he'll hurt you. Or maybe it's something as stupid as he'll make you incredibly sad because he'll break your heart. I'm afraid that you'll leave and Simon and I really will be alone."

"That's not going to happen." She brushed her hand through Mandy's hair. "Don't live your life in fear, sweetie. If that's what I've taught you and your brother these last years, then I am incredibly sorry."

"So you're going to help him?"

She smiled, knowing that she really didn't have a choice.

"Yes, Mandy. I believe I am."

25

Burton waited for Cowan at Versailles, a Cuban restaurant known for its authentic cuisine and ambience. Here, people gathered to eat and talk—in Spanish. Even the waiters stumbled over their English. The place managed to be homey despite its floor-to-ceiling mirrors, chandeliers and green vinyl chairs. It reminded Burton of the old days.

When he'd first come to South Beach, he'd spent his fair share of nights sleeping out on the beach or in hostels. He'd lived off cheap Cuban food that could fill a man for less than two bucks and beer that cost only pennies. He'd come to love the place long before the pulsing energy of Ocean Drive and restored Art Deco buildings had brought along the likes of P. Diddy and skinny models on photo shoots. So had Angel Barrera.

Burton sipped his Cuban coffee from its demitasse, thinking about the dark side of this paradise. How cleverly its neon glow and Latin beat could hide people like Barrera. Drugs. Prostitution. It was all here for the taking, making men like Barrera rich.

When he arrived, Cowan sat across from Burton, and spoke in fluent Spanish to the waiter, laughing over some joke. The guy could speak like a native, though he'd told Burton he didn't have a drop of Latin blood. He'd picked it up on the streets, growing up on Calle Ocho, also known as Little Havana. The man looked in his early thirties, and from what Burton could see, he'd long left his humble roots. It wasn't that he flaunted anything—quite the opposite. But it was there in the snazzy gadgets of his trade Burton had seen at his offices. Cowan had only the best. One thing was certain—he still liked his Cuban coffee.

When the waiter left, Cowan turned serious, getting to the heart of the meeting. "You asked me how I knew about you and Lydia Barrera." He slid an envelope across the white-topped table. "You'll find everything inside."

Burton didn't bother to open the envelope. The proof didn't really matter; he more or less knew what was inside. Still, once he opened the envelope there would be no going back.

Seeing him hesitate, Cowan added, "Burton. Anything I found out, it's a sure bet Angel already knows about it."

He glanced up, examining the guy's earnest expression. He couldn't help feeling Cowan was manipulating him somehow. But what was in it for Cowan? The guy didn't want money, he knew that much.

Angel, Burton thought. Burton had this feeling it all went back to Angel Barrera. For some reason, Cowan wanted to give Burton the heads-up, maybe get him to rat on one of Miami's most successful criminals.

Burton felt a tingling at the base of his neck. For an instant, he almost reached across the booth to check the guy for a wire.

At that moment, Cowan grabbed his BlackBerry, which must have been set on vibrate. He looked at the number.

"I gotta take this," he told Burton, sliding out of the booth.

Burton tried not to be offended, watching Cowan step outside, the BlackBerry pressed to his ear. Too many years on top, he told himself. He was used to everyone kowtowing to him.

He glanced down at the envelope, then looked away. He reached for his coffee instead. The stuff was thick, black and sweet, just the way he liked it.

He hadn't called Clay. He hadn't had the stomach for it. And now here was this envelope to deal with.

Would there be photographs of Lydia? he wondered. He remembered how beautiful she'd been, olive skin and dark, dark eyes. She was only Burton's age, a good decade younger than her husband.

Dear sweet Lydia, now dying.

He picked up the envelope, felt that it was thick with papers. Cowan's proof.

He could still hear Angel's voice.

Shame on you, Burton....

He didn't know what he was waiting for. He was a man already living in hell. But the moment felt like that day in his office with the Beretta on his lap. His hands started to shake.

Open it, dammit. Face the truth.

But before he could fumble with the clasp, Cowan returned to his seat across from Burton. The guy looked all business.

"Something's come up," he said, leaning forward. "I'm going to need your help."

Piper always started with breathing.

Clay had come to her house. They were in her office, Clay reclined on the couch and Piper sitting in the chair across from him. She had thought about this step very carefully, had wondered about her decision even as she'd invited Clay over.

Now she instructed him to take the air in slowly and exhale through his mouth. She told him to count to four in his head as he inhaled. One, two…that's right. Then exhale. Good.

"I want you to tense your right arm," she said. "Now release the muscles. Do you feel the difference? Now the left. Tense, then relax."

They were trying a more aggressive approach, hypnosis.

There was a lot of controversy surrounding the kind of traumatic amnesia she suspected Clay had suffered. The idea of memory loss resulting from psychic distress—as opposed to direct physical injury—had fallen out of vogue. At the heart of the dispute were the false memories of sexual abuse and the "Memory Wars" of the 1980s. A barrage of lawsuits followed the discovery that many of the "repressed" memories had been induced through highly suggestive psychotherapy. Authorities in the field now argued that people were incapable of "rediscovering" memories of traumatic events.

Even more contested was the use of hypnosis to retrieve such memories. The fear was that, through psychoanalysis and hypnosis, the therapist's own imagination guided and suggested the patient's perception, manufacturing memories. The process was similar to what happened when a person was shown photographs or told stories about themselves when they were very young. Eventually, they began to incorporate the image or story as a "memory," forgetting the origins weren't organic.

Piper knew she was on shaky ground. But one thing she'd learned these past two years: when it came to lightning injury, there were no rules.

The particular circumstances surrounding Clay's memory loss—lightning strike followed by the discovery of his wife's brutal murder—complicated matters. It would be impossible to tell if his amnesia had a psychic or organic cause. Piper had come to believe that, in all likelihood, his amnesia was the product of both.

"Your whole body is feeling heavy, so heavy. Your arms, your legs, your eyelids, so heavy. You are incredibly relaxed."

The fact was, Clay needed to remember. The last year, his life had been on hold, his guilt hanging over him. Which was why she now guided him toward an imaginary elevator, asking him to relax. Following her instructions, he would step inside and, starting with one hundred, count each floor backward as he ascended to the top floor.

"Ninety-two, ninety-one…you're very relaxed…ninety."

With each floor, he would continue to feel sleepier, she told him. Once he reached the top floor, the door of the elevator would open onto a beautiful beach.

"You're at the beach. The sun is high overhead, warming you. You can hear the waves crashing on the surf. Can you feel the sand under your feet? You lie down and sink into that warmth."

She watched his breathing, taking him into a deep trance, until finally she thought he was ready.

"Can you hear me, Clay?"

She knew how badly Clay wanted to know the truth about that night, how haunted he'd become by the possibilities. Her own fears hovered there in the room. Clay was part of their lives now, the main instrument in Simon's recovery. And here she was about to discover whom, exactly, she'd brought into their lives.

"Clay?" she prompted.

When he finally spoke, the sound was barely a whisper. "Yes."

"I want to take you back. Do you remember coming to my

house during dinner? Our session was interrupted by my daughter, Mandy. You were seated on the couch."

"Yes." Again, his voice was almost too soft to hear.

"Okay. Now let's go back a little further. The first time we met, over two months ago. You came here to my office."

She was slowly taking him back in time, searching for memories before the accident. She could see him shift on the couch, frowning when she brought him to the time of the trial.

"No matter what you remember, you don't need to be afraid. Nothing can hurt you, do you understand? It's like watching a movie. You're safe."

She had thought about where they should start. She'd read a good part of the court record courtesy of Grace Calderon. Her prior sessions with Clay also guided her. "It's the night of the accident. You're home with Jillian, packing your equipment, getting ready to go out. Jillian is upset."

"We're fighting," he said, his voice low and gruff. "She doesn't think I love her. She says I threw her into another man's arms. She blames me for what happened."

She felt a pang of conscience, familiar with her own complicated past. How easily she could put herself in Clay's situation, wondering how she'd failed in her marriage, angry that anyone—even Piper herself—could blame anyone but Kevin for his affair. But she didn't have the luxury of dissecting her motives now. She shut down that line of thinking, going on instinct.

"You try to convince her that she's wrong," she said, imagining how the conversation might have progressed. "Of course, you love her. She's your wife."

"Yes. But I'm tired. I'm yelling."

"What are you yelling?"

"That I'm sick of the lies. I tell her to go to him. I don't care anymore."

She felt her breath catch in her chest. *I can't do this. I'm too involved.*

"What does Jillian say?" she asked nonetheless.

Even with his eyes closed, the expression changed. She could only term that smile a smirk. "She's in love. She's going to leave me for him."

"Do you believe her?"

"Yes."

"You're angry."

"Very. But I'm also relieved."

He'd never talked about his emotions during their sessions together. He'd always managed to skate over the surface, never delving into what could have been, steering clear of such matters.

"Why are you relieved?" she asked.

"I'm done. I'm so done. I never looked at another woman, I never even thought about cheating on her. You marry someone, it's supposed to be forever."

She could feel the weight of his words. She couldn't have explained it better, knowing only too well about the pain of giving up. *I'm tired...I'm done.*

"How does the argument end?"

"It doesn't. I leave. The storm. I'm going to take photographs out in the Glades."

"What did Jillian say when she saw you were leaving?"

There was a moment of silence. Then he said, "She told me not to bother to come home."

Piper frowned. She could see now why Aidan Parks had been determined to keep Clay off the stand. Not a pretty picture for the defense. "You drive out to Everglades National Park in your Jeep," she said, speeding them forward. "You have your equipment and set up for the shoot. What do you see?"

"I'm standing in the middle of the storm," he said, now deep in a trance. "It's amazing. A perfect night. The sky lights up purple and magenta. It's going to be a great show, a lot of staccato flashes. The branching will be amazing. I'm setting up the camera. I set the focus to infinity, the shutter speed to B, preparing for the next strike."

She could see him visibly relax. He was in his element, more at ease, his face smooth and no longer crimped around the mouth.

"You're taking photographs. Tell me what's happening." She wanted to keep the questions open-ended, at the same time guiding him through the event.

"The storm, it's getting closer. The alarm just went off."

He had talked about an alarm before. She wanted to keep him in the moment, focus there. "What does the alarm sound like?"

"It beeps. Slow and steady, like a heartbeat. It's warning me to pack up. It's not safe. I need to leave."

"And do you leave?" she asked, already knowing the answer.

"No. I stay. I set up for the next shot."

"Why do you ignore the alarm?"

"I don't want to go home."

Because he'd been fighting with Jillian. Piper closed her eyes, the scenario a painful reminder of her own choices the night Kevin had died. "You're worried about Jillian?"

"She's with him. I know she is. I can tell."

That made her pause. "How?"

"The fight. She was arguing with me because she felt guilty."

Piper thought she understood. "Do you think she wanted you to fight for her? Convince her to stay with you? She told you about the other man. Did she want you to beg her to choose your marriage instead?"

"Yes." There was no hesitation.

"But you don't?"

"No. I don't care anymore. Not like before. I thought our love was forever. Now I know it was temporary. For Jillian, those emotions had run their course. We're through."

She thought of delving further into those emotions. It was no simple thing to give up on a marriage. He sounded so final. And yet, she knew that might just be a temporary reaction. He was angry and hurt.

She decided to forge ahead instead. She needed to get them past the storm and closer to the time of the murder.

"You're back in the middle of the storm, Clay. It's coming closer."

"Yes."

"You can hear the alarm."

"Yes."

"What do you see now?"

On the couch, Clay started shaking his head as if struggling with the question. She didn't know what he would be remembering, or why he chose to fight the memory. But she could see he was experiencing discomfort. It was time to bring him back.

"Clay, you're safe. You're back at the beach, heading for the elevator."

He started mumbling softly, still shaking his head. She couldn't understand what he was saying, but clearly, he was in some sort of distress.

"You're feeling more alert now, Clay, slowly rising to the surface of sleep as the elevator descends to the ground floor."

"No!"

Suddenly, his body stiffened and arched on the sofa, then dropped back. His legs began shaking, his heels thumping against the couch in a fast dance.

"When I count to three." Piper stood, for the first time truly alarmed. She tried to keep the panic out of her voice as she stepped to the couch. "You'll wake up refreshed with a sense of well-being. One."

On the couch, his arms began to flail. A guttural sound sputtered from his throat as if he were choking. Again, his back arched, stiffening horribly, then falling back to the couch.

She grabbed Clay by the shoulders, trying to support his body. "Two."

He was fighting her. Piper could taste her fear in her mouth as another convulsion rocked Clay, almost throwing Piper to the ground. The whole episode felt out of control, a nightmare. Nothing like this had ever happened.

"You're completely refreshed now, feeling wide awake. Three."

Suddenly, his whole body dropped onto the sofa, relaxed.

She caught her breath. She thought it was over, that he'd wake up now. That everything would be all right.

"Clay?"

That's when she realized he wasn't breathing.

"Oh, dear God."

Piper straddled his body. She checked for breath and pulse, then administered two puffs of air into his mouth.

"Oh, please. Oh, please, God, no!" she yelled, continuing to administer CPR.

She remembered the night Kevin had died, the ambulance lights flashing against the house. She'd come inside to find the paramedic working on Kevin. Now it was only her fighting for Clay's life.

After fifteen chest compressions, she pinched his nose for mouth-to-mouth. "Wake up!"

Beneath her, she felt Clay suddenly inhale, the sound shockingly loud, a drowning man breaking the surface to grab a much-needed breath of air. He sat forward, elbows to knees, throwing her off balance and to the floor.

He stared at her, obviously confused to see her there. He glanced down at his hand. He opened and closed his fist.

"What happened?" he asked.

She stayed there on the floor. She was still trying to let it all sink in.

She thought she'd lost him. He was dead. *Dear God.*

"Piper?"

She tried to sound calm, disguise her own panic...and exhilaration.

Because she knew. She just knew.

"I think," she told him, "you were just struck by lightning."

26

Clay sat at the table in Piper's kitchen, his hands cupped around a mug of tea. Half an hour had passed since he'd lain lifeless on the couch, Piper fighting to save his life. Now here he was at her table looking as right as rain.

She tried to take in everything that had just happened. The fact that she'd almost lost him.

"Hey," he said.

She smiled, knowing how easily he could read her. "I'm fine."

"Sure. I can see that. You do CPR on your clients every other session, right?"

"Interestingly enough," she told him, keeping her smile, "what happened tonight isn't about me."

He reached across the table. He touched her face, holding her gaze. "You're still sticking to that story, are you?"

He was right, of course. This *was* about her. More precisely, about them. Because she cared about Clay. More than she wanted to admit.

"Clay," she warned.

"Right," he said, dropping his hand from her face. "Change of subject."

He stared down at his cup. It was a mug Mandy had given

Piper for her birthday, a *Far Side* cartoon showing two scientists working over a missile. As one scientist delicately hammered on a nuclear warhead, the other held a brown paper bag next to his ear, ready to pop it.

Piper suddenly felt just like that unsuspecting scientist—only the paper bag had already popped, letting loose all its secrets.

She cared about Clay. God, did she. Tonight, she'd been given a taste of what it would be like to lose him.

"So," he said, forcing an upbeat tone. "Let's stick to the facts, then. Those tests I took. The pen and paper ones that you said would show if I'd been injured. I thought I'd flunked those?"

She nodded. "If the brain is affected by lightning injury, it's like a computer getting short-circuited. There is short-term memory loss, difficulty processing new information. Sometimes victims can't take on more than one task at a time. They're easily distracted."

"I had all that," he said.

"Yes. I know. But you got better. With lightning...some of the most serious symptoms become long-term, growing worse before they get better. If ever."

Again, the not-so-subtle possibility that he was faking reared its ugly head. "I still have trouble sleeping. The headaches, the hand tremors."

"There could be other reasons for that, Clay."

"Like?"

She was trying hard to keep her expression a professional blank slate. "If you saw your wife die. That's an incredibly traumatic event."

He frowned. "I'm not sure I follow you."

"There's a pretty famous case of a man who claimed he couldn't see color. I don't mean he was color-blind, that he couldn't tell the difference between green and red. He saw everything in black and white, like an old movie before color film. He claimed his color sight returned after he'd been struck by lightning. But that kind of color blindness isn't possible—the vision would be so impaired that you'd be legally blind. It turned out his disability was a hysterical complaint caused by a car accident that killed his mother. She died in his arms."

"Hysterical?"

"The mind playing tricks."

He sat back. She could see he didn't like the diagnosis. "As in psychosomatic?" he asked.

"Something like that."

"You think I have hysterical amnesia?" he asked.

"It's difficult to tell, but it is possible that you won't let yourself remember what happened that night."

He pushed the mug away. He stared outside through the window to the backyard. It was the middle of the day. He could hear birds chirping, the sound of cars on the highway that backed up to the neighborhood. They had palm trees in the backyard, the short kind that looked almost prehistoric. He stared down at his hand, opened and closed it.

"You were doing that when you woke up," she said.

"What?"

"Opening and closing your fist like that. You did it right after you woke from hypnosis."

He stared at Piper across the table. She was an incredibly beautiful woman. It's what he'd first noticed about her. Her beauty. At the time, he'd noted her extraordinary looks in a distracted way, like when a person flips through a magazine and sees photographs of models advertising alcohol or cologne.

When he looked at her now, he could still see her beauty.

Only he wasn't the detached observer anymore. There was nothing cool or uninvolved about his feelings for Piper.

"I remembered something else about the night Jillian died," he said. "Something more than hearing the storm alarm. It happened the day I came over and Mandy interrupted us. I didn't tell you. I don't know if I was scared you'd tell me to hit the road, or if I was still dealing with the memory myself. It was like developing film. Suddenly, there's the image. I could see it like a photograph in my head. A memory, I'm pretty sure. My hand holding a gun."

He could see he'd shocked her. It was shocking, the possibility that he'd killed Jillian.

"What else?" she asked.

He shook his head. "Nothing. Nada. Just the damn gun. It was my father's. I kept it in the nightstand drawer. As if I would ever use it, even if someone came sneaking in at night." He shook his head. "I didn't keep it loaded."

That's how he remembered the gun. Buried behind a bunch of crap he kept in the nightstand, the bullets there in a box beside it. He couldn't remember the last time he'd even looked at it.

He glanced at Piper. She was watching him, her eyes not even blinking, as if she were afraid she might miss some clue there on his face.

"I need to know the truth, Piper. I need to find out what happened."

"I understand."

Only she had this blank look on her face, like an animal staring into the headlights of oncoming traffic. "But you don't want to put me under again."

She shook her head. "Not in a million years."

"But that's what I need...if I want to remember."

"I'm not sure what you need."

He smiled.

"What?" she asked.

"Just now, you made it sound as if you wanted to say something like, what I need is a swift kick."

But she didn't get the joke. "You stopped breathing. I thought you were going to die."

"Yeah? Well I didn't, did I?"

She looked away. He could see she would need convincing. But before he could get started, she looked back and just nailed him. "You asked me about Kevin once. If he'd cheated on me. Well, he did. When you were under, when you talked about Jillian. Everything you said." She shook her head. "It sounded so much like my own marriage."

He could sense a change in the energy in the room. This wasn't a therapist talking anymore. Maybe she hadn't played the role for a while. Things had changed between them. Evolved.

"Go on," he told her.

"He was a widower, my husband. After I found out about the other women—and yes, there was more than one—I remember thinking that he'd never cheated on Tami, Mandy's mother, the one great love in his life."

She remembered the night Kevin had died, how she'd thrown the evidence of his infidelity in his face. She'd found a note folded in his coat pocket when she'd taken it to the cleaners. He'd countered with denials. And when that hadn't swayed her, he'd tried the truth, telling her it was just meaningless sex. That he was sorry.

The way he'd said it, she'd known right then and there it hadn't been the first time.

"I knew, I *knew* what he had to live with…the tragedy of that enormous loss. I'm a therapist, for goodness sake. I knew about the demons he was fighting. And still, I couldn't help making the comparison. Why wasn't I enough?"

He could see how upset she was. He hesitated. But then, thinking better of his caution, he reached across the table and took her hand in his.

"The other day when I talked to Simon," she continued, holding on to his hand, for the first time almost clinging to him. "Everything he said, all that stuff about thinking it was his fault. That's how I felt, Clay. I was so angry with Kevin that night. Right before I confronted him, he said he was going back to work. And I knew the truth. He wasn't going to work. He wasn't even on call that night."

He gave her hand a squeeze. "Come on, Piper. Your husband's death. That wasn't your fault—"

She reached up and pressed her fingers to his mouth, shutting off the words. She spoke very carefully. "I left to go to my sister's. I left so he couldn't leave Simon alone at the house to see his lover. And then he was dead."

Everything he was about to say rushed out of his head. He couldn't tell her, *Wow, I don't know how you feel*—he did. He knew exactly how she felt. He couldn't argue she wasn't responsible—it wouldn't matter.

But he could suddenly understand why—despite everything he'd been accused of—she was still willing to help him. And why it scared her to death.

"No. I didn't kill Kevin," she said quietly. "And I don't believe you killed your wife."

That blind faith. He tightened his grip on her hand, not daring to say a word.

"I keep thinking," she said, "I should know somehow. I should be able to see if you're telling me the truth, which is truly ridiculous."

"Those wonderful telepathic powers."

She laughed. "Apparently, they're sketchy at best."

He looked down at her hand in his tanned one, how small and delicate her fingers appeared. Only Piper wasn't delicate—that much he knew. "So what are you afraid of? Do you really think I could die if you hypnotize me again?"

"No."

But then he realized the truth. "You're scared I did it. That somehow those instincts of yours could be off."

"Not even close," she told him. And then, keeping her gaze steady on his, she said, "What I fear most is not your guilt. I worry—I'm terrified—that I'm working under extreme prejudice here. And if we keep at this, I think I could be guiding the outcome."

"How's that?"

She licked her lips. "Leading questions. A blatant desire for your innocence."

She let go of his hand. She reached across the table and cupped his face. "You saved my little boy, Clay. And more. It's not just gratitude that I'm feeling."

He thought back to their discussion earlier, the idea that he'd become some sort of obsession. How in many ways he felt the same. Only he wasn't so sure anymore. What he felt for Piper, it was so real.

"So now what?"

"Now?" She closed her eyes. She let out a deep sigh and dropped her hands. "Now, you go home."

"Just like that?"

The question lingered. He could see something there in her eyes even as he told himself he was wrong. Talk about wishful thinking....

"Yes," she said. "Just like that."

They walked to the door. He tried to imagine what she was thinking. He stopped and Piper turned to him. He was about to say something, reaching for some speck of brilliance to turn this around.

The next thing he knew, he was kissing her.

He felt everything sweep in, all the feelings he'd been holding back. He could feel her do the same. She didn't even hesitate, just leaning into him, letting those emotions consume her.

She stopped, resting her head against his chest. She laughed, the sound a release.

He touched her hair. He'd been thinking about that hair. How soft it would feel.

The look he gave her, he held nothing back.

"Can I see you tonight?" he asked.

"Are you asking me out?"

"Something like that."

"I'm your therapist."

"You're fired."

She shook her head, suddenly serious. "Don't do this. Don't take us there."

"Too late," he said.

And she knew he was right. It was too late for second thoughts.

"Come for dinner," she told him.

He stepped back, smiling, and gave her a salute. Piper watched him walk toward the Jeep parked in front of the house. She'd never seen that look on his face before. She hesitated to interpret it as carefree, as if a great burden had been lifted. She wasn't sure exactly what it might mean.

From where she stood in the doorway, she could still hear him whistling softly.

Clay sat in his car, the keys hanging from the ignition. Piper had already stepped back inside and closed the door. He leaned his head against the headrest.

"Wow."

When Clay had woken up from hypnosis, he'd felt this incredible weight. He hadn't been able to breathe. And the only thing that had eased that feeling of pressure had been seeing Piper right there next to him.

He hadn't wanted to fall in love. He hadn't wanted to invade her life. He would screw it up. Just like Jillian.

But he hadn't stopped that kiss. And now, it was too late. Because he'd want more. He'd want it all.

By the time he'd rolled up the driveway to his house, that all changed.

There was a beehive of activity. Several police cruisers were parked out front, the lights flashing. Men were entering and exiting his house, carting things out like ants at a picnic.

The door had been knocked down. Someone had propped it up against the wall outside. Police were everywhere.

He saw a woman in a suit waiting. He walked toward her, asking, "What's going on?"

The woman, a tall Hispanic with her hair tortured into the compulsory I'm-a-professional twist at the back, stepped toward him.

"It's called knock and notice." She gestured to the broken door. "You weren't home, so we let ourselves in. I'm Grace

Calderon, assistant state attorney. And this," she said, handing him a folded sheet of paper, "is a search warrant. Somehow I think you're familiar with the contents."

"A search warrant for what?"

She cocked her head like a bird, giving him an evaluating look. "Shawna Benet was shot and killed last night not far from here. She received a call right before she died. We traced the number to you. Shocker, I know. In the meantime, where were you last night, Mr. Chase?"

"But that's crazy." He could feel his heart hammering in his chest. "I didn't call her. Last night or any other night, for that matter."

"We've subpoenaed the phone records, so we'll know soon enough."

She stepped in closer. Clay braced himself, knowing there would be more.

"Shawna Benet came to me a couple of weeks back," she told him. "She said she had valuable evidence that would help convict you. Last week, she changed her mind. Now, she's dead. You connect the dots, Mr. Chase." She didn't even blink, a woman comfortable with intimidation. "In the meantime, this isn't an arrest warrant...yet. So let me ask again. Where were you last night between the hours of 10:00 p.m. and midnight?"

He felt the air rush out of his lungs as if he'd been hit in the stomach.

"I was home," he told her.

"Anyone who could vouch for that?"

"No." He wasn't going to involve Piper. No way.

"I repeat. What a shocker."

The woman's phone sounded. She flipped it open, bringing to mind images of Captain Kirk. *Beam me up, Scotty.*

She looked at him, her eyes narrowing. She put the phone away. Whatever she'd just heard, it wasn't happy news.

"Well, it looks like this is your lucky day, Mr. Chase. Burton Ward just vouched for you. Apparently, he's had you followed. The detective he hired corroborates your story. You're off the hook...for the moment."

The assistant state attorney walked back inside, returning to her capacity as supervisor. Clay just stood by as photo equipment and file boxes shuffled past, wondering why the hell they still needed to search his house if he was in the clear.

He thought about what had happened today. Piper's mouth against his, her arms holding him, clinging to him.

Another murder. Another trial. Round and round we go....

His lucky day?

Not hardly, he thought watching the cops continue to rummage through his house.

27

Grace stared at the man seated on the other side of her desk. Now things were getting interesting. And not in a good way.

"You've had a private investigator following your son-in-law since the trial ended in a hung jury?"

"That's right."

Burton Ward wasn't easily intimidated, but he didn't seem particularly happy to be Clayton Chase's alibi either—which of course made him a superior witness. Nothing the defense would like better than to call Burton Ward to the stand on their behalf.

Unfortunately, it wouldn't stop with the trial for Shawna Benet's murder. Burton's testimony spelled disaster all around.

Now that the cat was out of the bag, so to speak—under America's great system of law, Grace would be required to provide the defense with any exculpatory evidence—Burton's little P.I. extravaganza had far-reaching implications for the Chase murder retrial. Grace could practically recite Aidan Parks's examination on direct.

Permission to treat the witness as hostile, your honor.

Permission granted.

Isn't it true, Mr. Ward, that you had a private investigator following your son-in-law?

Yes.

Mr. Ward, wouldn't you characterize your quest to determine your son-in-law's guilt as an undertaking tantamount to the search for the Holy Grail?

No, I would not.

Interesting. But isn't it true, Mr. Ward, that despite the incredible resources at your disposal, at no time have you or your private investigator discovered one scintilla of evidence to show that Clayton Chase is anything other than completely innocent of your daughter's death?

I don't see how a lack of evidence proves—

And isn't it true that your investigator actually found Clayton innocent of another murder the state attorney tried to dump on his doorstep?

In that case, yes, but—

A murder in which, once again, the state attorney's office made a rush to judgment against my client, only to discover that the real perpetrator had slipped through their fingers?

Jesus.

And let's not forget Chris and his little episode out in the Glades. He'd been dead certain Chase wouldn't have left the photo shoot of his own accord.

It didn't sit well with Grace, the possibility that Clayton Chase was innocent. All along, she'd thought she could put it together. Oh sure, she'd kept an open mind, tried to remember all those MLFs nagging her along the way. But the truth was, she'd been hoping for that tidy little bow to wrap around the Jillian Chase murder.

"It must stick in your craw," she said, letting a bit of her own disappointment lead the conversation with Burton, "to be the one to come to the rescue for Clayton."

The big man uncrossed then recrossed his legs. She clocked the Armani suit he wore at about two thousand. Just casual wear for the great Burton Ward.

He shrugged, but didn't quite pull off indifference. "After I learned about Ms. Benet's death, I assumed you might think Clay was involved."

"The last call on her cell phone came from his house."

"That may well be, counselor, but according to my investigator, he didn't make that call," Burton said gesturing to the sheets of paper he'd placed on her desk. "That log gives the precise time of Clay's every movement. At the time of the phone call to Shawna, Clay was sitting outside on his damn veranda, no phone in sight."

She stared at the log provided by Burton's private investigator. "How convenient."

"Ms. Calderon, though it pains me to say it, there is no way Clayton Chase could have killed her."

She leaned back against her chair and dropped her pen to her desk. Not what she wanted to hear. "Your private investigator can account for his movements the *entire* night?"

"Would I be here if he couldn't?" Burton Ward leaned forward, fingers laced together as his elbows rested on the armrests of the chair. "Ms. Calderon, I didn't say Clayton Chase didn't kill my daughter. I just know he didn't kill Shawna Benet."

"I'll need the name of your private investigator."

"I'll have him call you, of course."

He stood, ready to leave, making a show of it. Burton Ward was not a happy camper to be called in like this.

He told her, "I suggest you find out who might have access to Clay's house in the Keys."

Grace frowned, watching Burton Ward walk out.

"I love it when people tell me how to do my job."

Cradling the phone, she punched in his number and waited for him to pick up. "Okay. Here's another fine mess," she told Chris.

Burton walked through the parking lot, anxious to get home. He'd come in at Calderon's request to say exactly what he'd told her office on the phone. Fucking waste of time.

She wondered if it stuck in his craw to be Clay's alibi? Just sitting there, listening to her bullshit questions, he'd wanted to explode out of his chair and scream his rage.

He pushed the unlock button on the remote, watching the Cadillac's lights wink at him. Now more than ever, he realized how naive he'd been. He'd allowed himself to fall into some sort of dream scenario where he played the hero for his baby girl, bringing her killer to justice. Now, he faced quite a different possibility.

Shawna Benet was dead.

After everything they'd lived through the last year—losing Jillian, the trial—had he become the villain in the story? Luring yet another young woman to her death? The fact was, he'd been using Shawna, manipulating her into urging Aidan into dropping Clay's case.

Before getting into the Cadillac, he looked around, trying not to appear too paranoid. By coming forward as the alibi witness, he knew he'd made himself a target...which, of course, was the point.

To bring him out. To force his hand. Burton had to take chances now. It's the only way he could think to get his nemesis to make mistakes.

Because Burton knew who the bad guys were now. There

was no doubt in his mind. And if he was right, he faced a formidable enemy, one the state attorney had no chance of prosecuting successfully.

It would be up to Burton to get justice for his baby. But this time, he wanted to be sure. No more mistakes.

He stepped into the Cadillac and turned into the busy street. He felt off balance, the traffic in front of him swimming, making him blink his eyes and refocus. He tried to catch his breath, feeling a sharp pain in his chest. He wanted to scream.

The last year, he'd been a man with a vision. Clayton Chase was that vision. Clayton the fraud. Clayton the murderer. Now, suddenly, Burton couldn't keep a fix on that target. He felt as if he'd lost his footing, lacked direction.

He hadn't slept last night. After he'd made the call to Calderon's office, as Cowan had instructed, he'd felt depleted. All night, he'd stayed wide awake in his bed. He'd debated getting up and doing work, trying to lose himself in the mountain of documents that had long ago lost its appeal. Instead, he'd just lain there, knowing what else waited for him in the office safe.

He knew Jackie watched him more closely these days, sensing his discontent.

He told himself to settle down. *One day at a time.* He didn't know where this investigation would take him. He only knew he had to follow it through. He shouldn't give in to that nagging voice inside his head telling him he'd screwed up. That it was too late to make good on his promise to his daughter.

He tried not to see his life as some bizarre Greek tragedy, his baby's murder, his just deserts. He focused instead on the road ahead. *Slow down, turn at the corner.* There was still more he could do. Another tack he might take. He couldn't stop until he had the whole story.

At a traffic light, he closed his eyes, reaching for the memory of Jilly Bean. She was smiling, telling him that she loved him.

Behind him, several car horns began to blare.

Burton opened his eyes. He wiped away his tears and pressed on the accelerator. He was moving forward again, focused.

I love you, Daddy.

His work wasn't done here, not by a long shot.

28

When Clay woke up that morning, he imagined his bed an island. As long as he remained here, the sheets kicked to the foot of the bed, the pillow under his head, he would stay afloat. He held out until almost noon.

Surrounding him was the flotsam and jetsam of the search warrant. Drawers lay emptied—files carted out—his laptop in custody. The rooms of his house painted the scene. A woman had died and he was once again under a microscope.

When he finally ventured out of the bedroom to eat, he was happy to see the cops had left the milk and Cocoa Puffs.

Last night, Jillian had crept back into his dreams.

This dream was different, not the horrific nightmare of the past. There'd been no repeat of the murder with Clay finding himself covered in Jillian's blood, holding her as his wife lay dying. The dream had somehow altered.

Jillian was still in his arms on the dining room rug, but she wasn't hurt. There was no blood, at all. Instead, she looked at him like a woman in love, resting in his arms like the old days, soaking it all in with her glorious smile.

All morning he'd been thinking about the dream. How it was like one of those Hollywood rewrites where the test audience thinks the ending too sad or morose and the director goes back to reshoot the final scene. In this version, they were still happy. They were still in love. She reached up and touched his forehead as she always did, pushing his hair back from his face. And just like all the other times, she whispered a single word.

There was no sound to his dream—there never was. No way he could decipher what Jillian wanted him to know...no way to know if she'd spoken at all.

Because it was just a dream.

There was no reason for him to believe that the scene had its genesis in real life. Those images could be the product of imagination rather than memory. The doctors had told him that lightning injury was like brain damage. He might never remember what had really happened.

He finished the cereal and put the dishes in the sink. He walked through his house, feeling like a ghost. He could imagine what he should be feeling, seeing his bookshelves in a jumble, chairs overturned and furniture in disarray. Violated. Angry.

He felt nothing. A ghost.

He made his way to the darkroom. Magazines and books had been knocked off the shelves. The cabinet doors lay open, the contents rifled through. Plastic gallon jugs of chemicals littered the floor.

He remembered one of the cops giving him a look as the man had wandered past carrying off a box brimming with Clay's belongings—all potential evidence now. The policeman had glanced at the broken front door still propped against the wall outside.

He'd told him, "You know, you can sue the city to get that fixed."

Right.

Clay glanced across the room to the locker that had housed his camera collection—*had* being the operative word. They'd forced the doors open, breaking the lock. Half the equipment was missing. Why the cops would take cameras devoid of film was anyone's guess. He wondered about the fine print on the search warrant. *Evidence of foul play and... entertainment?*

He took down the old Pentax, a 35 mm SLR he'd picked up secondhand when he was twelve. It was the first camera he'd bought for himself, saving up money from babysitting and working for his dad on projects around the house. Apparently, the Pentax was decrepit enough not to rouse suspicion. It alone remained with his collection of lenses.

Holding the camera, he wondered about Simon. The excitement on the boy's face when he'd captured lightning in his lens. How it would have felt to help Simon bring those photographs to life here in his darkroom. How that wasn't going to happen now.

Hysterical amnesia. That's what Piper had called his memory loss. He thought hysterical just about covered it. How out-of-control his life had become, the roller coaster of events and the overwhelming emotions.

This morning, he'd tried to remember.

Lying in bed, he'd pressed for a memory, any memory. Piper had made it sound as if the truth were there, just out of reach. He simply chose not to access the information because it was too painful. Hearing her explanation, he'd pretty much thought: *Bullshit.*

It didn't make sense. Not to him. Mind over matter, right? If he focused—if he tried—it should all be there. Instead, the answers felt jammed up inside his skull. Any attempt to press forward brought along a searing headache as reward.

He'd spent the morning trying different tricks. If he relaxed…if he focused on the days leading up to that night. It was like trying to remember where you last left your keys. All he needed to do was retrace his steps, follow the bread crumbs.

Nothing.

He remembered waking up from the hypnosis session to find Piper there with him…remembered that look of discovery on her face. She thought he was in some sort of danger if she took him under again. He had another opinion altogether.

In Clay's opinion, the danger lay in not remembering. Anything that could get him closer to the truth was well worth the risk.

He raised the Pentax to his eye, focused the lens. He pretended to shoot.

"Bang," he said.

The phone rang. He stared at it, remembering what the state attorney had told him. The call to Shawna's cell had originated from this house. He couldn't imagine how that was possible. The only other person who had had a key was Jillian, a key that was now in his possession after her death.

During the trial, he'd learned to lock up after a reporter had sneaked inside to rifle through his papers. There hadn't been any sign of a break-in. He would have noticed. Again, a lesson learned after the harsh spotlight of the media had landed on him.

The phone continued to ring. He walked over and checked the caller-ID display. Piper's number flashed on the LCD screen.

By now, she would have read the story in the papers. Maybe she'd even heard about it on the news late last night.

Once again, he was a person of interest. Clayton Chase, the murderer, under investigation.

She'd want to come forward. Clear up the facts. No way could he be responsible, she'd be thinking. He'd been with her around the same time. And while she'd been long gone at the time of the murder, she couldn't imagine that he'd sneak out after their time together to kill someone. She'd try to vouch for him.

She wouldn't realize how little what she had to say mattered. Not for one minute did he think the search last night had been to satisfy suspicions about Shawna Benet alone. A year later, the state attorney was still searching for the proverbial smoking gun for Jillian's murder.

He sat down in front of the phone, letting it ring. Piper wasn't one to give up easily. She must have kept at it for a good twenty or more rings.

When the phone finally stopped, he thought about the other mental exercise of the morning.

He'd considered confessing to Jillian's murder. Just getting it all over with and giving the state attorney a call to say he did it. In the end, he'd determined confessing might be just as big a cop-out as trying to get away with the crime.

If he hadn't killed Jillian, someone else had. And he owed it to her to find out the truth.

Which led him here. Back to the phone. Ready not to call the state attorney's office but to ring up the one man who just might be his ally in that search.

He picked up the receiver and dialed the private number he had memorized.

Burton answered on the second ring. Apparently, he'd been waiting for his call.

Piper stared down at the document she held in her hands. She felt frozen inside, unable to respond to this attack.

In her head, she wasn't just standing with her feet glued to the floor. In her mind, she ripped the papers in two, righteous indignation perfuming the air as she called her mother-in-law to give her a piece of her mind.

Unfortunately, real life turned out to be a much more placid affair. She had no response, too deep in shock.

Just minutes ago, she'd been focused on a completely different problem: Clay and the murder of Shawna Benet.

She'd read the story in the papers—once again, Clay had been implicated in a crime he couldn't have committed. She'd been on the phone calling him, frustrated when he hadn't picked up. Who in this century still didn't have an answering machine or voice mail?

That's when the doorbell had rung.

She'd hung up the phone to answer the door. A handsome young man had stood before her with a smile. He'd appeared in his early twenties, with dyed black hair gelled into stylish disarray. He'd worn a T-shirt that said Don't Kill the Messenger.

He'd had a package for Piper Jordan. When she'd answered that she was Piper, he'd handed her the paperwork.

She'd been served. By her mother-in-law. Leah was suing for custody of Mandy and Simon.

She still didn't know how to feel. Shocked? Frightened?

"No," she said out loud, crumpling the document in her hand. She felt angry.

Oh, yeah. She was good and pissed.

Piper picked up the phone and called the only other person in this world she could trust. "Crissa?"

She told her sister what had happened. It took Crissa only fifteen minutes to arrive on Piper's doorstep. She didn't want to know how many laws her sister had broken to make that kind of time.

"The bitch!" Crissa's first words as she swept into the house.

Piper followed her big sister into the kitchen, feeling suddenly as if her own personal cavalry had arrived.

"Don't you worry, honey. I have your back." Crissa had her cell phone to her ear, the documents in hand. "Mick Carstairs, please," she said into the phone. She shook her head, flipping to the second page. "This is absolute bullshit."

Something in Piper's chest swelled, then moved up to her throat, making it difficult to swallow.

"Mick." Crissa's voice dropped to dulcet tones. "How are Leslie and the kids? Well, of course, this isn't a social call, darling. Would I ever bother you at work if I weren't in just the very worst way?" She winked at Piper. "Everyone knows who to call when they need a knight in shining armor."

Piper knew Mick and Leslie Carstairs. She'd met them at dinner parties and at barbecues in her sister's backyard. Mick Carstairs had his own law firm, Carstairs and Associates, and a column in the paper. He was also a hired analyst for the local news station, their go-to man whenever some celebrity got in trouble and hit the six o'clock news. He was famous enough to have to make a guest appearance as himself on a nationally televised sitcom. Crissa also happened to be the godmother to his two-year-old son, Nathan.

Piper listened to Crissa break down the issues presented in the document. "I'll have Piper fax it right over, sweetie. I knew you'd take care of me. Tell Leslie I'm still salivating after that salmon recipe she promised. Shame on her for making me wait. Oh, and Mick? You are The Man, baby."

She slapped the cell phone shut in her hand and gave Piper a brilliant smile. "According to your new attorney, Grandma has about a snowball's chance." She picked up a pen and wrote down a number. She ripped off the page with a flourish and handed it to Piper. "Here's his fax number. He's waiting."

Piper took the number, then threw herself into her sister's arms. She didn't say a word, just held on tight.

Her sister whispered, "I know. I know."

Half an hour later, Piper and her sister sat at the table, the proverbial cup of tea steaming before each. The pages had been faxed, an appointment set for consultation, a phone call already logged in to opposing counsel.

Piper watched her sister flipping through one of Mandy's magazines.

"What do you think?" Crissa held up a photograph next to her face. The advertisement showed a model with black hair sporting bright magenta highlights.

Crissa sucked in her cheeks to look model chic. "Is it me?"

"Maybe. If you were going to a costume party."

"Ouch." She glanced at the photograph. "But maybe you're right."

Piper cupped her hands around the mug of tea. She let a few minutes pass.

"You told me to be careful," she said.

Crissa shrugged. "You always follow your heart. It's probably your best and worst quality."

"My heart has been wrong before."

Crissa reached across the table and tipped Piper's head up

to look at her. "Hey. That doesn't mean you're wrong this time, okay?"

"So you don't think I'm exposing my children to criminal elements?" she asked, quoting from the papers she'd been served.

Crissa put down her cup. "You know, there's this new Cuban intern. Sweet girl, really. You'd like her. I'm pretty sure she could put us in touch with someone who does voodoo or Santeria."

"The evil eye?"

"Okay. Let's skip the lightweight stuff. We hire a hit man."

Piper bit her lip. "What if Leah's right?"

"Look. You can second-guess yourself from here to kingdom come—let Witchy-pooh Leah shake your faith. But you believed in this guy way back when."

"Now suddenly you're on his side?"

Crissa leaned back in her chair and took a deep cleansing breath, yoga style. She made some interesting hand gestures around Piper, as if she were checking her aura.

She gave Piper a piercing look as if to say, *puleeze!*

"I know you, Piper. I'm on *your* side. You followed your instincts and they paid off. Big time." She leaned forward, making her point. "Simon. He's back. Your baby boy is talking again."

Piper closed her eyes, knowing her sister was right. The man she knew…the man she was falling in love with…he wouldn't hurt her children. And he didn't kill his wife.

"Honey," her sister said. "The only thing that man is going to do is break your heart."

Piper sighed. "That, I can handle."

The phone rang. "I'll let the machine get it," she said,

knowing it wouldn't be the kids or the attorney. They would have used the home line. This was a business call.

The message machine clicked on. She heard a stranger's voice.

"I'm trying to reach Piper Jordan. My name is Aidan Parks. I would like to speak to you about my client, Clay Chase. It's urgent."

Piper listened as Aidan Parks left a phone number where he could be reached. She could call anytime, day or night.

She stared at her sister across the kitchen table—imagined how she must look. The deer in the headlights.

Clay's attorney wanted to meet.

29

It had been a while since Clay had walked into a library. Maybe as far back as when the local branch had done a retrospective on his work and he'd been invited to the opening. These days, any research he did was online, relying on the convenience of the Internet. Now, God-knows-how-many years later, he'd actually had to look up the address to find the place.

The cops had taken his laptop. And he needed Internet access. The library was the quick and dirty answer.

The topic at issue: dreams and their meaning.

He was a little disappointed to learn that, according to the newest scientific theories, dreams were meaningless brain farts. Chemicals fired signals to the part of the brain controlling higher thought and vision. The cortex then attempted to arrange those signals along with real memories into a story. The resulting chop suey accounted for the strange nature of the images.

As for psychotherapy, the story wasn't much better. There were several schools of thought. Freud and his "free association" interpreted dreams to be the release of repressed elements. Jung picked up the baton and used dreams to achieve psychic equilibrium. According to Jung, dreams were the raw language of the unconscious and woe to the man who ignored his psyche.

And then there were the hocus-pocus theories of the New Age generation. Dreams were considered a supernatural event, a way for those who had "crossed over" to communicate with the living. Grab your crystals and give me an *om!*

He spent most of the afternoon sifting through cyber garbage. An hour into a Web site on the paranormal, he was so frustrated, the crossing over stuff started to make sense.

Why not? He'd been struck by lightning and survived (there was one site dealing exclusively with life-threatening trauma as a trigger to psychic powers). He hadn't been able to focus his camera until Piper had stood as the subject for his lens. Hocus-pocus to the nth degree.

Why not believe that dreams could be some link to loved ones? Why couldn't Jillian reach across that chasm between life and death to reveal to him how she'd died? Why shouldn't dreams be that window, the image of Jillian whispering to him, a key?

Clay pushed away from the cubicle and frowned at the computer screen. "Because it's bullshit," he told himself. And he didn't believe it. Not for one minute.

He wasn't so much a man of science, but he needed something more than what these Web sites offered. Which brought to mind another topic for his research.

He entered Google and typed in: Memory.

He couldn't accept Piper's slam-the-door and throw-away-the-key theories. It didn't make sense that he could hide the truth from himself, amnesia as some sort of protective mechanism. He was living in hell, for God's sake. How much worse could the truth be?

A few hours later, some time after he'd read about "synaptic storage mechanisms" in the brain, he started coming up with his own theory.

What he needed was a trigger—an image, a sound. Like when the vending machine won't give up the goods or your television refuses to show anything but horizontal lines. If he could give himself a swift kick or shake something loose.

What he needed was a mental Heimlich.

He logged off the computer and headed for the door. The trigger, of course, would be critical.

It took him half an hour to get to the flat in South Beach, the home he'd once shared with Jillian. It wasn't the most fashionable address, but Jillian had loved the Art Deco building. She always said the area reminded her of a big box of crayons with all its pastel colors.

He still had a key, but it shocked him when the damn door clicked open. The property had been a gift from Burton to his daughter. He'd thought Burton would have changed the locks by now.

Inside, the place looked eerily the same. Stark. Vacant. A beautiful view, sure, but that was it. He realized the house had always felt empty to him, its postmodern furniture and cream-colored walls giving off a sterile ambience.

Jillian had called the look "clean." She grew up with her mother's passion for gilded Louis XIV and baroque mirrors hearkening back to the Sun King himself. He tried to imagine when that sense of sterility from these rooms had leached into their marriage.

In the dining room, he dropped the key on the table. The Persian rug had been replaced, the floorboards scrubbed clean. The room retained a museum sensibility. He half expected to find Madame Tussaud's-type replicas in wax of himself and Jillian eating dinner.

He pulled out a chair and sat down. He often wondered what was in it for Aidan. In a sense, Clay had taken his girl. And still, Aidan doggedly defended him. Clay knew the trial had made the guy's name; Aidan had practically become a household word overnight. And still, Clay didn't think it was about the money or fame. This was about Jillian, losing her. Somehow thinking that if he could save Clay, he'd be keeping some promise he'd made. Yesterday he'd called, checking in. When Clay had told him about the hypnosis session with Piper, Aidan had gone apoplectic.

He wondered what Aidan would think about what he was doing now.

He stared at the floor, at the exact spot where he'd regained consciousness. He remembered vividly the sight of Jillian, her legs tangled at odd angles, her eyes staring up at him lifelessly—the blood, everywhere. Everything before that moment remained a perfect blank.

This, then, was the door he needed to jar open.

He started with the images from his dream, fixing on the sight of his wife in his arms. He examined the image in his head as he would a photograph he might develop. She was staring up at him, still very much alive.

But now he began to doubt the image that just an hour ago seemed so reliable. It was fading, disappearing into the realm of imagination. A false memory he couldn't trust even as he tried to recreate it.

He stretched out his hand, watching it shake. The tremors made him feel eighty years old.

"Exercise over," he said.

Most people came to South Beach to get away. The place had a hip nickname, SoBe, a sliver of land referred to by many as the American Riviera. Here, movie stars dined and gridlock carried a Latin beat. Here, all of his dreams had come to die.

And he couldn't remember. There was nothing there. Not even a faint shadow of something that he could run after. No hope. No answers.

And so many questions.

He glanced at his watch. He didn't want to be late for his meeting. But he saw he had plenty of time.

He made his way back to the Jeep, hoping that in the end, he could live with whatever happened next.

Burton stared at the gun.

He remembered when he'd bought it. For protection, he'd told Jackie. She hadn't liked knowing it was in the house. For her sake, he'd kept it in the safe.

The 9 mm Beretta felt almost hot in his hands. He passed it back and forth from his left hand to his right, mimicking some bad guy on television.

Jillian had been shot in the back. He'd always hoped she hadn't seen the blow coming, that she hadn't been afraid. He'd wanted that small kindness in the face of tragedy—the miracle that she hadn't suffered.

He'd been the one to identify her at the coroner's. She'd been covered with a sheet that the coroner had demurely folded back to show her beautiful face, only that. There hadn't been a mark on her, no allusion to any pain she might have suffered. She'd looked like a sleeping angel.

But he had nightmares. His little girl begging for her life. His baby gasping for a last breath as her lungs filled with blood.

After those dreams, and there were many, he'd wake up in a cold sweat. He'd come downstairs and opened the safe. He'd take out the gun. Just like now.

He felt his breath choking inside him. He was thinking how he could put an end to all the suffering, both his and his little girl's. The pain would immediately vanish. In his hand, he held instant relief.

He raised both hands, still holding the gun. He could taste the metal in his mouth, could smell it. His finger pressed on the trigger.

With a guttural shout, he threw the gun to the floor.

"Burton?"

Jackie stood at the door dressed in her tennis whites. He looked up quickly, imagined how he must appear to her, caught in the act. He tried to determine how long she'd been standing there. He hadn't expected her home until much later.

"What are you doing, Burton?"

He almost laughed out loud. He wanted to run to his wife and tell her that he didn't know—that maybe he hadn't known for a very long time.

She stepped into the office, usually his private preserve, but his wife wasn't the shy type. He followed her gaze to where the safe lay open. Jackie knew what he kept in that safe. She knew almost everything about him. The family back in Tennessee. The changed name. She even knew about Barrera. But not Lydia.

"Oh, my God, Burton."

Her voice now had the authority it had lacked before. She spotted the gun, walked to where it lay on the floor. She didn't pick it up. Not because she was squeamish. Jackie knew how to shoot.

She just stared at the gun. She didn't look up at him when she whispered, "Don't leave me, Burton. I couldn't bear it."

Burton dropped his head against the back of the chair and closed his eyes. "Honestly, my love. I've been gone for so long now. I thought you'd grown used to it."

He felt his wife's arms close around him. She knelt before him, crying as he embraced her. She wept openly in his arms as he stroked her hair, feeling her release flow over them both.

He knew he'd robbed Jackie of so much with his hatred and his guilt, dragging her into his nightmare because he couldn't let go. Couldn't live in a world without his Jilly Bean.

He looked over her shoulder at the gun on the area rug Jackie had commissioned for this room, some strange geometric design that supposedly complemented the furniture. The gun appeared surrounded by a starburst.

"I'm sorry," he whispered, kissing her hair. "I'm so sorry."

Jackie looked up. She wiped the tears from his eyes with her hands. "Whatever you do, Burton, you remember how much I love you."

She said it like a command, his brave little warrior. He pressed a kiss to her forehead. But Jackie wouldn't know the horrible possibilities he was running from. She thought he was a good husband and father. That he was blameless in their child's death.

He held her tightly, squeezing almost too hard. He knew it must hurt her. She felt so small in his arms.

"Jackie, my love," he whispered in her ear. "I have something to tell you."

30

Piper waited in the Lobby Lounge restaurant at the Ritz-Carlton, staring at the glass of wine on the table before her as if it were a crystal ball. She hadn't touched a drop even though she'd come early to order the drink. She'd wanted to brace herself for the meeting ahead, looking for courage.

Last night, she'd done the same thing, turning to a bottle of Barrilito rum her sister had given her as a Christmas present way back when. She'd downed a shot before bed. It hadn't helped. She hadn't bothered with pills, either. Instead of sleep, she'd spent the night going over all the different scenarios in her head.

He hadn't killed Jillian…he couldn't have. Whatever had happened—it must have been an accident, a mistake. He wasn't a killer. She would have seen something before now, a glimmer of violence, a clue.

But here was Aidan Parks, Clay's attorney—she recognized him from the television coverage during the trial—winding his way past the white-linen covered tables of the Lounge, coming to tell her *You're wrong!*

The blond hostess shrink-wrapped in this season's version of the little black dress—emphasis on little—led the way. Piper hadn't said anything to Clay about the meeting, per Aidan's instructions. She felt strangely disloyal, as if she'd somehow joined in what was looking more and more like a conspiracy against him.

Trust me, we all want what's best for Clay, Aidan had told her over the phone when she'd returned his call yesterday.

It seemed to be a theme in Clay's life, the idea that people needed to step in and take over.

She set aside the wineglass, realizing she didn't need courage. She wasn't looking for strength. What she needed were answers, which was why she'd come despite her misgivings.

"Thank you for meeting with me," he said, sitting down.

The man had dressed in his dapper best, the green linen suit looking crisp and cool on his athletic frame. He appeared calm…as if he hadn't implied on the phone to her that his client was a killer.

But then she imagined that was part of the gig as a criminal attorney. It was all smoke and mirrors, trying to manipulate the people they called the Black Box in the jury stand.

"Would you like something to eat?" he asked, glancing at the wineglass.

"I'm not hungry."

"That's a shame." He handed the menu back to the hostess. "I understand they have a lovely traditional tea here." To the hostess, he said, "Martini, VOX. Two olives, please."

He had very pale eyes and mousy-blond hair. She wondered for a moment if that helped in the courtroom. He was the proverbial blank canvas. He could, she imagined, become whatever was necessary for the moment, from angelic to avuncular—from dogged to sincere.

Apparently, he preferred the direct approach with Piper.

"I think what you're doing is dangerous," he said, not bothering to wait for the martini to jump in.

"I'm not sure I follow," she answered, on the defensive.

He thanked the hostess with a smile as she placed the brimming drink before him. When she turned to leave, he set the napkin and glass just a little to his right, then immediately removed both olives, almost as if he thought they might contaminate the vodka. He set the olives side by side on the napkin next to the glass, lining them up just so. The sequence had the appearance of a ritual. Piper thought, *Classic obsessive-compulsive-disorder behavior.*

He waited, making certain that he had her complete attention. She imagined that stare used to great effect in the courtroom.

"The hypnosis." He shook his head. "Not a good idea."

"Really? And here I thought your degree was in law," she said, hoping she sounded more confident than she felt.

Of course, Clay had discussed their session with his attorney. It only made sense. And still, she felt unsettled, nervous that she hadn't been able to reach Clay since the news reports about Shawna Benet's death.

"Clay needs to remember. I thought hypnosis might help."

Aidan smiled. "I'm only his lawyer. But it hasn't hurt him yet, his lack of memory."

"Maybe not in the courtroom, but in real life?"

He *tsked* softly. "Now isn't that rather naive of you? The courtroom is real life."

"He's haunted by what happened. He wants to know the truth."

"And the truth will set him free?"

This guy was really getting to her. "Something like that, yes."

He leaned forward. Suddenly the energy at the table changed. "Let me tell you something. In Clay's case, the truth is going to put his ass in jail for a very long time. And that would be the good news. Now that there's a possibility of a double murder, he's looking at the death penalty for certain."

"He didn't kill Shawna Benet."

"Really? And you know that because?" He knew she had no answer to his challenge because she'd left the house long before the time of the murder. "I thought as much. Listen to me carefully. I don't plan on repeating myself. Shawna Benet was a personal friend of mine. I feel her loss deeply."

She could hear his voice choke up. For the first time, true emotion clouded those pale eyes.

"After Shawna's death, even I have lost my faith in Clay Chase," he told her. "But I know how to do my job. I don't know what game Burton is playing," he continued, "giving Clay an alibi. Maybe he just wants vigilante justice. He's afraid to take us on in the courtroom again, that Clay will get off. Or more likely, he thinks the prosecution will drop the re-trial if they can get him on Shawna."

"Why are you telling me this?"

He leaned closer over the table, dropping his voice to a whisper. "I know what it's like to get close to your client, Piper. I've known Clay a very long time. He is a very charismatic man." He gave her a chilling smile. "I have a feeling you've crossed ethical lines."

She felt his words like a slap across the face. "That's none of your business."

He nodded, as if he agreed. "But here's the thing. It is. Because I am going to get Clay off."

He had her speechless. She couldn't imagine what he was saying. He believed Clay guilty of both murders and yet, he would defend him? Because it was his job?

Was that what this was all about? she wondered. Making sure that his golden goose—the man who had made Aidan's career—remained innocent in the eyes of the public?

"I'm not planning to stand in your way," she told him.

"Or so you think. The problem being, of course, that you won't be able to help yourself. You want to 'fix' Clay—you're already knee-deep in the process, helping him face his inner demons. But an innocent man doesn't *have* demons. He doesn't admit to having his fingers wrapped around a gun, either."

He smiled, apparently catching an expression of surprise on her face even as she tried to keep from giving herself away.

"Of course, he told me everything," he said.

"He's still not sure what he remembers," she equivocated.

"And you plan on changing that," he said, more than making his point. He paused, giving her a look. "Those ethical lines? Let me tell you something. I've crossed over those lines so many times for Clay, I can't even see a vague outline in the dirt. I plan to do it again."

She shook her head. "Why?"

"Because I can."

And there it was, that narcissism that fueled so many successful men. He had the power. He could do the job. And he would, no matter what he thought about Clay personally.

"No," she said, voicing out loud what she knew in her heart. "You're wrong. He didn't do this."

"Piper, he killed her. He killed Jillian. I can almost prove it."

She felt something heavy rest on her chest. She couldn't quite catch her breath.

"Almost?" She shook her head. "You don't know what happened that night. You can't prove anything."

"Really? You would know better than I how these things

work. Come off it, Ms. Expert Witness, he wasn't hit by lightning. No such thing. What he has is a convenient memory lapse. He can't allow himself to remember, and you damn well know why."

Because he killed his wife.

"These sessions are making him unstable," he continued in the face of her silence. "I think you're pushing him to the brink."

She didn't understand. Then suddenly, she did. "Of murder?"

"Back off, Piper. Before another innocent dies."

He stood, dropping money on the table for the drinks neither had touched.

"Be careful," he told her. "Be very careful. Clayton Chase is not who he appears to be."

Burton asked Clay to meet him at Everglades National Park, at the very spot where Clay had been taking photographs the night of Jillian's murder. Both men stood in the humid heat, Burton looking impossibly cool in a charcoal wool suit. Clay watched as his father-in-law walked around, wondering how this meeting would go.

"So this is where it happened?" Burton asked.

"The lightning strike, yes."

Burton stepped in close. He had both hands in the pockets of his trousers. The posture didn't suit such a powerful man. Clay couldn't remember ever seeing his father-in-law in anything other than Power Mode.

Burton squinted against the sun. "Do you remember any of it?"

Clay shook his head. "I wish to God I could."

Burton kept looking around. Clay imagined he was trying

to give off a sense of the casual. Just the two of them, having a word. Of course, he looked anything but.

"So you don't remember how you drove back to the house?" he asked, still looking around.

It sounded crazy, the idea that he couldn't remember getting in the Jeep and driving home. "That's right. I don't remember."

"As I understand it, the theory goes, you were in some sort of trancelike state after the lightning strike, right? Like a dog who gets hit by a car, you went on instinct, dragging yourself on home." He looked out over the horizon, his back to Clay. "Packed up all your gear, nice and neat—that must have been instinct, too—put everything in the Jeep and drove on back to South Beach."

Burton wasn't even trying for sarcastic. There was no special intonation to his voice. The words themselves did the job.

"I want to remember, Burton," Clay said. "I want to know the truth."

Burton nodded, as if he bought what Clay was saying. But suddenly, he turned.

Clay saw he had a gun in his hand.

"I want to know something, too," Burton asked quietly. "I want to know if she begged you not to kill her. Did you hesitate, at all? Was there a moment when that look of terror in her eyes moved you just a little and made you pause? Or did it happen without thought? A fight maybe? She pushed you to it, throwing her infidelity in your face? She questioned your manhood? She deserved it, goading you into pulling the trigger?"

He spoke with very little emotion. He walked toward Clay, the gun still on him. But up close, Clay could see there was nothing casual about how Burton felt.

"Here we are, Clay, just the two men who loved her most. Was it an accident, a fight that got out of hand? You tell me, and you tell me now. What did you do to my little girl?"

The pain now was coming through, Burton choking on the words. He stood directly before Clay. He pressed the barrel of the gun into Clay's chest.

"Tell me, you *fuck*. Tell me!"

"I don't know," Clay said.

Burton shook his head, smiling but keeping the gun on Clay. "The same old story. 'I don't remember.'"

Burton grabbed Clay in a waltz, the gun still in his hand. He swung them around and around, singing. "I don't remember…I don't remember." He kept them both spinning in his insane waltz. "I don't remember!" Turning and turning as he shouted the words.

When they stopped, it was Clay holding the gun. Now, the barrel pressed against Burton's chest. There were tears in Burton's eyes. He nudged Clay's finger onto the trigger and let go, letting Clay hold the gun on his own.

"Did you know I used to work for Angel Barrera? One of his hired muscle. These were his favorite hunting grounds," Burton said, motioning out toward the mangrove swamps. "Such a simple thing to get rid of a body in the Glades. A gator. A storm. The gun," he whispered, "if it ever surfaced, the cops would trace it back to me."

Burton raised Clay's hand, still holding the gun, and placed it against his own temple. "You could make it look like suicide. I'll leave my hand right here. Powder residue and all that. Just tell me the truth. Please, I'm begging you. It's worth it to me, Clay. Just to know the truth."

"I don't remember—"

"Tell me, dammit! Tell me if you killed her, if you hurt my baby. Just tell me the truth and put me out of my fucking misery!"

"I can't!"

"You owe me that much, you bastard. You tell me. And then you shoot me. Shoot me dead!"

Clay pushed Burton away and dropped the gun. Burton stumbled back, the two men facing each other. He shook his head, took another step back. He held his hands out wide and smiled.

"Shoot me," he whispered, losing his smile. He picked up the gun, and gave it back to Clay. He pressed the weapon into Clay's grip and wrapped Clay's fingers around the butt. "Because I sure as hell can't do it."

Clay looked into Burton's eyes. Jillian had had her father's eyes, a near-blinding sapphire blue. Only Burton's eyes had dimmed with age and despair. Clay saw now something he'd never seen before: the great Burton Ward was begging for his help.

Clay stared at the gun in his hand, about to explain that even now, he couldn't help Burton.

But suddenly, the picture in his head changed. A stab of pain at the back of his head made him stumble. Another blow brought Clay to his knees. He thought for a moment Burton might be responsible. That it had all been a trap. Somehow he'd been struck from behind.

Only Burton was still there, looking at Clay with a puzzled expression.

Clay blinked, trying to clear his vision. That pain again, like a sledgehammer going at his skull from the inside…until he recognized it for what it was. Resistance.

He told himself to relax, to stop fighting the pain. He slowed his breathing, just like Piper had taught him to do. He closed his eyes, falling into that vision hidden in the shadows of his mind. He searched for it, wrestling it out of the darkness, bringing the image into the light. A memory.

Jillian lying on the rug, blood everywhere, the gun in his hand—Jillian smiling, whispering a single word—someone behind him, just out of sight, a dark presence....

Clay dropped the gun. He grabbed the back of his head with both hands and fell forward, experiencing the most excruciating pain. He tried to go deeper, holding on to those images—tried to see who was there in the shadows by the door behind him.

Until suddenly the image vanished.

He tried to catch his breath, the pain ebbing as the memory slipped away. He looked up at Burton. Jillian's father had witnessed the whole thing, was staring at Clay as if trying to understand.

"What just happened?" Burton asked.

Clay sat on the ground. He could feel his heart pounding. He'd gone back to the flat in South Beach looking for a trigger, something to jolt him out of his fog.

Looking back at Burton, he told him the truth. "I think something just got jarred loose."

31

Grace sat in her living room. Photographs and three-by-five cards covered practically every inch of the floor. She'd started on the dining-room table, but the mess had spilled onto the carpet.

Grace had been a debater in high school. She figured that's when the card thing had started, a way to organize her thoughts. Each card had "evidence" summarized in pen. She used different colors to help distinguish the importance of the information and how it might be connected.

The Jillian Ward-Chase murder—those cards alone carried her to the floor—and the killing of Shawna Benet were clearly related. She hoped the cards would tell her how.

She'd been so deep in concentration, she nearly jumped out of her skin when she felt a hand on her shoulder.

"Whoa. Settle down, sport," Chris said when she jumped to her feet.

She thrust her hand out, palm up. "Give."

"What?" he asked, acting confused.

"The key." She gestured to her palm. "Give."

With an exaggerated sigh, Chris reached in his pocket and pulled out his keys. Attached to the chain was a mini Magic 8 Ball—she'd given him that key chain as a joke the day they'd first made love, after he'd claimed to have known through cosmic sources they were fated to be together. Ouch.

He slipped off the apartment key and handed it over. He took her hand in his before she could pull away.

"That's okay, Gracie. You'll always have the key to my heart."

She yanked her hand free. "I'm going to forget you said that."

But before she could step away, he grabbed her other hand and turned it over. As clear as day, a tan line on her ring finger showed where her wedding band used to be.

"Don't worry," she told him. "It will fade."

"Spoken like a true romantic."

"Haven't you heard? Romance is overrated. Now make yourself useful."

She handed him half her stack of cards and continued to place them like puzzle pieces. Eventually he joined her there on the floor.

"Grace?"

"Yes." She reached across to place another three-by-five on an open space.

"What the hell are we doing?"

"We're drawing a picture," she said, continuing what she was doing.

He sat back on his heels. "Visual aids?"

"You have your methods," she said, crawling on her knees to an open corner. "And I have mine."

When all the cards were spread over the floor and table, she stood and walked around her puzzle.

Chris followed. After ten minutes of silence, he asked, "What do you see, Grace?" When she ignored him, focusing, he added, "Because you know what I see? I see squat."

She frowned. "I'm missing something."

Chris shook his head. "You're a stubborn woman."

She was standing over the dining-room table where she'd placed a photograph of Jillian in situ. *Something there...*

"Chris?"

He came to stand behind her. He was tall enough to look over her shoulder at the photographs. "Yeah?"

"Does something in that photograph seem strange to you?"

He shook his head. "Nah. I just see the murder scene."

"You know, when Shawna Benet came to my office, there was something incredibly familiar about her. I couldn't figure out what it was."

"And now?"

She reached across the table to one of the newest photographs. Shawna Benet lay curled on her side, her hand next to her face, palm up. Grace put the photograph next to Jillian's.

"They look alike," she said. "That's why I thought I had met Shawna before. Going over the file, I'd been staring at photographs of Jillian Ward-Chase, dead and alive."

Next to each other, the photographs looked eerily the same. Chris stepped closer.

"Jesus, are they posed?"

"Yes," she answered.

"A serial killer?"

"No," Grace said, cocking her head, seeing the truth. "Just a guilty conscience."

When Clay called, Piper had just arrived home from the Ritz-Carlton. He wanted to talk—something important had come up. But she was still shell-shocked from her meeting with Aidan Parks.

She'd sputtered some excuse about needing more advance notice. To which Clay answered, "Bullshit. What the hell's going on, Piper?"

She'd always been a lousy liar.

By the time he made it to her door half an hour later, she hadn't gotten any better at it.

"I met with Burton. He had a gun," he said, standing on the doorstep. "He asked me if I killed Jillian." He could barely get the words out fast enough, as if he half expected her to slam the door.

"He put the gun in my hand," he continued. "He wanted me... He wanted me to tell him the truth and then he wanted me to shoot him. He said he couldn't do it himself. When he put the gun in my hand, that's when it happened."

He stopped talking, those beautiful eyes just shining with some knowledge.

"What?" she asked, swept up in the story.

"I remembered. Jillian was still alive when I was at the house. She'd been shot and she was in my arms. She was smiling at me, trying to tell me something. And then it just stopped. That's the last thing I remember, Jillian whispering something."

She closed her eyes.

"Piper?"

"Come in," she said.

Piper leaned back against the door as Clay paced in the entry hall. He looked pumped up, telling her about his meeting with Burton. The gun in his hand had triggered the memory, no doubt.

He came to stand before her. Gone was the fear she'd seen sometimes hidden in the twist of his mouth, the confusion about what might have been. The victim had disappeared. He was clear-eyed and ready.

"I need to go under again," he said.

She tried to remind herself that she was a professional. What he was telling her should trigger a comment, a strategy to help him. This wasn't the time to sit in silence.

But the words backed up inside her. In her head, she heard only Aidan's warning.

These sessions are making him unstable…you're pushing him to the brink.

"I can remember now, Piper. With your help."

She looked up. "Is that what you want?" she asked, voicing her own doubts.

Because she thought Aidan might be right. That she was forcing Clay into a crisis neither of them wanted.

"Of course," he said. "Why are you asking me that?"

She didn't know she'd been holding her breath. She didn't want him to remember—she wanted to live, even for just a little longer, in the bliss of ignorance.

She stroked his face. She hadn't understood how dear he'd become. She'd thought herself hardened against this kind of weakness. She had her children. There was no more room in her heart. She couldn't imagine herself in love again.

And still, she lingered, her hand on his face, enjoying just the touch, the sight of him so close.

"Are you sure?" she asked softly. "Are you very sure?"

He frowned, for the first time catching on to her reluctance. He took her hand from his face.

"What's going on?" he asked.

But she shook her head, trying to hold on to her fantasy.

"It might be too soon to go under," she said. "If you just

had this memory. I don't want to put you under and trigger another crisis. Clay, you stopped breathing."

He pulled away. He shook his head.

"Something's wrong."

On so many levels, she realized. With them. With those feelings she'd been nurturing all along despite the very good reasons she had for running scared. With the idea that *they* could happen, that being with him could somehow be okay…that she could fall in love because he wasn't a killer. He just couldn't be.

Only now they had to deal with more than faith. They had to deal with reality. His memory.

"Aidan called me," she said, giving in and telling him the truth.

It took him a minute to realize the significance of that phone call. She could see in his eyes the dawning realization, his body following the motion of his thoughts as he stepped back, away from her. He looked like a man ready to jump out of his skin. He had to move. Do something…instead he just nodded, shoving his hands into the back pockets of his trousers.

He stared at her, unblinking. "He told you I did it? I killed Jillian?"

The question surprised her. "No. No, of course not—"

"Don't lie to me."

For the first time, his tone turned harsh, cutting her off.

"Don't," he said, his voice now softer. He took his hands from his pockets and stepped to her. He placed both hands on her shoulders. "Just don't."

She didn't know how to control what was happening. Nothing about her relationship with Clay approached the professional, Aidan had been right about that much. She'd crossed that tricky ethical line and now she couldn't find her way back.

Once again, he stepped away. "I've known for a long time how Aidan felt. Maybe from the first. You have to understand how Aidan works. He does it all backwards. He puts the case against me together first. Once he knows how to convict me, he figures out how to beat the rap."

The energy was gone from him now. He looked almost casual. "So, do you believe him? Do you think I killed Jillian?"

She walked over to him. She reached up and cupped his face in her hands. He was almost a foot taller than her five feet four inches. His hair, a sun-kissed brown, just touched the collar of his shirt.

He had beautiful eyes. It's what she'd noticed about him from the first. Their color made up of bits of gold and green. And that dimple in his chin. The way he looked at her made everything just disappear.

She found herself pulling him toward her…kissing him.

He didn't stop her. Instead, he grabbed her with both hands and pressed her closer, deepening the kiss. She realized everything her sister had warned her about had come true, that she'd been imagining just this. Clay, a man who survived what her husband could not, was a weakness. A mirage. She wouldn't listen to reason. She couldn't. She'd listen only to her heart.

"This is crazy," she whispered, still kissing him.

"No. This is the first sane thing that's happened to me."

She couldn't disagree. She'd cut herself off from these emotions, and now they overwhelmed her. She couldn't control the need to stay in his arms, her mouth on his, her hands, everywhere, as if she could somehow find the truth with her heart.

When she finally pulled away, she leaned into him, catching her breath. She told him, "No. I don't believe you killed her."

"Then help me remember."

She looked up at him. "I'm scared, Clay."

"Yeah? So am I."

"I know what you want. To clear the slate and start a new life. But what if it doesn't happen like that?" she asked, choking on the words. "What if I hypnotize you, and you stop breathing again?"

"Or something worse?"

Like finding out that her heart was wrong. That Aidan and his theories would all prove to be true.

She felt the emotion welling up inside her, bubbling over until she couldn't control it. She didn't want her doubts. This man had given her back her son.

"What am I supposed to do if I lose you?" she asked.

He smiled and brushed her bangs from her eyes. She knew he loved her. Not even Kevin had managed this much emotion when he'd held her. She wondered suddenly if Kevin had ever truly loved her, the emotions he'd shown so mild compared to what she saw now. Maybe she'd been right all along—you could only love so fearlessly once. For Kevin, that had been Tami. After that, you always hold back, even if just a little. With Clay, she couldn't hold back.

"You're right," he told her, seeing how she felt. "It's too soon."

"You have to give me more time."

"Yeah. I know. Patience. Not my virtue."

"I can't help being scared."

"It's okay." He kissed her again, sweet and light. "It's okay. We'll go slower. There's no rush."

But they both knew that was a lie. They were running out of time.

"I want to help you remember," she said. "I do."

"Shhh." He pulled her to him, her head resting against his chest. He held her tighter.

When he finally pulled away, he kissed her forehead. "I'll call you, okay?"

She nodded. "Okay."

But when he walked out, she knew his departure was not a gentle meeting of the minds. They were both pretending, wanting that fantasy of hope to last just a little longer.

32

Burton waited patiently out on the streets of Miami. He remembered when he'd first come to the city, how the lights and sounds had fascinated him. But the show had gotten old, like one of those video games that at first captivates, but later turns into something rote that no longer satisfies.

He had known Angel Barrera would be here, at the opening for a new restaurant called Latin Infusion owned by a certain actress. Even at seventy-four, Angel wouldn't miss this sort of scene…the place to be seen by those who worried about that sort of thing.

It took a while—imagine, an old piece of shit like Angel out past his bedtime—but Burton was patient. He could wait him out.

Around ten o'clock, Barrera stepped outside with his entourage of men with cell phones and women in furs, ready to hit the evening's next gig. Burton stepped out from the shadows, blocking his path on the sidewalk.

"Angel."

Barrera stopped, suspicion turning to delight when he recognized Burton. The man's bodyguards had already closed in, but he waved them off. The change in expression made Burton the most uneasy. Angel wore the look of a satisfied man.

"I was hoping we could take a ride," Burton said. He gestured over to where his sedan and driver waited.

He watched Barrera's expression change again, this time to wariness.

Barrera stepped closer. "I'll tell you what, Burt. There's my ride over there." He pointed to a stretch Hummer. The driver waited by the opened door.

It was Burton's turn to look satisfied. "Works for me."

Both men walked over to the Hummer and stepped inside. They waited as the car turned into traffic. Angel offered Burton a cigar, which Burton turned down. Angel knew he didn't smoke. Angel took one of the cigars from the gold case and lit up.

Burton watched the lights of SoBe flash by. He was thinking about Jillian. How much she'd liked the nightlife, believing Palm Beach much too subdued for her.

"How's Lydia?" Burton asked.

"Dying," Angel answered. "And taking her sweet time about it."

Burton wasn't surprised by the cruelty in his voice, not after reading the report from his P.I. He hadn't seen Lydia in years, but he had his own way of keeping tabs on her medical condition.

He buried the guilt, knowing he was here with Barrera for a reason, the kind he'd pushed away for far too long. When he'd met Clay out in the Everglades, he'd already received the most damning piece of evidence from the detective he'd hired. A report from an orderly at the hospital that Lydia had confessed her sins to her husband. Burton knew he was Lydia's biggest transgression. Still, he needed this one last meeting to confirm his worst fears.

Perhaps all along he'd known the truth. He wondered if that's why he'd been so damned set on believing Clay had shot Jillian. If Clay wasn't the killer, that left only Burton's wide shoulders to bear the guilt.

"So," Angel asked. "What did you want to talk about?"

"A few years ago, I turned down your offer for the Indian gaming deal."

Angel's eyes lit up. "That's right."

"You said I'd regret it."

He let the words sink in, watching Angel's eyes narrow, his teeth clench on the unlit cigar.

Burton smiled. "Did you make me regret it, Angel?"

He removed the cigar, staring at Burton with a knowing smile. "What are we talking about?"

"My daughter," Burton said with deadly earnest. "We're talking about Jillian."

Angel stared out the window. Impossible to say if he was hiding anything.

"You want to talk about Jillian?" The lights behind Angel flashed by like a movie set. That's what it was like out here in Miami at night, a surreal circus.

Burton took out the paper he carried inside his jacket. He unfolded the page. He'd been doing the same thing over and over since he'd received the evidence from Cowan: unfolding the paper, rereading the orderly's account, putting the paper away again.

"For the longest time," he said, "I never questioned who killed my daughter. I focused on making sure the guilty party paid for her death. But recently, I started thinking about who my real enemy might be. Do you remember that day? How you threatened me and mine?"

He handed Angel the evidence he'd been given.

Burton said, "When my baby died, I think you finally made good on that threat...but for a very different reason."

Angel didn't read the paper. Instead, he crumpled the page into his fist and leaned forward in his seat to whisper, "You want me to tell you how she died? That I or maybe one of my men pulled the trigger? You want me to give you the answers you've been dying to hear for the last year?"

Burton was wrong about Angel not aging. The man looked suddenly very old as he sank into that cobra smile of his.

"Go ahead. Gloat," Burton said, knowing he was on the verge of finding out the truth. "You killed her, didn't you? You want to take credit, don't you? I know you that well, Angel. Come on, man. Don't you want to see me squirm?"

But Angel only deepened his smile around the cigar. "Lydia is dying one day at a time, her strength eaten away by the cancer inside her. I've watched you this past year, Burt. How close you've come to doing the same." He leaned closer. "There's only one thing I can't allow. Disloyalty. After everything I did for you, you son of a bitch. You turned your back on me? I want you to die one day at a time for your sins. Just like Lydia. So no, Burt. I will not answer your question. I won't give you the satisfaction of knowing the truth."

Angel signaled the driver to pull over. The two men watched each other in silence before Burton stepped out.

"Welcome to hell," Angel said, shoving the ball of paper back into the pocket of Burton's jacket. "Have a nice long stay, my friend."

Burton watched the glow of the Hummer's rear lights recede into the night.

* * *

Clay went straight to Aidan's. He knew it was a mistake to blow in there with this much emotion pumping through him. But damned if it didn't feel good.

He drove, fighting the urge to slam his fist onto the steering wheel until he couldn't, then punching the leather-covered plastic, setting off the horn.

Piper thought he'd killed Jillian. Aidan had more or less told her as much.

Well, it's what Clay had been thinking all along, right? Always fearful of the truth. And now when he wanted to find out—know what really happened—she'd lost faith. They both had.

He didn't bother with the doorbell, seeing Aidan's Jaguar in the underground parking lot. Instead, he pounded on the apartment door until it opened. Aidan stood there, a whiskey in his hand and a glassy look in his eyes—until he realized Clay wasn't feeling so friendly.

Clay went straight for Aidan, grabbing the glass he was holding and throwing it to the floor so that the tumbler full of scotch rolled across the carpet, spilling ice and booze. He grabbed Aidan by his silk shirt and slammed him up against the wall.

"I had to tell her," Aidan said, knowing immediately what had brought Clay to his door in such a rage.

"But not me? Keep the poor sick bastard in the dark. But here's the thing, Aidan." He pressed into him, whispering in his ear, "I…always…knew. I could see it in your eyes what you really thought. So now you tell me. Once and for all, we come clean, you and I. Why, Aidan? Why are you so fucking sure I killed Jillian?"

"Don't do this, Clay."

He slammed him against the wall again. Then again. "Tell me, dammit."

With surprising force, Aidan broke Clay's grip and shoved him off. He took a swing at Clay, but Clay ducked, punching his fist into Aidan's stomach and following with a right cross. Aidan crumpled to the floor, holding his head with a soft groan.

Clay waited, standing over him, catching his breath. When he finally could, Aidan rose slowly to his feet until both men stood face-to-face.

"That's not how this works, Clay," he said. "I'm the one who keeps your secrets. That's the only way I know how to do my job."

Clay slammed his fist against the wall, just missing Aidan. "Your secrets are killing me."

"You're wrong. It's what's keeping you alive, buddy. Trust me on that."

Aidan shoved past Clay and opened the door. He stood there, catching his breath. "Go home, Clay. Talk to me in the morning. After you've thought about what it would be like to spend the rest of your life in jail."

Clay came up to Aidan and stopped. He wanted to make sure Aidan understood what he was asking him to do.

"You think you're keeping me out of prison?" Clay shook his head. "Now who's lying to himself?"

He could hear Aidan call out to him as he made his way to the elevator.

"I'm all you have now, Clay. You just remember that tomorrow morning when the world makes sense again. I'm all you have, dammit!"

33

Clay wasn't sure what he'd expected. Had he really bought into some fairy-tale ending where Piper would proclaim her love and together they would discover his innocence? Did he believe that the life he'd once been so happy to throw away could now become sacred again?

No. Nothing that simple. He'd taken the fantasy even farther, he realized, believing he could step in to be a father to her children…that they might even have a child of their own. He'd clear his name and cleanse his conscience in one fell swoop and he and Piper would live happily ever after.

A nice dream, that. Only, it wasn't going to come true. Not by a long shot.

He parked the car on the access road. He grabbed his old Pentax from the front passenger seat and headed into the park.

He didn't stop to think about what he was doing—he tried to go on automatic, hoping to plug into some part of his brain that wouldn't put up roadblocks. It had happened here before, with Burton and the gun. Damned if he wouldn't make it happen again.

It was just after dusk. He set up the tripod, screwed the camera in place. He took a breath and stepped back, the cable release in his hand.

He shut his eyes and focused on that night. He didn't adjust the aperture—he didn't open his eyes. He just tried to remember, going back to the moment when lightning had split the sky.

He wasn't sure if he had it right, but he found himself ignoring his shaking hands and intermittently pushing the shutter button on the cable release, waiting a few seconds, then letting go. He was following the same instructions he'd given Simon. *Count to five, release*....

It wasn't long before he had established a rhythm of sorts. He kept his eyes closed as he shot the entire roll. He wondered how much of his inability to use his camera stemmed from sheer stubbornness. He'd always been a perfectionist; he hadn't wanted to settle for snapping shoddy photographs with shaking hands. He'd wanted it all back, every bit. No compromise. But he'd learned a thing or two from Simon, a boy willing to struggle with speech that had once been perfect and fluid. Now, it was Clay's turn.

He never opened his eyes. He just held the cable release like some stupid lifeline, taking timed exposures of the evening sky.

When he finished, he packed up and drove home. In the darkroom, he developed the photographs with new chemicals he'd purchased earlier in the day at one of his old haunts, a camera shop in town. The clerk had practically fallen over himself once he'd figured out who Clay was. Difficult to know what made him more famous in professional circles these days—his past work or the headlines.

He hung the proofs on the drying line. It didn't matter what the photographs showed, just the sequence of events. Piper and her hypnosis session had started the process. Burton had egged Clay along, confronting him in the Glades. Now, Clay hoped to push himself further out of the mental fog that had plagued him the last year. He knew that since the night he'd woken to find his wife's blood on his hands, he'd felt asleep.

Time to wake up. Hard and fast.

At eleven o'clock at night, the doorbell rang. He was in the darkroom, drinking a beer. He'd been staring at the images he'd developed, trying to figure out which could help him most. The doorbell rang again, insistent.

He put down his beer and left the darkroom reluctantly— until the front door opened like a magic curtain to reveal Piper.

Her hair was wet, as if she'd just stepped out of the shower. She had a trench coat clutched around her even though there wasn't a cloud in the sky. She wasn't wearing makeup.

She'd never looked more beautiful.

"I'm sorry," she said.

He leaned against the door, enjoying the sight of her. She'd always seemed tiny to him. A woman he could wrap up in his arms and she'd disappear there.

"I lost faith," she said. "I shouldn't have done that."

A rush of emotion filled him, grabbing him by the throat. He couldn't catch his breath, he felt so much.

"I won't do that again," she told him.

Once again, that face of hers told the story. Here was a woman whose faith couldn't be shaken. Everyone else might look at the evidence and point their finger, but not Piper. She'd judge him with only her heart and see everything he'd kept hidden. His fears and desires.

"Clay?"

She took a step toward him, then another. He didn't let her

take the rest, reaching for her instead. He cupped her face in his hands, holding her face up to his.

Looking into her eyes, he felt shaken to his core, realizing at that moment what it was he'd seen in his camera lens when he'd taken those photographs. He would never be just a project for Piper, something to be discarded and replaced. She could never hold back, even now, risking everything by coming here. In her eyes, he saw what he didn't deserve but wanted so desperately.

"Clay, it's all right," she whispered, seeing his doubts, conquering them.

He swept her up into his arms and kissed her. She kissed him back with the same passion he felt burning him up. It didn't take long to make their way through the living room, dropping clothes along the way. By the time they reached the bedroom, he couldn't imagine stopping.

He realized he'd been dreaming of just this. He'd visualized how she would look and feel naked in his arms. That her breasts would be this perfect...her waist impossibly small. Her skin tasted and smelled like vanilla.

Only, none of those visions included Piper crying...which was what she was doing as she lay alongside him on the bed.

He sat up and pulled her into his arms. He stroked her hair as he held her, letting her cry.

"Hey." He kissed her head. "It's okay. We don't have to do anything. Just let me hold you a little longer, okay?"

She raised her head to look at him. Slowly, she pressed her palm to his chest, where his heart beat fast and hard.

"I don't know if I can do this," she told him. "I don't know if I can fall in love again."

He smiled and turned her so that she lay beneath him. He settled over her, holding her head in his hands.

"The not falling in love part?" he said. "Too late for me."

She looked questioningly into his eyes. He hoped she could see everything he felt. She was a woman he wanted beyond what was rational. He knew all about those deadly impulses. His desire for her wouldn't show caution. It wouldn't keep her safe.

"I haven't made love to a man since my husband died."

"Are you afraid?"

"Not about that, no."

"What is it then?"

"What I fear is something really small, and stupid, and petty. That you'll wake up tomorrow and you'll feel different," she told him. "That it won't last."

He took her hand in his and placed it on his heart again. He kissed her softly.

He told her, "I'm not going to feel different. I'm never going to feel different."

She nodded, biting her lip. "Well," she said, managing a teary smile. "That's good to know."

They made love as if there had never been a past. They were only in this moment. There would be no one whispering in her ear of the danger. No rational thought whatsoever. There was only the touch of her hand, a kiss on her mouth…the endless joy and abandon of being together as man and woman.

"Was this a mistake?" she asked afterward.

He didn't answer right away. "You're talking to a man who has nothing to lose," he said finally, telling her the truth. "Things stopped mattering long ago. If I slept in late, if I drank too much." He turned on his side to face her. "Now, suddenly, everything matters."

"Ditto," she said, reaching for him, starting all over again.

They disappeared together into the fantasy, the idea that they could make love and be together without regrets. They both knew reality would come knocking soon enough.

An hour later, she stood beside him at the kitchen table, wearing only one of his shirts. They were staring down at the photographs he'd spread out on the table.

"Here," he said, pointing to one eight-by-ten. "That's what I remember best. That precise moment in the sky. After that…nothing."

"Then focus there," she said.

"I can't. I tried," he said, shoving his hands through his hair.

"You won't let yourself remember."

"My mind protecting me from the truth because I killed her?" He shook his head. "I don't buy it."

"Or watched her die. Anything traumatic enough to make you want to protect yourself from those memories."

"Even if your theory is true, there has to be a way to change what's inside my head. I can't just *not* remember." He sat down at the table. "How do I get it back? How do I break down that wall inside?"

She took his face in her hands and turned it to hers. She kissed him on the mouth, giving him everything.

"How do you remember?" she said. "We both stop being afraid, that's how."

He closed his eyes and pulled her onto his lap, thinking: *No truer words.*

34

Grace opened the door to let Chris into the Chase pied-à-terre in SoBe. A year ago, this place had been blocked off with police tape as crime-scene technicians scoured the rooms for evidence. Tonight, you'd never know anyone had been killed in these posh surroundings.

With Jackie Ward's help, Grace had tracked down Burton Ward on his cell phone. Luckily, he had been in the area and agreed to meet Grace at the flat with his key despite the late hour. She promised to call Burton if she discovered anything—any little thing—which was basically the only way she could get rid of the man. Chris had told her he had an errand to run. He'd catch up with her here.

"About time," she told Chris, shutting the door behind him.

"Hey. I was hungry."

She rolled her eyes. But she was happy to have his help, so she didn't push.

She took Chris into the dining room. She'd set up the chairs to look just like the photographs taken of the crime scene. It was a shot in the dark to enlist Chris for one of his reenactments, but her puzzle pieces still weren't coming together. Time to do it his way.

"All right, reenactment boy," she said. "How do we start?"

Chris looked around the room. "Hey, Grace. We should really get a place like this, you know? Nice view, furniture you never want to use. What do you say? You got a couple of million socked away?"

"Chris."

"I'm on it."

He began by studying the crime-scene photos that were spread out on the dining-room table. Grace waited, knowing Chris would take his time.

"Okay," he said when he was ready. "Tell me what you got."

"Well, I called Donnie Lincoln—because you were taking your sweet time getting here."

"And?" Chris asked.

She pointed out the photograph of Jillian Ward-Chase. It was a close up of her hand. "You see that? That's blood. Donnie ran tests, of course. Clayton Chase's blood. From a cut he'd sustained on his forehead."

He nodded. "Okay. You're the vic. Get on the floor."

They spent a good ten minutes talking about blood splatter and other evidence, trying to get it just right. Grace was lying on the floor. Her hand rested next to her face, palm up, just like Jillian in the photographs. Chris knelt down beside her.

"So, she bled out here on the carpet. Chase was covered with her blood." There were, of course, detailed accounts of the blood on his clothes, including photographs. Chris stopped to think about it.

"Here." He pulled Grace onto his lap, drawing her tenderly toward him.

"Don't get any ideas," she said, because she could feel her own heart racing.

"I'm a complete professional. Now focus. Given the blood

on his pants and shirt, he was probably holding her up like this," Chris said.

He closed his eyes. She could see that he was thinking about something, digging deep into his Ouija-board powers of detection. He opened his eyes and frowned.

"You said he had a cut on his forehead?"

"That's right," she answered.

"And the blood was on the tips of the vic's fingers. On her right hand? Only on the tips?"

"Correct. That's how it is in the photo."

"No other blood from Chase on her whatsoever?"

"Nada," she said. God, she loved working with him. And living with him. *Damn.*

He gave that beautiful smile again. "Grace, brush the fingertips of your hand on my forehead, like maybe you're checking to see if I'm hurt or something?"

The puzzle pieces snapped together in her head. "Why would she do that, Chris? I read the record, the testimony of all the witnesses. Jillian Ward-Chase was no pansy. She was a tough businesswoman who gave as good as she got," she said, doing what Chris always did, putting herself in the victim's place. "Why would she tenderly wipe away the blood of the man who just shot her?"

"She wouldn't."

"If she hit him, or pushed him away…"

"It would have been different," Chris finished for her. "There wouldn't have been just that tiny bit of blood on her fingertips."

Grace sat up, getting the whole picture. "Jesus. And Donnie knew it. But somehow he convinced himself he was wrong. Some other story could explain that blood on her fingertips, one that didn't mess with his theory of the case."

She looked up at her still-husband admiringly. This is what he did so successfully—reenacted the crime while taking on the point of view of the characters involved. Just now, putting herself in Jillian's place, she'd felt flooded by a powerful sensation of discovery. And all these years she'd pooh-poohed his methods.

"Hey," he said, reading her. "It just takes a leap of faith."

She could see he wasn't talking about the reenactment anymore. She stood, not having the luxury of getting off topic. They already had two women dead. And she was beginning to think it might not stop there, not if someone was trying to frame Chase.

She gathered up the photographs and stuffed them into the file. "At a minimum, we had an obligation to reveal those test results. Instead, Donnie buried them."

Chris stood by, giving her some space. "Donnie Lincoln stacking the deck? Say it ain't so."

"Exactly."

Her husband looked at her, giving her that smile that had gotten her into so much trouble the last four years. Time hadn't diminished its effect.

"Did I ever tell you how sexy you are when you're right?" he asked.

"Well, darling," she said, tempting fate as she leaned closer, "I'm about to get a whole lot sexier."

"How's that?" he asked, inching in but letting her make the call.

"Shawna Benet. I'm betting there's something there in the past with Clayton Chase. Whoever is setting him up for her murder knows what it is. And I'm thinking either Burton Ward or his private investigator knows more than he's letting on."

She gave him a quick peck on the cheek and smiled as she dialed up Burton's cell on hers.

"Mr. Ward? I think it's time we talk about Shawna Benet."

We stop being afraid....

Clay stared at his hand, watching it begin to tremble. *Stop being afraid.* He focused there, on his hand, willing it to stop shaking.

"Dammit," he said, making a fist.

He'd sent Piper home, assuring her that he'd come to see her first thing in the morning. They'd shared a tender kiss good-night. Only, after she'd left, the doubts had started pouring in.

What the hell did he think he was doing, falling in love with Piper? Who did he think he was, giving her hope? She had no idea what she was getting into. They were both pretending he was one of the good guys, doing the ostrich thing.

But the fact was, he'd do it all again. So he told himself to skip the mea culpas and get back on course.

He was back sitting at the kitchen table, looking at the photographs he'd developed. He'd been thinking about the last few months. Since the trial, everything had changed. He'd been waking up from a deep sleep, trying somehow to reach back to that terrible night and make things right. That's why he'd gone to Piper in the first place. Why he'd raged at Aidan, and had begged Piper to help him.

But the thing was, he was just asking people to do the job for him. He was standing on the side of the road with a flat tire, waiting for some good Samaritan to pull over and lend a hand. What he needed to do was grab the crowbar himself and get started. From what he'd read on the Internet, that's how this memory thing worked. It was up to him.

He stared at one of the photographs he'd taken at the Glades, the one that reminded him of the night Jillian had died. He took a deep breath, wondering if he had the courage to discover the truth.

He held a hand out. He smiled.

Steady as a rock.

35

The phone rang at her bedside. Piper woke instantly, that reflex of the dreaded middle-of-the-night phone call releasing its hair trigger.

Recognizing Clay's phone number on the caller-ID display, she picked up. "Hello?"

"I remembered," he said.

"Clay?" She was confused for a moment, his voice sounded strange, not like Clay at all.

"Meet me in the Glades." He gave the directions, sounding out of breath. "Do you know where that is?"

"Yes, but—"

"Be there, please."

He hung up.

She stared at the phone, her heart thumping in her chest. She was barely awake. She couldn't understand the urgency in his voice. It seemed so out of context.

And then, she did.

I remembered.

She jumped out of bed and dressed. She woke Mandy to let her know where she was going and how long she might be. She told her she'd have her cell phone on her at all times and that Mandy should call her if anything went wrong at home. She walked around as if in a dream, her mind hardly able to catch up with her next move.

I remembered. Such simple words that left so much unsaid.

In her experience, people didn't dive into accepting responsibility. They tiptoed into their guilt with simple statements. Later came the elaboration. The process was like peeling an onion one layer at a time...until the mind could accept the reality of what lay inside.

Driving down the empty streets, she realized she feared the worst had happened. That Clay had discovered he was responsible somehow for his wife's death—and he'd just remembered the grisly details.

Clay steadied his breathing, counting as he inhaled and exhaled. He clenched and relaxed his fists. It took a while before he thought he was ready.

He closed his eyes, trying to visualize Jillian.

His wife had been a striking beauty, the kind of woman who could walk into a room and cause a sensation. She'd loved fashion. But most of all, she'd loved the attention her money and breeding attracted. Her charm and connections had made the gallery. And him.

He pictured her now, imagining that strength. His wife had not been a woman to give up without a fight.

He could see her in his arms. Only now, that image was no longer dreamlike. It felt solid, a memory he'd reached for by focusing on his photographs, relaxing into a state that allowed him to move back in time to the night she'd died.

It wasn't so much self-hypnosis—there was too much effort involved, too much direction on his part, for this to be anything other than an act of will. To him, the key had been in the sequence of photographs he'd taken earlier, the sheer act of walking through each step in his mind.

When he reached that wall when everything disappeared into pain, he deepened his breathing. He pushed past the headache. He tried to imagine how he might have proceeded that night, thinking carefully about the next step.

He would have packed up his gear and driven himself home. *That's right, focus there.* He made up each step until he could pick up the thread to the images in his dream, realizing for the first time that he wasn't dreaming, after all. He was, in fact, remembering.

The whole thing felt different. The pain was there, yes, that sledgehammer having a go at the back of his head...but at some point the movie in his head had the sense of the familiar. It was like that sensation when you have a word on the tip of your tongue, and suddenly, it's there. A curtain parts. A certain word, a particular image, is revealed. You remember.

She was in his arms. He was covered in her blood, but her eyes were open and she was still very much alive. But he could see she was slipping away, her breath shallow and rough. She whispered something, reached for him until he drew closer...a woman who refused to die.

Until she named her killer.

He sat up, realizing what it was Jillian had been trying to tell him all along.

"Dammit."

He picked up the phone to call Piper. It was the middle of the night, but he knew this was important.

Only, he was too late. Mandy picked up and told him Piper was driving out to meet with him.

When he'd never called her at all.

36

Piper pulled up behind the SUV on the access road. She opened the car door, expecting to see Clay, even though she didn't recognize the car. There was no one else out here and she knew she'd followed his directions precisely.

But the man who stepped out from behind the shadows of the SUV wasn't Clay.

"Aidan," she said, moving toward him. "What are you doing here?"

But then she understood. That strange urgency in his voice on the phone that hadn't sounded like Clay, at all.

Because it hadn't been Clay.

He lifted his hand to reveal the gun he was holding. "Turn off your headlights."

When she did as she was told, he pointed the flashlight in his other hand toward a path heading into the swamps. "Over there."

Her heart pounded so loudly in her ears, she had a hard time hearing him. But the gun waving her toward the clearing was obvious enough.

"Move," he said.

She took a step forward, into the dark. He pointed the flashlight ahead, making it possible for her to watch only one step at a time as she crept past the foliage ahead. They were far off the beaten track. She couldn't even hear the traffic from the highway.

"Why are you doing this?" she asked, still moving ahead.

"You went to see him. You stayed late," he said, letting her know she'd been followed. "You weren't going to stop. You would have kept helping him. Eventually, he would have remembered."

He pushed her forward, forcing her farther up the path spotlighted by the flashlight. With each step, she started making the connections. Aidan, the attorney trying to get his client off, wouldn't go so far as to hold a gun on the woman who might change his client's fate. This was about Aidan, the man. What he might have done.

"You killed Jillian," she said, turning to face him. Once they reached the swamps, she didn't want to think about her chances of getting out of this alive.

He shone the flashlight in her face, blinding her. She raised her hand to try to block the light.

"I loved Jillian," he said, emotion flooding his voice. "She meant everything to me. I would never have hurt her if I'd had a choice."

She took a deep breath, telling herself to calm down. *Think, Piper!* This was Jillian's mystery lover, the man whose child she'd carried. All along, it had been Aidan.

"It must have been horrible," she said, remembering Clay's belief that Jillian had been killed by her lover. "To watch the woman you love die."

Much of his face lay in shadows, but what she could see of him showed crippling emotion. Aidan Parks loved Jillian Ward-Chase. And he'd killed her.

"It was supposed to be Clay," he whispered. "Angel never said anything about Jillian."

"Angel Barrera?" she asked, knowing Aidan's connection to the crime boss.

"He played on my vanity, offered me a position. Angel knew my story, how Burton had turned against me for Clay. And Angel needed something from me."

"He used you," she said, trying to encourage him to keep talking.

She had no idea what Mandy would do if Piper failed to return within the time she'd given. Piper's cell phone was back in the car in her purse. If Mandy tried to get in touch, she might get worried. Might even call Clay or the police. She needed to stall.

"He said he knew what it was like to get screwed over by Burton Ward." His voice cracked, emotion overwhelming him. "He'd just learned his wife had had an affair with Burton way back when. Apparently Burton wanted out of Angel's little enterprise and begged Angel's wife to intercede. Once Lydia got Angel off Burton's back, he dropped her. All along, he'd been using her. Of course, she couldn't come clean to her husband, not back then. Now that she's dying of cancer, she told him everything. She wanted to die with a clear conscience."

"He preyed on your sympathies. Burton used you both."

"Did you know Jillian and I were engaged? When she left me for Clay, I asked Burton to talk to her. One word—just one word from her father—and she would have married me. That's the way those two were. Thick as thieves." He brushed away tears with one arm, careful to keep the gun on her. "He wanted Clay to take my place." He shook his head as if in disbelief. "Clay didn't even love her."

"Not like you."

"God, that last year. I could see how miserable she was. A woman like Jillian needs to be cherished. She needs to be the center of attention. Always." He smiled, remembering. "So I saw my chance."

"She was going to leave Clay for you. She was having your baby."

Again he choked up. She could see such pain on his face.

She realized now why Aidan had defended Clay so vigorously. In his mind, he'd connected Clay's defense with his absolution for Jillian's death. He claimed to be helping Clay for Jillian's sake, but it was his own guilty conscience at work. "Angel found out we were seeing each other. He wanted to help...because of what Burton had done to him. I thought...I thought I could trust him. God, I actually believed him."

"Of course, you did," she said, sounding sympathetic. "And that's when it all went wrong," she said, knowing what came next.

"He wasn't trying to kill Clay. He wanted Jillian dead. Because she was Burton's heart."

He started crying openly then. She knew what he was doing, the release the confession would grant him. To his mind, it wouldn't matter what she knew. She wasn't walking out of here alive.

"Angel had one of his men out at the Glades keeping an eye on Clay," he continued. "When he was struck by lightning, the guy called Angel. He saw an opportunity."

Suddenly, the events of the night came into focus. "Angel's men brought Clay back to South Beach."

He nodded. "Clay was out cold from the strike. A couple of Angel's goons put him in the trunk of their car. They packed up his gear, got rid of the film in the camera, so there wouldn't be any evidence that he'd actually been there, and they drove Clay's Jeep back to the house."

He kept the gun on her, but his hands were shaking. She tried to come up with some plan, some way to divert his attention and disappear into the swamp.

"Don't," he said, steadying the gun, guessing her intent. He motioned ahead. "We're wasting time. Keep moving."

She wasn't sure how long they'd been talking. She tried to think of something more to do or say. This is what she was trained to do: get people to open up, to talk even when they were unwilling. "This wasn't your fault. You could still talk to the authorities. He tricked you—he forced your hand."

"Just keep walking."

But she had to press her point. "At the very least, tell me how she died. I know you didn't want to kill her. How did it happen, Aidan?"

He shoved her from behind. She landed on the marshy ground in a clearing. She stared up to see him standing over her, the light from the full moon shining on his face. He didn't look like a killer. He looked horrified, as if he, too, couldn't quite believe what he was doing. And still, the fact that he was scared or reluctant didn't make him any less dangerous.

"He put the gun in my hand—Clay's gun," he said. He dropped the flashlight and shoved the weapon into his hand as if reenacting the moment. "He had a gun to my *head*. I was so scared. I tried to talk him out of it. And Jillian. Dear God, Jillian."

"He made you choose," she said, hearing the horror in his voice.

"I was a coward. I picked my life over hers."

She shook her head. "No. He would have killed you both. He would never have let Jillian live. You said it yourself—Angel wanted to hurt Burton by killing the one person he loved most."

He watched her more carefully now. He crouched down beside her. She forced herself to hold still, not inch away.

"Angel wanted to hurt Burton," he said, his eyes intent. "Just as much as Burton had hurt him."

"That's why you helped Clay," she said, trying not to sound out of breath. She needed to keep playing on the inevitable human desire to confess and seek absolution. She had to keep him talking. "Because in the end, he was the only one you could help."

"I spent the last year of my life trying to keep his miserable ass out of jail."

"For Jillian."

He nodded. "She was still alive when he regained consciousness. She reached up and touched his face, real tender like. She whispered something to him. I couldn't hear what she said, but I knew in that instant she regretted our affair. That she loved Clay. I wanted to save him for Jillian. But then he started to remember."

She didn't say anything, knowing what he was thinking: Because of her.

"Shawna saw everything," he said. "She was always following Jillian around. That's right," he said, guessing what she'd just figured out. "Shawna was blackmailing me. She wouldn't stop until she had *everything* Jillian had—and I wasn't enough. She wanted Burton's money, too. If I saved Clay, that wasn't going to happen. But if Clay went down for Jillian's murder, Burton would turn to me, give me everything that once would have gone to Jillian. Or so Shawna thought."

"But the call to Shawna came from Clay's house," she said, remembering the information that had been leaked to the papers.

"Just like tonight," he said. "I called you from Clay's house out in Tavernier. Jillian gave me a key. We used to meet there, her own little 'take that' to Clay. Clay was in the kitchen when I called you, looking over his photographs, still trying to remember. The first time, when I called Shawna, you'd just left. Clay was sitting outside. Tonight, I took my chance, sneaking in when he wasn't paying attention."

She had the sense that she was teetering on a precipice. He wouldn't want to kill her. There was no gun to his head now, no threats of blackmail. She would be his first cold-blooded killing. "Don't do this," she pleaded as he checked the gun again. "Please, I won't tell anyone. I have children. Their father is dead. I'm all they have. I'll keep my silence, I swear."

But he shook his head. "I told you not to help him remember."

He raised the gun, ready to fire.

Clay drove into the Glades, hoping that Mandy was right, that her mother had gone back to where it all started.

He found her car first…parked right behind Aidan's.

His heart stopped in his chest as he put together what was going on. Aidan had lured her here, making her believe it was Clay she was meeting. He would kill her. Just like he'd killed Jillian and Shawna.

He parked and headed toward the Glades, following the path, seeing the footprints there in the dirt. From the clearing ahead, he heard voices.

Piper was pleading for her life.

Immediately, he dove past the growth. He raised his hands in the air as Aidan turned to point the gun at Clay. He made sure to keep his distance from Piper, giving Aidan two targets.

"Dammit. You called him before you came," Aidan said, pointing the gun at Piper.

"Don't be stupid, Aidan. Would she have walked out here if she thought she wasn't meeting me? I remembered, Aidan. That night she died, Jillian whispered your name to me," Clay said, stepping closer. "She named her killer."

Aidan tracked him with the gun as Clay circled him. At the same time, Aidan kept glancing back at Piper, letting her know that she was still a target.

"This last year," Clay said, trying to buy some time. "I could never figure out why you were helping me." He'd put a call in to the police, for whatever good it would do him. He was pretty sure no one believed him. And to Burton. Of all people, Burton should know the truth. "I thought it was for Jillian. To try to keep a piece of her alive. Jesus Christ, Aidan. You killed Jillian."

"It *was* for Jillian. Don't get sanctimonious on me. I could have let you take the blame, Clay. Angel framed you beautifully," he said, wielding the gun back and forth between Clay and Piper. "The gun had your prints on it—it was registered to your father. I dropped it on the floor the minute I shot her. When you came to, you picked it up, held there in your hand. But I promised myself I wouldn't let you take the fall. Angel tried to muscle me into letting you, just like Burton."

Clay could hear Aidan choking on his words, the tears there in his voice as he circled closer. "Do you know you were supposed to die? Angel wanted it to look like a murder-suicide. But there I was at my lawyer best arguing for your life. I convinced him, told him how much more it would hurt Burton if he thought his precious son-in-law killed Jillian...and got away with it. It was just the kind of twisted reasoning that would feed Angel's need for revenge. You asshole, I'm the only reason you're not rotting in prison for her murder."

"Piper isn't part of this," he said, keeping his eyes on the gun. "Let her go. You and I can finish this."

Following Clay's gaze, Aidan looked at the gun thoughtfully for a moment, as if thinking about his options. "I used this gun to shoot Shawna." He looked up, meeting Clay's eyes. "Now, it's going to be the final piece of evidence to put it all together." He raised his hand and pointed the weapon. "Your murder-suicide with the new woman in your life."

Clay raced for Aidan, screaming, "Run!"

Piper dove past the brush behind her, just before she heard the gun go off.

37

At the sound of the gun firing, Piper stopped. Clay! She scrambled back toward the clearing. He'd shot Clay. He'd killed him. Just like he'd killed those poor women.

But she forced herself to stop and turn around. She wouldn't help Clay by making herself Aidan's next victim. Soon enough, he'd come for her. Crying, she pushed back through the shrubbery, the soggy soil grabbing at her feet. She needed to keep going. She had to get help.

She knew she was making too much noise. She tried to get her bearings, figure out how to make her way back to the road and the cell phone in her car. Once she made the call, she would return to help Clay.

But even as she made her plans, she saw the horrible flaws. Aidan had a gun. Most likely, Clay had come unarmed. He would have revealed his weapon as soon as he'd entered the clearing, if he'd brought one.

Another shot hammered through the night.

Taking a breath, she doubled back toward the sound of the gunfire. She didn't know what she would do once she got there, but she knew she had to do something.

Only she wasn't going to get that chance. Someone grabbed her from behind. She tumbled to the dirt. Piper flipped on her stomach and tried to crawl away. She felt herself pulled back by her ankle. She turned toward her assailant, kicking, about to scream.

A hand was clamped over her mouth, stopping any sound that might warn Clay.

Clay threw himself forward, racing right at Aidan. The gun fired, just missing him. Clay tackled Aidan, downing him like a calf. He grabbed the hand holding the gun and raised it to the sky. The two men struggled, the gun turning first on Clay, then back around to Aidan. But Clay didn't have as strong a grip on the weapon. Slowly, the muzzle of the gun targeted him.

Gritting his teeth, Clay held on to prevent Aidan from pressing the muzzle to his temple. With incredible effort, Clay shoved the gun straight up into the air as Aidan fired.

Both men pushed apart and jumped to their feet. Aidan still held the gun, but Clay could see Aidan's hands were shaking.

"Listen to me, Aidan. You're not going to get away with this. The cops are on their way now. There won't be any place to hide if you kill me now."

"That's where you're wrong." Aidan held the gun with both hands now, trying to steady his aim. "You showing up here works beautifully. The poor lady who was trying to help you remember, she didn't know what she was getting into. You lured her here, killed her, then turned the gun on yourself. The guilt was too much for you. You couldn't keep up with the secrets."

"And you? Can you keep up, Aidan?"

"I have a plane waiting to take me to my new life. Angel's operation in the Caymans." His hands on the gun still shook. "Once you're gone, my reputation stays intact. I get away, and it's a clean slate."

"Okay," Clay said, raising his hands, inching closer. "I get it. A new life in a new land. But give me a minute, just a minute. I want to know how it happened." He was starting to think the police hadn't believed him. That no one would come to help. He could only hope he was buying time for Piper to escape. "Jillian. You were the figure in the shadows behind me, I remember that much. Christ, Aidan. Why? You loved her!" he screamed at him.

"Because I had a gun to my head! Angel found your Colt and bullets in the nightstand. One of his thugs loaded it and shoved it in my hand. He turned me to face Jillian. Jesus, they got such a kick out of it, seeing me squirm. Angel told me I had ten seconds to decide. My life or Jillian's. I was standing right next to her, looking right at her. Dammit, Clay, he started counting."

"Jesus," Clay said under his breath.

"I told her to run. She turned, thinking she could get away. And that's when I fired. I didn't want her looking at me. I couldn't bear it."

Clay shook his head, never hating Aidan more. He would never have fired that gun. Not in a million years. Even tonight, he hadn't brought a weapon. He didn't even own one, not since the trial, when his father's gun had been taken as evidence. It just wasn't the way his brain worked.

"I know what you're thinking," Aidan said. "I should have died. I should have taken that bullet for her. You would have, right? That's what you're thinking. I took the coward's choice. I became exactly what Angel wanted—his stooge, forever in his grip."

"And now? What choice are you going to make now, Aidan?"

He shook his head. "Now, I don't have a choice."

With a yell, Clay raced straight for him, head down. He wanted to stop him, keep Aidan from hurting Piper. At the same time, this was the man who had killed Jillian. He'd turned Clay's life into a nightmare, making him think he'd killed his wife.

This time, when the gun went off, Clay knew it hit its mark.

38

Mandy didn't know what to do. She'd been calling Piper's cell phone nonstop. She'd left urgent messages.

When she'd talked to Clay, he'd made it sound as if everything was going to be okay. But now she didn't believe him. Piper should have called by now.

Something was wrong. Piper knew how they all fell apart when they couldn't keep in touch. They weren't like a normal family, people who hadn't been touched by tragedy. In their lives, if someone disappeared, it was forever.

So she called Sean. He came over right away, listened carefully as she told him the weird happenings of the night.

"He's not answering either," she said, after trying Clay's cell phone, the worry inside her heart growing until she thought she would choke on her fear.

"Something's not right," Sean said.

"My mom wouldn't take off like this. No way. She wouldn't keep me in the dark either. And she's not answering her cell. She's like crazy about keeping in touch."

How many times had Mom complained about Mandy not answering her phone? It was like a religion with the woman.

"What?" she asked, seeing that Sean had a strange look on his face.

"You just said 'my mom.'"

"Yeah."

"That's the first time I've heard you call her that."

She could feel the tears welling up as she crashed into her fears. She couldn't lose Piper. No way. That just wasn't happening.

She ran into Piper's office. She remembered the day that lady had come over from the state attorney's office. Mandy had been in her room, but she could hear everything from her window.

She opened her mother's file cabinet. She found the thick folder from the trial easily enough. The woman's card was crushed and jammed inside at the bottom.

Mandy thought about calling 911, but she wasn't sure they would believe her. She really wasn't sure what was happening. And she didn't want to dick around with a bunch of questions. She figured this would be a lot faster.

Looking at the card, she punched in the number for Grace Calderon's cell.

Piper turned. The hand was still over her mouth, but now she could see who it was. Burton Ward put his finger to his lips, indicating the need for silence. He motioned ahead.

Now she could hear voices. She was back near the clearing where Aidan had taken her at gunpoint. She could hear Clay and Aidan arguing.

Burton dropped his hand from her mouth. He motioned for her to stay where she was, then turned for the clearing.

He had a gun.

She could hardly catch her breath, realizing that at least now there was help. But she didn't understand the complicated relationships at work—didn't know if Burton would want revenge against Clay or Aidan.

Even before she realized what she was doing, she found herself dropping to her knees and inching forward through the foliage, following Burton. When he saw her, he again motioned for her to stay. But she shook her head, crawling faster to catch up.

They both stopped just outside the clearing. She could barely make out the words, but Burton seemed intent on the conversation. She couldn't see too far ahead in the moonlight. But suddenly, Burton tensed, hearing Aidan's confession of how Jillian had died. Listening to those horrible words, she could feel herself getting sick.

And then she heard Aidan's gun go off.

She almost screamed, but managed to keep the sound inside. She jumped to her feet in time to see Aidan and Clay fighting on the ground. Everything was happening so fast, but she felt frozen in place. She couldn't move.

When the gun fired a second shot, she watched in horror as Clay crumpled to the ground.

Just as Aidan raised the gun for the killing shot, Burton shouted, "Aidan. Over here."

Burton stepped into the clearing. Aidan turned. Seeing the gun in Burton's hand, he turned to aim at Burton.

But it was too late. Burton fired. Again and again. With each bullet, Burton walked toward Aidan. With each shot, Aidan jerked in place as if pulled by strings in some sort of comical puppet dance...until the strings were just cut loose.

Aidan dropped to his knees then fell face first into the dirt. Burton Ward bent down and calmly checked for a pulse. Not far from the two men, she could see Clay sitting up, clutching his shoulder where he'd been shot. A circle of blood blossomed on his shirt.

Piper ran to Clay just as she heard the night come to life with the sound of sirens. Burton still stood over Aidan.

She thought she heard him whisper, "There you go, Jilly Bean. There you go."

39

Grace stepped inside her office to find Chris seated in the chair in front of her desk, his feet propped up on the corner. He had a self-satisfied look on his face. She walked around to the other side and took her seat. She shuffled through the piles waiting for her attention. She didn't say a word.

"I thought we could have lunch," he said.

"Because?"

"To celebrate. All's well that ends well, right?"

She stopped what she was doing and crossed her arms over her chest. "If you mean Clayton Chase, yes. There won't be a retrial."

"And there are witnesses to say the deceased, one Aidan Parks, was also responsible for the death of Shawna Benet. Two birds. One stone. Mystery solved. And you're the hero, leaving no stone unturned, unlike your predecessor. Promotion, much? Where do you want to eat? I was thinking Italian."

She cocked her head. "It does indeed appear as if Aidan Parks fired on Clay Chase. And it would appear that Burton Ward acted in the defense of his son-in-law by killing Parks."

"Listen to you, 'does indeed.' And…end of story, right?"

"It might be." She sat back. "There's just this one little thing that's bothering me. The private investigator Ward hired.

The guy was supposed to get in touch with me, but he never did. I was going to give it a couple days before I tracked him down. But now I'm wondering if maybe he told Burton about Aidan. That's why Burton followed him out that night with a gun—revenge."

She waited, giving Chris a chance. He looked at her long and hard. But he was the first to blink.

"I never told him it was Aidan Parks," he said. "He put it together when you called him about Shawna Benet. He knew she was sleeping with Aidan. Apparently, you weren't the only one to figure out Ms. Benet was playing a surrogate Jillian. I also understand that Clay Chase put a call in to his father-in-law on the way out to save his damsel in distress."

She nodded, having figured out who Mr. Ward's mystery detective was around two o'clock this morning. Unfortunately, that was well after she'd made love to her husband, who'd been sleeping there beside her in the bed when the therapist's kid had called her cell phone.

"I was going to tell you," he said.

"Sure you were."

"That's why I came here. I was planning to tell you everything over lunch."

"Convenient."

"And you're not buying a word of this."

"Not a single one."

He closed his eyes and took a deep breath. "I thought..." He looked away, shook his head. "I *would* have told you. Eventually."

"Eventually."

He leaned over the desk and grabbed both of her hands in his. "Don't be mad about last night."

"That we made love when in fact you were undermining several—and let me emphasize the word *several*—of my investigations? Gee, Chris, why would that get me upset?"

"I thought I could handle it."

"It didn't occur to you that Burton Ward would take out his revenge when he found out who killed his daughter?"

"I didn't point the finger at Aidan Parks," he said, raising his voice to match hers. "I was pretty damn sure that it wasn't Aidan. For God's sake, he was the guy's attorney…the only reason Chase wasn't convicted in the first place. The evidence I gave Burton pointed solidly to Angel Barrera. Apparently Burton had an affair with the guy's wife, and she made a deathbed confession to Angel. And trust me when I say that if Burton had gone after Angel, I didn't really give a shit. Burton is a big boy. He and Angel have history."

"Why didn't you tell me?"

He released her hands and sat back in his chair. "The man killed Burton's daughter. He had a right."

"To vigilante justice? Not in this country."

"Come on, how many times have you guys gone after Angel Barrera and come up with nothing but egg on your face? Besides, if I tell you anything about my clients' affairs, I might as well retire from the detective business—not to mention, as an officer of the court, you're under an obligation to report anything I tell you. Then some guy with an itchy palm sees his chance at a big payday and blows the whistle to Barrera—who puts a bullet in my client. End of story."

But he could see from her expression, he wasn't making headway.

"I was an ass," he said, shifting gears.

"A lying one."

"Technically, I never lied to you."

"Technically? Well, how about, technically, we never have sex again?"

"I owed him confidentiality."

"And what, pray tell, do you owe me?"

He stood, tired of the argument. "You know what, honey? I owe you my love. I owe you my heart. Hell, I'll even give you my happiness, because I will be a miserable bastard without you. But I can't keep telling my business to an assistant state attorney just because I share a bed with her."

She saw that he was going to leave. "Sit down," she told him. "We're not finished."

He smiled, returning to his seat. "I was hoping you'd say that."

"You're officially hired," she said. "No, it wasn't my idea. I would have shown your miserable lying ass the door. We need you to get Barrera. Whatever you turned up and more."

"What about Burton?"

"He's onboard. We're making a deal on the Parks murder."

"What? That was self-defense. If that man is making a deal, he needs the name of a good attorney."

"And he has one, which is why he's making a deal. Chris, he shot the guy five times in the chest. Self-defense?"

"Self-defense, defense of his son-in-law, defense of that poor woman that got dragged out to the Glades, deadly force in the face of deadly force... How the hell does that *not* add up to the world is down one scumbag and all is well?"

"Because there's still plenty of scumbags out there. A big one by the name of Angel Barrera, to be precise."

He grinned. "Burton wants to nail Barrera."

"Through the heart. Which is why we've offered a deal and he's taking it. Now, are you going to help or not?"

"Depends," he said. "Are you going to forgive me?"

"Chris," she said, finally letting it all out. What the heck. Life was short. "I love you. I don't know if I want to be married to you. But I do love you. With all my heart, I'm afraid."

He thought about it. "But here's a better question. Are you going to serve me with those divorce papers you keep threatening?"

She held out her hand. "Give me your keys."

He looked at her quizzically. "What?"

"Your keys, Chris. Hand them over."

"I thought we already did this." But he gave her the keys just the same.

She grabbed the miniature Magic 8 Ball at the end of the key chain and gave it a shake. She read out loud, "Ask again later."

She looked at Chris, waiting for his reaction. She rather liked how the Magic 8 Ball had summarized their marriage. *Give it time.*

He smiled. "It will do, Gracie. It will do." He took back his keys. "Okay, Counselor. When do we start?"

"Right now, Chris," she said, picking up on the double meaning. "We start right now."

Piper sat next to the hospital bed just watching Clay sleep. A monitor that showed his heart rate beeped next to his bed. He was wearing one of those funky gowns, the sheets tucked up under his chin. She thought he looked a little pale, but the nurse had told her that wasn't unusual after surgery.

"Don't worry. He's through the worst of it," she'd said, patting Piper on the shoulder and leaving her to her vigil.

When he finally woke up, opening his eyes, she thought she'd never seen anything so beautiful in her life.

"Hi," she whispered.

"Hi," he said, giving her a sleepy smile. "Are you okay?"

"Yup. More than. Only, I'm a little jealous."

"Why?" he asked.

"I don't have any cute little scars as a memento," she said, nodding to where his arm lay in a sling.

"Yeah, well. I like you without the cute little scars. And by the way, it's a manly scar."

She sighed. "I was scared, Clay. I was so scared."

"Me, too." He picked up her hand at his bedside with his good one. He kissed her palm and brought it to his face. She could feel the rough stubble of his beard growing in. "I don't want to even think about losing you."

"Yeah. I know the feeling."

"The kids?"

Of course, they would be the first thing he would ask about. *The kids.* She smiled, realizing they were all going to be okay. Even Leah had let up, having dropped her lawsuit in the face of Piper's bulldog counsel. "You won't believe this, but Mandy called the state attorney. The woman who came to see me left her card and I had it in your file. Mandy found it and called the woman's cell phone."

"Atta girl, Mandy." He gave her hand a squeeze. "I'm glad you're here, that I get to wake up to your face. You have a beautiful face. A lot of character. Very photogenic."

"I bet you say that to all your models, just so they'll sleep with you."

He kissed her hand again. "You must hate hospitals."

"I don't know. The horrible lighting, the meat-freezer temperature...the soft moans of the injured. It has a certain ambience."

"Not to mention the memories," he added with a quiet look that told her he understood.

"The last time, it wasn't a happy ending." She took his hand in hers and kissed all his fingers. "This will be different."

They sat in companionable silence. But after a few minutes, she stood. "You need your rest."

But he held on to her hand, not letting her go. "I remembered. I did the same thing you told me to do during the hypnosis. The counting, trying to relax during the stupid elevator ride. But I kept looking at the photograph, kind of falling into that picture in my head of the Glades. I remembered waking up in the trunk of a car, I think. I'm not sure about that. My head hurt. I think I hit it when I blacked out from the strike. But the second time I came to, yeah. I remembered everything after that."

"Angel's men brought you to the house."

"I woke up there beside Jillian. I saw the gun and picked it up. I was completely disoriented, like when you wake up from a dream and nothing makes sense. I saw blood. Everywhere. I remember throwing the gun away. I lifted her head onto my lap."

She didn't interrupt, but she held his hand tighter, knowing how these memories must affect him.

"She told me she was sorry," he said. "She reached up and touched my head where I'd hit it. And then she told me who killed her." He frowned and looked up at Piper.

"It's okay," she told him, pushing back his hair. She kissed him on the forehead. "Everything's going to be fine, now."

He reached with his good arm and pulled her down to him. He kissed her. In the end, he tried to pull her up on the bed. She thought he'd hurt himself if she fought him, so she curled up there beside him.

"It must have been awful," she said. "Remembering like that."

"Yeah," he said. "I'll need years of therapy. Years."

It took her a moment to realize what he was saying. She turned to look at him, smiling.

She whispered, "It's a good thing I know a therapist."

"I hear she's one in a million," he said, giving her another kiss.

**The newest book in the Cedar Cove series
by _New York Times_ bestselling author**

DEBBIE MACOMBER

This time around, a mystery is troubling Cedar Cove's private
investigator, Roy McAfee, and his wife, Corrie. They're receiving
anonymous postcards and messages asking if they "regret the past."
But not all is gloomy in our beloved small town. Romance is in the air
for Linnette McAfee, whether she likes it or not—and there may still
be hope for Cliff Harding and Grace Sherman. So pick up your copy
of _50 Harbor Street_ and find out what else is going on in Cedar Cove!

"The books in Macomber's contemporary Cedar Cove
series are irresistibly delicious and addictive."
—_Publishers Weekly_ on _44 Cranberry Point_

_Available the first week of September 2005
wherever paperbacks are sold!_

50
_Harbor
Street_

MIRA®

OLGA BICOS

32076	DEAD EASY	___$6.50 U.S.	___$7.99 CAN.
66732	SHATTERED	___$6.50 U.S.	___$7.99 CAN.

(limited quantities available)

TOTAL AMOUNT	$ _____
POSTAGE & HANDLING	$ _____
($1.00 FOR 1 BOOK, 50¢ for each additional)	
APPLICABLE TAXES*	$ _____
TOTAL PAYABLE	$ _____

(check or money order—please do not send cash)

To order, complete this form and send it, along with a check or money order for the total above, payable to MIRA Books, to: **In the U.S.:** 3010 Walden Avenue, P.O. Box 9077, Buffalo, NY 14269-9077; **In Canada:** P.O. Box 636, Fort Erie, Ontario, L2A 5X3.

Name: _____
Address: _____ City: _____
State/Prov.: _____ Zip/Postal Code: _____
Account Number (if applicable): _____

075 CSAS

*New York residents remit applicable sales taxes.
*Canadian residents remit applicable GST and provincial taxes.

MIRA®

MOB0905BL